MAKE MY HEART MALT

GIA STEVENS

If you ever find yourself locked in a storage room…
Make sure Garrett Dawson is with you.
It's more fun that way.

While this story is a romantic comedy there may be situations that are triggering to some. For a list of those content notes please visit my website and scroll to the bottom of the page.

Chapter 1

GHOST OF A MAN

Dessa

It's strange how a plain white envelope can make me so anxious. One might think it's a notice to report for jury duty or that I need to act fast, or my car warranty will expire. Side note: my car warranty has been nonexistent for eight years. It might be a letter from the police saying they finally figured out who stomped all over Mrs. Halverson's tulips, and now she's suing for damages. Sorry, Mrs. Halverson. But it wasn't all my doing. In fact, I was the only one who gracefully tip-toed across your flower bed unlike the other savages who stomped their way across. Either way, it's not that. It's worse. Much worse.

I flip the envelope back and forth between my fingers, the black calligraphy screaming at me on every turn. Screw you, black lettering. Who gives a wedding invitation to their ex? Or has their mom deliver it to my mom to deliver to me? It's a slap in the face. It's a blatant move that screams, "Look I've moved on, why haven't you?" I hate you, envelope. I *have* moved on.

Okay. That's not entirely true. Yes, it's true I've moved on from my ex-boyfriend who's now getting married, but there's someone else I've desperately tried to move on from. Every year, the start of baseball season is a stark reminder that he's still around, and he still hasn't said a single word to me. No phone call. No text. No email. I would even settle for a postcard at this point. It's better than being ghosted. Because of that, this wedding invite has hives sprouting all over my body. Not because of who's getting married, but because of who's going to be there. I'd hate to be the bitch who ruins the wedding by punching her former-best-friend-turned-most-hated-enemy in the face in the middle of "I do." I don't think the families would appreciate that too much, even though I would find great pleasure in it.

This envelope has haunted me for the past three months—ever since my mom handed it to me. If things didn't end the way they did all those years ago, attending this wedding might be a different story. Right now, I don't have time to replay the last ten years of my life because my best friend Rylee returns to work today from her maternity leave. As I toss the envelope, it slides across the coffee table before coming to a stop on the edge. I climb to my feet and stroll five steps into the open kitchen of my one-bedroom townhome. After grabbing my keys from the counter, I make my way out the front door.

As I arrive at Porter's Ale House for my bartending shift, my heart stammers in my chest at the highlights from the Seattle-Minnesota world championship game playing on the TV. Not only is it airing on the two TVs behind the bar but also on the projector screen across the room. Even though baseball season ended three weeks ago with underdogs Minnesota stealing the win from Seattle, they still like to show the missed catch by Seattle's star catcher. It became Minnesota's tiara on top of their Cinderella-story year. And I'm over watching it. Not over Minnesota winning because they played hard and deserve the win, but over watching Seattle. Most importantly, watching their star catcher. With a quick roll of my eyes, I snatch the remote. My hands tremble as I switch channels, hoping to escape seeing him again. A collection of boos echoes through the entire bar.

"Fine. Fine." I turn the channel back before everyone throws their drink at me. "Baseball season is over. Let's move on to a new sport," I mumble to myself. I'm certainly ready to move on. Yes, it's my favorite sport. Yes, I bleed blue and red for the Minnesota Mallards, but I don't need to watch every replay fifty times.

As Lach steps next to me, his light brown hair flops across his forehead, I catch a glimpse of his tattoo peeking out from beneath the rolled-up sleeves of his hoodie. He's an artist and drew all his own tattoos. "You don't want to piss off the die-hard fans. They've waited eighteen years to see their team not only make it to the playoffs but be world champions, especially against a team like Seattle."

A heavy sigh escapes my lips. The fans deserve it, but what about me? I deserve some reprieve from this torture. "For the past three weeks, that's all I've seen. And that doesn't include watching it live." A customer in front of me lifts his empty glass. I nod and get him a refill.

As soon as they announced the dates and times of the championship games, I was tempted to call in sick and bury myself under the covers with a bottle of vodka, but I couldn't do that to Jake. Instead, I hoisted up my big-girl panties and spent three hours watching my ex-best friend behind home plate. It was bittersweet watching Garrett miss the catch, allowing Minnesota to score the winning run and beat the top team in baseball. What really broke my heart was Garrett's press conference. He loves the sport, always has, and it shows in his emotions.

When he first started playing professionally, I refused to turn on any of his games. All the hurt and anger resurfaced again. A sport I love shouldn't cause me so much pain. By his third year playing for the Seattle Warblers, I had no choice since they were playing Minnesota. It was hard at first, but eventually I numbed myself to the pain. Eventually, each game got a little easier. I may hate him, but I still want to see him succeed. Even now, as the press conference replays on the TV, I have a hard time turning away.

Garrett's gaze fixates on the microphone in front of him. "You don't get many second chances. I really screwed up this time. It was my fault we didn't win." He lifts his head and stares directly at the camera, but it's like he's staring at me. "But next time I'm coming out one hundred twenty percent. I'll give it my all and make sure that next year we take home the trophy." His bright green eyes glimmer. I'm not entirely sure if it's because of the lights or if he's a little teary-eyed. Maybe both. Despite being a recording I've watched so many times I have it memorized, my heart still plummets to my stomach like I should care about his feelings right now. Then I remember he sure as hell didn't care about mine. Finally, I rip my gaze away from the TV as it cuts to commercial. He's dead to me and has been for the last ten years.

To keep my thoughts off Garrett, I busy myself with creating a fresh drink special. I tap the tip of my pencil on a notepad as I think of ingredients that will pair well together. Maybe I should name it "Asshole Baseball Players Who Have No Regard For Anyone's Feelings But Their

Own." I think it's catchy. But instead, I pick a more neutral name and call it "The Mallard."

"You know what I like about baseball?" Nora leans her butt against the edge of the beer cooler next to me, her long blonde braid draping over one shoulder.

Lach grabs a pint glass and pulls the lever down on the tap, watching the golden liquid fill the glass. "The hard work, dedication, and skill that goes into playing the game?"

"No. The baseball pants," Nora deadpans. She rests a hand on her hip and taps her chin. "Though I suppose filling out a pair of polyester pants perfectly does require a lot of hard work, dedication, and skill."

Once the beer is full, Lach passes it to a customer, then turns to Nora. "Yeah, that's the most important reason why you should like baseball."

"It's my 'why,' and you don't get to question it." Nora flips her braid over her shoulder. "What about you, Dessa? Why do you like baseball?"

I spin the bottle of vodka upside down and pour an ounce into the shaker. I've been bartending since I turned twenty-one, so I can eyeball a pour and only be fractions of an ounce off. We've tested my skills many times at the bar since no one believes me. It's a great bar trick that gets customers to buy shots. "Who said I like baseball?"

"Um, the baseball earrings and Minnesota shirt you wore all baseball season kind of gave it away," Nora says.

"Oh." I pause. "Like Lach said, I'm a fan for the hard work and dedication." Grabbing a bottle of coconut rum, I pour it into the shaker. I was once a fan of the baseball pants, but now they remind me of Garrett. Throughout our junior year of high school, he would always make sure there was a seat for me behind home plate, giving me the perfect view as he practically did squats on the field. Back then, I had a thing for baseball pants. Right now, baseball pants can suck it, along with the catchers who wear them.

"I'm not sure what you're making, but with that much alcohol, I'd think you're trying to take down an entire baseball team," Lach says as he unfolds a step stool, setting it in front of a giant chalkboard drink menu hanging on the wall and climbs the three steps.

His voice pulls me from my baseball pants thoughts. "Shit." I set the bottle of rum on the bar and stare at the shaker with four more ounces of liquor than I wanted.

"Distracted by baseball pants. It's okay." Nora pushes off the bar. "It happens to the best of us. In fact, I firmly believe the invention of baseball pants was intended to attract women to the sport. Spoiler alert: it worked."

I twist my head to face Nora as she saunters to the opposite end of the bar.

"So, what's the drink called?" Lach glances down at me.

While I create the drinks for the weekly menu, he writes them on the board and adds fancy doodles to go with them. I peer over my shoulder, the chalk marcher scritches above me while he finishes shading in the letters of the saying, "Have you met my friends Barley and Hops?"

"I don't know, since I screwed it up. Maybe there won't be a fresh drink this week." I throw my hands in the air and let them fall to my sides as my bottom lip juts out. Seeing Garrett on TV must have flustered me. That's the only logical explanation why my concentration is nonexistent. I dump half of the alcohol into another shaker and some pineapple juice into the first shaker. I shove the lid on top and give it a couple of shakes before I pour the liquid into five shot glasses and pass them to a few customers sitting at the bar. "Fruit cocktail shots."

"Are you giving away free shots again, Dessa?" Jake strolls between me and Lach behind the bar with a case of beer in his hands.

"I need taste testers since you're out." I glance at the row of customers in front of me, a hopeful expression on my face. Two guys and a girl all raise their thumbs, the other girl squishes her face like she sucked on a sour candy, and the third guy spits half of the cocktail back into the glass before pushing it away.

My shoulders drop. "I'm taking that as a no." I've never been this off on my game before. It's unsettling.

"We can always do an old one," Lach says. "What was the one from a couple of weeks ago? It had vodka, peach schnapps, and triple sec."

"The Backseat Smash," I answer on a sigh.

Lach points the chalk marker at me. "Yes! That one. Customers loved that one."

My shoulders deflate. I hate reusing a drink—especially when it was already featured. Plus, this is what I do. Wonder Woman is nothing without her superhuman powers much like a mixologist is nothing if they can't create drinks. "But we already did it."

"I'm sure half of the customers won't even know, and the other half won't care. We can do that again."

"I really wanted a 'Welcome Back Rylee' cocktail." I huff out a breath. "What time is it?" I glance at Lach.

He his gaze drops to his black watch. "Ten to eleven."

"Shit! I lost track of time." Or I got distracted with all the baseball talk. Either way, I need to get the decorations. Abandoning my cocktail for now, I race to Jake's office and collect the balloons, streamers, and the banner.

Rylee's been on maternity leave for the past month. Even though she has three months, she's opted to take one and work a few hours a day to make sure we're all doing our jobs. I know deep down, she misses me, her best friend, and perhaps it's to get a little reprieve from Trey, who's determined to have another kid. Who knew the man who claimed to never want kids, now wants enough to fill a baseball roster?

One hour and a sweaty forehead later, I peek my head over the ledge of the side window into the Porter's parking lot.

"She's here! Get ready!"

I scamper to the main bar area where everyone is gathered. A corner of the banner we got that says *Welcome Back Rylee* drops from the ceiling. I climb on a stool and re-secure it. As I step down, a sliver of light pours in through the front door as Rylee strolls in. A roar of claps and cheers rolls through the bar as everyone rises to their feet.

The widest grin takes over her face as pink tinges her cheeks. "What is all this?" She glances around the packed Porter's. She strolls toward the end of the bar where Lach, Nora, Jake, and I are standing. As she passes, everyone offers their congratulations. "You'd think I won a Nobel Peace Prize, not had a baby."

When she's within arm's reach, I squeal and pull her to my chest. "I'm excited you're back.

She giggles under her breath. "You've come over every week since I've been gone."

"I know, but working with those two," I hike my thumb between Lach and Jake, "has been boooring."

"Hey, I heard that," Lach says.

I glance behind me. "I wasn't trying to be quiet."

He rests his chin on my shoulder. "If I was gone for a month, you'd miss me."

I roll my eyes. "Hardly." I playfully jab my elbow into his chest.

He chokes out a laugh. "Son of a bitch. I need to find

some less violent friends." He rubs at his chest before wrapping an arm around Rylee. "Glad you're back."

"Me too." She smiles at him. "Now everyone, get back to work."

"Listen to the boss." Jake clasps a hand on her shoulder. "Glad to have you back."

Rylee and Jake stroll down the hall to his office while Lach tends to the opposite end of the bar. I grab a frosty pint glass from the cooler and hold it under a tap, pulling the lever down. Once it's full, I pass it to a customer and pour another. The front door opens, and a sliver of sunlight pierces through. I peer up. A tall, rugged man in dark jeans and a fitted white shirt that accentuates his toned arms, with a tattoo peeking out from beneath the sleeve stands a foot inside the doorway. A baseball cap is perched on his head, dark hair spilling out from the sides. His scruff-covered jawline rivals any stone statue. He turns my way and pulls the aviators off his face. A half smirk tugs at his lips.

Time stops. My breathing stops. Noise stops. Everything stops. All the people in Porter's disappear. Standing before me is a ghost of a man. One I knew years ago and hoped I would never have to see in person again. Stars burst through my vision, then my entire world goes black.

Chapter 2

IT'S NOT DESSA

Garrett

Three Days Earlier

My eyelids shoot open, and I'm met with inky darkness. My heart thunders in my chest. Cold sweats spread across my body, sending a shiver down my spine. I blink a few more times and twist my head to face the alarm clock. It's 2:52 a.m. Fuck. It was a dream.

I'm standing behind home plate. Abbott is running down the baseline toward me, a sinister grin on his face. My gaze drifts to the shortstop. His arm rolls back and sling shots forward. The ball barrels toward me, the red stitching almost hypnotizing as it rotates through the air. All I need to do is lift my glove and catch the ball. That will send us into another inning to fight for the championship. I glance at Abbott, who's now only a few steps away. I slide my foot to touch the edge of the plate and lift my arm, preparing to catch the ball, except I don't have a glove. In fact, my entire hand is missing. The ball soars past me, and Abbott crosses home plate, scoring the winning run. The entire Minnesota team runs out on the field and congregates at the pitcher's mound to celebrate. I'm rooted in place as fans throw hats, jerseys with my number, and trash at me until I'm standing in a knee-deep pile. From the opposing team's dugout, Dessa runs out onto the field. Her long, honey-colored hair flows behind her until she reaches the pitcher's mound and wraps her arms around a faceless Minnesota player.

Swinging my legs over to the side of the bed, I sit up, and rest my elbows on my knees. I exhale a deep breath and scrub my hands down my face. This is the third time I've had this dream or something similar in the past week, but it's the first time Dessa's appeared. I climb to my feet and amble through the darkness, across my bedroom, and into the hallway.

Once in the living room, I flop onto the couch and turn on the TV. As soon as the replay of my missed catch comes on the screen, I immediately hit the power button on the remote. The TV goes black. You'd think they'd find something else to play by now. Baseball players miss catches all the time, but they certainly like to torture me by showing mine at every opportunity. Twist the dagger in my gut a little more. It's fine. I should be celebrating a victory. It was mine to win. Inches from my fingertips, or in my case, glove. But instead, I'm sitting on my couch in my condo in a city that hates me. Most would say I'm overreacting, but I've seen the social media posts, the GIFs, and the memes. Fans are not subtle about it either.

Home Run Playboy… more like Chokes Behind the Plate.
His glove works better without a hole in it.
The ball must need to hit him in the face for him to catch it.
Dawson sucks.
We need a new catcher.
Trade him.
He's already past his prime.

He better not be back next year.

This is just in the last two days. I've been subject to their hatred for a little over two weeks. While I can brush most of the comments away, this time hits particularly hard. Maybe because I know I won't have too many more years left playing professionally. My contract expires in three years. Then it's either negotiate a new one or go wherever the trade is.

All season, everyone expected us to make it to the world championship and win, so it sucks that I'm the reason the entire team went home empty-handed. My missed catch can only be attributed to one thing, and that thing is missing. I searched the clubhouse, the dugout, my condo, everywhere, and it's nowhere to be found. It's the only logical explanation.

I shove the coffee table away and stand. A newspaper and a stack of magazines tumbles to the ground. "Fuck," I mumble. Bending over, I grab the fallen mail from the floor when a white envelope with gold embellishments catches my attention. My eyes widen in terror when I read my brother's name in black calligraphy. This has to be a wedding invitation—it's too fancy for anything else, especially coming from Tony. That means only one thing. Just my fucking luck. Apparently, the universe wants to kick me when I'm at rock bottom.

When I left Harbor Highlands, my brother was with the one girl who should have been mine. The heaviness in my chest intensifies. Add another dagger to my heart to match the one in my gut. My brother is getting married… to my girl. My gaze shoots to the left. Georgia LaBelle. Wait. It's not Dessa. He's not marrying Dessa.

I rip open the flap and check the date. December third. My brother is getting married in a little over a week. Most importantly, he's not marrying Dessa. It's been ten years since I've been back home. It's been just as long since I've spoken to her, but no matter how hard I fight it, she's always a recurring presence in my dreams, especially as of late. While I couldn't catch the ball to win the championship, maybe I can finally catch the girl. The one who should have been mine all those years ago. Time to go back to Harbor Highlands. Alright universe, it's one-one. Tied game.

Porter's
ALE HOUSE

After booking my flight, I spend the next two days ignoring everyone outside my condo. The entire city is still upset, or a lot upset, with me. Perhaps getting out of Seattle is exactly what I need. It will give everyone time to cool off. In the meantime, maybe there will be a football scandal to take the heat off me. I can only hope.

I pull into the driveway of my parents' house, the tires leaving tread impressions in the light dusting of snow before I park my rental car. Winter is ready to make her appearance. It may have been ten years since I've been back here, but not that long since I've seen my parents. Every year I send them round-trip tickets to visit me in Seattle. At least I don't have the guilt trip of never seeing them hanging over my head.

As soon as I push through the front door, voices echo down the hallway from the kitchen. Memories of my childhood flood through my mind. No matter how long I've been gone, the sweet scent of lavender will always remind me of home. I toe off my shoes and stroll toward the sound, not fully prepared for what I'm getting myself into since no one knows I'm coming.

My brother, Tony, comes into view first. We both have a similar build: broad shoulders, over six feet, though I have a few inches on him. But that's where the similarities end. His hair is lighter than my dark brown and instead of green eyes like mine, he has brown.

"Holy shit! Look what the cat dragged in." Tony rounds the corner of the kitchen island and wraps his arms around me in a half hug, half back pat. "What are you doing here?"

"I hear there's a wedding." I wrap an arm around his shoulder and return the back pat. Growing up, we were close not only in age, with him being a year older than me, but our relationship. We played all the same sports, so we were constantly either practicing or playing with each other. We were competitive, but that only drove us to be better, to try harder. At least, it did for me. All that changed the summer leading into my senior year of high school, when it was no longer about the sport.

"You're a little early. There's still a week to go," Tony says.

"I needed to get out of Seattle for a while." But mostly I want to see Dessa.

"Truth be told, I never actually thought you'd show." He laughs, then glances around the empty room. "Alright, who had Garrett coming to the wedding on their BINGO card?" When his gaze falls to me, his smile falters. "Just joking. We didn't place bets. But I'm glad we didn't because I would've lost." He nudges me with his elbow.

"If my team had won the championship, it might be a different story." I shrug.

"I saw that." He clasps my shoulder. "That's rough. You win some. You lose some. I'm sure you'll get them next year." He flashes me a half smile. It's cocky and condescending and I wonder if he's even referring to the game anymore.

Losing that game was a tough pill to swallow. Even

after three weeks, it still stings as if it happened yesterday. The replay constantly runs on a time loop in my head without the added help from the replays on TV.

The runner was rounding third, coming straight at me. I took my eye off the ball for a fraction of a second. The ball was soaring in the air straight toward my glove but tipped the edge, ricocheting off to the side, and Minnesota scored the winning run.

"Either way, I'm glad you could make it. It's good to see you."

I'd like to think he's telling the truth, but the wretched stench of bullshit wafts around from a mile away, especially his.

"Likewise." Mostly because I know he's not marrying Dessa. If it was her name on that invite, there's no way in hell I'd subject myself to that kind of torture.

"Since I didn't know you were actually going to show, I don't really have a spot for you in the bridal party." Tony shoves his hands in his pockets and rocks on his heels.

"Is that my baby boy?!" My mom's voice carries through the entire house until she comes into view through the arched doorway between the living room and the kitchen. There's a possibility the neighbors down the street heard her as well. "I knew eventually you'd come home."

Her voice is like a ray of sunshine, and her smile is just as bright. She wraps her arms around me in a big hug. It's the type of hug that engulfs you, reminds you of home, and lets you know everything is right in the world. I rest my chin on the top of her head as I wrap my arms around her shoulders.

"It's so good to have you here," she mumbles against my chest. "If I'd known you were coming, I would have postponed Thanksgiving a couple of days." She breaks away from our hug. Her smile even brighter than before.

Living in Seattle has been a perk for not joining in on family festive holidays. I always conjured up some excuse so I wouldn't have to see Tony and Dessa together. Do I feel like a terrible son for missing holidays? A little. But I had to do it for my own sanity. I shove my hands into my pockets.

"Now that Tony and Georgia are in town permanently, since Tony got a coaching position with the Harbor Highland Agates, maybe there can be more family holidays together." Mom's gaze dances between Tony and me, waiting for confirmation from either of us.

Instead, I deflect to avoid any more talk about family time. "The Agates… Aren't they an amateur baseball team? They play in the collegiate summer baseball league," I ask.

"They are." Tony squares is shoulders, puffing out his chest.

I nod. Tony didn't have the skills or discipline to go pro. I hope he's better at coaching, otherwise, I'll feel sorry for the players.

A few seconds later my dad and a woman who's about the same height, hair color, and figure as Dessa stroll into the kitchen. She stops next to Tony, and he wraps his arm around her shoulder. If I had to guess, this is his bride-to-be.

"Georgia, this is my brother, Garrett." His sharp gaze connects with mine. "Garrett, this is my soon-to-be-wife, Georgia LaBelle. Her family owns the LaBelle Hotel chain."

"That's my father's business. Not mine. Plus, soon I'll be a Dawson," she corrects while smiling at Tony.

I hold out my hand. "Nice to meet you."

"It's nice to finally meet the Home Run Playboy." She winks. Her hand is soft against mine.

I inwardly cringe at the nickname the fans and tabloids have given me. "The home run part is true. I don't know so much about the playboy though."

Last year, I had my best season with sixty-two home runs, most ever by a catcher. Ever since then, the tabloids coined me the Home Run Playboy. Living my best single life aided in the nickname.

"Weren't you dating that supermodel from Brazil?" Georgia taps her chin.

"Dating" is a far stretch. More like we enjoyed each other's company on and off for six months. If I needed a date to an event, she'd come with me and vice versa. It was more of an arrangement that often included sex. "We went to a couple of events together. Nothing serious," I say.

"Oh. Okay. I hope you'll be staying for the wedding." She steals a glance at Tony, who's glaring at me.

"That's the plan." I shove my hands into my pockets. Even though it's not the entire plan. It's more like an excuse for the plan.

My mom brushes the wrinkles out of my shirt. "I wish I would have known. I could have gotten your old bedroom put together with clean sheets."

"Along with your shrine of greatness," Tony mutters, but not quite loud enough for everyone not to hear.

"Don't worry about that. I got a hotel room." I wave her off.

"Nonsense. Your bedroom is still upstairs. Cancel your room and give me five minutes. I'll get it ready for you." Without another chance to argue, my mom is out of the kitchen and halfway up the stairs.

"Good to see you, son." My dad squeezes me on the shoulder. "Sorry about the loss."

"Thanks," I answer sheepishly. Maybe I should have

stayed home so I wouldn't be subject to all the pity. I've been here five minutes and I'm already over it.

"Oh! I got it!" My mom barrels into the kitchen, her face lit up brighter than the Harbor Highlands Christmas block party. "Garrett can be an usher at the wedding. There's always room for another usher. Since everyone missed Thanksgiving." Her hopeful gaze drifts between me, Tony, and Georgia.

A laugh rumbles from the back of my throat and I shake my head. Nothing like a good guilt tripping to start this wedding off on the right foot.

Tony's eyes meet mine, and I shrug. Once our mom gets an idea in her head, we all kind of have to run with it. He glances down at Georgia, and she nods.

"Yeah. We'd like to have you as an usher," Tony says with a flat tone.

Our mom claps. "This is so exciting to have both my boys here and at the wedding together." She wraps us both in a hug. She's aware of the rift between us but pretends it doesn't exist in hopes we'll go back to the way things were. Easier said than done.

Chapter 3

SORRY, I GHOSTED YOU

Garrett

Over the next hour, our mom plays mediator as Tony and Georgia tell me all about how they met and how Tony swept her off her feet. I'm hard-pressed to believe he has the capabilities to woo anyone, but to each their own. Georgia animatedly describes the wedding from the colors to the decor while Tony scrolls on his phone as if he'd rather be anywhere but here. Same, but I'm also not going to be an asshole about it either.

After they leave, my mom turns to me. "How have you been? And don't give me any of that 'I'm fine' crap."

I laugh. Leave it to Mom to not sugarcoat anything. "Of course, I've been better. When an entire city hates you, it's hard to walk around with a smile on your face." I don't mention my only saving grace is the possibility of seeing Dessa. She'd spend the rest of the afternoon fixated on our relationship, or lack thereof.

Her hand rests on mine. "You're an amazing baseball player. Everyone will soon forget all about it."

"Soon" can knock on my door any day now. Instead of dragging my mom to my pity party, I nod. "I'd like to think so, but right now it looks bleak. Enough about me. How's everyone here? How's Dad?"

"Wedding planning has kept me busy, and your father has found himself a new hobby." Her voice raises an octave at the end.

"Oh yeah? What's that? He's not collecting vintage fishing tackle again, is he?"

My dad tends to go through these phases, like mini mid-life crises, where he'll randomly start collecting things. Last year it was vintage fishing tackle. The year before that was old oil cans.

"No. Thank goodness." Her shoulders deflate. "We're running out of room to collect things. We need to downsize, not the other way around. Anyway, he bought himself a drone and found a flying club to join. Don't get me wrong, I love your father, but I need him to leave the house. This club gives me a few hours a week to have some peace and quiet."

I'm envious of my parents' relationship. For starters, they *have* a relationship. One that started in high school. Something me and Dessa should have had. Besides that, they have unconditional love for each other even if they're in each other's hair every now and then. A moment of silence passes between us.

My mom rests her arms on the table and leans in as she bites back a smile. "Are you going to ask me how she's doing?"

My eyebrows hit my hairline as my gaze shoots to my mom.

She swipes her hand in front of her. "Don't give me

that look. You know exactly who I'm talking about. I'm surprised you haven't asked about her yet. I figured it would have been the first thing out of your mouth when you walked through the door."

I cast my gaze downward to the white and gray quartz countertop. "I don't know what you're talking about." Playing coy is useless since she can read me like a book. Always has. She calls it a mother's intuition. I call it fucking creepy.

"Just because you don't talk about her doesn't mean you're not thinking about her. I know you." She rests a comforting hand on my forearm.

I fiddle with my phone on the counter, working up the courage to ask. I've never been a nervous guy, but when it comes to Dessa, she short circuits my brain. The corner of my lips curve into a smile. "How's Dessa? Is she still in town?" Fuck. It sounds so weird to say her name out loud. For so long, it's only been a thought in my head.

My parents have always known the reason I cut ties with everyone when I left Harbor Highlands. Having to hear about Tony and Dessa's relationship was always like a knife twisting in my gut. I didn't want to know how happy they were while I was stuck being a miserable piece of shit. She always respected my wishes. Until now.

"She is. She has a townhouse on the south side of town."

My heartrate spikes, knowing that she's still around. For the first two years that I was gone, I occasionally checked her social media but with every post of her and Tony together, I got angrier and more spiteful. Eventually, I couldn't do it anymore. I forced myself to stop looking and torturing myself.

"Her parents still live down the street?" I ask.

"They do. You should stop by for a visit. I'm sure they'd love to see you again."

I nod and rest my hands on the table. I pick at my thumbnail, working up the courage to pry some more. "So, is Dessa…"

"Single?" A knowing smile curves her lips. "The last I heard, yes, and she works at Porter's."

Again, I'm not thrilled my mom can read my thoughts. She always has the answers to the questions I didn't even ask.

"Now go freshen up." She swats my arm. "You can't make a good second-chance impression looking like that."

I laugh, then glance down at my stained hoodie and gray joggers. "What's wrong with this?"

"You'll certainly make an impression looking like that, but I assure you it won't be a good one." She quirks an eyebrow at me.

"Alright." I push away from the counter. After collecting my luggage from the car, I carry them up the stairs to the second floor. Once I'm at the top, I stroll down the hallway. The second door on the right is partially closed, so I push it open with my foot. Instantly, I'm transported to ten years ago. All the walls are still the same slate blue, and every single one of my high school trophies, medals, and plaques decorate the shelves scattered around the room. I drop my luggage in the far corner and glance around.

On the nightstand sits a baseball under a glass case. I pull off the top. The white cowhide is smooth under my thumb. This is the ball from my first ever home run my sophomore year, the same year I made the varsity team. We were only two games into the season when I hit the ball over the fence. As I rounded third, I spotted Dessa cheering in the stands. Our eyes locked and it was that moment I knew my feelings for her exceeded the best friend territory. After our crushing thirteen-to-five win, the entire team went to a friend's house to celebrate. Instead of going out, Dessa and I came back here, sat side-by-side on my bed and binged movies while eating movie theater butter popcorn. She claimed to hate the scary ones, but they were always her first choice when we were together. I'm convinced it was so she could curl into my side at all the scary parts. I wasn't going to complain.

I place the ball back in the case and set the lid on top. Strolling to the other side of the room, I pull out fresh clothes from my suitcase. It's now or never.

After I'm showered and changed, I jump into my rental car and drive across town to Porter's. Along the way, I spot several new businesses mixed in with a few familiar ones. While many things have changed, it's still oddly refreshing to be back home.

I pull into the parking lot and park my car in the first available spot. With a steady hand, I push the ignition button, cutting the engine. Fuck. With a heavy sigh, my hands fall to my lap—once again, my nerves getting the best of me. Even behind the plate with balls flying toward me at ninety miles an hour, I'm never this nervous. Maybe because I have protective padding. Now, I'm just flesh and bones. A lot more damage can happen. What is she going to say? How's she going to react? Will she be happy to see me or want to introduce her fist to my face? I should have packed my catcher's mask. I won't lie—after the way I left, I kind of deserve a punch to the face. But we're older and wiser now, so maybe she'll be understanding. Who am I kidding? She'll want to punch me in my face. Fuck. What if she's not here and I'm psyching myself up for nothing? More importantly, what the hell am I going to say?

"Sorry for ghosting you." Blunt, but a little insensitive.

"Sorry, I couldn't bear to see you with my brother, so I abandoned you." It's the truth.

"Sorry, I was a selfish prick. The idea of you with someone else, even though we were just friends, made me want to stab myself in the eye." Maybe too much truth.

"Sorry. I was in love with you but didn't have the balls to tell you. Hell, I'm pretty sure I'm still in love with you." Oh yeah. She'll definitely punch me in the face for the last one.

Inhaling deeply, I release a long, steady breath, hoping a sense of calm will wash over me, but it doesn't. Here goes nothing then. I exit the car. As soon as I walk through the door of Porter's, I'm instantly hit with nostalgia from ten years ago. The exterior has remained relatively the same, but the inside got a little facelift with a modernized, industrial atmosphere. Jake's done a lot of work here.

The buzz of the TV and chattering voices fill the air. Sweet laughter bursts forth, cutting through all the other noise. It's infectious. A sound I could never forget. I snap my head toward the bar, my heart hammering in my chest, as I spot Dessa. Her smile illuminates the entire room. Her appearance is slightly different. A little older, more mature, but she's still the most beautiful woman I've seen. A smile twitches at the corner of my lips as I pull off my sunglasses. Her smile falters, and her once rosy cheeks turn pale as all the color drains from her face. The whites of her eyes disappear as her body collapses to the floor.

Chapter 4

HIT A TATOR

Dessa

My eyelids flutter open, and I blink, adjusting to the light and bringing everything back into focus. Holy shit, that was some intense dream. It was so real. Garrett casually strolled into Porter's as if he didn't have a care in the world. Like nothing changed between us. And then he smiled at me. Not a bright, full smile, but his signature sexy half smirk. One that makes your nipples hard just thinking about it.

"Dessa, are you okay?" Lach's deep voice jolts me back to reality.

Shit, maybe that wasn't a dream. My gaze dances around the ceiling until Lach's face comes into view as he bends over me.

"You okay? You fainted. Here's some water." He unscrews the plastic cap before passing me a bottle.

Shit. Fuck. Is Garrett really here? The deafening sound of my pounding pulse fills my ears, fueling the half-anger, half-panic surging through my veins. I can't face him. If I do, I'll strangle him, and I don't need first-degree murder on my record. Can they read my thoughts? Would they know it was premeditated? Maybe I can get off with second-degree. Better yet, let's not murder anyone today, and I won't have to worry about prison time.

Slowly, I rise to a sitting position and glance at the edge of the bar. Everyone is facing away from me, their attention on the hometown baseball hero—better known as the Home Run Playboy. Now's my turn to run away, well technically not *run*, more like crawl away so I can bury myself in a hole and pretend he isn't here. Even better, pretend he doesn't exist because those emotions are best kept under lock and key than out in the open.

I scramble to my hands and knees. Lach lifts his brow but doesn't say anything. With my eyes wide, I hold my pointer finger over my lips. Garrett can't see me if I crawl along the back of the bar. All the surrounding noise dissipates as I concentrate on getting to the opening. It's only a few feet away. Then I can escape down the hallway. One hand in front of the other. With each step toward the opening, the pounding of my heart grows louder in my ears. I continue crawling with my head down until my hand lands on a sand-colored canvas loafer. My heart leaps into my throat, and I struggle to take a breath. My gaze lifts from his dark stone-washed jeans, travels to the hem of his white t-shirt, and then lingers on his muscular chest before finally landing on his familiar face, wearing a smug smile I want to slap away.

"I thought that was you." Garrett crosses his arms over his chest, causing his shirt to stretch across his pecs and biceps. If he flexes, the fabric is going to give out.

His voice is as smooth as Macallan whisky. It sends my head into a tailspin. Sure, I've heard him speak on TV, but it's been so long since it's been in the flesh. I'm pretty sure I'm still in a state of paralysis from him being here. In person.

"What are you doing down there?" He tilts his head.

A heavy sigh escapes my lips. So much for hiding. Time to feign ignorance since it's easier than the truth. My heart lodges in my throat as I pat around on the floor. "I—um— I lost a contact." I continue to tap the dirty tile floor, searching for my nonexistent contact.

"If I know anything about bar floors, you won't want to put that back in your eye when you find it," he says smugly.

"When did you start wearing contacts?" Lach asks from behind me.

I twist my head to face him and mouth, "I hate you."

Lach shrugs. "It's a valid question."

"With the way you're crawling on the floor, I suspect you're trying to avoid me," Garrett says.

The corner of his lips lift into a half-smirk. It's hot and sexy and shouldn't affect me the way it does. It's always been his signature look and can still make butterflies take flight in my belly.

Not willing to abandon my contact ruse, I pretend to pluck it off the floor. "Got it." I scramble to my feet, avoiding eye contact with Garrett as I shoulder past him. My footsteps echo off the walls as I storm toward the bathroom and slam the door behind me. I sag against the door, brushing my dirty hands on my jeans. What the fuck was that? I've known Garrett for half my life, yet he's turned me into a blithering idiot. I guess it's the not seeing him or talking to him for ten years that really did me in. Never in a million years did I expect him to show up here. If I had to guess, he got the same wedding invitation I did. Granted, it's his brother, so he would be expected to show, but it's not like Garrett to conform to expectations.

I push off the door and stroll to the sink. Taking a paper towel from the dispenser, I run it under the faucet until it's damp. I press the towel to my face, the icy chill seeping into my heated skin. Too bad there isn't a window so I can *Pretty Woman* my way out of here. Instead, I hike up my pants, figuratively of course, and give myself a pep talk. I can do this. I'm an adult and can handle the situation like the twenty-eight-year-old I am.

"Dessa?" His voice is deep as it penetrates through the door.

All the previous adrenaline dissipates as a blanket of red floods my vision. Nope. Screw the high road. Fuck him and fuck him for making me feel feelings I was not anticipating feeling today. He can now experience what it's like to have someone walk away. I yank open the door and he nearly topples through the doorway. I shoot him an icy stare as his hand flies to the doorjamb to regain his balance. His signature scent of citrus and amber fills the air, reminding me of happier times we once shared. It's both sexy and seductive. It could possibly be my kryptonite.

His gaze locks on mine. A crackle of electricity fills the air around us. "You dyed your hair."

Instead of bolting past him, I freeze. My eyelashes flutter while I process his words. "After not seeing me, not talking to me, not a single social media message with 'Hi, how are you? We should catch up!' for ten fucking years all you have to say to me is 'You dyed your hair'?"

He stares at me without blinking, as he realizes the words he said and how stupid they sounded.

His silence fuels the raging inferno building inside me. He thinks things can go back to the way they were? That's not happening. "Why are you here? Just so you can walk away without a goodbye again? Well, screw you. I'm doing the walking away this time."

I shoulder past him, leaving him standing in the doorway alone. Am I being childish? Probably. Would the adult thing be to talk this out? Absolutely. Do I care? Fuck no. He left the first time, and I'm making sure I'm the one leaving for the last time. Before I reach the end of the hallway leading into the bar, his voice echoes behind me, followed by his footsteps.

"Dessa. Wait. Talk to me," he pleads.

When I reach the bar, Lach glances at me and then to Garrett, who's still behind me. "Everything okay?"

"I can't be here anymore. I need to leave."

Without missing a beat, Lach says, "I'll cover the rest of your shift."

"Thanks. I owe you." I'm grateful he trusts me and doesn't ask questions, even though I'll have to tell him everything later. Right now, I don't have time. I need to get out of here. Mostly, I need to get away from Garrett.

"Dessa! Wait." Garrett's voice trails behind me.

My steps quicken as I continue to ignore him.

"Dessa! Can we talk?"

I pretend to tune him out.

"Dessa!" His hand grips my elbow, and I yank my arm away.

Spinning around, I almost collide into his chest. I drop a foot back to give myself more space. "You had ten years to talk and what did you do? Nothing. You don't get to waltz in here now and demand that we talk." I twist on my heel to leave, but his fingers brush my wrist.

"Tates. It's not what you think."

I freeze. It's like I smacked face-first into a brick wall. I guess I sort of did, and its name is Garrett Dawson. Ten years have passed since I've heard his nickname for me. A name that was once endearing now leaves a bitter taste in my mouth.

I remove the "Reserved for Dessa" paper sign left on the metal bleachers behind home plate and fold it before tucking it in my pocket. Every game Garrett leaves a reserved seating sign where he wants me to sit. For the most part, everyone leaves it empty for me. Seated behind me is an older couple talking about baseball, sacks, and taters. My eyebrows pinch together, curious what that has to do with baseball. Until the man explains that sacks are the bases, and a tater is a home run. I chuckle to myself at the comparison.

By the third inning, we're down three to one. Garrett steps out from the dugout wearing white baseball pants and a red jersey with a white number seven stitched below the Trojans name. He casually swings the bat back and forth, loosening up. I scream his name and clap. He glances up and flashes me a half smirk.

"Hit a tater!" I yell.

Before he reaches the batter's box, he halts in his tracks, tilts his head, and shrugs. I laugh and shrug mine as well. He steps up to the plate and gets into position. The pitcher winds up and throws a curveball to the outside. Garrett holds his swing. He has a knack for gauging the perfect pitch. The umpire calls a ball. Garrett takes a step back, rolling his shoulders before stepping to the plate again. A cloud of dust floats through the air as he plants his foot. With his concentration aimed at the pitch he waits like a cat stalking their prey. The pitcher winds up and throws the ball. He swings. A crack resonates across the field as the ball sails to center field and drops outside the fence. I jump to my feet, screaming and clapping, while Garrett rounds the bases. The Trojans came back to win eight to five.

After the game, I meet him outside the dugout to congratulate him on the win. I throw my arms around his neck and without missing a beat, he wraps an arm around my waist. "Congrats! And you got a home run!"

"Thanks." He pulls off his sunglasses. His piercing green eyes stare back at mine. "What was the tater thing?"

I giggle. "I overheard some people talking about home runs being called taters and bases are sacks. I don't know. I went with it."

I drop my arms to my sides, but instead of letting me go Garrett wraps his arm around my shoulder. "I guess I'll have to call you my Little Tater. Tates for short."

My nostrils flare. "You don't get to call me that anymore. You lost that privilege." Anger roars through me like an EF-5 tornado. He can't storm back into my life and expect everything to be rainbows and butterflies. Using my nickname from when we were kids doesn't instantly make things better. What he did hurt. A lot. Maybe one day I can forgive him, but that day is not today.

I reach over to a customer's table and, in a calm, hushed voice, I ask, "Can I borrow this? You can get a new one at the bar. Tell them it's on Dessa."

Before they can respond, I grab the glass of beer and hurl the liquid at Garrett. "No. It's exactly what I think."

He ducks, the bulk of the beer narrowly missing him, but a few droplets wet his shirt. His gaze drifts to mine. Amusement, not anger that I threw a beer at him, etches his features. "I see you haven't been practicing your throw."

Steam billows out as I flare my nostrils. I grab another customer's glass and throw the beer at him. This time hitting him in the face. The golden liquid drips down, soaking into his white shirt. "The first is always practice."

He wipes a hand over his face. "I deserve that one."

I huff, spin around, and storm out of Porter's. What happens when your hot as sin, former best friend, baseball-playing, ex-boyfriend's brother barges back into your life, wanting to talk? You're screwed. Royally and utterly screwed.

Chapter 5

YOU SMELL LIKE A BREWERY

Garrett

That could have gone better. On the plus side, it could have gone a lot worse. A beer to the face is a first for me so I can now happily cross that off my bucket list. In all actuality, I was expecting a fist instead of the beer. I haven't said her nickname in years. I don't know why I said it. The name tumbled out of my mouth faster than I was able to swallow the letters down. The real punch in the gut was her throwing my own words back at me. She once asked me why I rarely swing at the first pitch and I told her, "The first is always practice." I'm glad after all these years, she never forgot. Perhaps all the hatred she has for me is a ruse. At least that's what I'm holding onto with both hands. Despite her venomous tone, she did talk to me. I'll take that as a small victory. She has every right to hate me right now. What I did was shitty, but at the time I was hurting. The best thing for me to do was to cut ties and leave. All I ask is she give me a few minutes so I can explain everything to her. Preferably without glasses of beer present.

"Um. I'm not exactly sure what happened and how you know Dessa, but I'm a big fan. And not because of the missed ball or anything. You're still an amazing player." A guy with short brown hair and a Porter's t-shirt holds out a white towel.

"Thanks." I pluck it from his grasp and run it down my face and over my chest, absorbing what beer I can from my shirt.

"I take it she's not thrilled to see you." He takes the towel once I'm finished.

"Did the beer in the face give it away?"

"A little bit." He holds out his hand. "I'm Lach."

I grip his hand with mine. "Garrett. Thanks for the towel and sorry for the beer on the floor."

"No problem. Not the first time. Can I get Seattle's most hated guy a beer? I promise I won't throw it in your face. I'm sure every person here will also happily buy you a beer since you gave Minnesota their first championship win."

I exhale a bitter laugh because it's all true. Seattle does hate me, and I did give Minnesota their first championship. The last one is the silver lining, I guess. As much as I would love to drown my sorrows in a cold pint of beer, I need to remain level-headed so I can draw up a game plan on how I'm going to get Dessa to talk to me since my first attempt failed. Truth be told, I didn't have a plan, anyway. But what was I expecting, a hug and a hand job? Instead, I got a face full of beer, and it wasn't even good beer. "Thanks, but maybe another time."

After leaving Porter's, I drive back to my parents', mostly because I don't have anywhere else to go. When I walk through the rear door that leads into the kitchen, my mom is at the counter plopping a spoonful of cookie dough onto a cookie sheet. As I pass by, I press a kiss to her cheek.

Her nose crinkles. "You smell like a brewery! Have you been drinking?" Her hands slap the table as she swivels to face me. "Please tell me you didn't drive home."

"No, and it's a long story. Apparently, Dessa wasn't as excited to see me as I was hoping." I yank open the fridge door and pull out a bottle of water. Twisting off the cap, I swallow a big gulp. The sweet aroma of melted chocolate chips lingering in the air makes my stomach rumble.

Her shoulders sag before her eyes soften, a small smile gracing her lips. "She'll come around. Just give her time."

I huff out a deep breath and shake my head. "I doubt more time is what she needs." But I'm out of options. I rap my knuckles on the counter. "I'm going to take a shower."

"Leave your clothes outside the door and I'll throw them in the laundry," she calls over her shoulder. The oven door creaks as she places the cookie sheet inside.

I hike up the stairs two at a time to the second floor and to the bathroom across the hallway from my bedroom. After I strip out of my clothes, I deposit them outside the bathroom door and turn on the hot water. Steam billows from the top of the shower curtain, filling the room. As I climb inside, the hot water cascades down my body and swirls into the drain, kind of like my failed attempt at an apology. With a sigh, I scrub my hands down my face, defeat washing over me.

Dessa hasn't been this mad at me since the time in middle school when I ditched her to play kickball with the boys. She wouldn't speak to me for a whole week, and it was the worst seven days of my entire life. She thwarted all my efforts at giving her notes in class by tossing them in the garbage before even reading them. Every time I tried to sit with her at lunch, she left to sit somewhere else. Finally, I got her to talk to me with a peace offering of my mom's chocolate chip cookies. It worked all those years ago. Maybe it will work again. At this point I'm willing to try anything.

Chapter 6

L IS FOR LOSER

Dessa

Yesterday after leaving Porter's, I drove around aimlessly, still in disbelief that Garrett fucking Dawson is in Harbor Highlands. Never did I expect to see him in person ever again. As soon as I saw his boyish good looks, but with a rugged charm, an entire gauntlet of emotions smacked me across the face. Hurt. Anger. Betrayal. Surprise. Anxiety. Excitement. And back to anger. So much anger. It was information overload, and I blacked out. Luckily, Lach caught me before I smashed my head against the floor. Seeing and speaking to him is what did me in. Ten years of rage bubbled out of me. Anger I've been holding on to for so long erupted like a volcano. Garrett was the target. Rightfully so. It was all his doing from the start.

Eventually, my mood evened out. When I arrived home, I made myself my favorite drink, a vodka gimlet. Then I set off to create new drinks to calm my anxious nerves, but based on the wicked pounding in my head, it didn't help. I'm pretty sure I did more drinking than mixing. I rest my forearm over my eyes to shield the blinding sunlight, willing my stomach to jump off the merry-go-round.

The last I heard, Garrett and his brother weren't speaking, but again, that was years ago, so maybe they've made amends. It's been a few years since I've talked to Tony. We were civil after our breakup, but it still left a strain on our friendship. We rarely talked, only a passing like or comment on social media. For the most part, he stayed on his side of town, and I stayed on mine.

On a groan, I slide out of bed because rolling is not going to help my stomach situation. I pluck my bathrobe off the hook on my closet door, shrug it over my shoulders, and secure the tie around my waist. I trudge into the kitchen and open a cupboard door to find half a sleeve of saltine crackers. Something is better than nothing since I thought a liquid dinner would be a sufficient meal last night. On my way to the other side of the counter, I make a pit stop at the fridge and grab a bottle of water. I plop down on a stool and dump half the contents of the sleeve onto the laminate countertop. Picking up a cracker, I bring it to my mouth and nibble on the corner. Crumbs fall to the counter like snowflakes. I brush them into the sink and swallow the now cracker paste. My stomach clenches at the intrusion of food. Now is not the time to revolt. You need substance. No alcohol.

A muffled *ding* sounds from somewhere in the kitchen. Without moving my head too quickly, I glance around the counter and over at my dining room table, but my phone is nowhere to be found. It chimes again and I stand to follow the noise. I lift a couple of notebooks on the counter, push an empty bottle of cranberry juice to the side, but nothing. I freeze for a moment, willing it to sound again, but it's like waiting for the dying battery of a smoke detector to beep —it never happens when you're actively listening. Tired of waiting, I round the corner of the counter, but before I can sit, my phone chimes again. On a huff, I stroll back into the kitchen and pull open drawers and cabinet doors until I find my phone sitting next to a bottle of tequila. Seems like an appropriate place for me to leave my phone. Still better than the one time I found it duct taped to the side of a box of wine in my fridge. I must have figured I wouldn't lose the wine, so might as well make sure my phone was close by.

I unlock my phone, and a parade of messages floods the screen.

RYLEE

Lach told me what happened. Well, half the story, so you need to fill in the rest.

LACH

Just wanted to check on you and make sure everything is okay.

RYLEE

Why are you not answering?

JAKE

Are you coming to work today?

RYLEE

Pick up your phone.

RYLEE

Answer Me.

RYLEE

Okay. I'm coming over.

I hit respond, but before I can type a reply, a banging on the door startles me.

"Dessa, open up!"

I slide off the stool and groan, my body refusing the movement as I stumble to the entryway. Twisting the lock, I pull open the door and Rylee barrels across the threshold.

"Finally! I'm glad you're alive." Rylee wraps her arms around me in a hug.

I wince from her loud voice. "Alive might be a stretch. I'm physically here, and that's the best I can offer right now." I untangle myself from her and step out of the way so she can enter.

Once in the kitchen she drops her purse on the counter and spins to face me. "Explain. What happened yesterday? All I heard was you threw a beer at Garrett Dawson and Lach was covering your shift."

"Technically, it was two." Rylee's eyes widen to the size of a saltine cracker. I throw myself onto a stool next to her as she stands. "Let's say the ghost of ex-best friends past has made an appearance."

Her mouth falls open, then closes like a fish starving for water before she leans forward. "Hold your panties. You're friends with Garrett Dawson?"

I swallow a gulp of water, not entirely sure if I want to rehash our history so soon. "Past tense. We *were* friends. All that's left is hate and resentment."

She rests her elbows on the counter. "How did I not know this? Why didn't you tell me you knew Garrett Dawson?"

"Something happened ten years ago that I chose to block out."

Rylee takes the seat next to me and props her head on her hand. "It must have been serious."

"As serious as losing your best friend can be." I give

Rylee the CliffsNotes version of my friendship with Garrett since she won't stop prying until I do. I start with how I dated his brother Tony and end with how Garrett left without saying goodbye and basically disappeared from the face of the earth. The only reason I knew he still existed was seeing him on TV during baseball season and in the tabloids during the offseason, holding hands with this actress and that super model. It all got very tiresome.

"Damn. I can't believe you were friends with Garrett Dawson, and even more so that you never told me."

"You don't always need to refer to him as *Garrett Dawson*. Back then, he wasn't the big Home Run Playboy he is now." The home run part has always been true, but not the playboy. As far as I know, he didn't date during our senior year. He was always busy doing something baseball related, even during the offseason. Granted, all my time was spent with Tony, and I couldn't pay that much attention.

"Why is he back in town?" Rylee asks, pulling me from my thoughts.

"I don't know." I was too busy throwing beer in his face to ask. "If I had to guess, it's for his brother's wedding. The same wedding I got an invite to."

Her shoulders scrunch as her brows draw together. "You got an invite to your ex's wedding? Who does that?"

I shrug. "You got me. Clearly, I can't go. One: it's my ex. Two: Garrett's going to be there, and I'd rather not run into him any more than I already have."

Her phone chimes with an incoming message. She glances down and rolls her eyes. "Jake wants to know if you're coming to work today."

I laugh. "I'm doing wonderful, Jake. Thanks for your concern."

Her phone chimes again.

Another chuckle escapes my throat. "Put him out of his misery and tell him I'll be in."

She glances at the message. "Actually, it's Trey." She tilts her head as she reads. "He needs me to buy pink paint, popsicle sticks, baby carrots, glitter, and latex gloves."

I nod along to her list. "That's an interesting combination."

"If I had to guess, the paint, glitter, and popsicle sticks are for some artsy thing with the girls. The latex gloves will be for his hands, so his dick doesn't sparkle like a princess wand like last time."

"That's a visual I didn't need today."

"Trust me, I didn't need to see it either, but he insisted on showing me. It was every bit as hilarious as you would expect." She smiles fondly at the thought of Trey. On the outside they seem like an unlikely pair, but they bring out the best in each other. And my best friend deserves all the happiness after dealing with her ex.

"And the baby carrots?"

She huffs. "He'll want a snack. I wanted to stop by and make sure you're okay, but I better get going. I have to make sure the house doesn't turn into a real-life glitter bomb."

"Or he's turning your house into an actual princess castle." I shrug. Trey's the father of two girls. One is Rylee's that he adopted, but he treats her as if she's his own. Of course, he treats them both like the princesses they are, and Rylee is their queen.

"Alright. We'll chat later. If anything new regarding Garrett comes up, you have to tell me."

"You'll be waiting a while since I'm avoiding him at all costs."

"Either way, this is more interesting than my life." She wraps her arms around me in a hug, then grabs her purse.

When the front door closes behind her, I rest my elbows on the counter and pick up another cracker, shoving it in my mouth. I guess I'll stop being a miserable piece of shit and be productive.

An hour later, I'm stepping out of the shower feeling semi-human, at least human enough to go out in public. I haphazardly twist my hair into a messy bun, slide into a pair of black leggings, and shove an oversize hoodie over my head. It's not my worst ensemble, but definitely not my best. I apply a light dusting of make-up to at least disguise the bags under my eyes and avoid scaring small children at the grocery store. Saturday mornings are my favorite time to shop. There's always fewer people. But today I'm running a little later than scheduled and vodka is the only one to blame.

At the store, I push my cart full of spinach, onions, rice, avocados, and granola down the aisle. My last stop is the juice aisle to replenish my stock from last night. As I reach for a bottle of cranberry juice, I hear my name. When I glance over my shoulder, Mrs. Dawson, wearing a bright pink blouse, is waving her hand as if she's trying to stop traffic. She power-walks toward me, the wheel on her grocery cart squeaking louder with each turn.

"Dessa. I thought that was you. It was so hard to tell with the new hair color, but I'll never forget your face." Her cart comes to a halt next to mine.

"Hi, Mrs. Dawson. It's such a pleasant surprise to run into you here."

"Normally I'm not on this side of town—"

Which is precisely why it's the one I go to.

"But we were having brunch to talk about all things wedding. Speaking of which, I hope your mom gave you the invite."

"She did. Thank you." I force a smile. An invite to a wedding I really don't want to go to. Lucky me.

"I didn't have your address, so I was happy I ran into your mom to pass it along, but if I'd known I was going to run into you at the grocery store, I would have given it to you myself," she says cheerfully.

Janice Dawson has always been on the right side of optimistic. Growing up, I never once saw her mad or even slightly upset. The sun always shines in her world. It wouldn't surprise me if she carried the invite around just in case we ran in to each other. I'm sure she has a stack of invitations in her purse at the ready to pass out to anyone she forgot. She always hated leaving someone out.

"But your mom mentioned you have a townhouse on Chestnut Street. That's a pleasant neighborhood."

"I do. I've lived there for about five years."

"That's great. I hope you'll be able to make it." A hopeful expression fills her face.

"Oh. I don't know—" I lift my shoulders in a half shrug. I hate being put on the spot.

"The whole family is going to be in town. Everyone would love to see you again."

"I'm not sure. I'll have to check my calendar." Calendar checked, and it's wide open, but I'm still not going to the wedding.

"And you have to meet Georgia, Tony's soon-to-be-wife." She pulls her phone from her purse and flashes me a picture of Georgia and Tony. "She's such a lovely lady. You two would get along fantastically."

"They look beautiful together." I stare at the picture, mostly because all other words have evaded me. They look happy together, and I'm glad Tony's found someone, but hanging out with my ex-boyfriend's soon-to-be-wife sounds awful. A root canal sounds more enjoyable.

"It's great you stayed friends with Tony." Her eyes soften as she offers me a small smile.

I nod. If by "friends," she means the occasional social media comment, then sure, we're friends.

She rests a hand on my forearm, and her eyes light up with delight. "I heard you ran into Garrett."

My chest tightens. If "ran into him" is the same as yelling at him and throwing beer on him. Twice. Then yes, I totally ran into him. "I did." I give her a tight-lipped smile.

"It will be so great to have the three peas in a pod together again." Janice's smile is infectious even though I'm not in the smiley mood.

Since I was eight years old, Tony, Garrett, and I always hung out. The three of us were the only kids on our street, so it was natural for us to become friends. Things changed going into our senior year, then everything completely disintegrated after graduation.

"Oh, I'm not sure about that," I mutter under my breath.

"And feel free to bring a date. I'm sure some handsome man has snatched you up."

"Well... Um..." Actually no, but I don't tell her that. "I don't know if I'll be able to—"

"Everyone is going to be so excited to see you." She clasps her hands in front of her as if this is already a done deal.

Great. Only for them to learn I've been in the same spot as I was ten years ago, but now with dyed hair.

"It's been so long since the family has seen you, especially Nana. She always adored you. It's getting harder for her to travel. She won't be able to make too many more trips to Harbor Highlands." She flashes me a warm smile.

Dammit. If anything could guilt trip me, it would be

Nana. She's the sweetest woman in the entire world. Clenching my teeth, I plaster on a wide smile, hoping it looks genuine. "I can't wait to see everyone." I'm doing this for Nana. But I can't go alone. I need a date.

I'm screwed, completely, utterly, royally screwed—not the fun kind either. This is borderline backdoor-without-lube kind of screwed. Not that I know from experience; it just doesn't sound pleasant. Panic grips me as I scour through my contacts on my phone, desperately seeking someone, anyone, who could be my last-minute wedding date.

Lach walks past me. "Growing up did your parents ever tell you if you make a face for so long it will eventually stay that way forever?"

My gaze slowly lifts from my phone to Lach. "Probably."

"Okay. Because you have been scrunching your face for the past ten minutes, and I'm afraid it's going to become a permanent look. I assure you guys are not into angry eyebrows."

I purse my lips. "Fine then. You can help me. I need a favor."

"Anything." He sets a case of beer on the edge of the cooler.

"I need you to be my date to a wedding." I hold my breath, waiting for his answer.

"Anything but that."

I prop my hands on my hips. "Why?"

"It's a wedding."

"It's a date for a wedding."

"Single guys like me go to weddings to hook up with

the single bridesmaids. I can't do that if I'm going with you as a date." He quirks an eyebrow at me.

I shake my head. "I don't care what you do. Hookup with whoever you want, including the bridesmaids."

Without looking up, he places the bottles in the cooler two at a time. "But I look like the asshole for hooking up with other people while on a date with someone else. I have a reputation to uphold."

"Do you want me to write you a permission slip?" A figurative light bulb sparks above my head. "I got it! I could dump you at the wedding and then you could play the guy with the broken heart. Girls gobble that shit up. They would be more than willing to make you forget all about her or me in this case." I flash him a dazzling smile, praying he takes the bait. I need him to say yes. "Even though I would be hard to get over."

"Don't flatter yourself. But your idea could work." He rubs his chin.

"Great! So you'll do it?"

"No."

I roll my eyes and huff. "You're a terrible friend." I spin around and face my boss. "Jake. Want to help out your favorite employee?" I flash him a smile so radiant it could rival the sun.

"There are a lot of things wrong with your sentence. For starters, I don't do favors," Jake deadpans.

"Today is a good day to start. It's at the end of the week. You can pick me up or we can even meet there if you'd like. But dress nice. Like you care."

"Whose wedding is it, anyway?" Lach asks.

"Tony Dawson."

"Oh. So Garrett's going," Jake says. "Yeah, I'm steering clear of that."

"What do you mean 'steering clear of that'? There's nothing to steer clear of." I prop my hand on my hip.

Jake scoffs. "Nope. I'll be busy washing my hair that night."

"I hate you both," I mumble. "See if you ever get a favor out of me."

"Good thing I won't ask." Jake closes the cash register with a heavy thud. Then he and Lach stride toward the hallway, I'm sure to think of more dumb excuses for why they won't be my date.

Nora approaches me from the other end of the bar. "So you decided to go to the wedding?"

"It's not that I want to go, but Tony's mom conned me into going. If I arrive dateless at my ex-boyfriend's wedding, people will give me nothing but pity glances. Since I've known most of these people my whole life, I don't want to be that person." Arriving with a date at least gives the impression that I'm not a twenty-eight-year-old, single woman who's done nothing with her life and that I'm not in the same place I was ten years ago. Even though I am. I huff out an exasperated breath.

She rests her hip against the cooler. "Where do you expect to find a date?"

"That's a very good question, since my phone has produced nothing but duds and my two friends are jerks. The dating pool is severely lacking."

"You could ask Trey to hook you up with one of the guys from SBL."

I create a mental lineup of the guys who've been to Trey's Single Bros Life meetings. Even though he's no longer single he still holds meetings for a guys' night. As each guy flashes in front of me, I don't want to walk through the doors at my ex-boyfriend's wedding with any of them on my arm. Miles may be the only acceptable one, but even then, I don't get the vibe that he knows how to date. "Why isn't there an app for dating?"

"There's lots of apps, but are you willing to put out at the end?" Nora raises a questioning brow.

"No. Like an app to find a casual date for events like this. No hookups. No expectations. No strings attached kind of dates."

Nora taps her chin. "You might be on to something."

I rest my elbow on the bar top and slump my head in my hand. I'm going to a wedding where everyone has known me for years, and I've done absolutely nothing with my life. Might as well add a scarlet letter *L* to my dress for "loser." My gaze drifts to Nora. Desperation laces my tone as I ask, "You have a lot of friends—can I borrow one for a night?"

"Correction. I've gone on a lot of dates. Some have certainly gone better than others, but I might know a few guys. What kind of date are you looking for? Someone to make the ex jealous or perhaps the ex-best friend?" She wiggles her eyebrows and I roll my eyes. "Okay. How about someone to intimidate the ex? Or someone the parents disapprove of? Even better, someone so sweet he gives you a toothache?"

I tap my chin, contemplating my choices as if I were picking food items off a drive-through menu. Jealous could work. I don't really need to intimidate anyone, but I like the sweet guy who'll show everyone I found a great catch. "Do you have someone who is sweet, but not overly sweet, and successful?"

She unlocks her phone and swipes her finger over the screen. "I can ask Brian. He's super sweet, I think because he's a mama's boy, but he does own his own business. When's the wedding?"

"December third."

"That's coming up quick. I'll send him a text."

My fingers drum nervously on the bar and my heart pounds as I anxiously await the answer. I might not have to go to this wedding alone. I do an internal happy dance. Hallelujah.

Her phone chimes with an incoming message and her lips press together. Disappointment etches her features as her gaze meets mine. "Brian's off the market. He's wifed up. I'm sorry."

My heart plummets to my stomach. Cut the music. This dance party just got shut down. "That's okay. Thanks for trying."

"If I think of anyone else, I'll let you know."

I nod. I'd better get my scarlet letter ready.

Chapter 7

THE MIDDLE FINGER

Garrett

Monday: The sun rays shimmer across the bright blue sky. The air is fresh and crisp. Most importantly, it's a great day to convince Dessa to talk to me. I can feel it deep in my bones. Today is my day. Upon entering Porter's, I spot Dessa behind the bar. Her back is to me while Lach is on a step stool, writing on the menu board under Drink Special. The blue calligraphy reads "Ghost Catcher." My body jolts to a stop as my chest tightens. A part of me wants to believe it's a coincidence, but I doubt it. My confidence meter drops a fraction. I brush my palms on my jeans and will my feet to power forward.

At the bar, I find an empty barstool and take a seat as Lach and Dessa continue to bicker about the drink. A small smile flirts on my lips. She was never one to back down, and I'm glad she hasn't changed because that fiery spirit is one of the many things I adore about her.

The stool next to me scrapes along the linoleum floor

as an older man rises to his feet. Dessa glances over her shoulder, her dark hair flowing around her as she says goodbye with a warm smile to the customer. When she spots me, her gaze narrows and her lips curl into a sneer. Her once playful demeanor instantly evaporates. Without saying a word, she stomps to the other end of the bar. She didn't throw anything at me. I'll chalk that up as a win.

Tuesday: As soon as I open the front door to Porter's, all the noise and chatter floods onto the sidewalk. The place is wall-to-wall packed. Damn near every stool and table is full. I scan the entire bar, and Dessa is nowhere. I hang around for a few minutes longer hoping that she's in the back or something, but she never appears. It must be her night off.

Wednesday: I'm determined to get her to talk to me. Hear me out. After that, if she wants to continue hating me, she can, but I'm not going down without swinging. Until then, I'll try a new tactic. One that involves her favorite thing.

As I flip through the worn pages of my mom's recipe book, a pang of guilt hits me. I've lost a lot of years with Dessa. All I can do is pray these cookies will be the perfect apology gift. Or at least a peace offering. She's never been able to say no to my mom's cookies. As kids, whenever Dessa came over, Mom would always have cookies waiting for us. For a while, I was convinced she was only friends with me because of the cookies.

Since my mom isn't here to make them for me, I'll have to bake them myself. How hard can it be? I have the recipe. All I need to do is follow the directions. Anyone can do that. Pulling a white apron over my head, I tie the straps around my waist, making sure it's snug. Glancing at my chest, I see an upside-down cartoon pig holding a butter knife and a pitchfork with the printed words "Don't worry, I got this. I watched a YouTube video." That's right cartoon pig, I got this. I rummage through all the cupboards and drawers to find mixing bowls, measuring cups, and spoons. Once everything is set out in front of me, I go on a hunt for all my ingredients.

With the first batch baking in the oven, I stare at the timer, drumming my fingers on the counter as I count the minutes until they're golden brown. I continuously peer through the small window in the door. Seconds before the timer dings, I yank open the door. The sugary sweet aroma of melted chocolate assaults my nostrils. It's a grand slam on my first try. I pat myself on the back. With an oven mitt covered hand, I pull out the cookie sheet and my heart drops. What started as nine cookies has now morphed into one enormous, rectangular, flat-as-a-pancake cookie. Shit. The cookie sheet rattles as I toss it on the stove.

I try again with a new batch. When they're finished, I let them cool for a minute. They look like cookies and even smell like cookies. This might be the batch. I grab one, break it in half, and toss a piece into my mouth. While I'm chewing, I glance at the recipe, but something tastes off. Almost artificial. Panic sets in as I peer at the counter with my ingredients. It's then when the square, white container labeled baking *powder* instead of baking *soda* catches my attention. Shit. Why is there baking soda and baking powder? And why do they do different things? Baking. The first word. The most important word. But no. After some quick research on my phone, I learn one requires an acid while the other doesn't, and these chocolate chip cookies require baking soda, not baking powder. I guess you learn something new every day. Another batch in the garbage.

By the third batch, I'm on the brink of defeat. But I can't quit. This is too important. I triple-check all my ingredients. Follow the recipe line by line. Now I wait and pray to the cookie gods that they turn out. While they still don't resemble my mom's chocolate chip cookies, they're close. Which counts in horseshoes and hand grenades. I grab one and break it in half. A string of gooey chocolate stretches between the two halves. I toss a chunk into my mouth and chew. I moan. They may not be a grand slam but at least a triple, and that counts in my book. Once cool, I grab a plastic tray and place several cookies on it, securing them with plastic wrap. After I clean up my mess, I waste no time and head straight out the door, cookies in hand.

Porter's
ALE HOUSE

"Well, if it isn't my second favorite baseball player." Jake comes to a halt on the other side of the bar at Porter's.

I take a seat across from him. "Why am I only your second?"

"Play for a better team, or at least learn how to catch a ball."

I huff out a laugh. "Thanks for the pep talk. You really know how to boost someone's morale."

"If you came here for someone to stroke your ego, you came to the wrong place." Jake reaches under the bar, then slaps three darts on the bar top. My gaze drops to the two red darts and one yellow dart with plastic tips. "This time, how about you take it easy on my dartboard, so I don't have to replace all these tips?" His brow arches.

Since I was seventeen, I've been coming into Porter's to throw darts. Luckily, Jake allowed me to hang out and spend my money on the dartboard. But not without a threat if I tried to order anything but a root beer, I'd have to learn how to throw a baseball with my toes. Jake's a big guy. You don't take his threats lightly. Since he gave me a reprieve from my house for a few hours, I wasn't going to jeopardize the opportunity. Unfortunately, Jake's dartboard took the brunt of my anger the entire summer leading into my senior year.

I reach into my pocket and grab my wallet. "Let me give you some money for those."

"Don't worry about it. If you didn't come here for darts, can I get you a beer?"

"No, I'm good," I wave my hand, "but is Dessa around?"

"No."

Jake has always been a man of few words. "Alright. Can you give her these?" I slide the tray of cookies across the bar.

His gaze drops, then slowly meets mine with a raised eyebrow. Somehow, he can ask a million questions with only an arched brow.

I shrug. "I need Dessa to talk to me."

"And you think cookies will do that?"

"It's my mom's recipe and her favorite." At least, I pray the cookies are a big enough bribe. If not, my next option is dropping to my knees and begging.

He pokes at the extra crispy cookie through the plastic wrap. "Don't quit baseball to become a baker."

"Thanks for that vote of confidence. I'm hoping it's the thought that counts." I drum my fingers on the worn wood bar top. "Speaking of Dessa, I want to ask you about her."

"Oh, hell no. I want nothing to do with that shit." He rises to his full height and crosses his arms over his chest.

"Come on," I plead. "You're the only person I have here. Plus, you've known Dessa as long as I've been away."

"I don't get involved in her relationships, and as long as she keeps it out of my bar, I don't care what she does."

"So, she's not seeing anyone?" I try to keep the desperation out of my tone but fail miserably.

"I don't keep tabs on my employees." Jake rests his palms on the bar and leans in. "Look, I'm well acquainted with your past and frankly, that's more than I want to know."

I lean against the backrest of the stool, twisting to rest my arm on the back. "She wouldn't have freaked out as much as she did if she didn't care. At least a little."

"Fuck." Jake stands to his full height and scrubs his hands down his face. "You know who's really good at this shit? Rylee. You should ask Rylee."

"I don't know Rylee. You're my friend, so I'm asking you as my friend, what do you think?"

He huffs out a long breath. "Talk to her. She likes to talk, so she'll eventually talk to you."

A small smile forms over my lips as I nod. He described Dessa perfectly.

Porter's
ALE HOUSE

Later that night, I head to Porter's. As soon as I stroll through the door, the lively chatter and clinking glasses fade into the background when I spot Dessa pouring a beer from the tap. She glances up as if she can sense my presence. She holds my gaze for a brief second, her eyes revealing a mixture of curiosity and hesitation, before she averts her gaze, pretending not to see me. Between two other customers, I find an empty stool at the bar and take a seat. The guy on my right flags her over, and she serves him a beer. She then asks the guy to my left if he needs anything.

Before she can walk away, I ask for a beer. Her only acknowledgment of me is her middle finger. As she continues to stroll along the edge of the bar away from me, I jump off my stool and follow her.

"Dessa. Wait."

"I have nothing to say to you, Garrett. I said everything I needed to say before."

"That's not fair. You can't shut me out."

"Watch me," she spits through gritted teeth.

I continue following her, dodging and weaving between customers. "Did Jake give you the cookies? I made them from my mom's recipe. I remember them being your favorite," I say with a hint of desperation. Right now, this is all I have.

"There's a family of raccoons devouring them by the dumpster," she says nonchalantly before stopping in front of a customer.

I huff out a laugh. She's talking to me, so that's a plus. "At least something is enjoying them," I mutter. "But this whole situation… it's not what you think."

She jerks her head up, jaw clenched, as a furious glare burns a hole through me. "Not what I think? So, you're telling me you didn't leave without saying a single word to me?"

I rub the back of my neck. "Well, when you put it that way. Yes. But I had to."

"No, Garrett. What you had to do was at least say goodbye. We were best friends. It's the least you could've done." When she's finished serving the customer, she continues to strut along the bar while I follow until we reach the end and there's nothing separating us.

"It's complicated." I reach out, wanting to touch her, needing to touch her. The warmth of her skin brushes against my fingertips.

She jerks away. "It's not complicated. You saying 'it's

complicated' doesn't make it complicated. In fact, it's pretty simple. You ghosted me."

"Dessa. Please. Give me a couple minutes so we can talk this out?" I plead. At this point, I'm seconds away from dropping to my knees and wrapping my arms around her legs so she's forced to talk to me.

"Fine. We can talk right now. Why did you leave?" Her hands clutch her hips as her lips form a thin line.

My gaze shifts to her coworkers, who are now staring at us along with most of the bar, who's in earshot of our conversation. Leaning in, I whisper, "I'd rather do this in private."

She shoots a sharp glare over her shoulder, and they pivot on their heels, pretending to be preoccupied. Her gaze meets mine again. "Now's your chance." She crosses her arms over her chest and taps her foot on the linoleum floor.

Her brown eyes turn a shade darker as she waits for me to say something. Anything. But words are failing me. How do I sum up ten years of hurt and frustration in a single sentence?

Growing impatient, she drops her arms to her sides. "If you're not going to talk, fine. You can stand there like a fool, but I'm getting back to work. This is done." Her hair twirls around her as she storms past me.

Fuck. I jab my fingers through my hair. "This isn't done," I say to her retreating frame. I'll wait here all night if I have to, and I do exactly that.

Chapter 8

TEN YEARS' WORTH OF CHANCES

Dessa

"He's been sitting over there all night." Nora props her elbow on the bar, her blonde braid draping over her shoulder. "You're not going to go talk to him?"

"No. He had his chance. I have absolutely nothing to say to him. He knows how I feel. He can wallow by himself all night if he wants to." I busy myself with washing a stack of pint glasses.

Since I stormed away from Garrett two hours ago, he's been sitting at a pub table in the corner of the bar, his eyes fixed on the glass in front of him. All night I've been discreetly stealing glances at him while avoiding being caught. I'm torn between wanting to punch him in the face or rip his heart out, since that's what he did to me. Pirates' code and all. An eye for an eye. Or in my case, a heart for a heart. The first one seems less messy, but the second would certainly get the point across.

Nora peers at Garrett, then at me. "The man made you cookies. The least you can do is talk to him."

I slam the door on the glass washer under the counter, the sharp noise reverberating behind the bar. "He's going to need to do better than cookies after ghosting me for ten years."

Her head shakes in disbelief. "I don't think you're giving him a fair chance. He made you cookies that you fed to the neighborhood raccoons. I would swoon if a guy baked me cookies."

I roll my eyes. "You don't ghost your best friend for ten years and expect a fair chance. He had ten years' worth of chances, and you know what he did? Nothing. So, I'm going to do the same." I fight to keep the bite out of my tone since she doesn't deserve my wrath.

"I don't know how you have so much will power to resist him. Garrett Dawson on TV, gorgeous. Garrett Dawson in person disintegrates my panties." She twists the end of her hair around her finger as she stares wistfully at Garrett.

I hate that she's not wrong. Garrett's always been good looking. As a teenager, he always had a boyish charm to him. But now, somehow time has made him even more attractive. My nipples pebble beneath my shirt. Dammit. Traitorous body. I spin around, avoiding both of them. "But he's still a jackass."

For the rest of the night, he sits at a table tucked away in the far corner, alone. By one in the morning, the bar has mostly emptied, the faint sound of a melancholic song echoing through the deserted space. Garrett's still slumped in the corner, in the same spot he's been all night.

I lean across the bar to where Nora is sweeping under the stools. "Tell him he has to leave." I nod toward Garrett.

"He's your friend, you tell him."

"He's not my friend."

"You know him more than I do."

"Please do this one thing for me." I link my hands together, on the verge of begging.

"No, he's your problem and you're going to deal with him yourself. I have to run to the back." She takes the broom and saunters to the other side of the bar.

"Ugh. Fine." I huff. "See if I do you any favors," I mumble under my breath. I stomp to the corner where Garrett's seated, each footfall growing louder with every step. Crossing my arms over my chest, I come to a stop when I reach his table. "We're closing. You need to leave."

He lifts his head to meet mine. "Let's talk for five minutes."

"I have absolutely nothing to say to you." I refuse to let even a hint of vulnerability escape. He doesn't deserve it.

"After all these years, you really have nothing to say to me?" His lips tip up in the corner because he knows I have a whole lot I want to say to him, but it's not worth a single breath.

"I could spend hours, probably days, telling you everything you did to hurt me, but it's not worth it anymore. I've moved on." Technically, I haven't moved on. I'll never move on, but I don't have it in me to hash it out with Garrett.

He rests his elbows on the table and leans in. "So that's it. Just like that. It's over?"

"What do you want?" I drop my arms to my sides in defeat. "A parting gift? It's done, Garrett. I'm done."

Without saying another word, he rises to his feet, and I retreat a step to give him more room. With one last glance at me, his green eyes bore into mine. Then he turns on his heel and stomps out the front door.

Once the door slams behind him, I race over and lock

it. With a heavy exhale, I finally let my shoulders sag. I expected him to put up a bigger fight than that, since he's been doing it all night. At least it's done. Hopefully, I won't need to see him again until the wedding.

For the next thirty minutes, Nora and I finish cleaning the bar and restocking a few of the coolers. Once we're finished, I turn off the lights and punch in the security code before leaving.

We're halfway across the dimly lit parking lot when I catch sight of a dark figure leaning against my car. I reach into my purse and wrap my fingers around a small, plastic case, my thumb hovering over the trigger just in case. They have one ankle crossed over the other, and a baseball cap perched on their head. Immediately, I recognize that it's Garrett. When I'm several feet away, he lifts his head.

I release my grip on the pepper spray and roll my eyes. I guess I don't have to wait until the wedding. "Do you make it a habit of leaning against strangers' cars?"

He pushes off and takes two cautious footsteps toward me. "It was the 'I Don't Eat My Homies' bumper sticker that tipped me off it's yours and not some stranger's."

"Oh yeah. That's definitely not mine. I like meat," Nora chimes in.

I glare at Nora before turning my attention back to Garrett. "Go home. I told you I'm done. I want to go home and go to bed."

"This isn't done. Me leaving was a shitty thing to do, but please give me five minutes. That's all I ask."

I scoff. "It was more than shitty. Plus, five minutes is more than what you deserve." I open my purse and fish around for the martini glass key chain but I'm missing my phone. Shit. I glance over my shoulder at Nora. "I have to go back inside. I forgot my phone."

"Do you want me to wait for you?" she asks.

"No." I wave her off. "It'll be fine. I'll only be a couple of minutes. You can go. I'll be alright."

"Are you sure? I don't mind." Her gaze flits from me to Garrett.

"Yeah. I'll see you tomorrow." As she strolls to her car, I turn around and beeline it back toward Porter's.

Garrett's footsteps are hot on my heels. "Talk to me."

"I'm not doing this. I'm tired. I just want to find my phone and go home." My body jerks as I spin around, slamming into his hard chest. Citrus and amber invade my nostrils. My kryptonite. As teenagers I would always borrow—or steal—his sweatshirts because I was always cold. I had a habit of lifting the collar and inhaling the comforting scent. Then I'm reminded of the painful memory of him leaving and suddenly, it's not so comforting. As I rest my palms on his chest, his warmth radiates to my hands. Tingles bottle rocket through my body until I'm reminded why I hate him. I shove him away. "Why are you so close?"

His balance falters as he takes a step back, giving me a few inches of space. "Fine, if you don't want to talk, I'm going to talk, and you'll listen."

"I don't want to do that either." I shove the key into the lock and turn. With a hard push, I'm through the door, but before I can close it behind me, Garrett slides through the opening. I roll my eyes. With a twist of the lock, the deadbolt slides into place, and I stomp across the bar.

"Will you stop so I can talk to you?"

"I don't need to stop. I'm fully capable of multitasking, so if you have anything to say, you can say it now." I shrug out of my coat and set it on the bar, along with my wallet before stomping down the hallway. When I reach Jake's office, I punch in the code to prevent the alarm from going off.

"It wasn't supposed to be like this." His voice trails behind me.

I continue to storm down the hallway and into the employee break room. Once inside, I flip on the light switch. Harsh fluorescent lights illuminate the room. "So, what was it supposed to be like?" I yank open the small metal locker and rifle through a stack of papers and shove a bag of granola to the opposite side. Shit. No phone.

"I don't know, but not this."

The sound of metal slamming shut echoes through the room as I spin around. Garrett's leaning against a table, rubbing the back of his neck.

"Really? Is that all you have to say? You want to talk to me and all you have to say is, 'It wasn't supposed to be like this.' That's your whole five-minute speech? Guess what, Garrett? It is like this." I shoulder past him, turning off the light, shrouding him in the darkness. Once in the hallway, I head toward the bar again.

From behind me, I hear Garrett's voice, strained and full of tension. "I was going through a lot, and I needed to get away."

"Congratulations, you certainly got away. For ten years." My steps quicken as I enter behind the bar. I prowl the length as I peer underneath where the glasses are kept.

"I'm sorry about that."

I stop in my tracks and whip around to face him, my nostrils flaring. "Is that all you're sorry about?"

"What else do you want me to say?" He throws his hands in the air.

I huff out a humorless laugh. "Clearly, you're not sorry. Not at all." I glide past him again. He turns to follow me down the hallway. Swiftly, I veer right into the storage room and turn on the light. In front of me are three walls covered with shelves filled with bottles of liquor and other various supplies. I start on one side of the room and scan each shelf, hoping to find my phone. Out of nowhere, a hard thump echoes across the cement, followed by gritty scraping.

"Shit," Garrett mutters.

A second later, something smacks against my shoe. I glance down and a piece of wood is resting next to my foot. My heart pounds in my chest, its rapid beats echoing in my ears as panic sets in. It's not just any piece of wood, but the one keeping the door propped open. As soon as I glance up, the supply room door is halfway closed.

"Look, I'm here now trying to make amends—"

"Nooo!" I screech.

Chapter 9

THE LADYGASM

Dessa

I lunge past Garrett, shoving him out of the way, and toward the door. My fingertips brush against the doorknob as it clicks shut. "No! No! No! Dammit!" I grip the cold doorknob and jiggle and tug, but it doesn't open. "Why'd you do that?!"

"W-what did I do?" His voice is frantic as he scans the room.

I continue yanking on the doorknob. "You kicked the piece of wood from under the door!"

His head swivels from side to side, searching for the piece of wood. "I didn't mean to. Perhaps someone shouldn't keep a piece of wood on the floor."

I throw my hands up in frustration. "It was propping the door open because it's broken, and once it's closed, it can't be opened from the inside." I yank on the door again to no avail. Talking to Garrett was the last thing I wanted to do today, and being trapped in a room with him is even worse.

His face goes stoic. "Oh, shit."

"Yeah. Oh, shit."

"Let me try." He nudges me out of the way and grips the handle. With every twist and yank, it still doesn't move.

"Just because you're a guy with big, rippling, strong muscles doesn't mean you can magically open the locked door." I can't keep the sarcasm out of my tone.

He pulls the doorknob again. "I don't need your snarky commentary. At least I'm trying."

"If I wasn't trapped in a storage closet with you, I wouldn't need to be snarky," I snap, clenching and unclenching my fists before continuing my quest to find my phone. As I scan the shelves, a purple glitter case catches my attention. "Found it!" I lift my phone in the air like it's the Olympic torch. "I'll call Jake and tell him to come and let us out." I tap the screen, but nothing happens. My heart races as I repeatedly press the side buttons, but the screen remains dark. "Dammit. My phone's dead. Where's yours?"

He pats his pockets, then peers up at me as trepidation fills his eyes. "In my car."

"Are you kidding me?" I spit. "Who leaves their phone in their car?"

"Who leaves their phone dead in a storage room?"

My gaze jerks to his, and my eyes narrow into fiery slits. "I don't need your attitude right now. We're going to be stuck in here until morning."

His fists pound on the door.

I roll my eyes. "It's useless. No one can hear you."

Slowly, his fist connects with the metal door one last time in defeat.

I slump against the corner of a shelf. The metal digs

into my back, but I don't care. I'm trapped in a storage room with Garrett fucking Dawson. I want to scream, but it'll be a wasted effort. "This is your fault. Why did you have to follow me? Better yet, why did you even come here?"

He spins around to face me. "Maybe if you talked to me when we were outside of the storage room, we wouldn't be here." The hum of the florescent lights echoes through the room. "And how was I supposed to know a piece of wood I accidentally kicked was propping the door open because the doorknob is broken?"

"Don't shift the blame on me," I scold.

"Also, if you didn't forget your phone in the storage room, which is clearly something you still do, we wouldn't be in this mess. Two strikes for you."

Oh, hell no. Now he's turned this personal. "I don't always lose my phone."

He laughs, lightening the mood slightly. "How many times did you forget it in my car in high school?"

I scoff, crossing my arms and shifting my gaze away from him. "That's not the point."

"I think I proved my point perfectly."

"Don't be so smug."

He shrugs. "Actually, this is kind of perfect. Now you can't run away from me." He finds a five-gallon bucket in the far corner and tips it upside down. Before sitting, he pulls his hoodie over his head. His shirt rides up, exposing a sliver of tan skin and a delightful happy trail that disappears in the waistband of his jeans.

I jerk my gaze away, praying he didn't catch me. Don't get distracted by the sexy baseball player. "What don't you understand? I don't want to talk." Stomping to the opposite side of the room, I pivot my shoulder so I'm facing away from him. I need all the space I can get so I don't reach out and strangle him.

"Stop being so stubborn."

I eye him over my shoulder. "I'm not stubborn. I'm standing my ground."

He props his elbows on his knees and scrubs his hands down his face. "I'm sorry I hurt you."

"Hurt me?" I push off the shelf and square my shoulders. "You destroyed me. You left without saying a word. Not a single goodbye. Nothing. You just left. You were supposed to be my best friend, and you just left." I pace from one side of the small room to the other. Apparently, the flood gate has opened. It was only a matter of time before I exploded. "I called and called, and you never answered. All my calls went to voicemail. All three hundred and twenty of them. Yes, I kept count. Yes, I'm pathetic because I hoped my best friend would pick up the phone and talk to me. And you returned none of them. Nothing. Just shut me out. Forgot about me. Eventually, I stopped when I realized the number was disconnected." I blow out a deep breath, willing the tears welling up in the corners of my eyes not to fall. "You didn't even invite me to your draft party. We were best friends. I would have been happy for you, celebrated with you, but you pretended like I no longer existed. I had to hear about it from Kristen! Who was not subtle in her bragging."

He jumps to his feet, jaw clenching. "It was a big night for me. I didn't want to spend it being fucking miserable because I'd have to see Tony's arm around you the entire night!" His head tilts toward the ceiling and he blows out a deep breath. "I didn't invite her. That was Tony's doing."

"Either way, it doesn't matter." My shoulders sag. I wave my hand between us. "We were friends. Best friends. And you stopped caring."

He takes a step closer. "What don't you understand? You were dating my brother. I couldn't stand to see you. Be near you."

His words are like a sucker punch to the gut. For so long, we were best friends, and he had no qualms about throwing me out like day-old trash. My back goes rigid, and I square my shoulders. "You said your piece. Once we're out of the storage room, we never have to speak to each other. Again."

"Fuck. Dessa." His face falls, and he rubs the back of his neck. "It was my only choice."

"You act like it was a prison sentence." I roll my eyes, my hands shaking as I spin around so my back is to him.

"No, it wasn't." With his hand on my bicep, he spins me around. "It was worse." His tone is somber.

I yank my arm away from him.

"You don't get it." His gaze drops to the floor, and the harsh lines on his forehead soften. "That was supposed to be our night. It was me you were supposed to be with. Not Tony."

"What the hell are you talking about? What night?"

"At Jacobson's lake party after our junior year."

Recognition hits me about the night he's talking about.

Garrett rises from his camp chair next to the fire pit and stares down at me. "I'm going to take a walk to the lake. Want to join?"

"Oh. Sure." I stand.

Tony lifts his head and peers at us. "Are you sure you want to go down there? There could be bears or something in the woods. Plus, we're about to light the fireworks."

"Bears? Really? I'm sure they're more afraid of us than we are of them. Plus, I'll protect her." Garrett throws his arm over my shoulder, tugging me to his chest.

I wrap an arm around his waist to keep steady and laugh. "Like that time I had to kill the spider that you claim was ready to make you its next meal."

"That thing was huge, and it cornered me. It was ready to strike at any moment."

A burst of laughter escapes my lips as I playfully roll my eyes. "Okay. If you say so." Then I glance at Tony. "We'll be back in a few."

"Feel free to start the fireworks without us," Garrett says over his shoulder.

Once on the dock, I lean back on my hands, mimicking his pose. Our feet dangle over the edge as the moonlight dances over the ripples in the lake. For a brief moment, our pinkies graze. With the single touch, a delightful surge of electricity dances through my body. I spare a glance at Garrett from the corner of my eyes as he stares off into the distance. All I want to do is reach over and intertwine our fingers. Instead, I inch closer to him on the dock, but he doesn't do anything. He's as still as a statue. Distant chatter and laughter echoes across the lake as everyone else gathers around the fire pit. His gaze flits to mine and god, I wish I could read his mind. The moment our eyes lock, his gaze darts away and his body tenses.

"I can't believe this time next year we'll be the ones graduating from high school." He breaks the silence.

"Have you decided what you're going to do?" I ask.

His head falls back as he peers at the dark sky. "I have a baseball scholarship to Florida State, but Coach thinks I should go into the draft. He believes my skills are good enough."

All I can do is nod. Florida is so far away, but baseball is his dream. It always has been. "I'll have to come visit."

"You better." He winks.

"It's so quiet and peaceful here. I needed a break from all the noise. Thanks for inviting me."

"Of course. I know you always enjoy sitting by the lake. Plus, I wouldn't want you wandering down here by yourself in the dark. I'd be a little sad if you got lost or eaten by a bear." He smirks.

"*Only a little sad?*" I laugh.

"*Maybe a smidge more than a little.*" He holds his thumb and pointer finger together.

"*Are there actually bears around here?*"

"*Occasionally, but for the most part, they're more scared of you than you are of them.*"

"*I can assure you I would be the one more terrified if I came face-to-face with a bear. You'd have to come save me with your strong muscles.*" Reaching over, I squeeze his bicep. Mostly, it's an excuse to get close and touch him. I link my arm with his and snuggle into his side. He smells like citrus with a hint of campfire smoke. I steal a glance at him, and he twists his head to face me. Our eyes meet, and an electric jolt of happiness surges through me. I fight the urge to lean in and press my lips to his. But he clears his throat and drops his gaze. I blow out a small breath and unlink my arm with his. A thick cloud of tension billows between us.

"*Dessa?*"

"*Yeah?*" I turn to face him.

"*There's something I want to do—*"

"*There you two are.*" Tony's loud voice echoes across the lake as he clambers down the dock. The wood creaks and groans with every heavy footfall. "*You've been down here forever. Are you two having girl talk?*" He throws his arms around both our shoulders and sticks his head between us. "*Mitchell, we need you to settle a debate whether Harrison should either shave his head or go for a mohawk.*"

"*She has an actual name,*" Garrett mumbles under his breath.

Annoyance coils through me at the use of my last name. It reminds me of his teammates, one of the guys. Next thing he'll be slapping my ass, telling me great job. I brush it off. I'll deal with it later. "*You guys are shaving his head?*"

"*Yes. And your answer will decide his fate.*" He helps me to my feet.

"*Why am I the one to decide? Shouldn't that be Cara's job since she's the one dating him and will be stuck looking at him?*"

"She's not here at the moment, so it's in your hands."

I glance at Garrett and mouth, "Sorry." Garrett drops his chin as Tony drags me down the dock and toward the fire pit. When we reach the grass, Kristen races past us and onto the dock. When she reaches Garrett, she wraps her arms around his neck and settles herself on his lap. He wraps his arm around her waist, and I can't bear to watch them any longer.

"What I remember about that night is Kristen all over you as soon as I left."

He links his fingers behind his head. "I didn't want her. I wanted you. So fucking bad. You were supposed to be with me. Because," his hands drop to his sides as if he's holding lead weights, "I had feelings for you for so long. And you—"

"What?" I step closer to him, preparing for a fight. "What did I do?"

He blows out a breath. "Left with Tony."

"Because you blew me off! All night I was giving you signs. Touching you. Moving closer. And you ignored all of them."

"Those were signs? We'd always been like that."

"Exactly! I wanted to kiss you. I was so excited when you invited me to the lake because I wanted alone time with you. And you blew me off like you didn't want me!"

He steps closer so we're toe-to-toe. "I wanted to kiss you so bad that night. It was eating me up inside."

I bump my chest against his, getting in his face. "And I wanted you to kiss me!"

His nostrils flare as my jaw clenches. Seconds tick by as we stare at each other. My chest rises in time with his. Like a vacuum all the air is sucked from my lungs, and I can't breathe. After years of built-up tension, a fireball of heat and passion bursts through me. I'm surprised I don't spontaneously combust. There's only one thing that can extinguish the flame. I clasp his face between my palms and smash my mouth to his. The brim of his cap stabs me in the forehead, but it's the least of my concerns. I inch closer to him until the front of his cap pushes off his head. Hops and mint linger on his lips. I'm already addicted. His arm wraps around my waist, desperately clinging to me like if he lets go, he'll lose me again. All my thoughts are consumed by Garrett. Kissing him. Him kissing me. Having our bodies flush. It's dizzying.

I jerk away. My chest heaves as I work to collect my breath. His eyelids rise to half-mast. His normally green irises are almost black with desire.

"Fuck," he whispers.

"Double fuck," I murmur. Being trapped in such close proximity to him, touching him, and kissing him short circuited my head, heart, and lady bits. My gaze drops to his mouth. I suck in the corner of my bottom lip, desperate to have his mouth on mine again. His lips twitch. With one hand, he takes off his cap and flips it backwards. A guy wearing a cap, hot. A guy who flips it backwards turns my panties to ash. Some girls like forearm porn, but I ladygasm over the backwards cap. Before I know it, his lips are on mine again. It's hot. Desperate. Frantic. Needy. And everything in between. I moan into his mouth, and he deepens the kiss. With his arms wrapped around me, my steps retreat until my back hits one of the shelves, rattling bottles from the sudden jolt.

As I run my hands over his chest, I'm fixated on the firmness beneath my fingertips. His heart hammers under my palm and I know mine's doing the same. I'm drunk on Garrett Dawson, and I don't want it to stop.

His fingers curl through my hair at the nape of my neck, holding me in place as his tongue sweeps across the seam of my lips. I press my body closer to his, needing to feel him against me. A surge of pleasure courses through me as his growing erection presses against my stomach. I'm desperate for this. For him. I open my mouth and our tongues stroke against each other's. It's hot and needy. A cloud of passion envelops us, and I never want it to dissipate. I didn't know what to expect, but it wasn't this. It's better. So much better.

He pulls away and I gasp for a breath. Slowly, he drags the tip of his nose against mine. "Fuck. I've wanted to do that for a long time."

"Same," I murmur..

"I don't want to stop."

"Me either."

"The ball's yours, Tates. What's the call?"

If he can turn me on so much from a kiss, I'm desperate to know what else he can do.

"Fast ball. Right down the center." I hold my breath, waiting for his next move.

He releases his grip from my hair and trails his fingertips over my arm, causing goosebumps to prickle my skin. He moves across my shoulder and collarbone until his fingers wrap around the base of my neck. His fingers dimple my delicate skin. It's not tight, but just enough so I know he's there and, damn, it turns me on more than it should.

"Good answer." His mouth descends on mine in a searing kiss.

Chapter 10

I WANT IT BAD

Garrett

I've spent so many nights imagining what my first kiss with Dessa would be like, and it was nothing like this. Full of anger, yet passionate. I guess anger can lead to passion. Either way, we're kissing, and I. Don't. Ever. Want. To. Stop.

With one hand at the base of her neck, I reach around and tug the end of her ponytail with my other hand, forcing her head to tilt. She whimpers, then moans into my mouth and I swallow the sound. My dick twitches, so I do it again. This time when I tug, she not only moans but rubs her denim covered pussy against my thigh. I've waited years to have my lips on her, and damn, it's better than I could have ever imagined. She's all soft curves and even softer lips. My dick is five seconds away from Hulk-smashing his way through the teeth of the zipper. I break away and nip at her jaw.

"Tell me if you don't want this," I whisper over her skin.

Her fingers dig into my shoulder. "I want it. Oh god, I want it so bad."

"Good, because I've waited ten long, agonizing years to have you, and I don't want to waste another second."

"Garrett?"

"Yes?"

"Shut up and kiss me." Her hand grips my chin, directing my mouth over hers.

This time, the kiss is soft and sweet. A needy moan escapes her throat. It's the most amazing sound in the world, and I want more of it. I want to hear her scream my name, this time in pleasure and not because she wants to kill me.

"I'm warning you right now, this isn't going to be gentle and sweet." I know she deserves gentle and sweet, but I'm too desperate to give her that.

"Good. I don't want gentle and sweet."

"You're perfect."

Her laughter echoes in the room. "Shut up with your sappy bullshit." Her hand grips the back of my head and directs my mouth to hers.

My hand skates over the waistband of her jeans and under the hem of her shirt. Her breath hitches when my fingertips connect with her warm skin. I inch my hand higher and higher. Each movement causes her to press closer to me. When I reach the edge of her bra, my fingers trace the fabric, teasing her.

A soft moan escapes her lips. "Garrett. Touch me."

I reach around and unclasp her bra. The fabric loosens around her chest, enough to get my hand underneath. I cup her full tit and squeeze.

"Yes. More." My dick presses into her thigh as her hips gyrate against me.

I brush my thumb over her hardened nipple, and she moans. Fuck. I love her moans. Her fingernails dig into my shoulders. I need to see her. All of her. With my other hand, I lift the bottom of her shirt over her chest, taking her bra with it until her perfect tits are on full display. I peer into her eyes and lick my lips. My thumb brushes over her nipple again, and her mouth falls open. Fuck. I want her in my mouth, to taste her skin. So, I do just that. Bending down, I wrap my lips around her erect nipple, swirling my tongue around the stiff peak. She thrusts her chest into me as another throaty moan escapes her.

Her hand slides down my chest and to my waist. My dick twitches when her fingers brush over the bulge in my jeans. Slowly, she slides her hand up and down over the denim.

"Pull me out. I want to feel your fingers wrapped around me," I mumble against her warm skin.

Without wasting a second, her other hand drops to my waistband. She fumbles with the button of my jeans, but after a few tries, she gets it undone. With trembling fingers, she tugs the zipper and peels the fabric away. With help from, me she gets my pants to my knees along with my boxer briefs. My long, thick cock juts between us, pointing directly at her.

Her mouth drops open. "Fuck," she mumbles.

"This is what you do to me, Tates. You make me so goddamn hard."

Her dainty fingers wrap around me, and I suck in a sharp breath. Her fingers don't even come close to fitting around my girth. Her warm hand feels so good wrapped around me. So good that stars dance behind my eyelids. I can't even imagine what it would feel like to be inside her.

How her warm heat would feel wrapped around me. Slowly, I buck my hips into her hand, imagining it's her pussy. I continue to brush my thumb over her nipple, and she jerks me off. Her heated gaze is glued to my dick. It turns me on even more that she's watching.

"Fuck, Tates. That feels so good. You jerking me off." I continue to thrust into her hand. "Is it making you wet?"

She nods.

"Let me hear you."

Her hooded gaze flits to mine. "Yes."

"How wet? Show me?"

Her hand remains on my dick for a moment before my words register, and she releases her grip. I take over and leisurely stroke myself as she undoes the button on her jeans. She tugs them over her hips and shimmies them down her legs. All that's covering her pussy is a pair of light pink cotton underwear with a little dark pink spot between her legs.

I nod to my side. "Grab the bucket and use it to rest your foot on."

She positions the bucket next to us and props her foot on top.

"Move your panties to the side. I want to see you."

She does what she's told. Her pink pussy is on full display. I lick my lips, wanting to run my tongue up her center. To devour her. But I'll save that for another time.

"Touch yourself."

Her gaze jumps to mine.

"You've touched yourself before, haven't you?"

"Yeah. But not while someone else watches."

"Would you rather I do it for you?"

Her lips press together, and she nods.

"Say it."

"Touch me, Garrett."

"With pleasure." I drop my dick and slide two fingers down her slit, her arousal coating my skin. Her breath hitches the moment I contact her swollen clit. I continue to run my fingers up and down, smearing her wetness all around. I press my lips to hers at the same time as I thrust two fingers inside her. She gasps, and I swallow the noise. I continue to finger fuck her, pumping harder and faster with each pass as our tongues caress each other's. She breaks away and grabs my dick. With what little room there is between us, she still manages to find a way to stroke me as I continue to thrust my fingers in and out of her wet heat.

"Oh! Yes! Right there." She throws her head back, and I take the opportunity to kiss along her jaw and suck on her heated skin.

"Come for me, Tates. I want to hear you screaming my name." I murmur against the side of her neck as I brush circles over her clit with my thumb and she explodes.

"Ah! Garrett! Yes! Yes!"

I cover my mouth with hers as her pussy spasms around my fingers. When her orgasm subsides, I pull my fingers out of her, bring them to my mouth, and suck the wetness off. I release them with a pop. "Fucking delicious."

While she's still stroking my dick, she inches closer to me, and I glance down. She brushes the head of my dick through her glistening pussy lips. I groan. I'd die to be inside her right now. Thrusting. Hard. She continues to brush my dick up and down, covering my tip in her wetness. One perfectly timed thrust and I'd be inside her. Fuck. I want that. But I'll let her decide the next move. While she continues rubbing my dick on her pussy, I kiss along her jaw and to her ear. Her heavy pants mix with my shallow breathing.

"What the hell is going on in here?" Jake's booming voice echoes through the storage room.

Chapter 11

BANG-BANG PLAY

Dessa

My heart jumps to my throat and I freeze. Glancing over Garrett's shoulder, I'm met with a fuming Jake glaring daggers at me. Realization smacks me in the face about what I'm doing, where I'm doing it, and who I'm doing it with. Also, my pants are on the floor and I'm sure Jake has a front-row view of Garrett's extremely toned ass.

"Fucking hell. Put your fucking clothes back on. Why the hell does everyone think they can have sex in my bar?" His heavy booted footsteps descend down the hallway.

Oh god, what did I do? I wanted it to happen, but not like this. Not with so much unsettled business between us. He can't stroll into town, kiss me, and expect our friendship to go back to how things were. It doesn't work like that.

With my palms on his chest, I shove him away. He stumbles, almost falling over since his pants are around his ankles. I'm such an idiot. As modestly as I can, I bend at the knees and swipe my pants from the floor before tugging them on.

"Hey! What was that for?" He yanks his pants over his hips, but not before I steal a glance at his still very hard and very big cock.

"You can't show up here and kiss me and expect everything to go back to normal." I storm past Garrett and out of the storage room. The only logical explanation for what happened is all the chaotic noise in my head regarding Garrett—and being confined in such a small room with him didn't help the situation either.

When I enter the bar, Jake's standing in the middle of the room with his arms crossed over his chest. "Thanks for coming to our rescue." I flash him a small smile, praying he forgets everything he witnessed tonight.

"Well, it wasn't the four in the morning wake-up call I was expecting, but when I got a notification that the lights were still on and the alarm wasn't set, I figured it was best I come here and check it out."

"Sorry. Garrett kicked the piece of wood holding the door open, and it trapped us in."

"And you thought you'd occupy your time by having sex in my storage room?" He quirks an eyebrow at me.

"We weren't having sex." But if he didn't walk in at that exact moment, I might be telling a different story.

He stares at me harder, willing the truth out of me.

"It's… complicated." That word makes me inwardly cringe. Damn Garrett for getting in my head.

"Whatever it was, don't let it happen again." He drops his arms. "I guess it's a good excuse to finally fix the door."

Garrett strolls into the bar area, tugging on his hoodie, and Jake peers up at him. "So, I take it you two worked everything out?"

"No," I blurt out.

"Yes," Garrett says at the same time.

My gaze slingshots toward him, my eyes widening because we most definitely did not work things out. If anything, we made things more complicated.

"I kind of thought we worked everything out." He shrugs.

I huff out a breath and shake my head. "I'll see you later," I say to Jake. Then I scoop my coat and wallet off the bar before strolling toward the exit.

"Don't I get a goodbye?" Garrett yells to my retreating frame.

I flash him my middle finger instead.

Once I'm in the parking lot, the chilly air instantly freezes my warm, clammy skin. I can't believe I did that. I was seconds away from lining up his cock with my entrance and impaling myself. Thoughts of his long, thick cock stretching me invade my head. Son of a bitch.

Last night, well, technically this morning, I went to bed thinking about Garrett, and now I'm lying in bed still thinking about him. It was a mistake. The only thing we accomplished was giving me an orgasm. Don't get me wrong, it was a great orgasm. Unexpected, but great, nonetheless. It's been way too long since I've had a non-self-produced orgasm. I got lost in the moment. That's all it was. My hatred for him hasn't changed, maybe slightly diminished, but there's still a lot we need to hash out, without the orgasms, before we can go back to being friends.

When he confessed he wanted to kiss me all those years ago, just as much as I wanted to kiss him—mind blown.

Things could have turned out much differently, but they didn't. Now, it's like we're starting from the beginning.

Rolling my head to the side, I stare at the clock. I only have an hour until I need to be at work. Luckily, Jake only needs me for half a shift. Either way, I'd much rather lie in bed and contemplate my life choices. And by life choices, I mean Garrett.

When I arrive at Porter's, Nora's behind the bar and Lach's on the step stool preparing the board for the drink menu. Both their heads snap to me and freeze. Only a few customers are scattered around the room, and all of them are completely indifferent to my existence. I pull my sunglasses off my face and set them on top of my head. A smile spreads over Nora's lips as her clap slowly crescendos. Then Lach joins in.

"I hate you guys." I stroll the rest of the way into the bar. "My guess is that Jake already told you."

"He called me and asked if I could switch shifts and come in early because he had to come to the bar at four in the morning to find you getting it on in the storage room." A smug smile creeps over Lach's mouth.

"And then he told me as soon as I came in." Nora hikes her thumb at Lach. "See, I knew as soon as you two talked you would eventually bang it out and everything would be fine."

I roll my eyes. "We didn't bang. We accomplished nothing, actually."

"Because you were too busy banging," Nora sing-songs.

"I would consider a bang an accomplishment," Lach chimes in.

I blowout an exasperated sigh. I'm not winning this battle. With my white flag waving, I'm stepping away from this conversation.

"What's today's drink going to be called?" Lach asks. "Banging in the Storage Room?"

"Sliding into Home?" Nora quips.

"Oh, that's good." Lach points his chalk marker at Nora. "You got the baseball in there."

Nora smiles and nods proudly.

"Or Bang-Bang Play," Lach says.

"Rounding the Bases," Nora adds.

"What about Backdoor Slide?" Lach wiggles his eyebrows.

"How about You Both Suck?" I shrug.

Lach contemplates my answer by bobbing his head back and forth. "It's not really the vibe I'm going for."

"Wait!" Nora's eyes widen. "Was there backdoor action? You can tell us. We won't judge you." She playfully nudges me with her elbow.

"No! And if there was, I still wouldn't tell you." I shake my head. Not wanting to listen to them any longer, I strut across the bar and down the hallway to the employee room. I'm sure I'll have to hear about it for the rest of my shift. At my locker, I throw my purse inside. I was hoping for some reprieve from Garrett today, but that won't be happening. Damn Jake and damn Garrett for kissing me.

Chapter 12

WELCOME! DID YOU BRING BOOZE?

Garrett

Last night was not how I envisioned our talk playing out. Don't get me wrong, it was fucking fantastic, but it's like I took a giant step forward and two enormously awkward steps back. Now I'm confused. Does she hate me? Hates me but wants to fuck me? Or maybe we could move past all of this and go straight to fucking me. The latter would be ideal, but now I have to approach this more cautiously than before.

I loved her sweet lips on mine. Honey and vanilla. Her body was so responsive to my touch, especially when I wrapped my fingers around her throat. Her needy moans and whimpers are engrained on my brain. Fuck. My dick twitches from the memory. I slide a hand under the blanket and wrap my fist around my shaft. Slowly, I pump up and down as I replay last night in my head. Her hot breath against my ear as her moans grew louder and louder. I squeeze the tip of my dick, and a bead of pre-cum pools at the top. With my thumb, I spread it around and slide down my shaft. Her begging me to touch her might be my new favorite thing.

"Garrett!" My mom's voice echoes up the stairwell. "I'm going to the store. Do you need anything?"

My eyelids snap open, and my hand freezes on my now hard dick, a sudden terror coursing through my veins. My fantasy dissolves into nothing as I'm shoved back to reality. I'm lying in my too-small bed at my parents' house. Fuck. My hand gripping my dick falls to the mattress.

"No, I'm alright!" I yell back.

I blow out a frustrated breath. I should've kept the hotel room. Wait. I should do a take two with the cookies, except I won't make them this time. I jump out of bed and open the door wide enough to poke my head through. "Actually, could you make some chocolate chip cookies for me?"

"Sure thing!"

On my way home from an afternoon workout at the gym I found when I arrived in town, I drive past Porter's and I don't see Dessa's vehicle in the parking lot so I'm assuming she's at home. Now my plan has an entirely new set of problems. Where does Dessa live? After I return to my parents' and shower, I meet my mom in the kitchen. Waiting for me on the counter is a tray of freshly baked chocolate chip cookies, their warm aroma filling the room. I snatch one off the top and shove half of it in my mouth. I moan. Oh yeah. This is way better than the ones I made. Still soft and chewy. No wonder she fed the ones I baked to the raccoons. Leaning my hip against the counter, I finish chewing. Then, as nonchalantly as possible, I ask, "By chance, do you know where Dessa lives?"

She pulls out the last sheet of cookies from the oven and sets it on the stove. "When I ran into her at the grocery store, she mentioned a townhouse on Chestnut Street."

I wrack my brain trying to remember where Chestnut Street is. It's been a while since I've wandered the streets of Harbor Highlands. But I guess that's why every phone now has a GPS. "Do you have a house number?"

She taps her chin with her oven mitt covered hand. "Five oh two."

"Great. Thanks!" I push off the counter.

Her brows draw together. "Or it could've been five twelve. Or two fifteen. Wait. Did she tell me a number?"

"Don't worry about it. I'll find it." I press a kiss to her cheek and grab a plastic container for the cookies. After filling it to the brim, I loosely place the lid on top. "Thanks for these." I lift the container and race out the door.

When I get to Chestnut Street, there's a row of three townhomes with two units each. Luckily, it's on a dead end, so I have a one in six chance of picking the correct one.

Upon first glance, I notice a minivan parked in the driveway and children's toys strewn across the front yard. Going off the hunch of no mention of children, I assume that's not her house, so I stroll to the next one. I knock on the door, and a dog barks on the other side. She's always loved animals, so this could be hers. When we were teens, she loved playing with our golden retriever, Max, and always mentioned she'd love to have one when she got older since her parents didn't want pets. When there's no answer, I knock again, and two more barking dogs join the mix. Based on the high-pitched yipping, I believe the others are smaller dogs. I know she'd rather have a golden retriever than a chihuahua. Again, If I had to guess, this isn't hers. Since there's no answer, I move on to the next townhouse. As I stroll up the driveway, a brightly painted Minnesota Mallards sign hangs on the door. This is promising. She's been a die-hard fan since I made her watch all their games with me.

I gently rap my knuckles against the door. My heart thunders in my chest. I'm not fully prepared for what to say if she answers, but like many things during this whole situation, I'll wing it. As I raise my hand to knock once more, the door suddenly swings open. A young boy around ten years old comes into view. His eyes grow wide, and he's stunned silent for a moment before he yells to his mom over his shoulder.

"What?!" a voice sounds from another room.

"Garrett Dawson is at our front door!" he yells, but his eyes are still on me, afraid to move in case I disappear.

"Garrett Dawson is not at our front door!"

"Yes, he is!"

"What did I tell you about lying?" A woman with short auburn hair comes into view. As soon as she sees me, she stops dead in her tracks, the towel in her hand fluttering to the floor. "Holy shit. Garrett Dawson is at our front door."

I give her a sheepish smile and wave.

Using the mirror on the wall, she carefully finger combs her hair, before sashaying toward the door. A seductive smile forms on her lips. "What can I help you with, Mr. Dawson?" she purrs.

"I was wondering if you know where Dessa Mitchell lives?"

Disappointment takes over her features, upset that I'm not there to see her. "She's two houses down at five oh eight. Before you leave, can I interest you in a drink?" She straightens her shoulders, causing her green shirt to tighten over her chest.

"Can I get an autograph?" the little boy asks.

I give her a tight smile, thankful for his interruption. "I can do the autograph, but I'll pass on the drink."

The little boy scampers off. Seconds later, he returns with a baseball bat and a permanent marker. Quickly, I scribble my autograph and pass it back.

He stares at it in wonder. "This is so cool! All my friends are never going to believe this. Thank you!"

"You're welcome. But I best be on my way. Sorry to bother you."

"You're welcome here anytime, Mr. Dawson." She winks.

I give her a curt nod and barrel down the driveway. When I glance over my shoulder, her eyes are still on me, so I quicken my step.

Shit. Did she say five oh eight or five oh nine? I got distracted with autographs and her undressing me with her eyes. I was only half paying attention. At least there are only two more houses. My odds are fifty-fifty.

Once I'm at the next house, I press the doorbell button. The rumble of tires on pavement draws my attention. I whirl around wondering if maybe it's Dessa.

Suddenly, a thunderous voice reverberates from the doorbell speaker. "What do you want?"

I whip around.

"Holy shit! It's Garrett Dawson. I'm a huge fan. Some bad luck with that last catch."

"Yeah. Thanks." I lean forward toward the small round lens on the side of the door, feeling awkward talking to a doorbell. "I'm looking for Dessa Mitchell. Do you know where she lives?

"Sorry man. I just moved in. I'm not acquainted with my neighbors yet."

Now I know my answer. "Okay. Thanks. Have a good day." I lift my hand in a half wave.

"You too. Stop by anytime."

When I'm at the next house, I'm confident this one is hers. Not only by the process of elimination but also because her lights are on, and she never leaves her lights on. Plus the "Welcome! Did you bring booze?" door mat screams Dessa.

I raise my hand and knock. With the container of cookies firmly in my grip, I hold my breath, waiting for her to answer.

Chapter 13

BREAKUP DRINKS

Dessa

I'm mid-pour when a knock on the front door startles me, causing some of the vodka to spill on the counter. Shit. I set the bottle down and throw a rag over the vodka. I'll take care of that later. When I reach the door, I peek through the peephole. My heart jumps to my throat at the sight of Garrett standing on the other side. Of course, he looks hot as ever in his backwards baseball hat and hoodie that stretches over his broad chest. One look at him makes all my negative feelings toward him evaporate, but he doesn't deserve my forgiveness. What he did was inexcusable. Maybe I should even the score and ghost him. I spin on my heel and make it two steps before he knocks again.

"Dessa. I know you're home. Your lights are on. You never leave lights on."

Dammit. I hate that he still remembers so much about me. One time, or many times, in high school, he picked me up for a baseball game and after we drove a mile down the road I asked him to turn around because I'd left my bedroom light on. Of course, he did it with no hesitation because that's the type of guy he is.

"Plus, I've already been to every other house on this street except this one. So, I know it's yours."

After a few seconds of silence, I think he may have left, so I go back to the front door and peer through the peephole again. Nope. He's still standing on my doorstep, facing away from me. He spins around and closes one eye to look at the peephole.

Panic sets in and I jerk away, thinking he can see me.

"I'm not leaving until you open the door. I'm prepared to camp out here all night if I have to. But so you're aware, it is getting cold and there's a good chance hypothermia will set in by morning. And I have my mom's cookies. Not made by me this time, but you can only have them if you open the door."

I shake my head and wipe the small smile off my lips. He can't know I find him slightly amusing. I yank open the door and cross my arms over my chest. "You think the good cookies will fix the years of hurt and betrayal?"

His eyes go wide for a brief second, probably surprised I opened the door for him, then his features soften. "It's a peace offering." He holds out the container for me.

I eye him and then the cookies before snatching it from his hands.

"Maybe we can finally sit and talk. Oh! And this." He reaches into his hoodie pocket and pulls out a tiny white flag on a stick. He waves it back and forth. "I surrender. I'm sorry I was an asshole all those years ago. I know it's inexcusable, but I'd still like to talk."

I blow out a breath and step out of the doorway and wave my hand, motioning for him to come inside.

This is a bad idea. Close quarters with Garrett Dawson is a temptation I don't have enough restraint to fight. It's already happened once. Too late now. The corners of his lips tip up into a smile as he walks past me. His citrus and amber scent wafts around me, causing my nipples to pebble. I close the door behind him and stroll through the living room and into the open dining room and kitchen while Garrett follows close behind. I set the cookies on the counter.

His gaze wanders around my kitchen island filled with bottles of rum, vodka, whiskey, tequila, a variety of mixers, and slices of lemons and limes. He takes his time studying everything on the counter before taking a seat on a stool on the opposite side of me. "What's happening here?"

"I'm experimenting."

"And what's this?" He reaches across the counter and pulls my recipe notebook toward him.

I snatch it back before he can flip through it. "My recipes."

"And that's full?"

I nod. "Almost. I'll have to start a new one soon."

"Wow." He nods.

I tuck a strand of hair behind my ear. "While you're here, you can serve a dual purpose and taste test for me."

Plus, this conversation will be less awkward with alcohol. And even less awkward because I won't be the only one drinking.

"Okay." He rests his palms on the counter. "Hit me with your best drink."

I tap my chin, deciding what to make. With a bottle of vodka in hand, I pour an ounce into two copper mugs, followed by apple cider and ginger beer. I cut two lime wedges and squeeze each one into a mug. Behind me, I rummage through my spices and garnish each drink with a dash of cinnamon. When I'm finished, I slide the mug across the counter to Garrett.

"I was hoping to see you toss bottles into the air and spin around and catch them." His lips curl in the corners.

"I'm not a circus act. I'm a bartender."

"Touché." He takes a sip of his drink.

I study his facial features, wanting to read his expression. The scruff on his jaw twitches as he swallows. Then he nods. "That's really good. It's refreshing but also adds a little holiday charm with the apple cider. They should serve these at Fir Meadows Tree Farm instead of hot apple cider."

I laugh. "I'm sure that would go over well with all the families."

"Maybe it would encourage them to buy two trees instead of one. Anyway, what's the name of this drink?"

"I call it a Dirty Reindeer."

"See! That's perfect. It would fit right in at the tree farm." He takes another gulp.

I fiddle with the handle on my mug. While the small talk is nice, I need him to get to the point. "You wanted to talk, so talk." I take a drink.

"Shouldn't we ease into it a little? Maybe warm it up. Or are we ramming it right in?"

I half cough, half choke. Surprisingly, I don't spit my drink all over his face. With a napkin, I dab at my mouth and regain my composure. "At this point, I think there's already been enough warming up. You should be able to ram it right in." I half wonder if we're talking about why he came over here or something completely different.

He scrubs his hands down his face before dropping them to the counter. "What do I say? I had to leave. It was easier to go than to talk to you. I was young and thought I was doing the best thing." His gaze drifts up. Dark green eyes bore into mine. "I know it's not an excuse, but it's the truth."

I guzzle the rest of my drink, not ready for this conversation. "Need another?" I raise my copper mug.

"Sure."

I make us two more drinks. "What about our senior year? You were always gone and never said more than two words to me."

He blows out a breath. "Honestly, I hated you. Or wanted to hate you."

My heart plummets to my ass. Those are three words I never wanted to hear coming from Garrett. And I certainly never expected him to say them.

"I hated my brother. I hated you were with my brother and there wasn't anything I could do about it. I thought it would be easier to be the asshole." He takes a drink.

I nibble on my thumbnail, digesting everything he's saying. "That's why you spent our entire senior year ignoring me," I mutter, mostly to myself.

"I couldn't see you with Tony. Everyday felt like a rope around my heart, strangling me. It was easier to hate. Deep down I never hated you though. I convinced myself if I said it enough that it would be true, and I could stop feeling like shit." His gaze drops to the counter. "I was eighteen and thought I had all the answers. Clearly, I was wrong."

I swallow a giant gulp of my Dirty Reindeer. "Do you know how many times I called? How many messages I left with no response? That gutted me. Then when I got the automated message that your number had been disconnected, I was in agony. I didn't have my best friend anymore. Do you think that was fair to me?"

He reaches across the counter and rests his hand on mine. "It wasn't. I know that now. But at the time, that was the only way for me to process my feelings. I'm sorry." His thumb brushes over my knuckles. "I hope we can move past this. I'm here now and want to make amends."

It's exhausting holding on to a ten-year grudge. I press my lips together before a smile tugs at them. "I think we can take some baby steps to rekindling our friendship."

"I promise, I'll do whatever it takes to show you I'm sorry. I can't take back what I did, but going forward I'll be the best friend I once was and know I can be." He pulls his hand away.

Instantly, I hate the loss of his warm hand on mine. I shake it off. "Another drink?"

"Sure. Let's try something new."

I mix a new drink and pass it to Garrett. He takes a giant gulp. His teeth grit together as he sucks in a sharp breath. "That one has a bite to it."

"I call it The Heartbreaker." My gaze meets his. "Because it's a little painful, like a broken heart." The corner of my lips twitch into a smile.

He huffs out a laugh and shakes his head. "I see what you did." He takes a sip. "Did you go to school for mixology?"

"Well, if you'd stayed in touch, you would know."

He flinches. "Ouch. Someone's taking shots below the belt."

I shrug and swallow the last sip of my drink. "I've always enjoyed concocting new drinks. When I got old enough, I started adding alcohol."

"That's right." He tilts his cup toward me. "I remember you would always mix five different sodas into your fountain drink."

I brush a strand of hair off my forehead and tuck it behind my ear. This is one more thing he remembers about me from years ago. "I enjoyed testing out the different combinations and seeing what I could create."

"Everyone thought you were being weird. But I loved that you didn't care."

My heart leaps to my throat at the word loved. Shut up, brain. It's not like he's saying he loved you.

He swallows the last gulp of his drink. "What else do you got? Maybe something like a slippery nipple? Sex on the beach?" He flashes me a wink.

A laugh bubbles out of me. I rest my palms on the counter and lean toward him, locking my gaze with his. "What are you trying to insinuate, Mr. Dawson?" My voice is low and husky. I'd like to think I sound like a sexy vixen, but it's probably closer to a drunk cat. I was never good at flirting.

"Well, Ms. Mitchell," he leans forward, mimicking my tone, "my drink is empty, and I need a new one." He winks again.

I laugh and rise to my full height, all five four of it, and busy myself with mixing a fresh drink.

He taps his fingers on the counter. "You know, you should make a drink for the wedding."

"And call it what? The Ex-Boyfriend."

"The Wrong Brother?" His lips spread into a wide grin.

I raise an eyebrow. "Or The Jerk Who Left Without Saying Goodbye."

He laughs. "That's too long. People won't go for that."

"I haven't decided if I'm even going to the wedding." I pour the drink from the shaker to a lowball and slide it to Garrett and then fill one for myself. "Don't you think it'd be a little awkward for the ex-girlfriend to show up at the wedding?" I take a sip of my drink.

Garrett shrugs nonchalantly. "You could always be my date."

This time I spit my drink out onto the counter and floor. With my hand, I wipe my mouth before grabbing a napkin to clean my mess. "Because that would make things less awkward."

He laughs. "Who cares? The wedding seems like a sham, anyway."

"How can you say that when you've been out of town for ten years?"

"I know my brother, and he's never been able to make a decision and stick to it. In middle school and early high school he constantly flip-flopped between baseball, hockey, and football. Not to forget, the brief time he also played golf."

"It's normal for kids to play multiple sports until they find one they enjoy the most."

"But that's the thing, I don't think he truly had a passion for any of them." He leans back and rests his arm over the backrest. "I believe he only got serious about baseball and played for as long as he did was because I played too, and he resented the fact that I was better than him."

I yank open a drawer and pull out a safety pin. Unhooking it, I jab the pointy end into the air toward him.

His brows pinch together. "What are you doing?"

"Deflating your ego. It's starting to occupy too much room."

He exhales a boisterous laugh. "It's not ego. It's the truth."

I drop the pin in the drawer and close it with my hip. "Maybe he's changed?"

He drops his arm from the chair and leans forward.

"Tigers don't change their stripes. Chameleons maybe. He'll disguise himself until it's time to strike."

"You're not judging him fairly, especially since you've been gone all these years."

"Have you been in contact with him?"

The ice clinks in my glass as I swirl it, mostly to busy myself with… anything. "We've always remained acquaintances with the occasional small talk, but it's not like I'm running off whispering all my deepest, darkest secrets to him."

"So you can't say he's changed either."

"I'm giving him the benefit of the doubt. What kind of person would marry someone they didn't love?"

"I want to say my brother, because that's exactly something he would do."

"I still think you're wrong." I flip through the pages of my recipe notebook, searching for the next drink to make.

"When you said that was full, you weren't kidding." He nods at the notebook.

"It's kind of like my version of a diary. While some people write breakup songs, I created breakup drinks." I smile at him.

"How many are about me?" He smirks.

"We never dated, so I never made any about you."

"With all the hostility you're throwing my way, I'm sure there's one or two."

I continue thumbing through the tattered pages, a smirk on my lips.

"I know that look. That's the 'you're right, but I'm not telling' look."

I stop flipping pages and lift my gaze to his. "I don't have a look."

He drops his hands to the counter. "Yes, you do. You

get the little half smile and your eyebrow twitches. Tell me I'm wrong."

I rub the twitch out of my eyebrow. I hate he knows me so well. Even after all the years away he can still read me like an open book. Always has. Apparently still can.

I roll my eyes. "Whatever. Fine. Perhaps there's a drink or two named after you." Or seven, but I don't tell him that.

His eyes light up as if I'm giving him the secret to eternal youth. "Show me one."

"A drink?"

"Yeah. Make it. Let me taste your disdain for me."

I laugh. "Alright. Let me find one." The swooshing of paper fills the air between us as I thumb through the pages, looking for the perfect one. "I got it." This was three years after he left and had his phone number changed. It was then when I finally gave up.

"What's it called?"

"Runaway."

He laughs. "Alright."

I pour us both a shot of tequila, squirt the lime juice inside, and slide his to him.

"That's it?"

"Yeah. It's kind of like a sucker punch in the gut. Kind of like when your best friend leaves without saying goodbye."

He raises his shot glass, and I do the same.

"Well, here's to runaways getting a second chance."

I clink my shot glass with his and we both throw back the liquid. The tequila burns as it slides down my throat. My entire body shivers from the earthy flavor and tart lime as a wave of warmth flows from my belly to my cheeks. I shake my head and push off the counter. A sea of fuzziness floats through my head. I grab a bottle of vodka and pour two shots into a shaker along with blackberry schnapps. Next, I combine the other ingredients into the shaker along with some ice and give it a shake. I remove the cap and pour the cocktail into a lowball, the deep red liquid glinting in the dim light.

He lifts the glass to eye level, inspecting the drink. "So, what's this one called?" He takes a sip.

My tongue peeks out, wetting my lips. "Sex on the Couch."

He chokes on the drink. A small giggle escapes me as I pass him a napkin.

"There's a little hint of sweetness that caught me off guard." He holds his thumb and index finger in front of him centimeters apart.

"It's the agave nectar." I busy myself with making another drink before he can finish the last one. I roll the rim of the glass in pink sugar. Once it's finished, I slide it across the counter.

"What's this one?"

"This one is called Asshole."

He squints at the pink liquid. "I don't get it."

I bite my lips together to hide my laughter. "You slide your tongue around the rim and then toss it back."

His gaze jerks to mine. A slow smile plays on his lips. "Got it."

A hint of desire dances in his irises. Either that, or the alcohol is causing me to hallucinate. His tongue peeks out as he swipes it around the edge of the glass. With hooded eyes he wraps his lips around the rim, watching me the entire time before tipping back the shot glass. His Adam's apple bobs up and down as he swallows. Why's it so hot? I tug at the collar of my sweatshirt. When did it get so tight? I should hate him, not want to jump over the counter and ride his face like a jockey at the Kentucky Derby. I pour the rest from the shaker in a glass and swallow the last gulp. It's a desperate attempt to bring my body temperature back to normal, which I'm almost positive is caused by the dirty thoughts playing through my head. Either way, I need a distraction from Garrett. Or myself.

Vodka. Vodka is a good distraction. With the bottle in hand, I pour two shots into a shaker to make a new drink. Garrett's eyes are on me the entire time from the other side of the counter. My heart races as he tracks my every move. When it's finished, I slide it over to him. He studies the glass, then lifts his gaze to mine.

"Are you trying to get me drunk?"

"You're a lot more manageable when you're passed out."

He barks out a laugh, then swallows the pink liquid, and I do the same.

After he's finished, his tongue runs over his bottom lip, and I can't help shifting my weight, rubbing my thighs together.

"What's that one called?" he asks.

"Get Me Naked," I whisper softly.

His normally green irises darken to a hunter green, almost black, and his nostrils flare. I can only imagine he's having the same thoughts as I am. It looks like he wants to jump over the counter and maul me like a ravenous grizzly bear.

"Say the words, Dessa. Don't mask them behind drink names."

Is he reading my thoughts? The glass slips out of my hand and shatters on the linoleum floor. Shards of glass scatter across the floor.

"Shit." I bend down and grab the large pieces, placing them in my palm.

The stool scrapes across the wood floor as Garrett

races around the end of the island to help. He holds out his hand for me to put what I've collected in his palm. While he throws the pieces into the trash, I get the broom from the tall storage pantry and sweep the rest. When I'm finished, I return the broom to the closet and close the door. I whirl around and immediately collide with Garrett's very strong and muscular chest.

"I'm sorry." My words are barely a whisper as my fingers brush over the cotton fabric covering his pecs. Without saying anything, his fingers rest on my waist as he leans around me to throw a piece of glass into the garbage. When he returns to his full height, he doesn't move. His gaze wanders from my eyes to my mouth. I part my lips, wetting the bottom one with my tongue. He inches closer, his grip on me growing tighter. My breathing grows shallow. There's so much electricity flowing between us it could power the entire state. His fingers flex on my waist.

"Garrett," his name is a cross between a whisper and a plea.

His hand reaches up and cups my cheek as my chest heaves with every passing second. Then his mouth crashes onto mine in a fervent, desperate kiss. With a hand on my hip, he spins me around and without breaking the seal of his lips on mine, he lifts me onto the counter with no effort. My knees instinctively spread to allow room for his body to nestle in between.

He pulls away and runs the tip of his nose over mine. "Tell me you want this." His voice is deep and breathy as his words hang in the air.

Without hesitation, I nod. "Yes. I want this."

Then his lips are on mine again.

Chapter 14

DID WE...

Dessa

I don't know if it's the alcohol or perhaps I'm drunk on Garrett, but fuck, I need him. Ever since the night in the storage room, he's all I think about. I want him to consume me. With every stroke of his tongue against mine, I know he wants it, too.

I break apart from our kiss and find the hem of his shirt. With one quick tug, I yank it over his head. My fingertips graze over the tan skin of his shoulder and over the colorful ink decorating his chest.

"My turn," he whispers against the shell of my ear. His fingers grip the bottom of my shirt, and I lift my arms so he can remove it. He tosses the fabric over his shoulder. His hooded gaze slowly drifts to my lace-covered chest, his expression heavy with desire. He slowly leans down and places a tender kiss above my heart, sending a wave of warmth through my body.

My breath hitches. The gesture is sweet, and I don't

know how to process it, so I tell him the only thing I want right now. "Garrett. Touch me."

I tuck my thumbs into the waistband of my yoga pants and rock back and forth until I've pushed them down my thighs. Garrett takes over and yanks them the rest of the way off. His eyes greedily devour my almost-naked body, as if he's studying me to remember later. I gasp when his mouth is on mine again. My head is swimming in the clouds. It's either from all the alcohol I've consumed or from Garrett. Either way, I don't want it to stop. We're a mess of lips, tongues, and limbs.

His hand snakes up my chest, and his fingers wrap around the base of my throat. He squeezes, but not too tight. I moan into his mouth, loving his hand on me. It's almost possessive, and the thought turns me on even more.

"Tell me if this is too much," he whispers across my lips.

"No. It's good. I like it." My words come out in short pants.

"You're absolutely fucking perfect."

His mouth slants over mine again in a hot, demanding kiss. A burst of stars prickle behind my eyelids and lands directly between my legs. His other hand skates over my thigh, sending a wave of goosebumps to wash over my entire body. When he reaches the apex of my thighs, his fingers brush over my lace-covered pussy. Another moan escapes me before I inch myself closer to the edge, and spread my legs farther apart. He takes my invitation and rubs small circles over my clit. I rock my hips, needing him to touch me more.

He drags the lace to the side. "Hold this. Right here."

I drop my hand between my legs and hook my finger through the fabric, holding it in place.

His middle finger slides down my slit, causing my body

to tremble from the contact. I'm on the edge of begging him to fuck me.

"So fucking wet for me." He circles the pad of his finger around my opening before sliding in. Leisurely, he pumps his finger in and out. "Look how wet you are."

I peer between us, his finger glistening with my wetness. I never imagined Garrett would be a dirty talker, but I also never thought we would be doing this. Again. My breathing grows shallow as I continue to watch as his finger disappears inside of me. That's something else that shouldn't be so hot, but it is. He increases his pace, pumping harder and faster. My mouth falls open and my breath quickens. He pulls out and adds a second finger before he continues to finger fuck me.

"Oh! Oh! Garrett. That feels so good." My eyes drift closed and my head falls back. I imagine it's Garrett's cock inside me. The size isn't comparable to his two fingers, but when his thumb brushes over my clit, I don't care. "Keep going. Don't. Stop." My moans and pants increase with every thrust of his fingers.

"I'm not stopping until you come all over my hand. Then I'm going to lick you clean."

"Oh. Fuck." My nipples tighten. A bolt of electricity hits me straight between my legs. Both my fingers and toes curl as a tsunami of bliss washes over me. I cry out Garrett's name as he continues to spear me with his fingers.

His warm breath skates over my cheek as he murmurs, "I love my name off your lips."

After my orgasm subsides, he pulls his fingers out of me and brings them to his mouth. He licks every last drop of my orgasm off his fingers. "Now it's time to clean you up."

My pussy is still sensitive from the orgasm, so as soon as

his tongue hits my clit, it doesn't take long for a second to build. He positions my feet on the counter and spreads my legs even more. With one hand still holding my panties to the side, I use the other to prop myself up. Glancing down, I get a view of dark hair nestled between my legs—hair that belongs to Garrett—and he's eating me out like a starving man. He takes turns between licking me and biting my thigh. My hips buck every time his tongue swipes over my clit.

"I want you for my every meal." His tongue licks the sensitive skin on my thigh before his lips wrap around my clit and suck.

"Oh! Ah! I'm not going to last much longer."

"Come all over my tongue. I want to taste all of you." He continues to roughly lick and suck on my pussy. In a matter of seconds, another orgasm roars through me. This one is more explosive than the last.

He lifts his head, his dark eyes meet mine, and he wipes his mouth with the back of his hand. "Fucking perfection."

"That was… wow." I release the grip on my panties, and they slide back into place.

"How many more orgasms do you have in you?"

"I don't know." I bite down on my lower lip. "But are you going to find out?"

"I never back away from a challenge." With his hand on my waist, he lifts me and tosses me over his shoulder.

I squeal in surprise. "Where are we going?"

His large palm connects with my ass cheek. The echoing slap resonates through my townhouse. I'm enjoying the mixture of roughness and softness he's been showing me. He gently massages the muscle.

"Somewhere a little more comfortable."

When we reach the living room, he bends over and deposits me on the couch. I brush the hair out of my face and he's standing in front of me, the bulge in his jeans calling to me like a beacon. There's only one problem. He's wearing entirely too many clothes. I reach to the waistband of his jeans. My fingers brush over the button and when I glance up, he's staring at me, watching my every move. With my heated gaze trained on his, I pop the button on his jeans and pull the zipper down. Slowly, I peel the sides away and push them over his thick, muscular thighs until they hit the floor with a thud. I run my fingers over the outline of his cock. He sucks in a sharp breath.

"Is that a baseball bat between your legs?" I murmur to myself, but apparently not quietly enough.

"Only one way to find out." He hooks his thumbs under the elastic, and he pulls the boxer briefs down. His cock springs free, fully erect and right in front of my face. I lift my hand and do my best to wrap my fingers around his girth. With my thumb, I swirl the bead of pre-cum around the tip. Needing lubrication, I collect what saliva I have in my mouth and spit it onto the head. I move it around as much as possible until I've coated most of his cock and my hand. I slide my hand down to the base and then up to the tip.

"Fuck. I love when you touch me. Feels so fucking good." His fingers thread through my hair.

A stinging sensations spreads over my scalp as he curls his fingers in the strands, but I don't stop. I continue to stroke him while occasionally wrapping my lips around the crown and swirling my tongue around the tip. I'm desperate to see him loose control. He thrusts his hips, pushing his dick into my hand. With each pass he gains more momentum.

"Fuck. I'm going to come." His thrusting becomes more erratic in my hand until his hot cum spurts out, hitting me in my chest and sliding down my stomach.

Eventually, his movements slow and I drop my hand. When his breath evens out, he bends over and rests his hands on the back of the couch, caging me in. "I think you deserve one more orgasm."

I stir awake, but my eyelids have fifty-pound weights attached to them. My head throbs like someone played Wack-O-Dessa with a baseball bat for the last twelve hours. I groan and roll over. My hand brushes along something warm and my eyes snap open. A mop of dark brown hair, attached to tan, muscular shoulders, lays next to me. Fuck. Fuck. Fuck. Alarms blare through my head, which does nothing to help my massive headache. Flashes of last night flit through my mind. Garrett came over. We talked. Had drinks. Lots and lots of drinks. Kissing. Touching. Fuck.

I jackknife to the seated position, ready to bolt out of here, but it's my bedroom. Pinching my eyes shut, I rest my palm on my forehead as my head throbs in protest. Spots dot my vision as I hastily lift the blanket to see I'm wearing only my bra and underwear. I drop the blanket. What happened last night? I lift the blanket again only a little higher and I'm greeted with a tight and toned muscular ass. My eyes widen. Holy shit. He's naked. I drop the blanket. I have my underwear on. Did we have sex? I scan the room for any telltale signs like a condom wrapper, but nothing. Instead, I find my favorite dark blue Minnesota Mallards jersey lying in a pile surrounded by buttons. I didn't realize he has such strong, hateful feelings toward the team. I move past the now-ruined jersey, but don't see anything. Maybe we didn't use protection? I lift the blanket for one more peek. Is it wrong I want to sink my teeth into the firm muscle? It must be from all the squats he does behind home plate. I bite my lower lip. Of course, it's wrong. I scold myself. Releasing my lip, I pout. You can't go around biting people's asses. They taught you that in kindergarten. Maybe not the asses part but definitely the "no biting."

"How many times are you going to look at my ass?"

My heart rate spikes. I've been caught.

"There's a draft every time you lift the blanket. Plus, it's way too early. Go back to bed," he mumbles into the pillow.

"Why are you naked?"

He rotates his head to face me, causing his brown hair to flop over his forehead. "I always sleep naked."

"Even in someone else's bed?"

"The bed doesn't care."

"But I do."

"Fine. You want me to put my underwear on?" He faces away from me and lifts the blanket, exposing his right butt cheek.

I grab the blanket and cover him again. "The damage to my sheets is already done. I have to burn them now."

"I'm pretty sure your sheets enjoyed the company last night. By the way you screamed my name, you did too."

"No." I shake my head, but the movement makes my head pound even more.

"Oh yeah, you did. I'm sure all your neighbors know you had company last night."

I slide down on the bed, willing it to swallow me whole. "What did I do last night?" I murmur.

"You gave me a very sloppy hand job."

A boisterous laugh escapes me. I vaguely remember his face between my legs and our time on the couch. Pretty much everything after that is a blur. "I saw three different cocks. I did my best to pick the right one. I can't say you did any better. I couldn't tell if all the wetness between my legs was my orgasm or your saliva. You were like a Saint Bernard with a jar of peanut butter. I'm pretty sure you bruised my clit from all the sucking."

A deep laugh rumbles from his chest. "And if you check under your fingernails, you'll find some of my DNA from gripping my hair so tight. I'm surprised your voice isn't horse from screaming my name."

I shoot him a glare. "My voice is just fine." Twisting around, I roll out of bed to at least put on a shirt so I'm a little less naked. While sitting on the edge of the bed, I glance down. What the hell? I peer over my shoulder. "Why do I have bruises on my inner thighs?" Did I fall last night and smack my thigh against something? I inspect the blue and purple skin closer. Are those teeth marks? "What the…" Those aren't bruises. They're hickeys. "What are you? A vampire?"

The bed dips as Garrett moves to look over my side. "Huh. I guess last night I was."

"What's wrong with you?" I palm his forehead and push him away.

He laughs and rolls to the side. I rise to my feet and walk the few steps to my dresser. I pull open the drawer and find an extra-long t-shirt. Before tugging it over my head, I glance over my shoulder and catch Garrett's eyes on me. I turn away, mostly to hide the smile that's taken over my face. "Also, you owe me a jersey." I grab the now scrap of fabric from the floor and toss it at him.

He catches it mid-air and deposits it back to the floor on the other side of the room. "You thought it would be funny to put that on last night. But you didn't find it funny when I ripped it off. With how much you moaned my name, I think you forgave me."

I roll my eyes. "You still owe me a jersey." I walk to the

edge of the bed, and Garrett reaches over and tugs me on top of him.

He rolls us over and shifts the blanket to cover me. Once he's situated, he drapes his arm over my waist. "I'll get you a new jersey." His lips press to the spot right below my ear.

When we were younger, Garrett would also throw his arm around my shoulders while we sat next to each other on the couch. I never thought much about it. It was something we always did. But now, lying in my bed, me half-naked and him fully naked, with his arm around me, hits differently.

"So, about last night… We didn't…" I curl my fingers into an O with one hand and stick out my pointer finger and poke it through the hole, "last night."

His eyebrows draw together, a smirk flirts on his lips. "Did we… make hand gestures at each other?"

"No." I widen my eyes and raise my brows. "Did we…" I motion with my hands again.

He shrugs, feigning ignorance.

I drop my hands to the comforter and huff out a breath. "We didn't have sex last night." I pause. "Did we?"

"See? That wasn't so hard. Do you think we had sex?"

My eyes shift back and forth. I remember the kissing, and the couch, but coming into the bedroom is black. I imagine I'd be a little sore if he's as big as I remember. My nipples pebble at the thought of my hand wrapped around his thick cock. I shake the thought away. Now is not the time.

"I'm not sure. I'm assuming I would be smarter than that. But we consumed a lot of alcohol last night. Anything could have happened." I drop my head to my hands. "Chances are we did. Dammit."

He laughs. "Before you give yourself a coronary, I'll have you know your vagina is safe. We didn't have sex."

A wave of relief washes over me.

"Believe me, you'd remember if we had sex." He sits up, the blanket drapes over his waist as he leans against the headboard. "But you did beg for it."

I gasp. "No, I didn't." Shit. Did I? Honestly, I wouldn't put it past drunk me. She can be a little slut.

"You did, and I quote, 'Garrett? I want your baseball bat cock in me.'" He uses his falsetto voice on the last part.

"You're so full of shit." I playfully backhand his bicep. "I would not say baseball bat cock."

"But you did many times. Along with 'I'm so horny for you. Fuck me with your big dick,' and 'I want to play with your baseballs.'"

My cheeks flame red hot. "There's no way I said all those things. If I did, I'm blaming it on the tequila."

He leans over, the edge of the blanket shifting lower on his lap exposing his V muscle. His thumb brushes over my cheek. "You're fucking adorable when you blush, but there's no need to be shy with me."

My heart hammers in my chest, waiting to see if he's going to kiss me. The anticipation builds as I ache for him to kiss me, but instead he pulls away. "I have to get going. I have some rehearsal dinner bullshit to attend."

He rolls to the edge of the bed and throws off the blanket. His back muscles flex as he rises to his feet. Then there's his ass. I should look away, but like earlier, I can't. But when he bends over, I divert my gaze.

"I don't understand why you have to practice getting married before you get married. You stand in front of a pastor and say 'I do.'" He pulls his boxer briefs over his hips. The elastic waistband slaps against his skin once they're in place.

"Some people want the day to be perfect. Special."

"What would you want?" Next, he yanks on his pants.

At least he was smart enough last night to bring his clothes with him to the bedroom so I don't have to watch him parade across my bedroom—naked—to fetch them. "I don't know. I haven't really thought about it."

"Doesn't every girl envision her dream wedding when she's like five years old?"

I laugh. "Not five. Maybe seven." I shrug. "I'd want something simple, elegant. Nothing too flashy. Something in the moment."

"I've made a mental note." He smirks. Then he rounds the foot of the bed to my side. Bending at the waist, he rests his palms on either side of me. "I have to get going before I crawl back into bed with you and finish what we started last night." He kisses my cheek. "I'll see you at the wedding."

"Let me walk you out." My fingers grip the edge of the blanket and lift.

"Stay in bed. Go back to sleep." His lips press to my forehead in a soft kiss.

Before I can say to hell with this and drag him back to bed, he exits my bedroom and descends the stairs. I hear rustling for a few seconds before the front door opens and clicks shut.

He's chipped away a little more, okay a lot more, of the hatred I've held on to for so long. A friendship is inching closer to the horizon.

Chapter 15

WEIRD GRAY AREA

Dessa

One Day Later

A bead of sweat slides down my forehead and I wipe it away with my forearm. This is worse than losing my phone. I continue to tear apart my entire townhome, searching for my notebook of drinks. My drink recipes are like a window into my soul at that moment. Losing it is equivalent to losing a part of myself. Currently, distress signals are blaring. Flares have been shot. All is lost.

Collapsing onto the stool at my kitchen island, I rest my elbows on the counter and drop my head in to my hands. What did I do with it last night? That's years and years of work and right now it's missing. Sure, I have the majority of the recipes memorized and Rylee and Lach can help fill in the missing pieces since I've used most of them at Porter's for the Drink of the Week, so starting from scratch wouldn't be the end of the world. But even so, I'd rather have my notebook.

I remember I had it yesterday when Garrett was over, but there was a lot of alcohol consumed, and I have no idea where I placed it. Shit. A wave of panic washes over me. Did it accidentally get thrown in the trash? I'd cry. Next to me on the counter, my phone buzzes with an incoming message.

RYLEE

I'm on my way. I have your charcoal handbag for you.

DESSA

Thanks. Just come in when you get here. It's unlocked.

Five restless minutes later, Rylee's strolling through the front door. I lean back on the stool. "I'm in here!" She holds up the handbag. "You can set it on the chair."

She sets the bag down and continues her way into the kitchen. With my foot, I push out the stool next to me and she takes a seat.

"Thanks for letting me borrow it. I never imagined I would be the type of person to attend fancy galas, but they mean a lot to Trey and his career. The least I can do is raid your closet for something outside of jeans and t-shirts." Her brows furrow when she takes notice of my destroyed kitchen. "What happened here?"

"I can't find my recipe notebook. I'll have to put the search and rescue mission on pause, though, so I can get ready for the wedding."

With her elbow on the counter, she rests her chin on her hand and twists to face me. "I still can't believe you're going to this wedding."

I groan. "I know. A part of me wonders why I'm doing it. But I think it'll be good. It will show that we're all moving forward." I pick at the edge of my phone case. "I chatted with Tony and briefly met his soon-to-be wife. They stopped by Porter's on their way out of town for the wedding a couple of nights ago."

"And that wasn't awkward?" Her brows raise.

"No. It was good. We're all in the position to be friends again. I've known his family for so many years. It'll be great to see them again, especially his nana."

"The only one you failed to mention is Garrett."

"Yes. The giant elephant in the room wherever he goes."

"What's going on with you two?"

I bite down on my lower lip as I contemplate my answer. Mostly because I don't know the answer. We've fought, kissed, fought, and then drunkenly exchanged orgasms. A part of me is excited Garrett's back in my life. I can have my best friend again, but there's still a giant rift between us I'm not sure we can ever repair. "I'm not really sure. We're in this weird gray area of friends, but friends who've also touched each other's privates." We both laugh. "But we haven't talked it out at all. And honestly, after the past week, I'm tired of talking."

"That's hard to believe coming from you."

"I know." I sigh. "Everything involving Garrett is exhausting right now. I just want things to progress naturally. I mean, it's still complicated with Tony being my ex and Garrett being Tony's brother."

"I'd imagine it would be weird to be with two brothers." She laughs. "Maybe as long as it's not at the same time."

A rush of warmth spreads across my cheeks. "Yeah, definitely not that." An image of both Tony and Garrett flashes before my eyes, but there's only one I fixate on. I shake my head, forcing the image to disappear like an Etch-a-Sketch. "I know I want to establish the friendship with Garrett and then we can see where it goes from there."

"Do you think that'll be hard with you living here and him living on the West Coast?"

"Now you're getting ahead of yourself. It's only a friendship. Everything else isn't something I need to concern myself with at this moment."

"But you might eventually," she sing-songs.

"I'll deal with it then." If the time comes. He's only been back in my life for one week. In no way am I planning a long-lasting future with him.

Rylee's phone chimes and she checks it. "Oh shit. I have to leave."

"Okay. I should get ready anyway."

"Let me know how everything goes."

"Definitely." I give Rylee a hug and walk her to the front door. After I close it behind her, I race upstairs.

I run my hand down the navy blue bohemian empire waist long-sleeve dress. A collection of necklaces sways back and forth as I rummage through them on the holder until I find the silver knotted pendant necklace. It will pair perfectly with the V-neckline of the dress. I clasp it at the nape of my neck and fluff my hair so it falls over my shoulders. Here goes nothing.

Luckily, the weather is cooperating, and the two-hour drive north goes by quickly. However, I have to question the person who thought it was a good idea to have a wedding in December in Minnesota. I shake my head. I can guarantee I'll pick a warmer month for my wedding or not have it in Minnesota. Shit. Why am I even thinking of getting married? I'm missing a very important key component in order for a wedding to take place. A fiancé. But first I need a boyfriend to turn into a fiancé. At this rate, I'll be pushing fifty by the time I walk down the aisle.

When I'm fifteen minutes away from the venue, snowflakes flutter from the darkening sky. With every second that passes, the flakes grow bigger and fall faster. I ease up on the gas to slow my pace as snow accumulates on the pavement. My fingers grip the steering wheel as I glance at the clock. Shit. I'm going to be that person who walks into the wedding in the middle of the ceremony. As long as it's not right at the "I dos" because that would be awkward as fuck.

The Three Moose Lodge sign comes into view, and I exhale a sigh of relief. Winter driving is not my favorite, even though I've been doing it since I got my driver's license. At the first available spot in the parking lot, I stop and cut the engine. I still can't believe I'm here. Why did I think this was a good idea? I debate turning over the engine and driving back to Harbor Highlands. But Nana's here. And so is Garrett.

I push open the door and step out. My charcoal mid-calf high-heeled boot sinks into the freshly fallen snow. With every step to the front door of the lodge, my boots leave a breadcrumb imprint in the snow just in case I need to bolt out of here.

The property is comprised of a large timber frame main lodge with several hotel-style rooms, but there are also several cabins scattered throughout the woods for a more intimate getaway.

Once inside the lodge, I brush the snow off my shoulders and out of my hair. A large white poster board perched on an easel in the lobby directs me toward the ceremony. My heart pounds in my chest, mimicking my footsteps. I'm unsure if I'm nervous or eager to see Garrett again. Both are a possibility. When I glance up, my breath catches in my throat and I come to a halt. My palms grow clammy as the world around me freezes. All the quiet chatter and soft music around me dissipates. My breath hitches. Standing between the open doors is Garrett, looking hot as sin in a sleek black tuxedo, complete with a vibrant red pocket square. All thoughts of maintaining only a friendship with Garrett are tossed out the window.

Chapter 16

SAVE A DANCE FOR ME

Garrett

I slide the cuff of my suit jacket over my wrist and check my watch for the tenth time. The ceremony is about to start, and Dessa hasn't arrived yet. She said she was coming. Maybe she's changed her mind after all. Fuck. I was hoping to spend the evening with her arms draped over my shoulders, our bodies pressed together, as we slow dance through the night.

A middle-aged couple strolls to the doorway, pulling me away from my thoughts. I nod to Greg, the other usher who's standing across from me, to let him know I got this one. I escort them to their seats. Elation surges through me when I turn around and she's sauntering toward the entrance. Dark, loose curls cascade over her shoulders. A charcoal gray peacoat covers her navy dress. She looks absolutely stunning. Like an angel descending from heaven. I jog to the doorway.

I turn to Greg. "She's mine." There's no way in hell I'm going to let anyone else touch her.

Our eyes lock, and a fire ignites inside me, my smile widening with every step she gets closer.

When she approaches the entrance, I hold out my elbow for her. "Fancy seeing you here."

She laughs. It's soft and sweet. "Shut up. You knew I was coming." She loops her arm through mine. "You don't have to escort me to my seat."

I lean in so only she can hear. "It's my job as an usher to walk every guest to their seat, and one thing I always do is take any job I'm given seriously. Plus, it gives me an excuse to touch you." I wink.

She peers at me through her lashes, a small smile on her lips. "I can't believe they wrangled you into being an usher."

"This is the most important job at a wedding. I dictate where everyone sits. One wrong placement could lead to an argument between enemies, or rivals, or even two scorned lovers."

"Or ex-best friends." She smirks.

"That one is more manageable." I rest my hand on hers, loving the way her warm skin feels against mine. "Anyway, the best man position doesn't deserve all the hype. You look gorgeous, by the way. The dress looks amazing on you."

A small giggle escapes her. "You can't even see the dress under this heavy-ass coat."

"The bottom is visible, so I'm imagining what the top looks like, and it's stunning on you." I slow my pace, mostly so I can get a few extra seconds to talk with her. "What do you say? Since I'm wearing a suit and you're wearing a dress," I nod to the front of the room where the wedding arch is located, "should we ask the pastor if he'll do a two-for-one wedding special?"

Her head jerks to mine, and I wiggle my eyebrows. "You're so full of shit."

"You shouldn't say 'shit' in church."

"This isn't a church."

"But God is present." I lift my chin towards the pastor.

"Good try, but not happening."

"I had to shoot my shot." My grip around her arm tightens a little more. "I still can't believe you didn't want to be my date."

"That would be so awkward. Girl comes to ex-boyfriend's wedding as the date of his brother. People would whisper behind their hands about me." Sarcasm laces her tone.

"Who gives a shit what they say?"

Her gaze flits to mine, indignation written all over her face. Dessa has always tried to maintain a proper front. She never wanted to be on anyone's bad side and definitely didn't want to be on top of the gossip pole.

"You shouldn't say 'shit.' God is watching." She repeats my action by nodding at the pastor.

A laugh bursts out of me, drawing the attention of a few guests. I pretend cough into my fist as we walk by. "Fair."

"By the way, do you know what I did with my recipe notebook? I had it the night you were over, but now I can't find it."

Shit. Shit. Shit. "Uh. No. You must have misplaced it. You tend to do that a lot." She can't know I took it. That would ruin the surprise.

"Damn. Alcohol leads to bad decisions."

"There were some good decisions made that night." I

give her a flirty wink. She shakes her head but smiles at me.

Once we reach her seat, I reluctantly let her go. I love having her at my side. Before she sits, I bend and brush my lips across her cheek. "Save a dance for me."

She glances up at me from the corner of her eyes. "I'll see what I can do."

I flash her a half smile. "I'll see you at the reception." Before she can respond, I'm strolling to the entrance with a little extra pep in my step.

The wedding planner informs us that the wedding is about to start and to take our seats.

Reaching into the inside suit jacket pocket, I pull out a pen. On a table next to the door, I find a wedding program and rip off a blank corner piece. I scribble a note before folding it into a small square. On my way to the front of the room to sit with the rest of my family, I drop the note in Dessa's lap as I pass by. As soon as I take my seat, I glance over my shoulder. With her head bowed, she unfolds the piece of paper. A few seconds later, she lifts her head, and her eyes meet mine. Her eyebrows pinch together, but then a smile slowly graces her lips.

Chapter 17

THE TINGLES AGAIN

Dessa

As I enter the reception, the crimson fabric draped on the walls with shimmering strands of silver catches my attention. It's exactly what you'd imagine for a winter wedding. Even though there are a lot of familiar faces, it doesn't make being here any less awkward. Maybe I should've taken Garrett up on his offer to be his date. I could be with him right now. Instead, I'm alone in a room full of mostly strangers.

Two steps through the doorway, I hear my name called from the right. I turn that way and spot the only person I really wanted to see today. Smiling widely, I walk over to a table where Nana is seated.

"Oh my," she exclaims, her voice full of admiration. "Dessa, you look beautiful." Nana's short, silvery hair falls in perfectly curled waves, framing her face as she elegantly dons a silver and black drop waist dress. She always enjoyed dressing to the nines.

"Hi Nana."

"And you changed your hair."

I run a hand over my hair, smoothing the strands. Too bad it's the only thing that's changed since the last time I saw her.

"It's so wonderful to see you. You look beautiful as always." I bend at my knees and wrap my arms around her shoulders for a hug. Tony's dad pulls out a chair for me to have a seat next to Nana.

"It's so lovely to see you, dear. I was really hoping it would be you walking down the aisle toward one of my grandsons." Her eyes soften, but I notice a hint of disappointment in her voice.

I awkwardly laugh. "But Georgia's great. She's perfect for Tony."

"She is." She reaches over and rests her dainty hand on mine. "That means you get to be with the one you're truly meant to be with."

My cheeks warm, and I bow my head to hide my smile. Mostly, I need a few minutes to collect my thoughts.

At one time, I thought I was meant to be with Garrett, but Tony happened first. Now Tony is married, and Garrett's back in my life. It makes everything a muddled mess. I go with what makes sense right now. "I'm really glad that we all can be friends again."

"I've seen a few things in my life and let me tell you what you have isn't friendship. It hasn't been for a long time. We all know it. It's time for you to see it now." She gently squeezes my fingers. "It was you who always made him happy. You who always gave him the biggest smile. And it's you who has his heart. You and Tony were never a good match. You two were like oil and water. You'd never fully come together. Now with Garrett, you two always had chemistry like I've never seen before. Much like me and their grandfather. You two are like two delicate pieces of string. When woven together, you create something beautiful."

Her words swirl around in my head. Nana's known me for over half my life, and that entire time she's seen me with Garrett. But years have passed. Things have changed. Garrett's changed. I've changed. Maybe not so much me since I'm still in the same spot as when he left, only a little older. These feelings are only fleeting since it's been waaay too long since I've been with a guy. That's the only logical explanation.

The DJ's voice booms through the speakers and I'm thankful for the interruption. "It's time to welcome the bride and groom!"

An image of Garrett and me strolling through the doors hand-in-hand flits through my mind. As we enter the room, his green eyes fixate on me, his radiant smile infectious. I shake off the image as quickly as it appears.

Tony and Georgia strut through the doorway, hands laced together. Tony stops and twirls Georgia, her white dress flaring at the waist as the sparkles shimmy in the light. Soon after, the rest of the bridal party dance their way into the reception hall. Last to enter is Garrett, a half smile on his face. When he's a couple of steps in, he immediately turns my way, almost as if he knew exactly where I'd be. Our eyes connect, and his lips curve into a wide grin. I can't tear my eyes away from him. A sweet warmth fills my chest as he leisurely walks across the dance floor and finds a seat near the front.

"Nana, we should go take our seats. They're about to serve dinner," Mr. Dawson says.

"I'm much more fond of this seat. It's closer to the bar," Nana says.

"I'll make sure the server brings you whatever you'd like," Mr. Dawson reassures her.

Nana ignores her son and pats my leg, drawing my attention. "See, that smile was just for you."

After a few beats, Nana stands, and with the assistance from Mr. Dawson, she shuffles to her table near the front.

After dinner and all the tables are cleared, everyone socializes while I hang out off to the side. It was much easier when the conversation was contained to the small group of people at my table. Now, it's like free rein and I don't know who I'm going to bump into first. Luckily, I spot Georgia and beeline it across the room, so I don't stick out like a turd in a fruit bowl.

"Hi Georgia. It was such a beautiful wedding. And your dress is gorgeous." The long-sleeve, lace, V-neck dress is equal parts elegant and romantic. The subtle sequins sewn into the lace add a little sparkle that reminds me of the sun reflecting off freshly fallen snow.

"Thank you so much. I'm so happy you could make it." She wraps her arms around me for a brief hug.

As we break apart, Tony approaches. "Mitchell, I'm so glad you can make it." He leans in and kisses my cheek but lingers a little longer than a friendly kiss should last. "You look gorgeous."

"Thanks." I pull away. "The wedding was beautiful. And doesn't Georgia look absolutely stunning? Seriously, I can't get over your dress." I push the conversation away from me.

"She does." He wraps his arm around Georgia's shoulder, and she leans into the crook of his arm. He presses a kiss to the top of her head before excusing himself. I finished chatting with Georgia until her attention is needed elsewhere. As a server walks by, I pluck a champaign flute off his tray.

Before the ceremony, Garrett seemed so eager to be around me as he ushered me to my seat, yet he hasn't said a single word to me. When I glance across the dance floor, Garrett's standing next to the bar as Tony approaches him. I'm not sure what they're saying but both of them are laughing and smiling. My heart swells. It's exactly like old times. Things could be moving in the right direction in all of us being friends again. I cross my legs, lifting the glass of champagne to my lips, the bubbles tickling my nose.

Three slow songs have passed, and he has not yet asked me to dance. Every time I've thought about approaching him, someone stops me to chat. By the time I finish the conversation, he's vanished.

Now from across the room, I spot Garrett. His heated gaze lingers on me from over the rim of his whiskey glass. He's telling me everything with only a look. It sends tingles directly between my thighs. I'm torn between the fight or the want. Currently, the want is winning. As he watches me, it's as if he's seeing me. All of me. Real and raw. All these years away from each other could never break the connection we share. Somehow, the time apart made it stronger. Here we are, two people who can't keep their eyes off each other. As they say, the bigger the risk, the higher reward, but they always fail to mention how debilitating it is when it blows up in your face.

Chapter 18

STAY WITH ME

Garrett

All evening, I've kept a close eye on Dessa, waiting for the timing to be perfect. Moments can be fleeting, and she deserves more than one. She deserves all of them. On either side of me, a couple of guys chat among themselves, occasionally bringing me into the conversation, but I'm more interested in the raven-haired beauty on the other side of the room.

The one song I've been waiting for starts playing through the speakers. "If you'll excuse me," I say to no one in particular.

Turning around, I place my drink on the closest table and my gaze instantly shifts to Dessa, who is seated at a table with another woman across the room. "Don't You (Forget About Me)" by Simple Minds continues to play. I weave my way in and out of people on the dance floor. When I'm standing next to her, I hold out my hand. Her eyes wander from my fingers, up my arm, linger on my chest for a brief second, until finally meeting my gaze with a warm smile.

"Dance with me."

Her smile grows wider as she lifts a brow. "Are you asking or telling?" There's a playfulness to her tone.

"Does it matter?"

She tucks a strand of hair behind her ear. Without saying another word, she rests her hand in mine. A crackle of electricity jolts between us as soon as we touch. I clasp my hand around hers as she rises to her feet.

Wordlessly, we stroll hand-in-hand to the corner of the dance floor. While everyone else is swaying their hips to the upbeat music, I link my fingers around hers and move her other hand to drape around my shoulders and over the curve of my neck. We sway back and forth to the music, neither of us saying anything and instead letting our bodies do the talking.

After a few silent moments, I twist my head and raise our hands, placing a kiss on her wrist. "I told you this dress would look fucking stunning on you."

She smiles up at me. Even in the dim light, I can see the pink cover her cheeks. She's always been self-conscious about compliments, but at every opportunity I'll tell her she's beautiful until she believes it.

She presses her lips together, something she does when she's nervous. "So, I'm guessing by your note, this is the dance you wanted me to save for you."

"It is."

A soft laugh escapes her. "This isn't really a slow dance song." Her fingers caress the short hairs on the back of my head. Then her eyes go wide. "Oh! I get it! Junior prom. The note makes sense now. Don't you forget about me. You dragged me out on the dance floor to slow dance to a not-so-much slow dance song."

My lips curl into a smile. "I thought it was pretty perfect."

"Yeah." She laughs again. It's as soft and sweet as caramel. "Except my date didn't really think so."

My hand slides down her back, resting right above the curve of her ass. "I wasn't going to go an entire night without dancing with my best friend."

I rest my forehead against hers. My voice is low, so only she can hear. "I'm sorry I was a complete asshole. If I could, I would take it back. Maybe one day you can forgive me."

She blows out a slow breath. "What you did hurt. A lot. I'd like to believe we've grown up since then. We're older and wiser." She pauses. Her gaze drops to the center of my chest.

Seconds go by without her saying anything else. Fuck. I ruined it. My chance with her is gone and I have no one to blame but myself. Tilting my head, I stare at the ceiling. My jaw clenches, willing anyone or anything to give me the words to make everything better.

Dessa presses herself closer to me. "I forgive you," she whispers.

I exhale a slow breath. I don't deserve her forgiveness, but I'll do everything in my power to show her how much she means to me.

"It'll take some time for the wounds to heal, especially since you came back to town reopening them again."

"I get that. In the meantime, I'm here now." I press my lips to her forehead.

She tilts her head, peering up at me. "Why did it take you so long to talk to me tonight?"

"I wanted the anticipation to be worth the wait." With my hand on her lower back, I press her into me. "Since you've been thinking about me, I do believe my plan worked." I lean down, my breath a whisper against the shell of her ear. "Don't worry, I thought about you every second."

As the song ends, half the people on the dance floor leave while the other half wait for the next song. I'm rooted in place with Dessa in my arms. Neither of us moving or talking. After a few beats of silence, the next song plays through the speakers, breaking the trance between us.

"I need a drink," Dessa murmurs. She pulls away from me and struts toward the bar. Halfway there, she spots a server holding a tray of champagne flutes and abandons the bar. She grabs one, pauses, and grabs a second one with her other hand. She guzzles one down, followed by the other.

I step next to her. My fingers graze her shoulder before I slowly slide them to her waist. The hitch in her breath doesn't go unnoticed. I lean down and whisper, "I hope you're planning on staying with all the champagne you're drinking."

Her gaze flits to mine. "Shit. I didn't think of that." She tips back the last gulp. "I've had three drinks, plus the ones I had at dinner." She peers at the ceiling and taps her fingers together as if she's counting. "I should be good to leave by 2 a.m."

I scoff. "And get home at four."

"I do it all the time at work."

"But you also only have a ten-minute drive and not two hours."

"I'll sleep in my car."

"It's December." She runs her teeth over her bottom lip. I'm sure she's trying to conjure up any sort of excuse she can. "Stay here." My voice is low and gravelly.

"I'm not paying for a room."

"Stay with me. In my cabin."

She tucks a loose strand of hair behind her ear. "You can't be serious? It's a wedding. Isn't it customary for all the single guys to hook up with the single bridesmaids?"

"Are you one of the bridesmaids?"

Her eyebrows pinch together as if the answer to my question is simple. "No."

"Then I don't want to spend the night with a bridesmaid. There's only one girl I want to spend the night with, and I'm looking right at her." With my arm still around her waist, I slide to move in front of her so we're facing each other. "What do you say? It beats driving home at 2 a.m."

I'm not ready to let her go. I want to spend as much time with her as possible, even if it only involves sleeping, but I really hope it involves more. Even if it's only to feel her soft skin under my palms, her body pressed against mine, my lips trailing over the column of her neck. Fuck, if I don't stop thinking about her, the bulge in my pants will be a dead giveaway of what I want to do tonight.

"I don't have any clothes."

"I have an entire suitcase full, so you can borrow something of mine."

"I don't know." The air around us crackles with heated tension. "But I really like my pajamas." Her lips split in a slow smile. Now she's just teasing me.

"If you don't like what I have, you're fully welcome to sleep naked. I'll make sure to keep you warm." Her cheeks flush pink. We haven't seen each other naked since the night at her townhouse, but I've sure thought about it. Based on the current heated expression on her face, she has, too.

She grabs my lowball out of my hand and slams the last drop of the amber liquid. Her face scrunches and she shakes her head. "I don't know how you can drink straight whiskey but balk at a shot of tequila."

"I sip the whiskey. I don't sip tequila. So, what's your answer?"

Her tongue peeks out and wets her bottom lip. "Okay. I'll stay, but only because I don't want to drive home."

That's the biggest lie I've ever heard, or at least not the sole reason she's staying, but I'll take it. "What do you say?" I nod toward the exit. "Want to turn this into a party for two?"

A twinkle glints in her dark eyes. Maybe she wants this just as badly as I do. "Lead the way."

Chapter 19

I'M TAKING YOU WITH ME

Dessa

My future self better not regret this because right now my present self's vagina is in charge and gives zero fucks about future self. When he told me I could wear whatever I wanted from his suitcase, my nipples jumped to attention. As a teenager, I loved stealing—borrowing—his hoodies. I still have a couple in my closet, including my favorite Harbor Highlands Trojans Baseball hoodie. As much as I wanted to, I could never toss it in the garbage. Plus, they were too comfortable.

Damn. I wish I had more champagne right now. I'm on my last thread of controlling my willpower against Garrett. If I stay with him tonight, I know exactly how the night will end. But fuck. It's Garrett. At his brother's wedding. Who I also used to date. Garrett's wearing a suit and looking extra delicious. It's almost as hot as his baseball uniform. I wonder if he has that in his suitcase?

We could role-play with him as a pitcher and me as the catcher.

"Ready?" Garrett asks, squeezing my hand.

I nod. If I open my mouth, I'm afraid the next words out will be "Fuck me, Garrett. Wrap your hand around my neck and fuck me." So, it's best if I remain silent. At least until we're out of earshot of anyone else.

As we exit the reception, a shiver runs down my spine, and I hug myself tightly as we make our way to coat check. Garrett passes our numbers to the attendant and steps to move behind me. His warm, comforting hands glide up and down my arms, as if all the happiness in the world resides within his simple touch. I relax against his warm chest, loving his hands on me, even if it's as innocent as keeping me warm.

Georgia passes us. She eyes me before coming to a halt on Garrett. A knowing smile spreads across her lips. I was really hoping we would go unnoticed, but of course not. I'm sure she'll ask questions later. What I have to say to her will depend on how the night goes. Once we have our coats, Garrett holds up mine for me. I shove my arms into the sleeves, then he does the same with his. As we're walking out, he grabs my hand and intertwines our fingers. Something about the gesture screams "more than friends." But it's comfortable and familiar. I don't hate it.

When we're halfway across the parking lot, he says, "We'll take my car and get yours in the morning."

"Okay." I'm letting him lead the charge because my head is still swimming with the idea of staying with him again. Based on all the heated stares and not-so-innocent touches, this won't be a friendly sleepover. I'm being impulsive, and this could all come back to bite me in the ass, but it's so hard to fight the connection we have. I want to feel everything, consequences be damned. Because right now he's all I want.

At his vehicle, he opens the passenger door for me like a gentleman. As soon as I'm settled in my seat, he shuts the door and disappears around the rear. He climbs in the driver's side and starts the engine. As we meander through the woods, the moonlight casts a gentle glow on the snowy ground, filling the air with a serene ambiance. Garrett reaches across the center console and rests his hand on my thigh. Whenever he touches me, it's like a single fluttering butterfly morphs into a million. It's all consuming. It's never been like this with anyone else. I don't know if it's because I'm familiar with Garrett or if these feelings run deeper. I glance to my left, and in the moonlight, I can see his jaw clench, as if he wants to say something, but doesn't know what. The rest of the five-minute ride to Garrett's cabin is silent, but the crackle of sexual tension runs high. Especially with his fingers drifting between my legs. I don't know what tomorrow holds, but for tonight, there's only one thing I want. Garrett.

When we reach the cabin, he parks the SUV in the lone parking spot on the side. He pushes his door open, and I do the same. When he reaches the passenger side, again he holds out his hand for me to take and escorts me up the three stairs to the covered porch. He fumbles with the key in the lock, but he never releases my hand. After it's unlocked, he pushes the door open and turns on the light. Then he motions for me to enter.

Before he can fully close the door behind us, I spin him around. With my palms against his chest, I shove him against the door, and it clicks shut. I cup his cheeks, the short stubble tickling my fingers.

"What was that—"

I crash my lips to his, not letting him finish. The keys

clatter to the floor. One of his hands tangles in my hair while the other wraps around my waist. My pulse hammers in my throat. All night I've craved for his lips to be on mine, and it's better than what I expect. He walks me in reverse, my butt bumping into stools and a countertop. But both of us refuse to break the kiss. We come to a stop in a room past the kitchen.

I pull away. My chest heaves as I collect my breath. When I'm with Garrett, he makes me forget who I am and what I'm doing. He's hypnotizing. The moonlight shines on us through the large floor-to-ceiling windows like a spotlight on a stage.

"We're both wearing too many clothes." I slide his suit jacket off his shoulders, and it hits the floor with a thud.

Garrett's gaze drops. His lips part as my fingers fumble to undo his tie. In the meantime, his hands roam over my shoulders, my biceps, and around to my back, making it entirely too hard to concentrate. While I fiddle with the buttons on his white dress shirt, his fingers find the zipper on my dress. Slowly, he lowers it until it comes to a stop. When all his shirt buttons are unfastened, I move to his belt. My fingers shake as nervous energy courses through me. I've had sex before, but not with Garrett. Honestly, he's all I want right now.

He drops his hands to his sides. I glance at him through my lashes and his eyes are on me. Desire swirls through his dark irises. His chest rises and falls with each passing second. I make quick work of his belt, then move on to the button of his slacks. Frantically, I yank this shirt from the waistband. Once free, the sides of his shirt fall open, exposing his rippling abs and tattooed skin. His muscles flex as my fingertips brush over his warm skin. Now, that I'm experiencing his naked chest in a slightly more sober state, I love the feel of him under my hands.

With a finger under my chin, he lifts, forcing me to look at him. His mouth descends on mine in a gentle kiss at first, but as seconds pass, it becomes ravenous. His tongue presses into the seam of my lips, and I open, inviting him in. Our tongues curl around each other as our hands explore each other's bodies. His hands cup my cheeks, holding me in place. He tastes like whiskey and bad decisions. And I'm beyond ready to get drunk off him. My hands fall to my sides, and he takes over undressing me. His hand brushes my shoulder, sending goosebumps to spring over my entire body as he slides the fabric down my arm. Then he does the same with the other until the dress pools at my feet.

He pulls away, resting his forehead against mine. "Fuck. I'm fighting with myself whether I want to take this fast and hard or if I should savor your body." His voice is shaky and strained.

"How about both? We have all night."

The corners of his lips curve into a smile. He wraps his fingers around the base of my neck, sending a burst of hot pleasure between my legs. His towering frame moves forward until my back connects with the wall.

His mouth slants over mine, but he doesn't kiss me. Instead, he whispers, "You do always get what you want."

Before I can respond, his lips are on mine. It's rough and demanding. Almost as if he's giving me all of him in this kiss. My hands skate over his chest, feeling every inch of him. His other hand clutches my waist, his fingertips dig into my skin like sharp talons holding their prey. It sends a shiver of desire down my spine. Our tongues stroke and caress against each other. I moan into his mouth, and he swallows every sound. His hand moves from my waist and slides across my stomach and to the sheer fabric of my bra. His thumb brushes across my already hard nipple. I moan again and press into him, wanting him to do it again. And he does. I drop my hands to his waist and tug him closer. I grind against him like a cat marking their territory. The bulge in his boxer briefs hits my clit and my head falls back, and I moan.

"Is that what you want?" Before I can answer, Garrett bends at his knees, wraps his arms around my thighs, and lifts. Instinctively, I wrap my legs around his waist, and he pushes me against the wall. Slowly, he grinds his cock between my legs, hitting me in the right spot.

"Oh. Fuuuck." My nails dig into the hard muscles in his shoulders. I'm sure they'll leave tiny half-moon indents in his skin.

He nips and sucks on my neck as he continues to rub his cock between my legs. My panties grow wetter by the second. All I want to do is pull his waistband down and move my panties to the side and let him slide inside me. Filling me.

"Do you have a condom?" I choke out.

He stops and mumbles against my skin. "Upstairs."

"You should go get it."

He lowers me to the ground and jogs to the stairs that lead to the loft. Halfway up, he stops and turns around and races down the stairs just as fast as he went up. When he's standing in front of me, he bends and hoists me over his shoulder.

"Hey!" I giggle. "What are you doing?"

With his palm on my ass, he ascends the stairs. "I didn't want to waste any more time coming back downstairs, so I'm taking you with me."

In the loft, he deposits me on the floor at the foot of the bed and retrieves the condom out of his suitcase. I climb onto the bed, kneeling on the edge.

"Also, there's more than one for later." He tosses it onto

the comforter, and with a hand around my waist, he pulls me to him for a heart-stopping kiss.

With our lips still fused together, the bed dips as he crawls on top. His hand snakes from my waist and past my chest to around the base of my neck. He reaches around my back with his other and with a flick of his wrist, he unhooks my bra. It falls to the edge of the mattress and tumbles onto the floor.

I inch closer to him and deepen the kiss. My heart beats wildly with every passing second. Sweet with Garrett is amazing, and this has been sweet, but it's time for the spice. I hook my thumbs in the waistband of his boxer briefs and yank them down his thighs. His long, thick cock springs free and I wrap my hand around his girth. A deep growl resonates from the back of his throat, and it only spurs me on. I continue to stroke him as I brush my tongue against his in the same manner.

Pulling away, he says, "Turn around." His voice is deep and strained.

I shift my weight to spin around. With my back to him, his hand skates over my stomach, sending goosebumps to sprout over my skin. My heart thumps in my chest as his hand continues upward. He cups one breast as his thumb brushes over my hard nipple.

My head falls against his chest as I moan.

His lips drag across my shoulder, licking and sucking. "I fucking love how responsive you are to my touch."

He pinches my nipple, and I whimper. "I love when you touch me." My words come out in breathy pants. My breasts feel achy and full.

"Good. Because tonight I'm going to make sure there isn't an inch of your body I haven't kissed, licked, or sucked." His other hand drifts to the base of my neck. As he kneads my breast with one hand, his fingers on his other hand curl loosely around the soft muscle. My pulse beats under his fingertips as I suck in a sharp breath.

His hard cock presses into the crack of my ass, and my mouth falls open. Reaching around, I wrap my hands around the shaft. He hisses through his teeth when I make contact. With one hand still around my neck, he slides the other down my stomach before dipping into the waistband of my panties and directly to my pussy.

"Fuck. So fucking wet for me." The pad of his finger circles my clit and my body jolts. My stroke on his cock falters. "Am I distracting you?" His hot breath brushes the shell of my ear.

"N-no. I got this." He chuckles before continuing to nip and suck on my heated skin while his fingers leisurely slide up and down my now even more soaked pussy. With added pressure, I continue to stroke his cock. Somehow, I swear he grows harder with each pump.

"Fuck Tates. Your hand feels so good wrapped around me. But I don't want to come on your ass. I want to be inside you." He pulls his hand from my panties as his other hand drops to his side. I whimper at the loss. "You won't be needing these." He slides my panties down my thighs. I lift my knee for him to slide them farther, then I do the same to the other side. Once they're off, he tosses the lace fabric on the floor. The head of his cock slides across my inner thigh and I arch my back, wiggling my ass, so he's fully aware of what I want right now. My body is buzzing for him to be inside me. If he doesn't push into me within the next ten seconds, I swear I'm going to spontaneously combust.

His laugh is low. "You think I'm going to give you want you want?" He kisses me right below my ear.

"Mmm. Yes."

"Think again." The tip of his cock slides through my slick folds.

I arch my back and push against him. This reminds me of the night in the storage room. I was doing the same thing, sliding his cock through my wetness.

"Garrett. Please," I whine. "I've already waited too long. I need you."

The bed dips, and I hear the condom wrapper ripping open. A second later, I peer over my shoulder as he lines himself up with my entrance. A beat later, he's pushing in.

"Ah!" My body jolts forward as all the other words get caught in my throat.

Chapter 20

HOME RUN STALLION

Garrett

Once I'm fully seated, I pause, because fuck, I can't breathe. I can't think. Hell, I don't even know my own name right now. This isn't real. This can't be real. Nothing this amazing can be real.

"Oh. Garrett." Dessa's low moan jolts me back to reality.

Oh. Yes. That's my name. "Yeah Tates?"

"I need you to fuck me."

"Right." Slowly, I slide out and thrust back in. I peer down and watch my dick disappear inside her. I've died and gone to heaven. That's the only logical explanation for this. All of this. Having sex with Dessa. Being with Dessa. Her moans and whimpers grow louder, and I increase my pace. She feels incredible. Soft and wet. I roll my hips, hitting her G-spot.

"Ah! Oh god! Fuck me. Harder. Harder. Don't stop!" Her pussy grips my dick, and I see stars.

I reach around between her legs and rub circles over her clit. "Come all over my dick, Tates. I want to feel you."

"Yes! Yes! Right there!" She screams out my name as her pussy spasms around me. After a few seconds, her breathing evens out.

I pull out and move up the bed. "Come here. I want you to ride my dick when I come."

On her hands and knees, she crawls across the bed. A devilish smirk forms on her perfectly plump lips until she's hovering over my body. When she's poised over my hips, I slide my hands up her thighs. She glances at me and tucks a strand of hair behind her ear. My heart nearly bursts out of my chest at her beauty. Not because she's naked, straddling my waist, but because she's perfect. In every single way possible. To me, she always has been.

With one hand on her waist, I grip the base of my dick, holding it steady for her. She sinks down on me, and my eyes roll back. Fucking hell. She's strangling my dick.

"Oh my god. You're so big like this." Her hands roam over my chest, using me for balance as she gyrates her hips, sliding me in and out. Her movements grow harder and faster with each passing second. A curtain of dark hair falls over the side of her face. Reaching up, I push it out of the way. I want to see her, all of her, as she impales herself on my dick. Pleasure consumes me, and I'm seconds away from exploding inside her. I drop my hand to her waist. My fingers digging into her soft skin. I need to hold on for just a little bit longer. With her bouncing on my dick, I reach up with my other hand and cup her full tit. She arches into my palm as I brush my thumb over the tip of her hard nipple.

"Oh! Fuck. Garrett. I'm going to come." Her pussy spasms around my dick.

I groan. She feels too good. Too tight. My dick is ready

to explode. I clasp the back of her neck and pull her to me for a long, deep kiss. She moans into my mouth, and I swallow all her sounds. I buck my hips, pounding into her from beneath. Fast and hard thrusts.

She breaks away, her moans and whimpers filling the loft. Good thing there's plenty of distance between the cabins, otherwise I'm sure the neighbors would hear.

"That's it, Tates. Come for me again. Come all over my dick." My balls tighten, and I can't hold on any longer. Another orgasm rips through her at the same time as I pinch my eyes closed and explode inside her.

She collapses on my chest, all her body weight resting on top of me. I run my hands up and down her back as it rises and falls while she collects her breath with my semi-hard dick still inside her.

"I think I'm going to need a week to recover from that."

I laugh. "I can't promise you a week, but I can give you the night."

She smiles at me before resting her cheek on my chest. Slowly, I drag a hand over her spine until I'm palming her ass. I love that she's here right now, with me. Being with Dessa was everything I'd imagined. No. It was better. Our connection is undeniable. It was strong years ago, but it's one hundred times stronger now. "Before we get too comfortable, I need to dispose of the condom."

"Oh. Yeah."

She rolls off me, and I slide off the bed. On my way to the bathroom, I yank off the condom and throw it in the trash. When I'm back in bed, I drape an arm over her waist and snuggle my head against her warm stomach as she leans against the headboard. The tips of her fingers brush back and forth over my shoulder.

I trace my fingers over her other hand, alternating

between pressing my fingertips against hers and intertwining our hands. "This right here is perfection."

"Lying in bed post orgasm?"

"Lying in bed post orgasm with you."

She giggles, causing my head to bounce.

"In all seriousness. I'm glad you stayed." I brush my thumb over her palm. "And I'm really glad we could… rekindle… this… friendship."

"If I'd known it was going to be like this, I might not have resisted for so long."

"Is that so?" I tickle her sides, and she squeals with laughter. Both of us wiggle and squirm on the bed. I roll to my back and take her with me so she's on top.

She props her chin on my chest. "What's next for the Home Run Playboy?"

"Can we drop the 'playboy'? I could be the Home Run Stud? Home Run Beast? Home Run Stallion?"

"Stallion?" She lifts an eyebrow.

"I mean. You rode me like one."

She throws her head back in laughter as a pink blush washes over her cheeks.

"I've never noticed your tattoo before." Her fingers trace over the half baseball, half compass inked over my heart and then follow the outline of the words as she whispers, "What is lost can always be found."

"I got it when I was twenty." She continues to run the tip of her finger over all the lines permanently etched into my skin.

A part of me wants to tell her that it's for her. That I was lost all those years ago, but being with her again, I feel found. She's the missing puzzle piece that makes me whole. Instead, I stay silent, not wanting to scare her away when we've just reconnected.

"I like this one too." A shiver races up my spine as her

finger trails down my rib cage and over the words *Rise from the Ashes*. She giggles. "And you're ticklish."

Her fingers dance over my skin, and I squirm before I trap her hand against my side. "I wouldn't start something you don't stand a chance at winning," I warn, but the corners of my lips curve into a smile.

The tips of her fingers slowly dance over my ribs, and I quirk and eyebrow, daring her to continue.

"Okay. Okay." She laughs. "I better not poke the bear."

"That's right. This bear pokes back." I wink.

"When did you get this tattoo?"

My gaze drifts to the ceiling as I think back. "I was only a few games in during my rookie year playing for Seattle and I was shit. Nothing was going my way. Missed catches. Strike outs. After the game our pitcher at the time pulled me aside and told me not to dwell on it. We all have bad games, but it's how to rise above those losses to do better in the next. Later that week, there was a break in our schedule, and I got the tattoo."

"I love that. And do you think it's helped you overcome those bad games?"

"It puts me in the right mindset." But it's not like my lucky penny. I run my finger over the top of her hand. There's been something on my mind for a while, and it involves Dessa. As of late, everything revolves around her, so that's nothing new. "I think I know why I missed the ball. During the championship game."

She props her chin on my chest, peering up at me. "Why's that?"

"I didn't have my good luck charm."

"Like a lucky rabbit's foot?"

"No. Yes. Kind of, but it wasn't a rabbit's foot. Do you

remember in middle school when we went on that field trip to Elmer's Logging Camp up the shore?"

She nods. "The place that has all the old logging machinery and gives tours and history lessons?"

"Yeah. Inside they had one of those machines where you put a penny in, turn a knob, and it flattens the penny while it imprints an image on it."

"I remember that."

I brush my thumb over the top of her hand, kind of feeling silly for what I'm about to say next. Only because something so small holds so much meaning to me. "During that field trip, you gave me a penny to put in the machine. You told me it was your lucky penny. Since that day, I kept that penny with me for every game. That year we won the State Little League Championship, and I attributed that win to your lucky penny."

Her eyebrows pinch together. "That's absurd."

"The championship game where I missed the catch," I blow out a breath, "I lost the penny. I think that's why I missed, costing us the game."

She rolls off me and leans against the headboard. Her fingers grip my chin, forcing me to look at her. "That's just a superstition. A penny won't make you win or lose a game." She drops her hand as her gaze falls to the blanket. "I'll be honest with you. It wasn't my lucky penny. I found it in the parking lot ten minutes earlier."

My head flinches back. Now it's my turn to be confused. "If the penny wasn't lucky," I rest my finger on my lips, "then there's only one other logical explanation."

"What's that?" Her eyebrows raise.

"*You're* the lucky one." I sit up, my lips splitting into a wide grin, and lean against the headboard next to her. I wrap my arm around her shoulder and tug her into the crook of my arm. "From now on, I'm going to need you to come to every game of mine."

She giggles.

"You laugh now, but I'm serious."

"What are you going to do? Shrink me until I'm two inches tall and put me in your pocket?"

"Since no one has developed shrinking technology yet, even though they did it in *Honey, I Shrunk the Kids*, I'll settle for a kiss before each game." I lean over and press my lips to hers. The kiss is soft and entirely too short.

"As much as I would love that, I do have a job and a life, but maybe we could get you another lucky penny. Last I heard, Earl's is still open."

She just made my entire night. Again. Now I have to return the favor. "We can do that tomorrow. But first, I need more of you. I have ten years to make up for."

"And you have to do that all in one night? I thought I was getting the rest of the night off."

"What I meant to say was I'm going to spend the rest of the night getting you off." She giggles as I lift the edge of the comforter and slide under and between her legs.

Chapter 21

IT'S ONLY A SUPERSTITION

Garrett

Earlier this morning, we left the cabin with a plan to meet back in Harbor Highlands to go to Earl's in hopes the penny machine is still there. After the two-hour drive and another thirty minutes to shower and change, I'm desperate to see Dessa again. I'm consumed by her. It's great to have my best friend in my life again, but now that we're taking our friendship to the next level, I'm here for every fucking second of it.

I rap my knuckles on the front door before entering Dessa's townhome. "Hey, I'm here!" Earlier, I texted her I was coming over and she told me to let myself in.

"I'll be down in a couple minutes!" she hollers from the second floor.

"Take your time!" This is the perfect opportunity. "I forgot my phone in my car! I'll be right back!"

"Okay!"

I jog out to my car and grab her notebook from the

back seat. Once inside, with quiet ninja skills, I toe off my shoes and hang my coat on the hook. I race through the living room and into the kitchen. I'm an asshole for taking it, but it was for a good reason. One I think she'll forgive me for. I hope.

Frantically, I scan the kitchen for anywhere I could place it while simultaneously listening for her to come down the stairs. I'm constantly jerking my head from the kitchen to the living room, and it's making me dizzy. I need to hide it in plain sight. Maybe she doesn't check these drawers. I rip open the first drawer and the tray of silverware rattles. That one won't work. I try the next drawer. Tupperware lids. I think she uses those too often with her drink garnishes. I slam it closed and try the next one. Kitchen towels. Fuck. I spot a small shelf filled with vegetarian cookbooks sitting in a light coating of dust. While she's amazing at creating cocktails, her culinary skills are subpar.

"What is all that noise?" Dessa yells.

"Oh. Um. Nothing!" I kick the leg of the barstool and flinch. "I just stubbed my toe!" Shit. That hurts. I limp out of the kitchen and throw myself onto the couch just as Dessa descends the stairs.

"I know it's kind of late, but do you think Earl's is still open?"

She sits next to me on the couch and tucks her legs underneath her as she snuggles into the crook of my arm. "If you didn't insist on giving me an orgasm while still in bed and then another because one wasn't enough, we might have left sooner."

"I told you, I have ten years to make up for. Plus, you looked too beautiful with the sun shining in through the large windows, and I knew you'd look even more beautiful with my head buried between your legs. But I won't lie. My favorite was your lips wrapped around my dick."

She laughs. "And that is why we got home so late."

A rush of emotions floods over me as my heart leaps in my chest upon hearing the word "home." She's my home. My comfort. My lifeline. The only thing I need in life. While she was using home as her house, I hope one day she'll think of me as her home.

She taps her chin. "It's been close to twenty years since I've been there. We can go check it out." She grabs her phone from the coffee table in front of us. Her fingers dance over the screen as she types before glancing at me. "It says it's open for thirty more minutes."

"Shit. How long does it take to get there?"

"With the snow, probably close to thirty minutes."

"Let's go!" I jump to my feet from the couch and Dessa topples over, bracing herself with her forearms on the cushion, since her weight was resting against me. "We have to do it now. I'm leaving tomorrow."

She giggles. "Okay. Okay."

I grab her wrist and pull her off the couch. She stumbles to her feet before regaining her balance. In two long strides, I'm at the front door. I throw her coat at her, and she barely catches it before it smacks her in the face.

"Slow down, Turbo." She giggles as she shoves her arms through the sleeves.

"We don't have a second to waste." I jam my feet into my shoes. I toss one boot at Dessa and then the other. She does a juggling act with both boots before they hit the floor with a thud. Shaking her head, but with amusement written on her face, she shoves her feet inside. "Do you have a penny?"

"Shit. No. I need one from you, anyway. You're the one

who gave me the first one, so you have to be the one who gives me lucky penny two-point-oh."

"Wait here." She jogs up the stairs with her coat and boots on. The jingling of change as it hits a hard surface echoes down the stairs. "Got one!" With the penny held high, she rushes down the stairs, her breath coming in heavy gasps from the winter coat zipped tight around her. "I'm surprised I had this."

I open the front door and usher her outside and to the car.

"Earl's should be coming up on your left in a quarter of a mile," she says.

At record speed, we raced across the city. Fortunately, the snowplows had cleared the earlier snowfall. I glance from the windshield to the clock—4:56 p.m. We have four minutes. Surely if we arrive before five, they won't kick us out. I step a little harder on the gas pedal hoping to buy us a few extra seconds. The enormous Earl's Logging Camp sign comes into view. Turning left into the empty parking lot, I secure the spot right in front of the door. As I peer into the dark interior, a wave of disappointment washes over me. I leave the car running and step out to read the open hours sign on the door. Four o'clock. Closed. My head falls, along with my shoulders. A deep sigh escapes me. Dammit, according to the online hours, we still have a minute to spare.

The snow crunches next to me as Dessa appears, resting her hand on my arm. "I'm sorry, Garrett."

"Me too," I sigh, my voice heavy with sorrow. As I spin around to go to the car, I notice a house with lights on a hundred yards through the trees. "Do you think the owner lives over there?"

She glances at the dark driveway, then back at me, and shrugs. "We're here, so it's worth a shot."

Both of us get in the car, and I reverse out of the parking spot to drive toward the plowed driveway. The silhouette of the trees casts an eerie shadow over the snow as we approach the house. One thing I hate about winter in Minnesota is that it gets dark by five o'clock. Approaching a stranger's house in the dark, with the closest neighbor miles away, causes my hackles to raise. At this point, the possibility of getting a new lucky penny outweighs the possibility of anything bad happening. I park next to a sidewalk that leads to the house.

My fingers grip the steering wheel, my knuckles turning white. This is my only hope. "You stay here. If anything happens to me, jump in the driver's seat and take off."

"And what about you?"

"I'll fend for myself."

She digs into the pocket of her coat. "I'll come with you. I have this." She holds up a can of pepper spray. "After Rylee's scare with her ex-husband and a former Porter's bartender, I got cans for my car, purse, and coat."

A smile twitches on my lips. I love that she's prepared. "Let's do this." We both exit the SUV and walk the shoveled walkway side-by-side. When we reach the stairs, I drop Dessa's hand and continue toward the door. With each step, my hand grows clammy, and the anxiety builds up inside me. I'm not sure if I'm more nervous about whoever lives here being a serial killer or if they'll have the penny machine I'm looking for. I tap my knuckles against the solid wood door. A few seconds pass before the murmuring voices come from the other side. Then the light above my head flickers to life.

The door opens, and an older man with a full head of white hair and deep creases around his eyes greets me. "What can I do for you?" His voice is hoarse and raspy.

"I was wondering if you're the owner of Earl's Logging Camp?"

"Yes. I am. But we're closed for the day. You'll have to come back tomorrow."

He starts to close the door, but I stop him with my hand. "I was really hoping for a huge favor."

He pulls his glasses down the bridge of his nose. "Wait. Are you Dawson? Garrett Dawson?"

A glimmer of hope sparks inside of me. Maybe he's a fan, and I can bribe him with an autograph.

"Tough break, kid. During the championship game, but you secured the win for my team."

Then the little glimmer dies a smoldering death. "Well, at least something good came out of it for someone."

"What can I do for you?"

I'm thankful he's at least willing to hear me out. "Strange as it may sound, when I was in middle school, we came to Earl's for a class trip. Inside the main building, you had a penny machine. If you put a penny in, and turned a knob, it would flatten the penny and imprint it with a mallard."

His eyes light up with recognition. "Oh yes, I remember that. All the kids loved that machine."

"When I was here, I did one and it kind of became my lucky penny. Then I lost it. So, I'm here to make another one, hopefully. I'll be real quick."

Sorrow washes over his face. "I wish I could help you. But I got rid of that machine years ago. It stopped working, and I didn't want to bother getting it fixed."

My heart plummets into my gut. This was my only chance of replacing my lucky penny. I don't know of any other place that would have the same machine. "Thanks for your help. Sorry to bother you." I turn on my heel.

Dessa's waiting for me at the bottom of the stairs. When I reach her, she wraps her arms around my waist. "I'm sorry, Garrett. You're more than welcome to take this penny, even though it's just a regular penny. Maybe I can rub it on my boobs for good luck."

A small laugh escapes me. "Thanks." I lean down and press my lips to her forehead. "It's just a penny, right? Losing it doesn't mean I'll be cursed with a lifetime of bad luck, does it?"

"It's only a superstition. Your skills are all you and not because of a penny."

While her words are meant to reassure me, I'm still convinced it's what caused me to lose the game.

"Perhaps I can take your mind off the penny." She drags the tip of her finger down my chest.

"You might have to try really hard." I smirk.

"I'm up for the challenge." A lust-filled glint shimmers in her irises. "Even if it takes all night."

Chapter 22

THIS ISN'T GOODBYE

Dessa

Last night, we came back to my place and for the rest of the night I made sure he forgot all about lucky pennies while he made me forget my own name. Several orgasms later, we passed out in my bed.

Now, as the morning light seeps in through the curtain, I snuggle closer to Garrett, absorbing all his warmth because in a few hours it will be gone. He'll be gone. My hand slides over his bare stomach. "Why do you have to leave, again?"

"I have a couple of endorsement photoshoots and commercials to shoot this week."

"Like Calvin Klein. Will I be cutting out full spread magazine ads of you in nothing but a pair of white boxer briefs to hang on my bedroom wall?" I rest my chin on his chest and peer up at him.

He laughs. "No. Nothing like that. I'll save that for the younger guys."

"Younger guys? I guarantee your body trumps any of theirs." Growing up, Garrett was always lean and fit. But Garrett in his late twenties with his broad, muscular shoulders and tapered waist makes my pussy weep. New spank bank material unlocked. With him having to go back to Seattle, that's how I'll have to occupy my nights from now on. The two weeks he's been here have been amazing. I never expected for us reconnect so quickly and seamlessly, especially after ten years apart. It proves we've always had a deep and powerful connection. It's the kind of spark that starts fires. I'm not ready to let him go. Mostly because I don't know what's going to happen next. I finally got my best friend back, only for him to leave again. "What endorsement deals do you have?"

His hand slowly slides over my spine. "I have a shaving cream commercial."

I gasp, reaching up to run my fingers over the light stubble on his cheek. "You're telling me this is getting shaved? This should be a patented look."

"You like the scruff."

I nod. "Especially when it rubs against my inner thighs."

"I'll be sure it grows back by the next time I see you."

My chest tightens. It's another reminder that he's leaving. "So, what else do you have?" I ask, needing a distraction.

"I have a commercial for a sports drink and a photoshoot for athletic apparel."

"No underwear?"

"Less exciting than underwear."

"A girl can dream."

"As much as I want to stay in bed with you for eternity, I'd better collect the rest of my things from my parents' house and say goodbye."

A heavy sigh escapes my lips. I don't want to say goodbye. I'm not ready. "Will you stop by before you leave for the airport?"

"Of course." He presses his lips to my forehead before untangling himself from me and rolling out of bed.

My gaze fixates on his flexing biceps as he collects his boxer briefs and yanks them up. All I want to do is tug him back into bed, tie him to the mattress, and never let him go.

Once he's dressed, he bends down and presses his lips to mine. "I'll be back in a few hours," he whispers against my lips.

My eyelids flutter open, and I nod. Then he disappears out of my room. A minute later, the front door clicks shut. Never in my wildest dreams did I expect to not only see Garrett again, but also sleep with him. Several times. My thigh clench together at the memory.

Two hours later, I'm shoveling the light dusting of snow from the sidewalk when I spot Garrett's black SUV in the distance. He pulls into my driveway and kills the ignition.

"I wasn't expecting snow today." He closes the car door.

Snowflakes continue to flutter from the sky. "Maybe they'll cancel your flight."

"I think there needs to be a little more snow than this for that to happen."

"So what? I guess I'll see you in another ten years?" Right now, it's either I make a joke, or I cry. Since it's cold outside, I'd rather not cry and have the tears freeze to my face.

In two quick steps, he's standing in front of me. He grabs the shovel out of my hands and tosses it onto the small mound of snow. Then his arms wrap around my shoulders. "I'm not leaving again. Well, technically I do have to leave, but I won't go radio silent. Not this time."

"So like nine years?" I mumble into his chest.

He laughs, the deep rumble vibrating both our bodies. "You never had a smart mouth before. But I kind of like it." He brushes a thumb over my cheek. "I'll call you every day."

"That's a little excessive, don't you think? I might have to screen my calls."

"Two for two. You certainly know how to knock me down a peg or two. When did this happen?"

"When my former best friend left without a goodbye."

"Never. Again," he murmurs, his arms tightening around me with a desperate tenderness.

"I hate this. I hate saying goodbye. But I guess at least this time I get a goodbye." The tear I've been fighting to hold back finally breaks free and rolls down my cheek. We've come a long way over the past two weeks. Some bonds can never break. Despite ours being tattered, we managed to repair it. I'm glad we could, and we even came out stronger on the other side.

"Look at me, Dessa." He rests his finger under my chin, forcing me to meet his eyes. His warm thumb brushes away the wetness on my cheek. "This isn't goodbye. It'll never be goodbye. I'm never making that mistake again. Got it?"

I nod. Anything I try to say gets lodged in my throat.

"I'll call you every day. Or text when I can't call, and when we both have a few minutes, we'll FaceTime."

"Only a few minutes?"

"We'll make it several long minutes." A rush of cold smacks into my body as he pulls away. My arms drop to my sides. He cups my cheeks and presses a light kiss on my lips. With our lips still touching, he whispers, "Something to think about until the next time we're together."

He gets in his car and reverses out of my driveway. I keep my eyes glued to his vehicle as it gets smaller in the distance. He comes to a stop at the stop sign, and I fully expect him to turn left and disappear down the road, but instead white reverse lights illuminate behind him. My brows pinch together. Did he forget something? He pulls into my driveway and jumps out.

"Did you forget—" Before I can finish, he kisses me again. My brows shoot to my hairline in surprise until I settle in and wrap my arms around his waist. The kiss is soft and gentle. I want to spend the rest of the day doing this.

He moves away a fraction of an inch. His voice is low as he says, "I told you it would be sooner than that."

I chuckle. "I don't know if five minutes really counts."

"Oh, it counts, and I'll show you exactly how much it counts."

"But don't you have a plane to catch?" I peer into his piercing green eyes.

"Yeah."

"And aren't you going to miss it?"

"I'll reschedule."

"Isn't that going to cost a fortune?"

"Probably. But it's worth it for a few extra hours with you. I wasted ten years not kissing you when I had the chance. I'm not wasting another second."

And his lips are on mine once again.

Chapter 23

SENTIMENT IS FOR SUCKERS

Dessa

I miss Garrett. When did I become that girl? The one who wants to bury herself under the covers and never come out because she misses her… I don't know what we are, but I miss him. It's been two days since he left, for real this time, but he kept his promise to call and text. He even called me the second the wheels touched down in Seattle. Luckily, it was a slow night at Porter's, so I had a few minutes to chat with him.

"I still can't believe you slept with two brothers!" Nora exclaims.

"I didn't sleep with them at the same time or back-to-back, so the situation is a little different." Stupid Garrett and not being able to keep his lips to himself gave it away that we were together. Since he was unable to keep his vampireness below the belt, when I walked into work yesterday, Rylee immediately zeroed in on the hickey on my neck. Within five minutes, everyone knew I had sex with Garrett. Granted, they were all super happy about it, but now I'll never hear the end. Which is fair, I guess, since we all razzed Rylee when she got together with Trey. Payback's a bitch, and Lach and Nora will get theirs. It's all a matter of time. Jake's the only innocent one here, but he's always kept himself on the outside. He likes to play the ignorance-is-bliss card, at least, when it comes to his employees' relationships. Or sex life, in Nora's case.

"You'll be thinking, 'That's not how your brother does it.' Or even comparing styles and size." Nora moves the palms of her hands back and forth to show a difference in length.

A warm blush washes over my cheeks. "Shut up. I hate you so much right now."

"I'm only pointing out the obvious. So, which is the better brother?" Nora leans on the bar top, wiggling her eyebrows.

I laugh. "I'm not going to pit them against each other in the sex department. What kind of person do you think I am?"

"I would totally compare them. I'd have charts and pie graphs. You can't sleep with brothers and not compare them." Nora stares at me with the Cheshire grin on her face.

Garrett. It's Garrett. He wins by a double-digit shutout. All those years ago, I picked the wrong brother. I want to tell her that, but instead I keep it to myself and only give her a smile.

"This is why you don't hook up with an ex's sibling. And don't think about hooking up with a best friend's sibling because they're practically family, and that's one line you shouldn't cross. It leads to nothing but bad news. Shit gets ugly. Feelings get complicated. Friendships collapse," Lach says as he strolls past us.

"But you can't help who you fall in love with," Nora counters.

I throw my hands in the air. "Why are we talking about love? No one loves anyone."

"Either way, I'm not going to be a dick to my best friend," Lach rebuttals.

I'll give it to Lach. He's one of the most loyal friends I've ever had. He would never be a dick to me or anyone else working at Porter's.

"I think this is different," Rylee says. "Yes, they're siblings, but Garrett and Dessa were friends before all of this happened. What if they were meant to be together? It's fate that Garrett came back to town for the wedding."

"The universe wants them together," Nora chimes in.

"If she wants to bang him out of her system, that's cool. Just know things will only get weird." Lach pulls out the step stool from under the counter.

"Please continue talking about me as if I'm not here." I prop my hands on my hips.

"Feel free to chime in at any time." Lach waves his palm in front of him, urging me to say my piece.

"It's hard to explain. It's like we're two opposite ends of a magnet. We're instantly drawn to each other. It's a force you can't fight, so I just let it happen. All I can do is wait and see where it goes."

"And by the blush on your cheeks, you're having fun while it's happening," Rylee sing-songs.

"That's beside the point. We're getting to know each other again and enjoying each other's company."

"While also enjoying the company of his dick. It's a win-win in my book." A wide smile covers Nora's face. "But speaking of Tony, what happened between the two of you all those years ago? Why'd you breakup?"

I cross my arms over my chest, propping my hip

against the cooler. "We just sort of… drifted apart, I guess. At the three-year mark, we grew distant. Both of us were busy with work and a year later we agreed to part ways."

"Which clearly was the universe telling you he was the wrong brother." Nora lifts a perfectly arched eyebrow.

"You need one of those cute couple names like…" Rylee taps her chin.

I spin to face Rylee, who's sitting on a stool on the other side of the bar. "Why? You never got a name. No one called you Tylee."

"That's because no one thought of it. You can be Gessa."

"Or Derrett," Lach adds.

I roll my eyes and huff. "One: those are terrible names and two: we're not even dating."

Lach shrugs. "Get better names and you'll have a better couple name."

I shoot daggers in his direction.

Jake storms out into the bar from the hallway, his eyebrows forming a deep V. "What is going on out here? There's more talking than working happening." He drops a stack of papers in front of Rylee. "Inventory lists. Double check it."

Rylee nods.

"Oh, we're only discussing Dessa's new man," Nora says.

"And that's my cue to leave and for all of you to do some work around here." Jake hoofs it toward the front door.

"You don't want all the dirty details?" Nora yells to his retreating frame.

"Nope!" Then Jake disappears through the doorway.

"The other day, I tried to talk to him about vibrators,

and I actually saw his cheeks turn a dusty rose." Nora throws her head back in laughter.

"I'm going to need a replay of that conversation." I hike my purse higher on my shoulder. "I'm going to put my stuff away."

"And I'm out for the night. You kids have fun." Rylee pushes her stool out and rises to her feet. With the stack of papers in hand, she's out the front door, and I make my way to the employee room, dropping off my purse and coat.

When I return to the bar, Lach is standing on the step stool in front of the chalkboard. "What do you think?"

Nora and I twist our heads at the same time. Nora laughs and I shake my head, but I can't hide the smile on my face as I read the words "Dessa Needs A Cocktail Minus The Tail."

Sadly, he's not wrong, but there's only one cock I need. I miss Garrett.

"You're missing a person." Nora tugs Lach off the stool and moves it a few inches to the right. Underneath she writes, "Garrett's Cocktail."

For the rest of the night, I steal glances at the board and think of Garrett. How can I not? His name is front and center. He told me I can always call him when I'm off work. My 2 a.m. is his midnight, so it's not so bad for him, but also I have work hair and that's just not always sexy.

After a few hours, the crowd quiets. Lach restocks the coolers while I run a rag over the bar top.

"So, Garrett's convinced he lost the game because he didn't have his lucky penny."

Lach peers at me. "Lucky penny?"

"Yes. Apparently, players have superstitions when they take the field. Some have a routine, or in Garrett's case, he had a lucky penny he's always had with him. The day of the game, he lost it."

"What's so lucky with his penny?"

I give him all the details about where the penny came from and the machine that made it.

He closes the cooler and breaks down the box. "I've seen those kinds of machines. They make like a little souvenir trinket."

"Yeah, he got it at Earl's Logging Camp just north of Harbor Highlands. After the wedding, we went there, and the owner said he got rid of the machine because it was broken." I toss the rag under the counter and refill a pint glass for a customer. "It would be a pretty bad ass present if I could get it for him," I muse as I stare off across the bar.

"That seems like a fun task, trying to track down that machine."

An older man, well into his sixties, clears his throat at the end of the bar. "I know someone who's done a lot of picking for antiques and collectibles throughout the years. There's a chance he might have what you're looking for, or maybe knows someone who does."

My eyes widen. A tiny glimmer of hope sparks inside me. "Are you serious?" I stroll to the end of the bar where he's seated.

"I can give you his number."

"That would be amazing and better than what I had, which was nothing." I grab a coaster and a pen and pass it to him.

He scribbles a name and number and passes it back. "You can tell him Otto told you to give him a call."

A delighted smile lights up my face as I stare at the number on the coaster. I hold the key to possibly the best

Christmas present ever. "Thank you so much. This means a lot to me." I tuck the coaster into my back pocket.

The next day, I called Jack and describe the penny machine. He knew exactly what I was talking about, and he's pretty confident that he has one. The only caveat is I'll have to come out and rummage through his five storage buildings, hoping to find it. Since I'm making it a habit of visiting strangers' homes who live in the middle of nowhere, I convince Lach to come with me. Plus, he also has the day off.

"Thanks for coming with me. I really appreciate it," I say, glancing at Lach in the driver's seat. I did a little research on penny machines, and I wasn't sure if we'd be able to fit one in the rear of my SUV, so I asked Lach to use his truck for easier hauling.

"No problem. I'm glad I could help. Even though I was your second choice." He smirks.

While at Porter's, I asked Jake to come with me, but he had plans. No one knows if Jake ever actually has plans or if he says he has plans to avoid doing things. Either way, Lach was standing right there, so he became my second option.

"It's not that I didn't want you to come. Jake's just a little more intimidating if things go… awry."

He tears his gaze from the road to turn toward me. "Hey, I can handle my own."

"And I don't doubt that, but Jake has an intimidation factor. Plus, he has a little more muscle than you."

He chuckles. "Thanks for the boost of confidence."

"That's what I'm here for." I smile brightly.

A short while later, we're pulling into a desolate

driveway out in the middle of nowhere. A giant white farmhouse with various sized buildings scattered across the property comes into view.

Lach slows his truck to a crawl as he peers out the window to scope out the various buildings. "Well, this shall be fun."

"I'd appreciate a little more enthusiasm because this will be fun. Do you want to get lunch afterward?"

He parks his truck close to the house. "This is worth way more than lunch. Just know you owe me. I'll figure out the details later."

"Ugh! Fine." We both climb out and stroll up the shoveled sidewalk. At the front door, I knock while Lach stands behind me. A few seconds later, a man with white hair and a bushy beard to match greets us. If he doesn't moonlight as Santa Claus, he really should.

"Hi, are you Jack? I'm Dessa. I called about the penny machine."

"Yes. I am. Let me grab my coat and I'll be right out." He closes the door while Lach and I retreat down the sidewalk. A few seconds later, he emerges wearing a black and gray flannel jacket and a walking cane.

"Thanks so much for letting us come out here," I say.

"No problem." His voice is a little weathered and rusty. "You'll be doing all the work trying to find it, though. As you see, I can't get around that great anymore. The snow makes it even harder."

"Of course. I brought a helper. This is Lach." They shake hands.

Jack gives us the rundown of the various buildings. He opens the garage door and pulls out a shovel, passing it to Lach.

"You'll need this." Then he walks past us and down the driveway.

Lach leans over and whispers, "You owe me. Big time." He lifts the shovel to rest against his shoulders and trots after Jack.

"How long have you been collecting, Jack?" I ask.

"Close to twenty years. At this point, I don't even remember what I have anymore."

"You hear that, Dessa? Twenty years." Lach's voice is dripping with sarcasm.

I flash him a wide thank-you-for-helping-me grin.

Jack points off into the distance with his cane. "I suspect it's in one of the medium size buildings. The red one has a really tricky door. You need to wiggle and jerk it at the same time."

Lach glares at me and mutters, "That one way over there, completely buried under the snow?"

"Yep. That's the one. That's the reason for the shovel."

"You so owe me," Lach mutters before he steps over the snowbank and trudges through the shin-deep snow. Following his footprints, I embrace the "work smarter, not harder" motto.

I'm praying his memory is as sharp as a tack because it's cold and I don't want to spend my afternoon digging through buildings full of junk. When we reach the large metal sliding door, he grips the wooden block handle and slides it halfway across. My eyes widen as soon as the bright light floods in through the opening. I underestimated how much junk a person could cram in a storage building. Every inch of the dirt floor is covered with stuff. Not only that, but it almost reaches the ceiling. This was a stupid idea. Garrett doesn't need a lucky penny.

Lach turns to me. "Let's get digging."

Luckily, there are a few pre-made paths to meander through. It's like a corn maze but constructed out of junk. Lach goes right, and I go left. I click on my flashlight and scan everything, praying it'll be out in the open and easy to see.

"Holy shit! No way!" Lach's voice echoes through the steel structure.

"What is it? Did you find it?" I'm crossing my fingers and toes he found it so we can leave.

"He has the exact bicycle I had when I was a kid!"

All my hope dies a junk-filled death. "That's great, but not why we're here." I continue scanning everything my flashlight beam passes over. I lift a box and set it down on an unsteady stack of other boxes. A cloud of dust and dirt plumes into the air. Covering my nose and mouth with my sleeve, I swat the cloud away with my other hand. It's going to be a long day. Once the dust settles, I resume moving boxes, praying I find it buried, but I come up empty-handed.

After an hour and still no penny machine, we moved on to the next building. Then the next. And the next.

Standing between two piles of junk, Lach wipes his brow with the back of his hand. "It's getting dark, and as much as I would like to find this machine, I also don't want to turn into a human popsicle."

"There's only one more building. We'll make it quick," I plead.

He blows out a deep breath. "Did I mention you owe me?"

A wide smile covers my face.

"Good. Just checking."

Ten minutes into the search, and I'm ready to call it quits. All my adrenaline has worn off, and I'm tired and cold. I tug my knit beanie farther over my head. My shoulders slump, and I blow out a deep breath. A silvery cloud forms in front of me before dissipating. "Lach?"

"Yeah?" His voice carries from the other side of the steel building.

"I think we should—"

"I think I found it!"

I perk up, rising to my full height. "For real?"

"Yes!"

I race past stacks of boxes, several old cars, and even more boxes until I find Lach. I shine my flashlight through a gap in several boxes, and I spot a brown rectangle with Souvenir Penny written in script across the top. "That's it! That has to be it."

Adrenaline surges through my body as we frantically move boxes, buckets, and other scraps of metal out of the way, piling everything on the sides until we have a clear path.

When it's finally exposed, a wave of elation washes over me. It looks like the exact machine from years ago, including the mallard stamp. I can't believe we found it. This entire trip was a crapshoot, but we actually found it.

I wrap my arms around Lach's shoulders. "Thank you so much for coming with me and helping me find it."

"Of course, but remember, you still owe me." He smirks.

"Yeah. Yeah. Let's get this thing out of here."

Lach borrows a dolly from Jack to move the penny machine out of the storage garage. I use the shovel to widen the path through the snow. Once we're next to his truck, Lach sets the dolly down. We exchange hopeful glances before turning our attention to the machine.

"I wonder if it works," Lach says.

"Earl said it was broken, but maybe this is a different machine. Do you have two quarters on you? And a penny?"

Lach exhales a deep laugh. "After all my hard work, you're now asking for money?"

I cross my arms over my chest and pop my hip.

He laughs again and digs into his pocket and pulls out a couple quarters and a penny. Taking them from his palm, I place them in the designated spots on the machine. I push in the quarter tray, the quarters clanking inside as they fall into the coin hopper. I grip the hand crank, but it doesn't budge. "Shit. It's not working."

"Let me try."

I step out of the way, and Lach jiggles the crank, but nothing happens. "Something must be broken."

"What do you want to do? I mean, we can fix it, right? Maybe?"

He shakes his head. "Don't look at me. I'm better at breaking things than fixing them."

I wrack my brain, trying to think of who I could ask. Trey's half brother, Ledger, is a mechanic, so he must be good with his hands. He could possibly fix it. Two phone calls and ten minutes later, I'm disconnecting the call.

"Ledger says we can drop it off at the shop and he'll check it out, but he makes no promises." Frankly, that's all I have, so I'll take it. I pay Jack two-hundred dollars and we finish loading it into the bed of Lach's truck.

During the ride home, I stare out the window, imagining Garrett's face when he sees it. He's going to freak out.

"I can't believe you paid two hundred dollars for something that doesn't even work."

"It's the sentimental value, and that's worth way more than two hundred dollars."

"Sentiment is for suckers."

I bark out a laugh. "You're such an asshole. I know Garrett will like this."

He glances over at me. "What's going on with you two, anyway?"

I suck my lower lip into my mouth and shrug a shoulder. "We're rekindling our friendship?" Aside from the friendship, everything else is up in the air. "Right now, we're taking it day by day. Seeing what happens. Garrett and his brother, Tony, had been a part of my life for so many years, and then we all went our separate ways. It's nice having everyone back together again."

"Including the sex."

Heat creeps up my neck. "Then there's that."

"Either way, you deserve all the happiness."

"Thanks. What about you? When are you going to find your happiness?" I shift to face Lach. "Or have you been holding out on me?" In the several years I've known him, I've never seen him with a steady girlfriend.

"My happiness is being single."

"Just wait. Your turn is coming. You're going to meet a woman who sweeps you off your feet."

"It's like the movie *Scream*. 'But wait, there's more!' Because it fits with the whole relationship idea. They come back for one last scare before trying to kill you. That's what relationships do. They kill you."

I roll my eyes. "You're being dramatic."

He shakes his head. "We all can't find baseball players to sweep us off our feet."

After our laughter dissipates, only the rumbling of the tires on the road fills the cab and I stare out the passenger side window at the dark sky.

Lach breaks the silence. "By the way, you also owe me fifty-one cents."

I smile and shake my head. "Yeah, you're definitely an asshole."

Chapter 24

IT'S COMPLICATED

Dessa

Ledger calls to tell me the penny machine is working. Immediately, I race over to his garage with a roll of quarters to test it out.

Upon entering his shop, Ledger and Jay are off to the side, huddled around the penny machine. Ledger's signature man bun holds his dark hair in place and tattoos peek out from beneath the sleeve of his navy work shirt. Olivia certainly lucked out with him. The clacking of my boots on the cement draws their attention.

"It should be in working order," Ledger says. "Jay's been making pennies all morning."

Jay pulls out a handful of flattened pennies from his pocket and shrugs.

I laugh. "This is amazing! Thank you!" I run my finger over the front plexiglass still in awe that he got it working.

"So I was able to rig it—"

Jay clears his throat.

Ledger rolls his eyes. "Jay was able to rig it so it doesn't need quarters to work. Give it a try." He passes a penny to me.

I place it in the slot and push the tray in. Slowly, I turn the crank and the gears inside rotate meticulously together until it spits out a flattened penny. "This is the best. How much do I owe you?"

"Don't worry about it. I think Jay had more fun playing around with it than anything," Ledger says.

"Do you mind if I keep it here for a little bit? Maybe until after Christmas, then I can figure out a place for it."

"Absolutely."

"Thank you." I place another penny into the slot and turn the crank.

A roll of pennies later, my phone chimes with an incoming message. I unlock the screen and my lips curve into a smile. We haven't talked since the wedding, so the message is a surprise, but a pleasant one.

GEORGIA

Want to meet me for lunch?

DESSA

Lunch sounds amazing.

GEORGIA

Great! Want to meet at the Lakewalk Café?

DESSA

Sounds perfect! I'll meet you in about fifteen minutes.

GEORGIA

I'll see you then.

As I walk into the quaint café, I spot Georgia sitting at a table near the windows overlooking Lake Superior. I inform the hostess I'm meeting someone and stroll into the dining room. When I'm halfway to the table, Georgia's head lifts, a smile on her bright red lips. I offer a smile of my own. Once at the table, I shrug out of my coat, hang it on the back of the chair, and take a seat.

"Thanks for coming out to lunch with me." She crosses her hands on the table.

"Thanks for the invite. I'm starving."

"Being new in town, I don't have many friends, and dining alone isn't as fun. But also, I don't want to assume that we're friends after one wedding invite and now lunch."

"No." I wave her off. "We're friends. I mean, the friendship has to start somewhere." Both of us giggle.

"Why is it so hard to make friends as adults?" she asks over her menu.

I nod. "It really is, isn't it."

Her shoulders drop in relief. "I'm really glad you came to the wedding too. It was nice to finally meet Tony's friends and family."

Carefully, I place my menu on the table, my mouth going dry. "I won't lie. I was a little apprehensive about going. The thought of attending my ex-boyfriend's wedding gave me hives. Not literal hives, but close." I swallow a sip of water. "Even though I've known Tony for so long, we spent so many years not talking, so it was a surprise more than anything. But it's nice to have him back as a friend and now you too, of course. I wasn't sure if my history with Tony would be awkward between me and you."

"No. Not at all" She shakes her head. "Tony told me everything, especially how much he misses your friendship. So, I'm happy you came. Plus, it was years ago."

I nod. It feels like a lifetime ago. "Me too. Everything turned out good. Really good." I smile mostly because I spent my night with Garrett and that made going to the wedding worthwhile.

A slow smile spreads across her face. "And I saw you cuddling with Garrett."

Heat creeps up my neck. "Yeah. We've known each other for such a long time. It was nice to have a friend there."

"From what I saw, I would have guessed more than friends." Her brows raise.

What did everyone see? I thought we kept our hands to ourselves, for the most part. "It's complicated." I repeat Garrett's words.

"I hope I'm not overstepping by saying you two looked cute together."

I smile because I don't know what else to do. Garrett and me as a couple? I never imagined it would be a possibility, especially after the last ten years. Luckily, the server makes an appearance to take our order. I order the vegetarian falafel while Georgia orders a smoked salmon, avocado, and tomato salad.

I use the extra few minutes to put all my thoughts back together. Once the server leaves, I link my fingers together and rest them on the table. "Enough about me. How did you and Tony meet?"

Her eyes sparkle with love and adoration. "He was working as an assistant recruiter for the Chicago Thunder, a Double-A minor league team, and they hosted an event at one of my father's hotels that I was also attending. From there, the rest is history." Her eyes crinkle in the corners at the mention of Tony. I'm happy he's found love.

I take a sip of my water. "What brings you to Harbor Highlands?"

"Tony said he wanted to move back. When he got the job for the Harbor Highlands Agates team, it was the perfect opportunity."

"I'm glad he's been able to stay within the baseball organization even though playing didn't work out for him. He's always loved the sport."

In high school, their lives were consumed with nothing but baseball. That's all they did, and they dragged me to all their games. While Garrett found success playing the game, Tony veered off in a different direction.

"Now that the wedding is over, what's the plan for the honeymoon?"

She unclasps her hands and sits up straighter. "Tony's taking me to Hawaii for two weeks." She squeals with delight. "We'll leave after Christmas. He thought it would be too chaotic to do it after the wedding, but before Christmas. Plus, we get to spend New Year's in Hawaii."

"Oh my god. Jealous! That sounds amazing."

For the rest of lunch, we enjoy our meal, and Georgia tells me she designs and sells custom handbags, purses, and wallets online. Currently, she's working toward building a physical storefront. Then she asks me about bartending at Porter's and how I create custom drinks. The entire conversation is light and fun. It's exactly what I need after all the heaviness surrounding Garrett.

Once we're finished eating, Tony saunters to our table and pulls out the chair between Georgia and me. "When you said you were going to lunch, I knew you'd be here." He leans over and presses a kiss to her cheek. He turns his attention to me. "Dessa. It's always a pleasure." A warm smile forms on his lips. It's a friendly smile, but the way his gaze lingers, it may be too friendly. With his eyes still locked on mine, he asks, "What's today's topic of conversation?"

I sit up straighter in my chair. "Georgia was just telling me how you're taking her to Hawaii for your honeymoon."

"Yes. That was a fun surprise. It was my wedding gift to her. Have you ever been, Dessa?" Tony asks.

I shake my head. "I haven't. But based on the pictures I've seen, it looks gorgeous. I've never been outside the Midwest."

"It's beautiful with the lush rainforest and pristine beaches. You should go sometime," Tony says, his gaze locked on mine.

"I'll put it on my bucket list." I give him a tight smile.

"I was telling Dessa that it was so great to see her at the wedding," Georgia chimes in.

"Absolutely. It was wonderful you could attend." Tony smiles at me. "Now that I'm in town permanently, we should hang out more often."

"That would be great. I'd love to hang out with the two of you. It'll be like old times."

"Yeah. The two of us. Of course." Tony nods.

Georgia rests her hand on Tony's. He glances down, and his eyebrows twitch, almost in displeasure. "I was telling Dessa that she and Garrett looked really cute together at the wedding."

Tony's gaze snaps to mine. "Are you two dating or something now?" A sharp bite stings his tone.

Georgia squeezes his hand to get his attention, and she scowls at him.

"What? It's just a question." He pulls his hand away from hers and drops it in his lap.

"We're friends," I say.

"Are you going to stay in contact now?" His voice grows heavy. "You know he has a busy schedule, especially once spring training starts."

Am I being interrogated? Where's the steel table and

two-way mirror? Tony seems more invested in my relationship with Garrett than I am. "I'm well aware of what his schedule will be like," I grit out through my teeth, my irritation growing exponentially with every question he asks.

"Remember, he's the Home Run Playboy. He has women falling over him left and right." He picks a piece of salmon from Georgia's plate and tosses it into his mouth.

"Tony," Georgia scolds. He shrugs a shoulder as he continues chewing.

"I'm well aware of who he is." I lean against the chair, crossing my arms over my chest.

"Good." Tony nods before peering over at me. "I'm sorry if I'm coming off a little assertive. I just don't want to see you get hurt. Again. And Garrett's exactly the type of person to do that."

Tony and I were dating when Garrett left after high school. He was by my side to brush away the tears. At every opportunity, he made sure to distract me from Garrett. He did it with no questions asked. I'll always appreciate that he could be the person I needed when I needed it most.

His phone chimes. After glancing down, he turns to Georgia. "We better get going. We have that appointment with the realtor."

Tony flags down the server for the bill. When he arrives at our table, Tony passes him his credit card. "You can put the entire meal on that."

I reach for my wallet. "Let me pay for mine."

Tony waves me off. "I got it. That's what friends do."

"Thank you," I say softly. I turn to Georgia. "It was great having lunch with you."

"It really was. Hopefully, we can do it again sometime."

A bright smile takes over her face, and I can't help but give her one in return. "Definitely."

Once Tony gets his card back, they both rise to their feet and exit the restaurant.

What the hell was that?

Chapter 25

MY NUMBER LOOKS GOOD
ON HER

Garrett

My phone buzzes on the coffee table, and I immediately glance at the screen, hoping it's Dessa. When I see the name, my chest goes hollow. It's not her. I debate on answering, but if I don't, there's a good chance Sam Henderson, the third baseman for the Warblers, will only keep calling or worse, stop over. I pick up the phone and press talk.

"Hey, man. What's up?"

"Are you back in town now?" Muffled electric dance music plays in the background.

"Yeah, I flew in earlier this week." I lean against the couch and kick my feet onto the coffee table.

"And I'm just finding out now? I'll forgive you since this is perfect timing. Come out with me and Stallman tonight." Marcus Stallman is the left fielder and on most nights is Henderson's wingman and vice versa. In fact, they try to convince every single guy on the team to go out with them.

I scrub my hand over the scruff on my chin. "I don't know. It's been a busy day. I want to relax at home." And drown myself in misery since I'm not with Dessa.

"Are you still moping about the championship game? Look man, it happens. We'll kick all their asses next year. In the meantime, I have a couple of ladies who are excellent at making you forget all your woes." Faint chatter sounds through the phone speaker.

"Nah, man. Thanks, but I'm not feeling it tonight. I'm just going to stay home."

"Are you sure? These girls are ready to go."

I laugh. Any woman he picks up is ready to go. All he has to do is mention he's the third baseman for Seattle, and they flock to him like seagulls. With that power comes a lot of responsibility, but that's not a word in his vocabulary. Like the one time he unknowingly hooked up with the coach's daughter of our biggest rival.

"Yeah. I'm good."

"Alright. You're missing out. I guess I'll have to occupy both these ladies."

Everyone likes to call me the Home Run Playboy, but Henderson is the biggest playboy in the entire league. He lives by the potato chip motto: you can't have just one.

"Well, actually, I'm kind of seeing someone," I spit out for no reason, because we are seeing each other, right? I'd make her my girlfriend in a heartbeat, but I'm not entirely sure where her head is at.

"Shit! Are you back with the Brazilian model?"

"Camila."

"Yeah. She's smokin'."

"No. Actually it's not her."

"Oh shit. You should give me her number."

"That's not happening. She's way too good for you."

A boisterous laugh sounds through the speaker. "You're probably right. So, who's the mystery woman?"

I sit up and rest my elbows on my knees. I scrub my hand down my face, trying to determine how much information I want to feed him. "Actually, I know her from my hometown. We grew up together."

"Like a childhood sweetheart?"

"Something like that. I don't know. We're seeing where things go." That's the truth. While we've never discussed our relationship, we definitely have the orgasms down pat.

"Enjoy your night alone, jerking off to some childhood crush fantasy. I'll be out having someone else jerk me off."

I huff out a laugh. "You're such an asshole. Keep your dick in your pants."

"It's more fun when it's not."

I shake my head. He's going to find himself in a heap of trouble, and I'll laugh in his face when he does. "Later." I disconnect the call.

As soon as I set down my phone, it rings again. I'm convinced it's Stallman trying to convince me to go out, but instead, Dessa's name flashes on the screen with a FaceTime call. A wide smile spreads across my face.

"Hey, Tates."

Dessa's beautiful face fills the screen. "Hey. How are you?"

"Much better now that you called."

Her sweet laugh sounds through the speaker. "So, you've been waiting around for me to call?"

"Do I sound desperate if I say yes?"

"Desperate looks good on you." She gives me a sweet smile. "Don't feel bad, I've been desperate to talk to you too. Oh! And I found my notebook earlier today."

I fake cough into my hand to fight the smile that wants to break free. "Where did you find it?"

"It was on a shelf in my kitchen I never use, wedged between two cookbooks. Apparently, my drunk self wanted to play a cruel joke on my sober self." She giggles. "Also, thank you for the present. I got it today. In fact, I'm currently wearing it."

After I ruined her Minnesota jersey, I told her I'd buy her a new one. A better one. Mine.

"Let me see."

She slowly lowers the phone. Her slender neck comes into view, followed by her ample chest. The buttons on the jersey are undone, exposing the valley between her tits. My dick twitches, knowing she's wearing nothing but my name on her back. I reach down and adjust myself in my gym shorts.

"Fuck. Tates. You look amazing. Number seven looks good on you. My dick went instantly hard."

A sparkle twinkles in her dark irises as she nibbles on her bottom lip. "Show me."

"You want to see how hard you make me?"

Her lips press together as her head jerks up and down. "Yes."

I pan the camera to the bulge tenting my shorts. With my hand, I tamp down the fabric to give a better view of my dick. I pull my phone away just enough to catch her tongue peeking out between her luscious lips and sliding her hand over her chest. Her fingertip caresses the edge of the jersey. When she reaches the middle of her chest, she slides the fabric away, exposing her plump breast.

"What are you doing, Tates?" I growl.

Her lashes flutter closed as her fingers circle her nipple. "I wish you were touching me right now."

Somehow, my dick grows achingly harder. I groan, palming myself in need of a little relief.

"I miss you so much, Garrett," she purrs, her teeth sinking into the corner of her bottom lip.

"Fuck, Tates. You look so hot touching yourself while wearing my jersey." I slide my hand into the elastic waistband of my shorts and wrap my fingers around my dick. I squeeze the head, and a bead of pre-cum pearls at the top. Smearing it over my crown, I realize this won't be enough. "If I was in bed with you, what would I be doing to you right now?"

"You'd kiss my neck and then move to the swells of my breasts."

"Show me." While she talks, I rise to my feet and stroll to my bedroom to get more comfortable. I prop myself on my bed against my headboard and bend over to pull a bottle of lube from the nightstand. My gaze follows the trail of her finger over her soft and creamy skin.

"You'd wrap your lips around my nipple and suck." Her back arches when she pinches her stiff nipple.

With one hand, I flip open the top of the bottle of lube and squirt a generous amount on my leg. My body flinches at the cold, but it's better than squirting it directly on my dick. I swipe one hand through it, doing my best to collect it in my palm while still holding my phone with the other. With my fingers wrapped around my fully hard dick, I leisurely stroke myself. "What do I do next?"

"You continue to kiss your way down my body until you reach my pussy." Again, her hand runs down her body until she reaches the apex of her thighs.

My grip on my dick tightens as I continue to leisurely stroke myself. "Is that all I do?" My voice is strained as I anticipate what she's going to say next.

She slides two fingers down her slit. Her breath hitches when she brushes over her clit. "N-no. You run your tongue across my pussy, nipping and sucking me."

"Fuck." I groan. My grip tightens as I increase my speed. "You taste sweet as hell. You got me so hard for you." I lower the phone as I continue stroking myself, so she can see how much she turns me on. When I lift the screen, she has two fingers inside her, thrusting in and out. They're glistening with her arousal. Somehow my dick grows harder. "Keep fucking yourself with your fingers. Pretend it's my dick inside you."

Her head falls against the headboard, and she moans. "Oh! Garrett!" She alternates between rubbing her clit and spearing herself with her fingers.

"Tates. Just like that."

The camera trembles as she moans out her orgasm. I can't take my eyes off her plump lips as they fall open. My name is a whisper on her lips. I imagine it's my fingers thrusting in and out of her pussy, giving her pleasure. I squeeze the base of my cock, picturing her mouth wrapped around me, sliding up and down. A tingle starts at the base of my spine and catapults to my balls as my orgasm roars through me. Ribbons of cum erupt over my stomach.

When we've both catch our breaths, she tucks a strand of hair behind her ear. "That was… wow. I can't say I've ever done that before."

I slide my shorts over my hips and use them to wipe off the cum before tossing them on the floor. Tomorrow will be laundry day.

"That was a first for me, too." I grab the edge of the blanket, covering myself from the hips down.

"Is this how it's going to be? You on the road. Me at home. In bed all alone. We'll call each other for phone sex one hundred sixty-two days out of the year."

"I'm sorry. I know it's hard. I want nothing more than to be there with you right now. To hold you in my arms, kiss your neck, and bury my face between your legs."

This time, she lets out a full laugh. "I want that too, so bad."

"It won't be forever."

"You have at least ten more years of playing baseball in you. If that's the case, it's like one thousand six hundred and twenty days of this."

"Are you planning on doing this for ten years?" Maybe she does want more. You don't talk about being in someone's life ten years in the future if you don't expect to be in it.

A pinkish hue flushes over her cheeks. "Hypothetically speaking."

"I have three years left on my current contract, then I don't know what will happen. If I play well enough, they might offer me a new one, or I could get traded."

"Perhaps to Minnesota?" She flashes me a hopeful smile. "Then you'd be somewhat closer."

"Maybe. Their catcher sucks." I wink.

A downward smile tugs at the corners of her lips. "Now I miss you even more. This talk has taken a sharp turn down Depression Drive. How about a change of subject?"

"How about this? Soon I'll see you wearing my jersey, with nothing on underneath, in person."

Her eyes go wide. "Wait. Are you coming back?"

"I'll be in Harbor Highlands on the twenty-third for Christmas." My plan was to surprise her with a visit. Show up unannounced and lock us away in her bedroom for at least twenty-four hours, but the wide grin on her face right now is worth spoiling the surprise.

She squeals. "I might have to buy another Minnesota jersey, so you can rip it off me."

"I will gladly rip off anything you have on. It's like unwrapping my very own present."

Chapter 26

WOOLLY MAMMOTH STATUS

Dessa

I chalked up my lunch date with Georgia, and the awkwardness with Tony to mercury being in retrograde. We haven't seen or talked to each other in several years, so we needed to shake off the rust. Tonight, I invited them over for dinner and drinks at my house as a take two. With an oven mitt covered hand, I open the oven and pull out a vegetarian lasagna. The savory aromas of garlic and fresh melted mozzarella fill the kitchen. I set the restaurant purchased lasagna on the stovetop. As it cools, a knock on the front door startles me. Striding out of the kitchen and through the living room, I twist the knob and pull it open. Georgia and Tony greet me with friendly smiles.

"I'm so happy you could make it!" I step out of the way and Georgia wraps her arms around me in a hug. As she steps away, Tony does the same.

"It smells amazing in here. My stomach's already rumbling." Georgia rests a hand on her belly.

"Also, we got you this." Tony raises a bottle of gin in the air.

"Thank you. This is way better than a bottle of wine." Tony passes the bottle to me as I take both their coats and they slip off their shoes. I escort them into the kitchen. "This is perfect. I'll make us some drinks."

Tony pulls out a seat for Georgia before sitting down himself. I stroll around to the opposite side and set the bottle on the counter.

Georgia rises on her stool to peer over to the stove behind me. "Did you make that?"

Spinning around, I glance at the lasagna, wishing I could make something that delicious. "If by 'made it,' you mean 'picked it up from Le Uve to warm up in my oven,' then yes. I made it." My lips upturn into a sarcastic smile.

Georgia laughs, and I join her. "We'll that's the hardest part, getting it from the restaurant to the oven without dropping it."

"Then call me a master chef." I playfully brush my shoulder. "Since I can't give you a home-cooked meal, how about a homemade cocktail?" I twist the cap off the bottle of gin.

"I won't turn that down." Georgia's eyes light up as a perfectly curved smile covers her face.

"Is that an Isabella Rossi drink book?" Tony reaches across the counter. His fingers curl around the glossy cover and pull it toward him.

I pour gin, lemon juice, and simple honey into a shaker. "It is."

Georgia turns to Tony, "Isn't she the mixologist with the chef husband? You took me to their restaurant in Chicago."

My eyes widen as my breath stalls. "You've been to Poco Grande?"

"I've been there a few times," Tony says before facing Georgia, "I took you a couple of months ago when we were in Chicago. I've known Isabella and her husband Chris for several years."

"Holy shit." I slam my palms on the counter. "You know Isabella Rossi? Like know her, know her? Not I-have-a-friend-who-knows-someone-who-lives next-door-who-knows-someone-who-walks-her-dog know her."

A laugh escapes him. "Yeah, I know her, know her. Along with Chris."

A lightness fills my chest. "I'm only obsessed with her show on the Cooking Network. Seriously, she can turn anything into a drink. She's amazing." I press my hands to my chest. "She's been my idol since I started mixing drinks. I follow her show religiously and pre-order every recipe book she publishes. How in the hell are you friends with her?"

He laughs. "Years ago, we met through some mutual friends. Every time I'm in Chicago, I go to Poco Grande."

My shoulders drop as I sigh and stare across the room at an invisible spot on the wall. "That would be a dream." What I would give to meet her and pick her brain about her drinks. But it will have to remain a dream. "In the spirit of Isabella, here's one of her favorite drinks. A bees knees." Lifting the shaker, I pour the cocktail into three low ball glasses. I slide two of them across the counter to Georgia and Tony.

Over the next two hours, we eat dinner, make drinks, and laugh. It's such a fun evening with friends. No one mentions Garrett and me, so I steered clear of talking about it myself mostly because everything is still unknown. Before they leave, we make plans to do it again.

Like a contestant on *Supermarket Sweep*, I race the grocery cart up and down the aisles, grabbing whatever I can off the shelves. I only have two hours before Garrett comes over. I still need to clean my house, shower, and shave. Everything is approaching woolly mammoth status. With Garrett not being around, I haven't needed to shave my legs since he can't see them during our FaceTime calls. On the plus side, it helps keep me warm during the cold winter nights. I toss two cans of chickpeas into my cart.

"Hey Dessa!"

With a quick spin, a small smile spreads across my face as I lock eyes with the familiar face. Tony's waving at me from the end of the aisle with a wide smile of his own. He struts toward me.

"Hi, Tony. What are you doing here? This grocery store is on the opposite end of town from you."

"This is the only store that has the sunflower seeds I like." He lifts a bag of barbecue flavored sunflower seeds from his basket.

I chuckle. "You and Garrett are obsessed with sunflower seeds. I remember your mom would yell at you for always leaving piles around the house."

"I wouldn't call it yelling, but it was a stern talking to."

A laugh escapes me. "That's true. Your mother doesn't have a bitter bone in her body."

"Thanks for inviting me and Georgia over again for dinner. It's great to see you two become friends."

"Of course. I love having you two over. And Georgia's great. You lucked out with her." I've spent weeks avoiding the elephant in our relationship, and with the holiday approaching, might as well point it out. My fingers grip the cart handle. "And you and Garret seem to have worked out your differences, since he was involved with your wedding and all." I hate knowing I'm the reason they stopped talking all those years ago. I had no idea either of them, let alone both, had feelings for me until Tony kissed me that night at Jacobson's party. All that's in the past now. We've all moved on. Or at least Tony has. Garrett and I are still undecided.

He shrugs. "Something like that. Did you know he's back in town?"

"I do. We're hanging out later."

His lips flatten into a thin line. "So, you two still talk?"

I nod. Heat creeps up my neck and over my cheeks. We've done more than talk, but he doesn't need to know that. "We've kept in contact."

"Even with the distance between you two?" He sucks in a sharp breath through his teeth and shakes his head. "That must be hard."

"We're just friends. We text, make the occasional phone call, and FaceTime whenever we can." My grip tightens on the handle of the grocery cart. I'm not used to the Tony interrogation. Things were never like this in the past. I pinch my brows together. "Why?"

With quick, jerky movements, he swings his head back and forth. "No reason. I just know him. He likes to keep his options open, and with there being so much distance between you two, it leaves those options even wider." He takes a step forward and brushes his hand over my shoulder and comes to a stop on my bicep.

This is the second time he's warned me off Garrett. He acts like I don't know him. Perhaps he's being a concerned friend. Or does he know something I don't? "Thanks for your concern. I know Garrett pretty well. I'm sure I can handle him." The corner of my lips curl into a smile. I'll handle him. He'll handle me. Naked, of course. "No need to worry about me."

"I just don't want to see you get hurt. That's all." He drops his hand and it falls to his side.

"How's Georgia? Is she with you?" I ask, peering over his shoulder. In the short time I've known Georgia, she's become a great friend. I love learning about her handbag business, and she enjoys learning about my less exciting bartender life. Plus, I want to be done talking about mine and Garrett's relation-whatever-we're-doing-ship.

"She's at home packing. We're going to go visit her parents in Chicago for Christmas. Also, I have some business to take care of while I'm there."

"Working over the holidays?"

"You know me." He playfully winks. "I always have something going on."

I laugh. "It must run in the family. Garrett's the same way." His name is out before I can stop it. I pinch my lips together to keep anything else from spewing out. Even when I tell myself not to talk about him, I still talk about him.

His lips turn downward at his brother's name. "Yeah."

Now I made it awkward. "Well, it was good to see you. Tell Georgia I said hi and we need to get together soon."

"What about me?"

"You can join too, of course. Take care." He leans in and places a kiss on my cheek. It's a little startling, for the fact that we've never been the type of friends who did that kind of thing. I brush it off. It's only Tony.

I grip the shopping cart handle and continue my way down the aisle, and Tony leaves in the opposite direction. Glancing at the time on my phone, I realize I only have a an hour and a half before Garrett arrives. The rest of my shopping will have to wait until later.

After I got home from the store, I threw everything into the fridge, spot cleaned the kitchen, and now I'm sitting on the edge of the tub, shaving my legs. I check the time on my phone. Shit. Thirty minutes. My phone rings, startling me. Garrett's name flashes on the screen. My wet fingers fumble to press the talk button while I simultaneously avoid pushing my phone into the tub. Somehow I manage to tap the speakerphone.

"Hey, you."

"What are you doing? Have you had dinner?"

"No. I just got home a little bit ago."

"Why is it echoing? Are you in the bathroom? Did you answer the phone while on the toilet?"

"No! I mean, technically, yes, I'm in the bathroom, but I'm not *going* to the bathroom. I'm shaving my legs."

"Oh yeah? Plan on getting lucky tonight?"

His voice is deep and sexy which causes goosebumps to prickle my skin. Shit. I'll have to shave again. "Either way, I'll be getting off with or without you."

"Fuck that. I'll be the one getting you off," he growls.

His words cause my nipples to pebble. "What if I were to start right now?"

"Fuck. Are you trying to get me hard? My dick is throbbing, and I need to pick up the takeout."

"Then you better get here quick before I finish."

"Food's not important, right? I'll get there much faster if I don't stop."

I laugh. "Don't worry, if I finish, we can always start again."

His deep groan echoes through the phone before it disconnects. For the next twenty minutes, I frantically dash around the rest of my townhouse tossing junk into drawers and closets, anywhere so it's out of sight. A knock startles me before Garrett steps through the door. When I catch sight of him, my heart leaps to my throat. I sprint, meeting him in the doorway and throwing myself into his arms. He wraps one arm around my waist, holding me tight.

"I'm so happy you're finally here."

"Me too, Tates."

He presses his lips to mine. I cup his cheek, my thumb brushing over the stubble. A round of butterflies take flight in my belly when he calls me the nickname. This friendship could develop into more, but again, he lives halfway across the country. While FaceTime is fun, I'm hard-pressed to believe it's sustainable.

Slowly, I pull away. "Let me help you with that."

"I got it. How about you show me how good my jersey looks on you? Then, after I'm finished eating my dinner, I'll have my dessert."

I flash him a seductive smile while I drag my finger down his chest. "Only because I'm excited for the second part." I wink and turn to climb the stairs. When I glance over my shoulder, Garrett's staring at my ass. I give it an extra wiggle before climbing the rest of the way to the second floor.

Once in my bedroom, I yank the jersey from the hanger in my closet and strip out of my clothes. With nothing on underneath, I shrug the fabric over my shoulders and fasten the buttons. The cool fabric grazes my nipples, turning them to stiff peaks. Garrett's jaw is going to hit the floor when he sees me. I twirl around. The hem of the jersey kisses the top of my thighs. If I bend over too far, I'll be flashing my butt cheeks. I'm fully prepared to skip dinner and dive into straight desert.

As I enter the kitchen, Garrett's on the other side of the island setting out containers of food along with plates and silverware for us. When I cross from the carpet to the linoleum, he peers at me and freezes. His gaze roams over my body as if he's studying me for later. My body temperature rises twenty degrees from his heated stare.

"By the way you can't stop staring, I'm guessing this is what you wanted."

"That's more than I wanted. More than I could ever dream of." He steps out from behind the island and stalks toward me.

My chest rises and falls with each of his footsteps. Get ready for desert.

He comes to a halt in front of me. His hands cup my cheeks, and his gaze bores into mine. "Seeing you wearing my jersey in person… There's no comparison to anything I've ever seen. You're just… wow. I'm five seconds away from saying forget dinner, I want dessert."

A deep rumbles sounds from my belly. Would it be weird if he has desert while I eat dinner? Yeah. That's most definitely weird. "We have all night for everything else. First food because it smells delicious." I rise on my tippy toes, breaking his grasp on me, and peer around his shoulder, wanting to see the spread.

Garrett laughs and spins around. At the counter, he pulls out a stool for me. "Have a seat. What do you want?"

The enticing smell of all the food makes my stomach growl again. "Everything. Just put it all on my plate."

"Here's some vegan muhammara, some garden pesto tortellini, fried noodles, and charred eggplant tian." He scoops a little of each on my plate.

"Did you order all the vegetarian dishes on the menu?"

"Maybe." He flashes me his signature panty-dropping smile.

Oops. Too bad I'm not wearing any.

How I feel about Garrett is equivalent to a thousand-piece clear jigsaw puzzle. All the pieces are there, but how do we put it together? It should be easy, right? We've known each other for so long, we were best friends, but he left and shattered those thousand pieces into a million pieces. Our chemistry is undeniable, but is what we're doing all we'll ever have? Or how do we navigate the uncharted territory of more? I drop my fork to the plate, and it clatters against the ceramic.

"Garrett, what are we doing?"

His fork stops halfway to his mouth, and he turns his head to face me. "I'm feeding you and counting down the minutes until I can be between your legs."

A small smile plays on my lips. "No, not that. What are we doing?" I wave my finger between us. "You and me. What is this?"

He sets his fork on his plate and turns to fully face me. He grabs my hand and intertwines our fingers. My heart rate spikes at his touch.

"We're rekindling our friendship. I have a lot of years to make up for."

My gaze casts downward. "But is it only a friendship?"

"What do you want?"

Loaded question. Do I even know what I want? "One thing is certain, I want this." I lift my head to meet his eyes. "You. *Us.* But what happens when you leave again?" He's still here, and my heart's breaking thinking about him leaving again.

"Then we'll continue this over text and FaceTime like we have been."

"So long-distance? I feel like I'd be having a more intimate relationship with my hand than with you."

"Tates." My name sounds like a plea. "Think about it this way, the time we do get to spend with each other will be that much sweeter." He presses a kiss to my knuckles.

I nod. "You're right."

"Let's not talk about this now. I'm here. You're here.

Let's focus on the present. We can worry about everything else tomorrow." His lips pull into a smile. "In the meantime, want to open your Christmas present? I know it's early, but I think this will help your mood."

"You got me a present?" A flush of adrenaline tingles through my body, and a wide grin takes over.

"You didn't think I'd come here empty-handed, did you?" Twisting around, he grabs a red box with a gold ribbon secured on top and passes it to me.

"You already bought me this." I point to the navy blue jersey I'm wearing.

"That's more of a present for me than you. Go on. Open it." He nods at the box sitting in my lap.

"Did you wrap this yourself?"

He nods. "I'm a man of many talents."

Shit. He's going to be sorely disappointed when I hand him his unwrapped present. Hopefully, he'll be too amazed by what it is to care. I tug on one end of the ribbon, and it comes undone. I peel away at the pristine wrapping paper, not wanting to rip it. After lifting the lid, the crinkle of tissue paper fills the room as I push it to the side. When I reach the bottom, I freeze. All the air escapes my lungs, and I forget how to breathe. Tears well in the corners of my eyes as I slowly lift my gaze to meet Garrett's. "What is this?" I choke out.

"You know how your recipe book went missing for a few days…"

I nod, brows pinched together.

"I may have borrowed it so I could make copies of your recipes and create a book for you."

My fingers trace over the glossy words *The Drink Menu*. I'm in complete disbelief that he did this.

"If you don't like the title, we can always make you a different one. I just wanted to give you something."

"Oh! No! This is… I don't know what to say." My voice quivers as a tear breaks free and slides down my cheek. I swipe it away. "That's a happy tear." A laugh bubbles out of me.

"You love it?" A hopeful smile flirts on his lips.

"Garrett, I more than love it." I set the box on the counter and jump to my feet, throwing my arms around his neck. "This is the most thoughtful gift anyone's ever given me. Thank you so much."

"You're welcome." He presses a kiss to my forehead. "But you have to look inside. That's the best part."

While standing at the counter, I flip through the pages. Garrett presses his front against my back as he looks over my shoulder, his hands resting on the counter, caging me in.

"This is amazing! And you have pictures. How did you do all this? This must have cost a fortune."

"Only half a fortune."

I twist my head to look at him, wide-eyed.

He laughs. "It wasn't that much. I called in some favors. My agent's sister knows self-publishing, so she helped me create the book. She also hooked me up with a formatter, and a friend of a friend is a photographer. Another friend knows a thing or two about mixing drinks, so she helped me try to make the drinks look as authentic to your recipes as possible."

"Garrett, this is amazing. I can't believe you did this." I continue flipping page after page. As soon as my eyes scan the name of one of the recipes, I freeze. A boisterous laugh bursts out of me. "What is this one?" I twist to face him, my finger resting on the glossy page.

A boyish grin covers his lips. "I got creative and made my own cocktail."

I stare at the name. "G Plus D," I whisper.

"Sorry, the name isn't as cool as all yours." He lifts one shoulder and lets it drop. "They say it really helps to get the clothes to fall off."

I throw my head back with laughter and point at the recipe. "Well, it's the tequila." I'm still in utter shock he did this for me. "Thank you so much. This is the best present I've ever gotten." I wrap my arms around his neck and press my lips to his. His hands slide over my waist and his arms drape on my hips, holding me to him as if he never wants to let me go. A chill runs up my spine when his fingertips tickle the back of my thighs right below my butt.

"Since we're exchanging gifts now, I have to give you yours."

"My undressing you while you're wearing my jersey isn't my present?"

"No. That's like the bonus present. For both of us. Wait right here. I'll be right back." I saunter out of the kitchen and add an extra sway to my hips, since Garrett's watching me.

He groans. When I glance over my shoulder, he's adjusting himself in his jeans.

I grab his present from my bedroom and return downstairs with both of my hands behind my back. "I didn't wrap it as beautifully as yours. In fact, I didn't wrap it at all, so don't judge me." He smiles and sits up in his chair. "Close your eyes and hold out your hand."

He does as I say. "You're not going to club me upside the head with a baseball bat and shove a ball down my throat and give me what I deserve after all these years, are you?"

I laugh. "That's a really good idea. I should've gone with that." He lifts one eyelid and smirks. I slap a hand over his eyes to make sure he can't see. "I promise no bats or balls."

"I'm kind of disappointed in the no balls."

"Maybe later."

"I'm holding you to it."

"Are your eyes closed? No peeking."

"It's pitch black in here."

I swing my hand to my back and pull his present from a bag before depositing the flattened penny into his palm. "You can open your eyes."

Slowly, his eyelids open. Without saying a word, he lifts his hand to get a closer inspection. Several quiet seconds tick by. "How did you find my lucky penny?"

"I didn't find your penny, but I did track down a machine that makes them and it just so happened to be just like the one from Earl's."

"Where is it?" He glances around my townhouse.

"Currently, it's sitting in a friend's garage."

"They had one the whole time?"

"No, a customer at the bar overheard me talking about it and said he might know someone, so Lach went with me and sure enough, in the back of the storage shed was the machine. I bought it from him, but it didn't work. I figured with my friend Ledger's mechanic background he must be good at fixing things and sure enough he got it working."

Garrett stares intently at the mallard impression on the copper. "This is awesome."

"It gets better. Not only do you have one lucky penny..." I bring my other hand in front of me and drop an entire plastic bag of pennies into his palm. "Now you have spares. And don't worry, I touched every single one of them."

Chapter 27

THE TRUTH

Garrett

The last few days I've spent with Dessa have been some of the best days ever. Every day she's becoming more and more of my everything. We spent most of our time together in her bed with the exception of her needing to work one day and me spending Christmas with my parents. Luckily, Tony was out of town, so he wasn't there to ruin my holiday.

There are zero issues with our physical relationship, but there's still a little hesitancy with her when it comes to our emotional one. Every day, I'll continue to show her I'm not going anywhere this time. I'll wait for as long as she needs because she's worth it.

Earlier today we said our goodbyes before she left to visit her parents. Like Dessa, I'm really starting to hate goodbyes. Unfortunately, it's what we have to do for now. We've made plans for me to fly back to Harbor Highlands in January. Then, as a surprise, I plan to fly her to Arizona for spring training in February, followed by a trip to Seattle for a home game.

In the meantime, I find myself killing time at Porter's, the sound of darts hitting the board echoing through the air. I opted for a late-night flight in order to have a few extra hours with Dessa. I'll be tired as hell tomorrow, but it's worth it.

"Holy shit, I never expected to see your ex-girlfriend at your wedding."

"Yeah, man. Dessa looked good too."

The dart slips from my grip, crashing to the floor at the mention of her name from a familiar voice I wasn't expecting to hear. Plus, there aren't too many girls named Dessa and ones who attended their ex's wedding. I bend over and collect the dart off the floor and continue to eavesdrop a little more intently. When I arrived, the bar was quiet so I figured I would have the dartboard area to myself. Little did I know I would have company. I lower the brim of my cap to shield my face. Placing the dart to the pub table, I lean closer to the half wall separating us as Tony and his friend talk.

"I can't believe you broke up with her all those years ago," a guy I don't recognize says.

"Truth be told, same. She was always the good girl. I kind of felt like an asshole for cheating on her," Tony says.

My jaw clenches as an inferno blazes through me. He fucking cheated on Dessa? How could he do that to her? She never said anything to me.

"Maybe if I didn't have a brief second of guilt, she would've been the one walking down the aisle toward me," Tony says as they both laugh.

What the fuck? He didn't tell her? I push off the table and nearly topple the stool over. I stalk around the half wall and to the table where my brother is sitting with one of his friends.

When I'm only a few steps away, Tony spots me. The confusion on his face quickly turns to panic. I come to a stop at the edge of the table and face him. My pulse races as I clench and unclench my fists, desperate to keep my temper at bay, but it's going to be a losing battle. "You cheated on Dessa?" I seethe.

Once the reason for my anger slaps him across the face, which I would like to do with my fist, he laughs and shakes his head. He lifts his chin and squares his shoulders. "I see you're still eavesdropping on my conversations, just like the little brother you are." He takes a swig of his beer.

I grit my teeth so hard I'm surprised I don't crack a molar. "Fuck you. Answer the question."

"There may have been a time," he glances at his friend and laughs, "or two." He shrugs, a half smirk on his face I want to brush off with my fist.

"You are a piece of shit," I spit.

His stool screeches across the linoleum as he jumps to his feet so we're chest to chest. Tony may be older, but I have a couple of inches on him and more muscle.

His face is inches away from mine, beer lingering on his breath. "Why the fuck do you care? You left her to go be a hotshot baseball player. You discarded her like day-old trash, so I made sure to comfort *my girlfriend.*"

My nostrils flare as my fists clench. I despise she held that title with him. But it's in the past. I'm determined to make her my future.

"Then I was done." He shrugs a shoulder, a half smirk on his face as he turns to his friend like it's something to be proud of.

My blood boils. He has zero remorse for his actions. He only thinks about himself. Typical Tony. Just like when he kissed Dessa, knowing I liked her. "It doesn't matter what I did. She didn't deserve that."

"Look, baby bro." He clasps his hand on my shoulder, his fingers piercing the muscle. I jerk away. "You're the Home Run Playboy, go find a chick and score yourself some home runs tonight. Quit holding on to something you never got." He flashes me a condescending smirk.

There's only one girl I want, and she's not here right now. My jaw clenches as my fingers flex. He's a narcissistic asshole who thinks he can get away with whatever he wants.

"Wait." His laugh is sinister before he narrows his eyes at me. "Are you going to run and tell Dessa since you two are besties now? Remember, you left for ten years. Left *her*. If you think she wants you now, you're delusional."

"Fuck you! You don't know shit." My fist clenches. Rage flows through my veins like lava. Years of hurt and betrayal are seconds away from exploding out of me. Everything Tony has done. "You've always been jealous of me. Wanted everything I had but you weren't good enough. Didn't work hard enough."

He exhales a barbed laugh. "Give me a fucking break. I'm not jealous of shit. Most of all, I'm not jealous of you!"

My jaw hardens as I shake my head. That's the biggest lie I've ever heard. "Then why did you kiss Dessa?" I raise an eyebrow, waiting for an answer, but I shouldn't expect one. He'll just deflect like he always does. I inch closer to him, not the least bit intimidated by him. "Because I can guarantee the only reason was because I liked her and you couldn't stand the idea of me having one more thing that you couldn't have," I grit out so only he can hear.

"So, the golden boy has come back to town to save the day? Why don't you go back to missing catches? You seem good at that. Probably did it on purpose." He turns to his friend and both cackle with laughter.

As kids, our mom always reminded us we are brothers, and family sticks together. She wanted us to get along, and for the most part we did. Everything changed in high school. It hasn't been the same since and never will be. For once, it's time for him to own up to his actions. It's not even for me. It's for Dessa. "You have two days to tell her yourself. She deserves that. She deserves the truth. And to hear it from the piece of shit you are. If you don't tell her, I will," I sneer.

He takes a step closer to me, his chest bumping into mine, desperate to appear tough. His cheek is inches from mine. I glare daggers at him from the corner of my eyes as he says, "And who do you think she's going to believe? I'm not the one who left her." He pulls away, and his lips curl into a half smile. "And we've rekindled our friendship, so I guess while you're away, I'll be spending more time with her."

Nothing but red fills my vision. I've finally reached my boiling point. I should have done this years ago. My fingers curl into a ball of steel. The air between us grows thick with tension. I pull my arm back and surge it forward, like a bullet firing out of the barrel. My fist connects with his cheek with a sickening thud. His head snaps to the side, his body following the momentum.

He stumbles back as his hand flies to his face. "What the fuck, Garrett?!"

"That's for being a piece of shit to Dessa," I spit.

He drops his hand. "And that's it? You just want to defend her honor? Well aren't you a fucking pussy."

My pulse pounds in my ears and I lunge at him, but an arm across my chest halts my movements, and I'm yanked back.

"What the fuck are you doing, man? Don't do this. He's not worth it," Jake grits out next to my ear. Once I'm out of arm's reach of Tony, he spins me around and pushes me toward the bar. He pulls out a stool and points at it. "Sit."

Jake turns around, his voice commanding as he yells, "Listen up! Everyone better put their fucking cell phones away. No one is going to go spilling any bullshit to the tabloids. If any photos or videos pop up on social media, you best believe I'll find out who you are, and you won't be allowed in my bar or any other bar in Harbor Highlands." He returns his attention to Tony. "You can also get the fuck out of my bar."

Tony throws his hands in the air, the imprint of my fist visible on his cheek. "What the hell? He punched me."

"You started it. He just finished it. So, there's the exit." Jake points across the bar.

"Whatever. This place is bullshit, anyway." Tony shoves a stool, and it hits the floor with a thud.

Tony clenches his fists as he and his friend storm out of Porter's, their eyes narrowing at me while Jake escorts them out the door. Once they're gone, Jake turns around. All the customers turn their heads away from him, afraid they'll be the next subject of his wrath. When he makes a demand, people listen. He's the best person to have on your side. On the other hand, if he's standing across from you, you're fucked. Because of him, my one bad decision may stay under wraps. Slowly, Porter's returns to its normal noise level.

Jake taps me on my shoulder and nods for me to follow him. I climb off the stool. I feel like I'm about to be scolded by the principal for fighting, even though I never got into fights. In his office, he points to the chair in front of his desk while he takes a seat on the other side. He doesn't even need to say a word—his actions say them all.

Jake rests his elbows on the desk, eyes narrowing. "What the hell was that? People eat that shit up for their five minutes of fame."

I scrub my hands down my face. "I know. Unfortunately, it's been a long time coming. He's always been a piece of shit, and him cheating on Dessa was my tipping point. She doesn't deserve that."

He blows out a breath. "No, she doesn't. But you need to think about your actions and the consequences. You have a lot more to lose than he does."

I nod. He's right. If this didn't happen here, it would be all over social media and blasted to the tabloids by now. I don't need the headlines to read "Star Warbler Player Punches Brother in a Fit of Rage."

"Also, Dessa's pretty good at handling her own." He raises an eyebrow.

I know she is. She always was, but I have the urge to protect her, and it's not going to go away anytime soon. Since Dessa's with her parents, I'm not going to ruin her night tonight. I'll tell her tomorrow, since Tony won't, and she deserves to know even though it would be better coming from the piece of shit's mouth instead.

Chapter 28

THE AFTERMATH

Dessa

I throw my coat over my shoulders and grab my purse to head out the door for work, but a knock startles me. Peeking through the peephole, I see Tony's standing on the other side. My brows draw together, unsure why he's at my door, so I twist the knob and pull it open.

"Hey, what are you doing here? I was just about to head out to work."

"I tried calling you, but you didn't answer." He rubs the back of his neck.

"Sorry. I forgot my phone at my parents' last night." Something about his posture and expression is off, but I'm unsure what it could be. Maybe he's having issues with Georgia?

"Do you have a few minutes?"

I check the clock on the wall. "Yeah, I could spare a few. What's up?" I open the door wider and motion for him to come in. Once he's inside, I close the door behind him.

"I need to talk to you." His tone is serious.

I huff out a laugh. "That doesn't sound ominous or anything."

He turns around and pulls off his sunglasses. A dark shade of purple and blue covers the skin under his left eye.

"Oh my god! What happened?" Shock and disbelief flood my body as my hand flies over my mouth.

With a heavy sigh, he releases a long, weary breath. "Garrett."

My eyebrows knit in confusion as my hand drops to my side. "What does Garrett have to do with your black eye?"

"He's the reason I have it." He points to his face.

"What are you talking about? What did he do?"

"Last night, I was at Porter's with a friend. We were talking, minding our own business, and Garrett was there. He overheard us talking about how great it was seeing you at the wedding. How you and Georgia have become friends. He got toe to toe with me, jealous that you and me are friends again and have been hanging out. He told me to stay away from you. When I told him he can't pick my friends or yours, he punched me."

My jaw drops to the floor. He wasn't even alone for six hours, and something like this happens? I can't imagine Garrett would do this. He and his brother have a rocky relationship, but he wouldn't punch him. Would he? While we've rekindled our friendship, a person can change a lot in ten years. I'm certainly not the same person as I was then, so I can't imagine Garrett is too. But getting jealous and punching someone? Especially his brother?

"I... I just want to let you know he's unpredictable. Borderline dangerous. If he'll punch his own brother, who knows if he'd do anything to you?" He rests his hand on my bicep. "Now I have to go on my honeymoon with a black eye. At least it was after the wedding." He huffs out a laugh.

Garrett would never hurt me, but I never expected him to punch Tony either. For him to be jealous is absurd. He has no reason to be jealous. Yes, he can be a little protective. That's always been his personality. Would protective morph into possessive? At the wedding, when I was talking to Tony and Georgia, Garrett was always close by, watching. This seems so out of character for him.

"I'm so sorry, Tony."

"It's not your fault."

"This happened because of me, so I kind of feel like it is."

He pulls me in for a hug, wrapping his arms around my shoulders. My cheek rests against his chest. "I wanted to let you know. But it might be better to steer clear of him. Take anything he has to say with a grain of salt. He'll do whatever he can to pry apart our friendship."

I nod my head. "Thanks for telling me. Again, I'm sorry."

"I better get going." With one hand, he sets his sunglasses on the bridge of his nose. "We'll chat later though."

"Yeah." I nod. "Text me or something."

Tony pulls open the front door and slowly closes it behind him. I take a few steps and peer out the peephole as he gets into his car. I turn around and sag against the door. What the hell? Garrett wouldn't do that, would he? Since this all happened at Porter's, it's time to get my ass to work.

When I enter through the door at Porter's, Lach and Jake are behind the bar.

Lach holds up my phone. "Your mom dropped this off."

I snatch it from his hands and quickly scan for any messages or phone calls from Garrett. Messages from Lach and Rylee litter my phone, and there is also a missed call from Tony. My heart sinks to the floor. Nothing. Why didn't he try to call me?

"What happened last night?" I ask Lach as I set my purse on the bar.

"Your Home Run Playboy is just as good at hitting faces as he is baseballs."

Jake shoots Lach a death glare. "Go make yourself useful over there." He points at the opposite end of the bar.

"What am I supposed to do?" He shrugs with his hands in the air.

"Figure it out," Jake deadpans.

Once Lach has retreated to the opposite end of the bar and is no longer a distraction, I ask Jake, "What happened?"

Jake stacks glasses under the bar. "Just like Lach said, Garrett punched Tony. I didn't hear the conversation, but I witnessed the aftermath."

"Why would he do that? Not only to Tony, but potentially to his career?"

"I've never known Garrett to do something without a solid reason. So, if you want answers, you need to ask him."

"Thanks, Jake." I stalk to the employee room and throw my purse into my locker. Grabbing my phone from my back pocket, I pull up Garrett's number and hit talk.

After a few rings, he answers. "Hey, what's up, Tates?"

I freeze. His nickname for me catches me off guard but I shake it off. I can't get distracted. "Did you punch Tony?"

A heavy sigh echoes through the phone. "He told you."

"Yes. He did." I spin around and lean against the

lockers. "But I really think you should've been the one to tell me."

"Why would I tell you? He needed to be the one to tell you. This was all his fault."

"You punching Tony is his fault? Did he accidentally fall face-first into your fist?" My tone is defensive. "He now has to go on his honeymoon with a black eye."

"Wait. Did he tell you why I punched him?"

"Yes! I understand we're all navigating our relationships after not talking for several years. We're adults, and there's no need to be jealous."

He barks out a humorless laugh. "That's what he told you? He's such a piece of shit," he mumbles. "I guarantee you whatever he told you was a lie."

"But you punched him. That's not a lie." I pace back and forth, sidestepping a table and chair in the employee room.

He blows out a deep breath. "Yes. I punched him. Is that what you want to hear?"

I don't even know what I want to hear at this point. "But why? Things were going back to normal. The way they used to be. When we were all friends. I want our lives to go back to how they were. The three of us. That can't happen when people are punching other people."

"You're delusional if you think things will ever be like how they were. That ship has sailed, exploded into millions of tiny pieces, and sank to the bottom of the ocean. Too much time has passed for any amends to be made. As long as you're involved, it will never be how it was."

"So, this is my fault?"

"No. Technically yes. It started because of you, but it's been simmering for years. You were just the accelerant. Tony's and my relationship was going to implode either way. It was only a matter of time." He blows out a deep breath. "So, what? You believe him?"

"He didn't ghost me for ten years." As soon as the words are out, I pinch my eyes shut. I regret them as soon as they pass my lips.

"Yeah. I thought we moved passed that, but apparently not." His tone is dejected.

My head is a massive knot. I squeeze my temples, willing the throbbing to stop. Everything was going well, or so I thought. "I didn't mean that. I'm tired of being the rope in yours and Tony's game of tug of war. I need time to sort all of this out. Everything happened so fast. You're in Seattle and I'm here. And all the drama with you and Tony. I don't know. We dove headfirst into this... relationship. Maybe we should slow things down."

"Is that what you want?" His voice is low.

"I think it's for the best. At least right now."

"I'll give you space for now, but know that this thing between me and you isn't over. It's far from over. We both know it. But also, so you know the truth, the real truth, not the fabricated shit Tony gave you, I punched him because he cheated on you and only dated you so I couldn't."

The call goes silent.

Chapter 29

FROM BEST TO WORST

Dessa

It's been over a week since I talked to either Tony or Garrett. Tony's been on his honeymoon, and Garrett's been MIA. On New Year's Eve, loneliness sucker punched me in the gut as I watched all the happy couples in the bar lock lips at midnight. All I could do was sip my glass of water—I couldn't even drown my misery in alcohol because I was working. To be fair, he sent me a text at midnight, ten o'clock his time, wishing me a Happy New Year. I didn't respond, mostly because I didn't know what to say.

I'm still conflicted about their fight. Rylee and Nora both agreed Tony deserved the punch to his face, and it was sweet for Garrett to defend my honor. But Lach thought it was dumb since Tony cheating happened years ago, and it's not worth the fight. Plus, there's the whole Tony-dated-me-so-Garrett-couldn't situation that seems too far-fetched to believe. Who would spend four years with someone they didn't like? Either way, I don't know who's actually telling the truth yet. This would be better if we didn't have such a complicated history.

I'm stocking the beer cooler when the front door opens, the sliver of light catching my attention. Tony strolls in wearing a dark gray wool pea coat. He runs his hand through his chestnut-colored hair, brushing the snowflakes away while the ones that linger melt from the warm temperature.

"Hey, Tony. I wasn't expecting to see you." I throw the empty box onto the floor as he takes a seat on a stool in front of me. "Looks like the shiner is finally starting to go away."

"Yeah and just in time."

I point to the beer taps with a raised brow, silently asking if he wants a beer. He shakes his head. "Just in time for what?" I ask while reaching inside the cooler for a bottle of beer for another customer.

"I'm heading to Chicago for work next week. I have a couple of recruiting meetings and meetings with coaches. You should come with me."

My head snaps back. "Go with you to Chicago? Shouldn't that be something you ask your wife to do?"

He chuckles softly. "That sounds bad, doesn't it? Let me start over. Over Christmas, Georgia and I ate at Poco Grande. Georgia thought it would be a fun surprise to arrange a meet and greet between you and Isabella. I made a phone call and she was thrilled with the idea."

The bottle of beer slips from my hand and hits the bar with a heavy thud. Luckily, it didn't break, but I set it to the side and grab another one. "That would be a dream!" I fight hard to not climb on the bar and dance and scream right now. It might frighten the customers, otherwise there's a good chance that would be happening.

With a firm grasp on the second bottle, I pass it to the customer.

"Let me talk to Jake and see if I need to change anything with my schedule. What days?"

A wide smile splits Tony's face. "Thursday through Saturday."

"And what about Georgia? Will she also be going?"

He frowns. "No. She's busy with the interior designer for her new shop."

A part of me would be more comfortable if Georgia was going. "Are you sure Georgia is okay with this? The last thing I want to do is step on anyone's toes."

"Of course. It was her idea." He waves me off.

His words are reassuring, but I'm still asking her myself. "I'm meeting Isabella Rossi!" I can no longer contain my squeal. My hands shoot up in the air, and I twirl in a happy dance. "What am I going to wear? I need to compile a list of questions because I'm going to forget everything once I meet her. Should I bring a gift? What if she asks me questions? I don't think I'll be prepared for that."

"Dessa, calm down. She's a really chill person. You'll get along great with her."

I nod in an attempt to simmer my excitement. I round the end of the bar and wrap my arms around Tony. "Seriously, this is amazing. The best thing that's ever happened to me."

"Well, I'm happy it could be me who can make this happen for you."

Once Tony leaves, I text Georgia to confirm the trip. She said this is an amazing opportunity for me and she wishes she could join us. Now that I have her blessing, I feel so much better about going and meeting Isabella Rossi!

Porter's
ALE HOUSE

After clearing my vacation with Jake and only needing to switch one shift with Rylee, I secured three days off. He booked all our travel, including the plane tickets and hotel rooms. I made it clear to get separate rooms and that I would pay for mine, but he said the rooms would be comped since Georgia's family owns the hotel chain. When I looked up the price, I nearly fell on the floor. Six hundred dollars a night for two nights was a little out of my price range. I'd be living off ramen noodles for the foreseeable future to afford that bill.

From my closet, I stare at my empty suitcase lying open on my bed. Unable to decide what to wear, I throw ten different outfits, along with five different pairs of shoes, into my suitcase. I sit on top, bouncing up and down, willing it to close. Once the zipper's in place, my phone chimes with a message that Tony's in my driveway.

I drag my suitcase down the stairs, huffing and puffing with each step. Once I'm out the front door, Tony's waiting inside his truck.

When he sees me, he steps out. "We're only going to be gone for three days. Did you need to bring your entire closet?" He stalks toward me and grabs my suitcase.

"I also have a carry-on. I was undecided on which outfits I want to wear. If I want to go comfy and casual or sleek and stylish. This gives me options." A gust of wind blows the loose snow through the air, icing my warm cheeks.

"You were always so indecisive." When we reach the side of his truck, he hoists my suitcase into the bed along with my carry-on bag.

I pat my jean pockets, coat pockets, then check inside my purse for my phone. "Shit, I forgot my phone. I'll be right back." After I find my phone on the kitchen counter, I race outside, hop into the passenger seat, and we take off to the airport.

When the car stops in front of the hotel, I peer out the window and look up and up and up. "I'll be honest, I've never stayed at a hotel with so many floors." I tear my gaze from the window to turn toward Tony, who's watching me.

"I'm just taking all your firsts."

A ghost of a smile tips the corner of my lips. Years ago, Tony was the first guy I slept with, but for him to make a comment now creates an unease in the pit of my stomach. I brush it off because I'm in Chicago to meet Isabella Rossi.

When we step out of the car, a bellhop immediately greets us to collect our luggage. A gust of wind blows through, and I tighten my coat around myself. With a hand on my lower back, Tony escorts me inside.

A dark, rich mahogany wood reception desk is a focal point against the light tile floor. At the counter, the front desk receptionist greets us with a warm smile. Her name tag reads *Kelly*.

The clacking of the keyboard echoes through the lobby as Kelly types Tony's name into the computer. "I have you in a king suite for three days and two nights." Her voice is polite and professional.

I lean in. "Excuse me? One room? There should be two."

She glances at the screen again to confirm the details. "I only have a reservation for one room."

Tony interjects. "That can't be right. I booked two."

"I'm sorry sir, it's just the one room."

"Can you add another room?" I ask, crossing my fingers.

"I'm sorry ma'am, we're fully booked." She gives me a pitying glance.

I blow out a deep breath, trying to keep my irritation at bay.

Tony looks from me to the receptionist. "This is unacceptable." His tone is sharp. "Do you know who my wife is?"

Her wide-eyed gaze drifts to me and then to Tony. "I'm sorry. No, I don't."

"Oh. It's not me. I'm not his wife," I quickly interject, waving my hands. Shit. That sounds bad. She probably thinks I'm the mistress. "We're friends." I blurt out. "We've known each other since we were kids. I'm just on the trip to meet my girl crush. Isabella Rossi. Do you know her?"

Kelly nods.

I pinch my lips shut and drop a step back. She doesn't need my life story.

Tony rests his hands on the counter and states very matter-of-factly, "My wife's father own's this hotel, and I'm going to make sure he hears about this." He narrows his eyes at her.

Tears well up in her eyes as her chin wobbles.

"Tony," I whisper. "That's not necessary."

"Yes. It is," he snaps. "The service should be better than this."

"Tony," I grit through my teeth. "Really. It's fine." I turn to Kelly. "It's fine. Whatever room you have will work." Today is supposed to be a good day. I don't want the bad karma of getting someone fired hanging over my head. Plus, this isn't her fault. She's only doing her job.

"I'm sorry. I swear I booked two rooms," Tony says to me.

"Being a suite, the room does offer a pullout couch outside the bedroom," Kelly offers.

"Great! Sounds perfect." I'm trying to stay optimistic in this entire situation, but sharing a hotel room with Tony was not on my to-do list for the day.

"You take the bed, and I'll take the couch," Tony says.

"You don't have to do that."

"No, I insist. This is my fault. I'll take the couch." He flashes me a sympathetic smile.

After checking in, we head to the twenty-fifth floor. When we enter our suite at the end of the hallway, the bright, natural sunlight shines in through the enormous wall of windows facing Lake Michigan. The view is absolutely breathtaking. The bellhop follows us inside and deposits our luggage in the bedroom. I almost correct him, but it's not worth the hassle. We can move our suitcases later.

Tony plops down on the couch and throws his arms over the back. "We have a couple of hours until we need to meet Isabella—"

"I have to get ready!"

"For the next hour and a half?"

"Yes! I need to freshen up, pick out my outfit, and make sure I have all my questions." I spin around and dash into the bedroom. I move Tony's suitcase to the other side of the door, then close it behind me.

I rummage through my entire suitcase and try on every different outfit combination imaginable. Once that's done, I do the same with the shoes. I finally settle on black skinny jeans with gray wedge booties and a cream blouse. I style my hair in a half updo with loose curls. An hour later, I emerge from the bedroom, and Tony's still sitting on the couch. His suitcase is sitting next to the armrest, and he's looking at his phone. He's changed into a fresh, black button-down shirt, but kept the same jeans.

The clacking of my boots on the tile floor draws his attention. He glances up, dropping his phone to his lap. "Wow. You look stunning."

"Thank you. I need to make a good impression for Isabella."

"Well, she won't be the only one left speechless." His gaze wanders down the length of my body and lands at my feet. "Shall we?"

Even though the restaurant is only two blocks away, we opt to request an Uber since it's windy and twenty degrees outside. The car stops at the curb in front of a large, dark brown building with floor-to-ceiling windows. Back lit letters stick out from the side of the building spelling out Poco Grande. Tony holds the front door open for me, and we walk inside. The dark brown flooring matches elegantly with the cream drapes. The maître d' greets us and checks our coats before showing us to the private bar section where Isabella is waiting.

My heart pounds in my chest as my palms grow clammy. No matter how many times I wipe them on my jeans, it's futile. I'm a giant ball of anxiety, nervousness, and excitement all rolled into one. I pray I don't make a giant ass out of myself.

When we reach the bar, Isabella is standing on the other side pouring a drink into two glasses. My hands shake as spots dot my vision. I inhale a deep breath, willing myself not to pass out. When she notices us, she looks up and smiles. Oh god, she smiled at me. I give her what I think is a bright, beautiful smile, but if I had to guess, it resembles a Chandler Bing smile.

"Hi. Welcome to Poco Grande." She slides the two glasses in front of us. "Tony. Always a pleasure to see you."

Tony nods. "Likewise."

Isabella turns to me. "You must be Dessa?" She holds out her hand.

My cheeks grow warm. She knows my name! "Hi! Yes!" I say entirely too cheerfully. Tone it down, Dessa. Discreetly, I wipe my palm on my jeans before reaching up to shake her hand.

"Please take a seat. I'm so happy you two could come." She gestures to the two stools in front of her.

Tony pulls out my stool, and I take a seat. "I am a huge fan." Let the fangirling commence. "I have all your books. Your show is always on my TV. I even have your mixology set."

She rests a hand on her chest as pink tints her cheeks. "Thank you so much. I'm so honored."

I made Isabella Rossi blush. "No. Thank you. Would it be weird if I asked you to sign my arm so I can get it tattooed later?"

She laughs as if I'm joking. I'm not, but I play along and laugh as well so she doesn't think I'm a stalker on the brink of tracking down her phone number and home address.

"I do have a brand-new book that comes out next week, and I'd be happy to give you a signed copy."

I've died and gone to cocktail heaven. Best. Day. Ever. "That would be amazing! Thank you!" I glance at Tony with the widest smile on my face. He's watching me intently with a half smile of his own. I turn my attention back to Isabella. "What is this drink?" I point at the glass in front of us.

"This is a palate cleanser drink to open your tastebuds to all the flavors you'll experience tonight. It's called a Negroni. It's made of an Italian bitter, sweet vermouth, and gin. Then garnished with an orange peel."

I raise my glass, and Tony does the same. We clink our glasses before swallowing our cocktails. Hints of both bitter and sweet dance over my tastebuds.

Isabella claps her hands together. "Now to the fun stuff. This is something new I've been trying. It's a smoky whiskey." She gives us a play-by-play demonstration of how she makes the drink. "First, I insert a tube into the shaker and cover the top the best I can and turn on the smoke gun. I'll let this sit for about two minutes. You can adjust it for shorter or longer depending on how strong you want the smoke flavor." She turns on the smoke gun, and a cloud of smoke rolls from the top and down the sides of the shaker as she infuses the whiskey. The whole process is mesmerizing.

I stare in wide-eyed fascination. "I never would've thought to add smokiness to a drink before."

"You'd be surprised by the flavor that it brings out of the whiskey."

"I bet." I make a mental note to add a smoke gun to my shopping list.

Once finished, she passes us a sample glass of the whiskey. "You need to try the whiskey by itself, first."

I take a sip. The smoky flavor adds a rich and savory element of smoothness to the dark liquid. "This tastes amazing. I can picture myself drinking this curled up next to the fireplace on a cold winter night." Garrett would really like this. Fuck. Why am I thinking of Garrett? I push the thoughts away.

Isabella nods excitedly. "Yes. Exactly. It gives it a cozy feeling." Then she starts on the next drink.

Unable to contain my excitement, I rise to my feet for a better view of everything she's doing. Tony continues to sit on the stool next to me. She uses a paring knife to delicately slice the orange peel into a twist for garnish. I lean in closer to examine her technique. From his stool, Tony does the same. His hand rests on my lower back and my body stiffens for a moment. Not wanting to give anyone the wrong idea, I inch away from him and his hand drops. I continue to watch Isabella intently as she places the garnish delicately on top of the drink when she's done, then she slides it across the table to us.

"So how long have you two been married?" Isabella wipes a rag over the bar as she prepares to make the next drink.

I choke on my drink. "O-oh! We're," I point between me and Tony, "not married."

"I'm sorry. My mistake. I saw his ring and assumed."

"We're just friends. We've known each other," I glance at Tony, "for close to twenty years."

"That's a long time," Isabella says.

I keep the info about us dating to myself. I don't want to give her the wrong impression or fuel the impression she already has. "He's just a really good friend."

Tony wraps his arm around my waist and pulls me closer to him. "Good friends."

I slide out of his grasp. Again, I don't want her getting the wrong idea. "So, what's the next drink?"

"This one is my favorite." She grabs a collection of various bottles and liquors and pours them into a shaker. "So, are you guys going to stay for dinner?"

"Dinner's an option? After all these drinks, I could use something to soak up the alcohol."

"Definitely, I'll arrange a table for you guys. You're in luck. Chris is in the kitchen tonight, so he'll make you anything on or off the menu."

"Please tell me you'll join us."

Tony sits up straighter on his stool and clears his throat. "I'm sure Isabella has a lot to do."

She shakes her head. "I don't want to impose."

"No imposing. I would love to pick your brain some more. Please join us for dinner." I plead. I'm only seconds away from climbing over the bar and getting on my knees to beg her to have dinner with us.

"If you don't mind—"

"Of course not." I turn to face Tony. "Right? You don't mind."

His gaze flickers upward and his nostrils flare. "No. Not at all."

Over the next two hours, I ask Isabella a million different questions, and she happily answers all of them while Tony leans against the chair and stares at his phone screen. Chris, Isabella's husband, made me the most orgasmic mushroom risotto. I'd try to make it myself, but there's no way I could come close to replicating the dish. I wasn't going to waste a single second of my time with Isabella. She's my rock star of mixology and just in the short time with her, I learned so many new techniques and new flavor combinations that I'll be implementing. She even gave me referral codes to a couple of local shops to buy products. As if that wasn't enough, she also gifted me a set of her signature stainless steel shakers that I'm almost too scared to ever use because they're so nice, but I will shake the shit out of drinks with them. Of course, she also gave me a signed copy of her upcoming book that I will cherish forever. When I die, I want to be buried with this book.

When we arrive back at the hotel, Tony sits my gift box from Isabella on the table. I'm still riding the high from the evening and probably will be for the next year. "Thank you so much for today. It was absolutely amazing. It was like a dream come true. I don't know how I could ever repay you." I shrug out of my coat and Tony does the same.

"Seeing your smile is the only repayment I need."

"Thank you again." I wrap my arms around his shoulders and give him a hug. When I pull away, his hands tighten around my waist. I glance up and his dark eyes bore into mine.

His hand slides down, resting on my lower back. "I miss this," he whispers.

"Me too. I'm glad we could become friends again." I give him a tight-lipped smile.

"No. I miss you. Us." His other hand reaches up and tucks a strand of hair behind my ear. "I miss this. What we had."

"Tony." My voice is low. "You don't mean that. I think all the whiskey's gone to your head."

"No. I know exactly what I mean." His hand brushes my cheek before it snakes to the back of my neck.

Alarm bells blare inside my head as my hackles rise. "Tony, you're married."

"It can be our friendly secret." He bends down, his lips centimeters away from mine.

"Tony. No." My voice is firm. With my palms on his chest, I shove him away. He's resistant at first, but I shove harder until he stumbles back. "What the hell are you doing? We're just friends! You're married!"

He runs his hand through his hair before his dark, stormy eyes meet mine. "I bring you here, pay for everything, set up a meeting with your idol, and this is how you repay me?"

I flinch at his words. Was he expecting me to have sex with him? Bile rises in my throat.

"Is this about Garrett?" He snarls.

"What the fuck, Tony? This has nothing to do with Garrett. Why are you even mentioning him?"

"You're dating him, aren't you?"

"What the hell does it matter?"

"Are you dating him or not?" he grits out.

"We're taking," I pause, "a break." Hell, I don't know what we're doing anymore. I don't know anything.

Tony stomps away, but after a few steps, he spins around and charges me. "It's always about him. The fucking golden boy. Everything is handed to him on a silver fucking platter. Anything he wants, he gets. Including you."

My entire body trembles. Either from rage or fear, I'm not sure. Maybe a combination of both. I've never seen Tony like this. Maybe what Garrett told me was the truth. "Did you cheat on me? When we were dating?" I tilt my head, studying him.

He huffs out a humorless laugh. "Is that what he told you? And I suppose you'll believe him because you're fucking now."

"Yes or no, Tony." I glare at him. "That's the real reason he punched you. Not because he's jealous." His hard eyes stare at me for a long minute. His silence gives me the answer I was looking for. "Or how about you only dated me so Garrett couldn't. Is that true too?" The throbbing vein in his neck gives him away. Everything Garrett told me was the truth. Once again, I'm made to look like the fool. My head throbs. "I don't want to deal with this right now. We can hash it out in the morning." I side step Tony, but he stops me.

"Get out!" He roars out the words like a dragon's breath.

I flinch. "You're kicking me out?" My chest tightens. It's strangling me so much I can't breathe.

"Yes, now get out of my goddamn hotel room!" He stomps toward the door and yanks it open. "I don't want dirty sluts in my room."

Tears prick the corners of my eyes, and I fight to keep

them at bay. What is happening right now? Like a flip of a switch, he's changed into someone completely different. "What am I supposed to do? Where am I supposed to go?"

"Figure it out." He grabs my wrist, and I yelp in surprise. He pushes me out the door. I stumble a couple of steps until my palms hit the other side of the hallway and I regain my balance. The echo of the door slamming races down the corridor. This time, I can't hold my tears back. Gravity takes over, and they slide down my cheeks. My suitcase. I stomp to the door and pound my fist against the wood. "At least let me collect my stuff!"

When he doesn't answer, I pound again. A minute later, the door flies open. He tosses my half-open suitcase into the hallway. I barely have time to move out of the way. My shoes and underwear topple out and scatter across the carpet. Next, he throws the box from Isabella, the contents inside rattling around as it smashes into the opposite wall.

"There's your shit." The door slams behind him.

My entire body trembles as I frantically shove everything into my suitcase.

A hotel guest from across the hall peeks her head out the door. "Is everything okay?" Concern laces her voice.

I nod as I attempt to choke back a sob. "I-I'm fine. Thank you."

Once my suitcase is packed again, I grab the box and tuck it under one arm. I roll my suitcase behind me to the bank of elevators. This was one of the best days of my entire life, and now it's the worst. When I reach the lobby, I plop down on a couch, defeated, and set the box next to me. I'm the world's biggest idiot. How did I not see this coming? What the hell am I going to do? I can't afford to stay here alone. Plus, I'd rather not stay anywhere near Tony. Since I'm unfamiliar with the city, I pull out my phone and dial the first person I can think of.

Chapter 30

DUH. IT'S FIVE IN THE MORNING.

Garrett

I'm a miserable piece of shit. I throw myself onto the couch, wearing stained sweatpants and a holey t-shirt. It's 8 p.m. on a Thursday night, and I'd rather sit at home than go out. The guys invited me to some new club in town, but I wasn't feeling it. In fact, I haven't been feeling it since my fight with Dessa. I've been numb. I hate that she's mad at me. I hate she won't talk to me. I was only trying to do the right thing. She deserved to know, and apparently, I'm the asshole for telling her.

For the past month, I've given her space, except for the New Year's message I sent. I wanted her to know I was still thinking about her. Dessa needs time to figure things out on her own. That's the way she's always been. Growing up, you could give her the answer and she'd still work it out herself. I don't want to push her, but fuck, not talking to her is killing me.

My phone buzzes on the coffee table, and I ignore it.

I'm sure it's one of the guys trying to convince me to go out tonight. If it's important, they'll leave a message. The ringing stops for a second, then starts up again. This time I glance at the screen, and Dessa's name flashes at the top. I lean forward and scramble to pick it up, hitting the talk button as I press it to my ear. "I'm so glad you called."

"Garrett," she whimpers, followed by a sniffle.

"Dessa. What's wrong?" I jackknife off the couch. "Are you hurt?"

"No." She sucks in a sharp breath. "But I need your h-help." Her voice cracks at the end.

"What do you need?"

A heavy sigh sounds through the speaker. "This sounds so stupid."

"What is it?" My concern skyrockets with every second she's not telling me what's wrong.

"Your brother invited me to Chicago to meet Isabella Rossi. Everything was going good till he tried to kiss me." She sniffles. "I pushed him away and then he kicked me out. I have nowhere to go. I don't know where to go."

Fucking Tony. Rage courses through my veins. I can't believe he would do this. I pace back and forth in my living room. "Where are you right now?"

"I'm sitting in the lobby of the LaBelle Hotel. I-I don't know what to do, Garrett." She sniffles again.

"I know exactly where that's at." I race into the office where my computer is. I pull up the website for a hotel nearby. I'll book her a room for the night and figure out the flight situation later. "Are you able to request an Uber?"

"Yeah."

"I'm booking you a room at the Four Seasons. It's five blocks away." I put the phone on speaker while I book the room online.

"I can't ask you to do that."

"You're not asking. I'm just doing it. Call an Uber to take you there. They have your name and will take care of you."

"I don't know what I would do without you."

"I'll do anything for you. Call me when you check in."

"Okay. Garrett?"

"Yeah?"

"Thank you."

"Anytime, Tates."

The call disconnects. Fuck. I wish I could be there right now, hold her in my arms, and tell her everything will be okay. It kills me I'm halfway across the country. Fuck it. I search for the next available direct flight to Chicago. There's a redeye leaving in three hours for two grand. Right now, I don't give a shit about the money. Dessa's alone, and I need to be with her. I charge the flight to my credit card, throw some clothes in a backpack, and race out of my condo to the parking garage.

After two hours of sitting in traffic and getting through security at the airport, I'm finally sitting on the plane. Dessa called me after she got checked in and to her room. At least I know she's safe. My leg bounces wanting to get to her. I can't believe Tony did this. He's an even bigger piece of shit than I thought. I'm fighting the urge to track him down in Chicago, rip out his jugular, and tell him what kind of asshole he really is. But he's not worth it. Dessa needs me more, and I won't disappoint her.

The plane finally lands in Chicago at four in the morning—Chicago time. My eyes are bloodshot from no sleep, not for the lack of trying, but every time I closed my eyes, I saw Tony and thought of how much I wanted to give him another black eye. Once the plane's stopped at the gate, I request an Uber, so there will be one waiting as soon as I'm outside the airport. Luckily, it's early in the morning and traffic isn't horrible, but it's still not ideal when I need to get to Dessa. When I arrive at the hotel, I'm out of the car before it comes to a complete stop. I'll be sure to leave the driver a generous tip.

At the front desk, I strum my fingers on the counter, willing the receptionist to work a little faster on getting me a key card. After what feels like hours but is only minutes, she slides the card to me. I race across the lobby to the elevators, and once inside, I jamb my thumb against the button for the fifteenth floor. My foot taps against the elevator floor as I watch the number rise. I pray no one else needs an elevator. I've been waiting long enough to get to Dessa, and I don't want to wait a second longer. Before the elevator doors fully open, I jog out and down the corridor. Once I reach the door, I pull out the key card and pause. Maybe I shouldn't just barge into the room since she has no idea I'm here. The last thing I want to do is terrify her. I tuck the card into my back pocket and knock instead. It's silent as I wait. After several seconds pass, I knock again. I hear the deadbolt click and the door opens a crack.

"Garrett? What are you do—"

Her hair is in a disheveled ponytail. Her eyes are still hooded from sleep, and she's never looked more beautiful. I push through the door, clasp her cheeks in my hands, and press my lips to hers. She gasps in surprise, then her hands wrap around my waist, holding me close to her. I break away and rest my forehead against hers.

"I didn't want you to be alone."

"You flew all the way from Seattle to come here? Did you get any sleep?"

I brush my thumb over her cheek. "I needed to know you were safe."

"You could have called me."

"I needed to see you."

"I needed to see you too." She lifts her chin and kisses me. It's soft and sweet, but also filled with promise and maybe hope.

She pulls away and wraps her fingers around mine, leading me through the living room and into the bedroom. I shrug off my backpack and toss it in the corner. Spinning around, her fingers grip the hem of my shirt, tugging it up over my chest. I help her remove it and toss it near my backpack. Her fingers push at the button of my jeans until it unfastens. She hooks her thumbs under the waistband and pulls them down past my thighs.

"Dessa. What are you doing?" My voice is strained. She's been through a lot in the last twelve hours, and I doubt sex is the answer right now, but if that's what she wants, I'll give it to her. I'll give her anything.

She peers up at me, and her lips curve in the corners. "I'm getting you ready for bed. You look like you haven't slept in days."

I'm going on twenty-four hours, but I had too much adrenaline coursing through my veins to sleep. But now that I'm here and Dessa's safe, I could crash for about a week.

"And you're coming to bed with me?"

"Duh. It's five in the morning."

I step out of my jeans and hook my thumbs under my boxer briefs, tugging them down until they hit the floor. Dessa's gaze drops as the elastic slides over my semi-hard dick.

"Not now. First sleep," she murmurs.

I don't know if that was for me or more for herself. But with her staring at my dick longingly, I could pass on the sleep for at least twenty minutes. She climbs into the bed and folds the blanket over, inviting me in. So, I follow her. I would follow her anywhere. She snuggles into my chest, and I wrap my arm around her. Her sweet vanilla honey shampoo invades my senses, and I drift off to a peaceful sleep.

"It's 10 a.m. Check out is in an hour. We should get going," she mumbles against my chest. Her voice is warm and soft. Everything that is comforting in the world.

I wrap my arms around her waist, snuggling deeper against her. "That sounds like a terrible idea."

She giggles. "Just because you're a hotshot baseball player doesn't mean you can do whatever you want."

"Hmm. I'm comfortable, just like this."

"But we need to check out. And I need to figure out a flight home."

I lift the hem of her shirt and place a kiss right above her belly button. "When I came in this morning, I booked another night. How about we worry about the flight later?" My hand skates over her skin under the fabric of her shirt. My thumb brushes along the underside of her breast. "Plus, I'd rather concern myself with something else right now."

She nibbles on her bottom lip. "And what's that?"

"You."

She runs her fingers through my hair. "I can tell you're pretty comfortable. Your cock is poking my thigh." She giggles.

"What can I say? He knows what he wants."

"Is that so?"

"It is, but the more important question is, what do *you* want?"

She slides out from under my arm and peels back the blanket. I roll over as she climbs between my spread legs, a smile curving her lips. She wraps her hand around the base of my dick and a deep groan rumbles in the back of my throat. Bending down, she runs her tongue along the underside of my shaft. When she reaches the head, her lips wrap around me like a lollipop. She swirls her tongue over the crown, and I suck in a sharp breath. I push her hair to the side for a better view as her hot mouth bobs up and down on my dick.

"Fuck Tates. I love watching you suck my dick. Your pretty lips wrapped around me. How much do you love it?"

She moans around my cock, causing vibration to soar directly to my balls. She keeps a steady pace, and I'm not going to last much longer. She uses her hand, trailing after her mouth, alternating the pressure between her lips and her fingers. I'm seconds away from coming down her throat, but I'm not ready yet.

"Come up here and sit on my face." She releases my dick with a pop. "Take your shirt off. I want to see your tits." She does as I say. The fabric drags over her hard nipples until they're fully exposed, begging to be pinched. Sitting up, I brush my thumb over the hard peak. She arches into my touch and moans. "Come here. I'm so damn hungry for your pussy." I drop back to the mattress.

She crawls up the side of the bed till her hips are at my shoulders. She lifts a leg over me and straddles my face. I slide my hands up her silky, smooth thighs and around the curve of her ass.

"You don't need these." I grip the thin strip of elastic and tug. Both sides rip apart, and the fabric falls to my chest. I brush them away before grabbing her hips and positioning her right where I want her. Starting at the bottom, I lick up her slit with the flat of my tongue. Her body jolts when I reach her clit, so I give her another teasing lick.

"Oh. Garrett." Her fingers wrap around the fixed headboard. "Mmm."

"You like my tongue on you? Lapping at your pussy." With my fingers, I spread her open and continue licking her.

"Yes. I love your tongue on me." Her hips grind against my face in time with my licks.

I spear her entrance with the tip of my tongue, and she whimpers. I continue licking and sucking. With my thumb, I circle her clit as I lick hard, roughing my tongue over her pussy. Her moans and whimpers grow louder with each swipe. I speed up my movements, desperate for her to come and scream my name while she does it.

"Ah! Yes! Garrett. Right there." Her hips rock over my tongue. With one hand, she cups her tit before pinching her nipple.

"Come all over my tongue, Tates," I mumble against her inner thigh before wrapping my lips around her clit to finish the job I started.

"Oh! F-fuck! Garrett." Her legs tremble, and her orgasm races through her. But I don't stop. I continue to lap at her pussy until I get every last drop.

Chapter 31

TAKE THE TRASH OUT

Dessa

Over the next twenty-four hours, Garrett and I stay in bed, have sex, order room service, have sex, book our return flights, have sex, go to bed, wake up, and have sex. Thankfully, with online grocery delivery, we were able to order in some condoms. Even without, I'm sure we would have gotten creative. I snuggle deeper into his chest. My finger traces the intricate half-compass-half-baseball tattoo on his chest as I inhale his comforting scent. Being in Garrett's arms makes me feel safe. He's my safe space. If I think about it, he always has been. It's hard to say if we didn't spend those ten years apart if I would come to realize that or not. Things happen for a reason. Maybe we needed to go through that in order to be where we are now. Right now, there's nowhere else I'd rather be.

"I'm sorry."

His hand freezes on my arm. "For what?"

"For everything." I peer up at him. "For not believing you about Tony. That he cheated on me."

"He actually told you?"

"No. But his silence was pretty damning."

"Go figure. He can't even own up to his mistakes. It's the same old Tony, but somehow, he's managed to get worse."

I roll to my stomach, resting on my elbows, and look up at him. "What do you mean?"

His fingers caress my face as he tucks a lock of hair behind my ear. "He says I'm the jealous one, but it's the other way around. My sophomore year, I made the varsity baseball team. It was the same year Tony also made varsity as a junior. I got a scholarship to play Division One baseball at Florida State, but I went into the draft instead. Tony didn't get any scholarships and if he wanted to play professionally, his only chance was to try out for any league and hope he got scouted. The Seattle Warblers selected me as the first overall pick. For two years, I played in the minors until I was called up. Tony quit playing and went into coaching instead. He couldn't stand the idea that he was older than me, but I was better. He wanted everything I had, including you. When I told him I was interested in you, he swooped in and took what I wanted." His head falls back as he stares at the ceiling. "Back then, I didn't notice it. I thought it was more of a brotherly competition, but now it's more obvious than calling water wet."

My head falls. "I fell right in his trap."

He rests his finger under my chin, forcing me to meet his eyes. "It's not your fault. I've changed. You've changed. The only person who hasn't changed is Tony. If anything, he's an even bigger narcissistic asshole than he was before. He lies and cheats his way through life."

"Yeah, he lies like a Persian rug." I blow out a deep breath. "Also, I'm sorry for the ghosting comment."

He bends down, resting his forehead against mine. His thumb brushes against my cheek. "It's okay," he murmurs.

I shake my head. "No. It's not." I pull away from him. "I don't know why I said it. You've shown me time and time again how sorry you are, and I keep throwing it in your face. I'm sorry. Please know that I forgive you for what we'll no longer talk about." I huff out a humorless laugh before I bite my lips together. My stomach churns as I wait for his response.

With his finger under my chin, he forces me to meet his gaze. "I forgive you too."

He presses a soft kiss to my lips. When he pulls away, I blow out a sigh of relief. The dark cloud looming over me finally dissipates, but soon enough, another rolls in.

My shoulders slump. "I need to tell Georgia what happened. If I was in her position, I'd want someone to tell me. Tony can't get away with this."

"Based on his track record, it's best to tell her sooner rather than later. I'm sure he's already spun up a web of lies to make you look like the bad guy and him the victim."

"You're right. It's time to take the trash out." I reach over to the nightstand and pick up my phone. I pull up her number and send her a message, seeing if she'll meet with me once I'm back in Harbor Highlands. When I finish, I set down the phone. "We have a few hours before we need to be at the airport. What should we do?"

"I can think of a few things, and they'll all have you screaming my name." He rolls us over so he's on top and his mouth slants over mine.

Two hours and several orgasms later, we're at the airport. People rush past us while Garrett has his arms wrapped around me in a hug. Goodbyes with Garrett are the worst. It's my least favorite thing in the entire world. I swear we spend more time saying goodbye than actually being with each other.

"I'll call you when I land, since you'll arrive home first."

I nod into his chest. He presses a kiss to the top of my head. "Are you sure you can't come back with me to Harbor Highlands? I promise to make it worth your while."

His chest rumbles with laughter. "As tempting as the offer is, I have to meet with my agent, and the team has a big charity event at the local children's hospital before we start spring training."

I huff. "I guess the kids can come before me." I give him a teasing smile.

"Thanks for being so understanding. The kids appreciate it. But we'll text, call, FaceTime, and we'll plan for whatever we can in between. Okay?"

I nod. I'm afraid if I open my mouth, I'll tell him I love him. That I've always loved him. Our first time shouldn't be standing in the middle of a bustling airport saying goodbye.

He rests his finger under my chin, forcing me to look at him. "Later, Tater." His lips curve into a smile before pressing against mine. It's something I'll have to burn into my memory since it will be a while until the next.

"Later, Home Run Playboy," I whisper against his lips.

"Remember, it's Home Run Stallion." He winks.

When I'm in Harbor Highlands again, I head to Porter's. Rylee's working, and I need to tell her everything and ask for advice on approaching Georgia about the Tony's-a-fucking-idiot situation.

When I stroll through the door, she does a double take before her eyebrows pinch together. "I thought you were in Chicago?"

I flop down on a stool in front of her. "Do you want the long version or the short?"

"I want every detail."

In between customers, I fill her in on the whole Tony situation and how he tried to kiss me, but I finished it with Garrett coming to see me. "But my biggest issue is telling Georgia." I rest my chin on my hand. Rylee has always been our resident problem solver. While most of the time it revolves around relationships, any advice she has is worth listening to. Hence, why I need her now.

"No one wants to be the bearer of shitty news. On the other hand, she deserves to know. Your best approach is going to be honesty, and you need to do it without Tony around."

"I know. That's the plan. Georgia is amazing and I love our friendship. I'd hate to lose that."

"Unfortunately, it's up to her to decide who she wants to believe." She shrugs.

I nibble on my thumb nail, contemplating my game plan. "There's no way I'll go to their house. I have no idea if Tony is there or if he's still in Chicago. Considering she has her storefront now, I'll try there first. I'll be happy if I never see him again."

"But isn't that going to be hard when you're dating his brother?" She flashes me a wide grin.

I drop my head to the bar. Complicated comes back and rears her ugly head. "It's not like Garrett is super close to Tony. Their relationship has been teetering on the edge since before I dated Tony. I'll leave that one up to Garrett on how he wants to navigate it, and I'll back him."

"Awww. Look at you being in a relationship and making decisions. Soon, you'll be the proud owner of the baby balloon arch and declaring your love for your man."

When Rylee was pregnant, we sat in her kitchen prepping for her baby shower, and I got her to admit she loved Trey. *Pats self on the back.* "Let's back the baby balloon train up. Even calling this a relationship is a stretch."

"You light up like a Christmas tree every time you talk about him. You might not realize it yet, but I saw this happening months ago." She grabs a pint glass and pours a beer from the tap before passing it to a customer. She rests her palms on the bar and leans in. "Tell Georgia about Tony," she pushes off and rises to her full height, "and then dive headfirst with Garrett."

A laugh bubbles out of me. That's exactly what I want to do. As I push away from the bar, the sound of my stool scraping across the linoleum floor fills the air. "Wish me luck. I hope she doesn't shank me or something."

"Call me from the hospital if she does!"

I give her a wave and a hopeful smile over my shoulder as I exit Porter's.

It's still been radio silence since the first message I left Georgia. I'd hate to do an uninvited drop in, but I have to tell her. While sitting in my SUV, I pull out my phone and call her number, making one last attempt to reach her. The call goes straight to voicemail, so I try again, and voicemail. This time I leave a message. "Hi, Georgia. It's Dessa. Please give me a call. We need to talk. It's really important." I press end and blow out a breath before dropping my head against the headrest. No doubt Tony has already told her some bullshit story.

I drive downtown to where her store is located. I cross

my fingers that she's there and she's alone. At the curb, I shift my SUV into park. A plain black awning hangs over the front as brown craft paper covers the windows, but they're illuminated by a light inside. She's here, or at least someone is. I step out and tug my coat tighter around me as my boots crunch in the snow on the sidewalk. Once I reach the door, I pull off my mitten and knock. Several seconds pass until Georgia peeks through a lose flap in the paper and glances at me. Then she disappears. I think for a moment she's walked away, but instead the lock clicks and the door swings open. I step out of the way and glance up at Georgia. Her hair's pulled back in a high ponytail and a purple cable knit sweater drapes over one shoulder.

"What do you want," she leans against the doorframe, crossing her arms, "besides trying to kiss my husband?"

I cringe at the words, not because I did anything wrong, but Tony now just gives me the ick. "That's not how it happened at all. I don't know what Tony has told you, but he is the one who made a pass at me. When I said no, he threw me out. I swear that's what happened."

Her face softens a fraction. "Why should I believe you, someone I've only known for a month, over my husband."

"Honestly, I understand it's hard to believe, and if the roles were reversed, I'd be hard-pressed to not believe my husband as well. But I know Tony. Right now, I have nothing to lose while he could lose everything." The tension leaves my shoulders. "This is what he does. Garrett punched Tony because when Tony and I dated, he cheated on me, and Garrett overheard him talking about it. Yes, it was in the past, but it definitely shows on his track record." I inhale a deep breath. Georgia stands in front of me, motionless as she absorbs my every word, her blank expression not telling if she believes me or not. But I continue anyway. "After the fight, Tony lied to me and said

Garrett was jealous of my friendship with him, and that's why Garrett punched him." She drops her arms and wrings her hands together. I'm crossing my fingers that she believes me. "You're a great person, Georgia. We've only known each other for a month, but I love the friendship we've built, and I don't want you to get hurt. That's why I'm telling you all this. I'm sorry. Please call me if you need anything. Anytime." I flash her a tight-lipped smile. "Thanks for hearing my side. Bye."

With that, I stroll down the sidewalk and toward my SUV. Halfway down the block, I hear my name, and I twist around.

Georgia is only a few steps away. Her arms envelop my shoulders in a warm, tight embrace. "Thanks," she whispers. Hurriedly, she lets go and practically sprints back to her store.

Things may be okay between Georgia and me. Or I really hope so anyway.

Chapter 32

WRONG BALLS

Garrett

It's been over two months since I saw Dessa in person. Held her in my arms, kissed her sweet lips. Granted, I've loved building an emotional connection with her and not just a physical one. But fuck, I need the physical. My hand can only be a poor substitute for so long. I pull up our spring training schedule.

During the eight weeks of spring training, there are three breaks in our schedule. The perk of spring training being in Arizona is the warm weather. No one wants to play ball in Seattle, or any northern state, in February. The day off in the middle of an away game and a home game will be perfect for Dessa to come visit.

At the start of my career, they told me which games I was playing, and I went, no questions asked. Now because of my status in the league, I've been able to negotiate which games I play and which ones I don't. Not traveling for the away game, I'll get an extra day with Dessa.

First, I make a phone call to Jake. Since I want this to be a surprise, I arrange to get her the necessary days off before purchasing the plane ticket.

I peer at the time on my phone. Dessa should be off work and at home by now. She gave me her work schedule, so it's easier to coordinate phone calls, especially surprise ones with happy endings. I pull up her number and press talk, and it rings a few times before she answers.

"Hey! I was just thinking about you."

"Happy thoughts, I hope."

"The happiest. I just bought a new bra, and I think you'd approve."

"Send me a picture or it didn't happen."

A few seconds later, a picture text pops up on my phone of Dessa wearing a black sheer bra. The outline of her hard nipples is prominent as they push against the fabric.

"Fuck. Tates. You look absolutely amazing."

"You mean my tits look amazing since that's all the picture was?"

"No. I'm picturing you, your whole body, in this picture."

She laughs. "What's up?"

Shit. I had a reason for this phone call, then I got sidetracked with nipples and sheer fabric. "What are you doing in two weeks?"

"Let me check my calendar. Oh, look at that, I'll be washing my hair."

I laugh. "Well, how about this? You come to Arizona, and you can wash your hair here."

"Arizona?"

"Yeah. In two weeks, we have a day off between games. That's the perfect time for you to visit for a long weekend." I cross my fingers she doesn't fight me on this. I need to see her. Touch her. Feel her.

"I'll have to check my work schedule."

I smile. "It's already taken care of."

"What do you mean?"

"I already talked to Jake and convinced him to give you Thursday through Monday off so you can come visit me."

"Wait, I didn't agree with this yet."

"Are you telling me no?"

"No. I mean, I'm not telling you no, but I need to book a plane ticket and a hotel."

"Already taken care of. Check your email. I'll wait." There's rustling, followed by the clacking on the keyboard.

"You bought me a plane ticket. You can't keep buying me plane tickets."

"This is more for selfish reasons than anything. In fact, this is really for me. And you don't need a hotel. I have an apartment."

"Okay. With the airfare and sleeping arrangements taken care of, what am I supposed to do while you're busy?"

"I'll have two days off so I can show you around the city, or I can show you my bed. Either or." She laughs, and it's the most beautiful sound in the world. "Then you can come watch a game."

"So, I get to watch you play with your balls all day?"

Now it's my turn to laugh. "And you can play with them later that night."

"Am I supposed to watch the game by myself? I'm not going to know anyone."

"I'll introduce you to some of the other players' wives and girlfriends."

There's a moment of silence and I pinch my eyes shut at the word "girlfriend." While we've never had the talk, I consider her my girlfriend. There is no way in hell I want to be with anyone else. If I had to guess, she feels the same way.

"Since you have everything mapped out, I can't wait!"

I'm standing in baggage claim waiting for Dessa to come into view on the escalator. Her plane landed eight minutes ago, so I should see her soon. Her sleek black hair glistens as the sun streams in through the atrium. When she glances up, our eyes connect, and I do everything in my power to not shove people out of the way to race up the escalator so I can wrap my arms around her a few seconds early. Instead, I reach down and hold up the sign I made for her. Her gaze wanders from me to my sign before a laugh bubbles out of her. She shakes her head and buries her face in her hand. When she's a few steps off the escalator, I drop my sign to my side. With a hand around her waist, I haul her to me, turn my baseball cap backwards, and press my lips to hers. Since we're in public, I keep it PG.

"I'm so happy you're here. I've missed you so fucking much," I whisper against her lips.

"I missed you too. But you could have done without the sign." She glances down.

"What? You didn't like it? I worked so hard on it." We both stare at the neon green poster board with thick, black lettering that reads "Have you seen my Taters?"

"Oh yeah, I could have definitely done without the sign." She giggles.

"How about you hold this," I pass her the sign, "and I'll take your luggage?"

When we arrive at my apartment to drop off Dessa's

belongings, I give her the real greeting I wanted to give her at the airport, which involved me stripping her out of her clothes and burying my face between her legs. I'm pretty sure she forgave me for my sign after the two orgasms I gave her.

After we're dressed again, I take her to my favorite gastro pub in town. We grab a seat on the outside patio. I order a Cubano sandwich, while Dessa orders the black bean and brown rice burger. We share a plate of Korean cauliflower.

"So, on top of your place in Seattle, you also pay for an apartment in Sedona?"

"I do. It's more comfortable than a hotel room for two months. I get my own space with my own things. Plus, two of my buddies are in the same building, so it's nice." The server drops off our drinks. I swallow a gulp of my beer while Dessa sips her Arizona spiked tea.

She crosses her leg over her knee. "What do you do with it for the other ten months of the year?"

"Wilcox, Salter, and I hired someone to handle sublets for us. With all of us being in the same building, it makes it easier."

"That's really smart."

I take a sip of my beer. "Have you talked to Georgia lately?"

She cuts a piece of cauliflower in half with her fork. "She texted me to say it was over between her and Tony. I didn't want to pry for details. I figured if she wanted me to know, she'd tell me." She stabs the cauliflower with her fork and puts it in her mouth.

"I get that. Fucking Tony. I can't believe he did that." I sit up and rest my elbows on the table. "I mean, I can. I just figured he would have grown up by now. You can't play puppet master with people's lives. Even though he likes to try." I pluck a piece of cauliflower off the plate and pop it in my mouth.

"Maybe when I'm back in Harbor Highlands, I'll call Georgia to check on her and see how she's doing. Invite her over for drinks or something."

"I bet she could use a friend right now." I reach over and place my hand on her thigh, running my thumb back and forth over the thin fabric of her leggings.

"Yeah. She doesn't have anyone. We can bond over how much of an asshole Tony is." She half smiles. "We could make little voodoo dolls or something."

"Remind me not to piss you off." I squeeze her leg and wink. The server delivers the rest of our meal, and we chat about my spring training schedule.

When we're finished, Dessa leans against her chair. "That was so good. You might have to roll me out of here." She rests a hand on her stomach.

"But you have to carry me out of here first."

She laughs. "Like I could carry you. What is that?" She points off into the distance. "The tall fence."

I follow her finger. "That's a batting cage."

She turns to me, brows pinched together. "They still have those?"

"They do. Want to go hit some balls?"

Her eyes light up. "Yes!"

I pay for our meal, and we stroll around the block to Strike Zone. The setup for these batting cages is a little different from most. They have different tiers from beginner to expert. We opted for the expert with a sliding net, so we can either have a pitcher behind a net or use a pitching machine. Since this is for fun, I opt to pitch the balls to Dessa. Once I'm in position behind the net, I tilt my head at Dessa on the plate. Her feet are too close together, and her hand position is wrong. I drop my arm to my side. "What are you doing?"

"Getting ready to hit the ball."

"No. You're not. Your stance is all wrong."

The bat drops to her side. "What's wrong with my stance?"

"Everything." I toss the ball to the ground and jog toward her. I position myself behind her. "For one, your feet are too close together." I rest my hand on her hip and slide it down the side of her thigh until I reach the back of her knee. With her help, I slide her foot out. "Your feet need to be about shoulder width apart." I slowly drag my hand up her side.

She glances over her shoulder and wiggles her ass against my dick. "Like that?"

A guttural groan escapes me. My head falls back as I stare up into the sky, willing all the blood in my body to head north again. "Yeah, something like that."

She twists to face me, and her head bumps into the brim of my hat. I lift it and turn it backwards.

Her tongue peeks out, wetting her bottom lip. "I don't know why, but it's hot when you wear your cap like that."

I lean in, my mouth centimeters away from the shell of her ear. "Does it turn you on?" She slowly nods. "Trust me, if there weren't other people around, I'd take care of that, but in the meantime, we need to fix your grip."

Her mouth drops open as if she's offended. "What's wrong with my grip?"

"You're choking the bat."

"I thought it liked to be choked." She smirks.

I lean in so only she can hear. "No, that's you."

She laughs. "I can't deny that I like your hand on my throat."

My dick twitches. Fuck, all it takes is one sentence for

her to turn me on. I clear my throat. I'm getting distracted from the task at hand. Her presence is a distraction. The best fucking distraction. I correctly position her grip on the bat and stroll behind the pitching net.

With her knees bent, her perfectly round ass sticks out. There's determination on her face, and it's the sexiest fucking thing I've ever seen. I step to the side of the net and throw her an underhand pitch. With all her might, she swings the bat and hits nothing but air.

"You were close, but a little high!"

"Maybe your pitch was low!" She kicks at the dirt, planting her foot before perfecting her stance. This time she does it without needing my help.

Again, I throw the ball, and she swings. *Crack.* The ball sails over my head before hitting the net and falling to the dirt.

She drops the bat and jumps up and down. "I did it! Did you see that?!"

"You're a pro! We'll sign you tomorrow!" I toss her a few more balls, and she's about fifty-fifty with her batting average.

Once she's done, we switch spots, but I opt to use the pitching machine instead. Dessa stands on the other side of the fence behind me.

"I like the view from back here."

I glance over my shoulder. "Are you looking at my butt?"

She tilts her head and taps her lips as if she's considering her answer. "It's a nice butt."

"I see how it is." I pop my hip and stick out my butt even more. "You're only with me so you can look at my butt."

"Among other things. But this is certainly a perk. It ranks high up there with the orgasms."

I draw even more attention to my ass by rubbing small circles over one cheek with my hand while also giving her air kisses. "I never took you for an ass woman."

A giggle bubbles out of her. "This whole performance solidifies yours is the only one I want."

I drop the bat and spin around. I slam my palm against the stop button for the pitching machine before stalking to the opening of the fence. Her brows shoot to her hairline as I cup her face in my palms. "Good answer." My lips are on hers. Firm. Hot. Demanding. If we were alone, it would last much longer. "I'm definitely hot for your ass." My hand slides down her back until I'm cupping her curvaceous ass.

She wraps her arms around my waist, mimicking my pose with a hand on each ass cheek. She shrugs. "It's only fair."

"You're not wrong." I stare into her deep brown eyes. Three words dangle on the tip of my tongue. I just need to spit them out. I've known she's the only woman for me since we were teenagers. If I were granted an additional minute for every thought of her, time would stretch into eternity.

"Are we just going to stand here all night, holding each other's butts, or are we going to hit some balls?"

Her words pull me from my thoughts and slap me back to reality. "You can definitely play with my balls."

She giggles, and with both hands she shoves at my chest, pushing me away.

"You're welcome to stroke my bat as well." She picks up a baseball and throws it at me. I catch it and toss it up in the air. "Wrong balls."

Chapter 33

BEST. WORKOUT. EVER.

Dessa

I twist my head on the pillow. The other side of the bed is empty. I sit halfway up and peek at the clock before flopping down and throwing the blanket over my face. It's way too early to be up, especially after the sex coma Garrett put me in last night. To say he's making up for lost time is an understatement. I'm pretty sure if I try to walk, I'll be a little bowlegged. Who knew baseball players had so much stamina?

Besides the sex, I love being with Garrett. It's like having my best friend back. We joke, we laugh, we chill, and it's all so comfortable. But the distance sucks. Long-distance relationships…er, friendships, or whatever we are: zero stars. Do not recommend. At this point, I'm one hundred percent invested. He's my one. My only. My forever.

A door clicks shut followed by footsteps. As they grow louder, I peek my head over the edge of the blanket. I'm greeted by a six-foot-four baseball Adonis wearing black gym shorts that hang low on his hips. I suck my bottom lip in my mouth. He lifts the hem of his shirt to wipe his face, exposing his chiseled abs and the dark strip of hair that disappears under his waistband. Instantly, my nipples grow hard. This is what I want to wake up to everyday.

After I finish drooling, I finally weave together enough words to form a complete sentence. "You worked out this morning?"

"Yeah. A workout is a great way to start the day." He yanks his shirt over his head.

Let more ogling commence. "But it's like nine in the morning." I sit up a little farther on the bed and prop myself against the headboard. "Your idea and my idea of working out are two completely different things. I prefer my workouts without clothes and in bed." A sultry smile plays on my lips.

Lust fills his irises as he stalks toward me. His palms rest on either side of my hips and he leans in, his lips inches from mine. "I could get on board with the no clothes." His mouth slants over mine in a brief kiss. Then he presses a kiss to my cheek and down to my jaw. His hot breath sends a chill through my entire body. "I could give you a workout right now," he murmurs against my skin.

I lift my chin and turn my head to the side to give him better access as he places open mouth kisses on my neck. "Does me watching you work out count as a workout? Because I'd totally be down to watch you do some pushups." I drag my fingers over his forearm and up to his bicep.

"That could work." He untangles me from the blanket. His heated gaze rakes over my bare legs, my navy blue lace panties, and stops at the Warblers logo across my chest. My hard nipples stretch the dark gray fabric. "Get on the floor." His voice is deep and gravelly, like he's fighting the need to ravish me right this second.

I scoot to the edge of the bed, and he helps me off. I sit cross-legged in the middle of the expansive bedroom floor. "What are you doing?"

"Just trust me. This will be enjoyable for the both of us. Spread your legs."

I inch my legs apart.

"More than that." He grips my knees and spreads my legs until I'm practically doing the splits. Then he situates himself in the pushup position between my legs.

My eyebrows pinch together. "What are you doing?"

He smirks. "We're both going to enjoy my workout." He bends his elbows and lowers himself to the ground. When his face is hovering inches above the apex of my thighs, instead of pushing up, he runs the tip of his nose over my lace-covered pussy. My breath hitches as a scattering of goosebumps covers my arms. When he pushes up, he peers up at me and winks before he lowers himself again. This time he peeks his tongue out and presses it against the lace. A shiver runs up my spine. He does it again and again. Each time the thin fabric grows more damp.

Before he descends again, he says, "Take them off."

Without hesitation, I lift myself up and slip one leg through the waistband and let them dangle around my ankle on my other leg. He dips again, this time licking up the length of my pussy. I moan from the contact.

He pushes up. "Spread yourself with your fingers. I want to see you glistening for me." With two fingers, I do what he says. "Fucking gorgeous. Just waiting to be devoured." When he lowers himself again, he holds his position as his tongue laps at my pussy. I cry out his name as I buck my hips, wanting more of him. He pushes up.

"Fuck, my girl is greedy. I better give her what she wants."

"Yesss." My teeth sink into my bottom lip. The anticipation of his mouth on me again drives me wild.

This time, when he lowers himself to the floor, he drops to his elbows and wraps his arms around my thighs, holding me in place. He continues lapping and sucking at my pussy. With two fingers he spears my entrance, filling me, and my hips jerk.

My mouth falls open on a gasp. "Oh! Oh yes! Right there. More. I need more." I reach up and dig my fingers into his hair, holding him in place. With every stroke of his tongue, every curl of his fingers inside me, my body lights up like a firework display.

"I'll give you everything, Tates. Everything." He wraps his lips around my clit and sucks.

My body jerks as my grip on his hair tightens. With the flat of his tongue, he gives me another teasing lick. "I want. To give. You. Everything. I—I—I love—" My eyes roll to the back of my head. The slow burn that started in my belly finally explodes as pure, blissful pleasure roars through me. "Oh. God. Garrett!" I clench around his fingers as waves of pleasure crash into me. My breathing slowly returns to normal as my orgasm subsides. Garrett crawls up my body, and I cup his cheek with one hand, the short stubble tickling my fingertips. His lips press to mine. I taste myself on him and for some reason, it turns me on even more.

"How was that work out?" he murmurs against my lips.

"Every morning should start with a workout."

"You know what needs to be done after a workout?"

I shake my head, still recuperating from my orgasm.

"Shower." He pushes off the floor and stands.

Desire pools between my legs once again when I catch

sight of his cock tenting his shorts, the loose fabric doing nothing to conceal his hard-on. He holds his hand out and I wrap my fingers around his before he tugs me up. We enter the en suite bathroom, a long two-sink vanity sits on the right, and along the far wall is an enormous walk-in tile shower with glass walls. He turns on the hot water and when he returns, I wrap my fingers around the hem of my shirt to lift and then he takes over, the fabric dragging up my body and over my head.

He cups each breast, his thumbs brushing over each stiff nipple. "All I want to do is wrap my lips round your tight nipples and suck." His tongue peeks out, wetting his bottom lip. Slowly, his hooded gaze drifts to mine. Steam billows out of the shower surrounding us in a haze. "But if I start now, I won't stop. And I have so much more planned for you."

"If that's the case, you're still wearing too many clothes." I hook my thumbs into the elastic waistband of his shorts and yank down. The thin, silky fabric drops to the floor. His long, thick cock juts out, brushing against my hip as a bead of pre-cum glistens at the tip. His hand clasps around the nape of my neck and he hauls my mouth to his in a searing kiss. With our lips fused together, he pushes forward until hot water rains down, cocooning us from the outside world. My hands roam over the planes of his body, over every dip and curve of his chest and abs, until my fingers wrap around his cock.

A low, rough sound comes from the back of his throat. "What do you want, Tates?"

I stroke him once. "I want this." I stroke him again. "In me." Three times. "Fucking me."

He spins me around, pressing my back to his front. His cock slides in the crack of my ass as his hand snakes up my belly, past my tits, until his fingers wrap around my throat.

My head falls back, hitting his chest, and his other hand lands between my legs. His finger runs up and down my slit.

"How do you want it?" His words are a whisper against my ear. "Should I bend you over and fuck you from behind? Or should I pick you up and thrust my dick into you?" My breath hitches at the last one. "I got my answer."

He nips and sucks on my skin below my ear as the water from the rain shower pours over us. It's exotic and sensual at the same time. I press my ass into him and bend my knees slightly, so his cock slides between my cheeks.

"Fuck," he growls, slow and deep, "I need to be inside you." He spins me in his arms and lifts me like I weigh nothing.

My legs wrap around his waist, anticipation building as I wait for his cock to fill me, but nothing happens. I drop my gaze as I run my hand over his cheek. "What's wrong?"

"Condoms are in the other room."

I press my lips together. This is Garrett. I trust him wholeheartedly. "I'm on birth control. We can go without."

"Are you sure? I get tested regularly. I'm negative." The tip of his nose brushes against mine.

"Same." With my hand, I move his head, lining my lips up with his, and kiss him. It's gentle and sweet. My tongue curls around his, sliding back and forth. He presses me against the glass wall and reaches between us. He lines himself up with my entrance before pushing me down. His cock fills me, stretches me. I break away from our kiss so I can breathe.

He continues to thrust into me, keeping a steady rhythm. "I love this between us. No barriers. You feel so fucking good."

My nails dig into his shoulders. I'm almost positive I'll leave permanent indents. "Yes! Yes! Me too." My clit rubs on his pubic bone in just the right way sending waves of euphoria rippling through me, causing my body to come alive. The pressure builds and builds inside me like a pressure cooker. "I'm not going to last much longer."

"You feel too good. Your tight pussy is choking my dick." His grunts mix with my moans.

"Garrett. Oh. Garrett."

"Let go, Tates, I'm right behind you."

Somehow, he pushes deeper, and I cry out. My moans and whimpers echo across the tile. A second later, his dick twitches, and his hot cum spills inside me. He continues to pump his hips until every last drop is gone. I brush a strand of wet hair off my forehead. Holy shit. Shower sex needs to be added to the rotation. Garrett pulls out of me and sets me on my wobbly feet.

He cups my cheeks and rests his forehead against mine. His breathing is still slightly labored. "That was…"

I smile. "Best. Workout. Ever."

"That's what I was thinking too." He presses his lips to mine in a soft kiss. We finish the rest of our shower while keeping our hands to ourselves, mostly. Once we're finished, Garrett wraps a towel around me before grabbing one for himself. He steps into the bedroom while I dry my hair. A booming voice echoes through the apartment, and I freeze.

"Put your dick away, Playboy! We have to get to the stadium!"

"You're the only one who needs to put his dick away!" Garrett yells back.

"If you didn't want me entering, you should have put the dripping ice cream hair tie on the doorknob. That's what it's for," the other voice says.

He pokes his head through the doorway. "Don't worry about him. That's Randy Wilcox. We call him Smokey. He sounds like a chain smoker, yet he's never touched a cigarette in his life. Between me, him, and Joe, we kind of have an open-door policy. Unless there's a certain hair tie on the door, but it resembles more of a dripping cone of jizz than ice cream." He shakes his head and I laugh. "When you're finished getting ready, come out and I'll introduce you to everyone."

I nod. Why does meeting the friends seem so serious? Maybe because I'm new to this entire side of his life. Both nerves and excitement twist in my gut. I'm nervous because I've never met them before and excited because we're taking a new step in our relationship. My hands tremble as I delve into my suitcase, sifting through the contents until I find a pink Warblers shirt and a pair of jean shorts. I shove my feet into a pair of strappy sandals while I run a brush through my hair. After I apply a light covering of make-up, I blow out a deep breath. Here's to the next step.

Chapter 34

MY NEW LIFE

Dessa

When I stroll from the bedroom into the living room, I'm met with six sets of eyes watching me. I sheepishly smile at everyone and give a small wave, slightly self-conscious. Garrett turns to me, his eyes full of affection, and in a few steps, his fingers entwine with mine. He gives my hand a comforting squeeze, simmering my nerves a little.

He bends down and whispers, "Don't be nervous. Everyone will love you." He turns his attention to his teammates and friends. "Hey everyone, I'd like to introduce you to Dessa." Over the next several minutes, I officially meet Randy, the center fielder, and his pregnant girlfriend, Tori, along with second baseman Joe Salter, his wife Melanie, and their two kids. Cora is an adorable four-year-old with curly red hair and Blake, who's six years old, has a mop of thick, dark brown hair like his dad.

With a swift motion, Garrett snatches his backpack off the floor and effortlessly tosses it over one shoulder.

Turning his attention to me, he says, "We have to head to the stadium for our pre-game workout and meetings. These lovely ladies will take care of you." He presses his lips to mine. My heart jumps to my throat as my eyes go wide. This is the first time we've kissed in front of other people. I'm unsure if he meant to do it or if it was out of habit. He pulls away a fraction of an inch.

"Did you mean to kiss me—"

"In front of everyone? Yes." He gives me another chaste kiss.

"Enough with the making out. You'll have plenty of time to do that after we win," Joe teases.

Garrett holds up his hand, about to give him the middle finger, thinks better of it with the kids present, and waves him off instead. He cups my cheek. "I'll see you at the stadium."

The guys leave and Tori and Melanie turn to me, wide, knowing grins on both their faces.

"Tell us everything," Tori says.

"We've never seen Garrett so invested in someone. Even when he was with that one girl. The model," Melanie adds.

Months ago, I remember seeing Garrett in the tabloids with a model on his arm, and every time, I'd roll my eyes. I don't know if it was jealousy or spite seeing him with someone else when it was so easy for him to leave me. But looking back, he was never smiling. He never looked at her like he looks at me now. It solidifies what we're doing, what we have, what we share, is real.

Cora tugs on her mom's shirt. "Okay. Let's go get lunch, then we can interrogate Dessa." Melanie winks, then adds, "Only if you want."

"Sure. Even though there's not much to tell," I say with a shrug.

Tori's dark eyebrows raise to her hairline. "With the way he looks at you, I'm sure there's a lot to say."

We all climb into Melanie's SUV, and she drives us to a restaurant a few blocks from the stadium.

After we're seated and food is ordered, Tori turns to me. "How did you and Garrett meet?"

How complicated do I want to make this? I'm not really one to share my life story with strangers, so I go with a simplified version. "We were friends a long time ago and then we lost touch for ten years before reconnecting at his brother's wedding." I take a sip of my water.

"Oh, so there's a lot of history." Tori rests her chin on her hand and leans in.

Cora sits on Melanie's lap while Blake sits next to her drawing in an activity book when she asks, "So you haven't experienced the full baseball life yet?"

I shake my head. "I get the gist, but no, I've never actually done it. What's it like? What's the game-day routine?" This is something that's always fascinated me. Garrett's told me about his day-to-day routine, but I don't know how it is from a partner's perspective.

"It all depends on where we are. Sometimes we'll go out for food before a game, sometimes we'll eat at the stadium. We'll watch the game, and then afterward we'll hang out in the family room while the players finish their post-game interviews and workout. Then we do it again the next day."

I nod along with everything Melanie's saying. I know baseball is a grueling schedule. Could this be my new life? "Do you two also live in Seattle?"

"We have a condo in the city, but we also have a house in Florida. Joe and I both grew up in Melbourne, so that's where we like to go in the offseason," Melanie says.

My eyes go wide. "Wow. So, you have three different houses."

Melanie nods.

"Same here," Tori adds, resting a hand on her small baby bump, "except we stay in Seattle during the offseason. Also, I'll add, we don't necessarily go to every game because it can be a lot of travel, especially once the baby comes. Instead, if the team has a charity event, the wives or girlfriends will attend those in lieu of a game. It lets us be supportive outside of just being at the game."

My mind is blown. I never would have imagined the significant others would play such a prominent role at these events. "Was it hard to adjust to living your life on their schedule? Did you give up your own careers to follow theirs?" Now that the floodgates have opened, I have all the questions. Things I never thought about before. I don't know if I want to give up who I am to follow someone else's dream.

"I won't say it's easy," Melanie says, "but it's gotten easier over time. It's become our routine. A part of our daily life now. They play one hundred sixty-two games a season, then more if the team makes the playoffs. But the four or five months Joe's not working is the most amazing time. He's home and so attentive to the kids. We get a lot of family time in during those months, so it kind of makes up for the time he's away."

I nod along, hanging onto her every word. This could be my life someday. "It's especially hard for Garrett and me right now because he lives in Seattle, and I live in Minnesota. We wouldn't necessarily have those four or five months together."

"When you date a baseball player, you date baseball." Tori laughs. "I didn't expect everything to be like this. I readjusted my work schedule as a fashion blogger so I could do it remotely. I've been super lucky with that."

"I'm a bartender. It's not something I can do remotely." I laugh.

"Then it becomes a personal decision and one you'd have to talk out with Garrett. I will say you'll develop a bond with all the wives and girlfriends over time. We're like family. Melanie has helped me a lot with what to expect with having kids and traveling." Tori rests her hand on Melanie's. "We've become like sisters." Melanie gives her a warm smile.

Over the next hour, we chat about their lives and mine. There's definitely a bond between the baseball wives and girlfriends that not everyone understands. If this becomes my life, it will be great to know I'll have an entire support system waiting with open arms.

After lunch, we head to this stadium. I follow Melanie and Tori's lead since I'm the newbie. At the box office, we collect our family seating tickets the guys had set aside for us. A security guard escorts us to our entrance. As we stroll through the tunnel, the sunlight grows brighter as it opens to the field. This stadium, being their spring training field, is smaller with less seating, but there's still a decent size crowd. We hike up the stairs to our seats a few rows up behind the Warblers' dugout. Sitting on the edge of the folding seat, I scan the field until I spot Garrett. A rush of emotions, from excitement to sadness, flows through me at seeing him in his uniform and a backwards Warblers cap. I hate that we lost so many years away from each other. But I love seeing him in his element. He was always meant to play baseball. Watching him on the field, it's clear this is his dream. Bonus points, him wearing his uniform is a total thirst trap.

Over the next several minutes, I'm mesmerized by

Garrett as he catches balls and tosses them back to another player. The kids yell for their dad and wave when they have his attention. Before the game is about to start, each team goes to their respective dugout. The Warblers are up to bat first. After the first batter strikes out, Garrett walks out onto the field. He swings the bat, loosening up his arms before he steps up to the batter's box. He bends his knees, hands slightly parted, gripping the bat. The pitcher for San Diego throws. The ball crosses the plate a little high, but the ump calls a strike. My foot bounces against the concrete. Come on, Garrett. He retreats a step and loosens his shoulders before returning to the plate. Once again, he gets into position. The pitcher slingshots the ball toward the plate and Garrett swings. The bat connects with the ball, sending it soaring to center field. It bounces off the ground before the San Diego player catches it. Garrett rounds first base and sprints toward second. The outfielder throws the ball toward the second baseman. When Garrett's a few feet away, he dives, sliding on his stomach. His fingertips graze the base just as the second baseman tags him with his glove. The ump waves his hands, signaling safe.

The Warblers finish their at bat with one run scored by Garrett. Now I get to watch him do what he does best. He saunters onto the field and stands behind home plate. He laughs with the ump before crouching down. I can't help but drop my gaze to his ass. Seconds before the pitcher throws the ball, Garrett moves to his knees and kicks his leg out. As the ball sails through the air, the sound of cheering fills the stadium. The batter swings, but the ball lands directly in Garrett's glove. The ump calls a strike. I clap my hands and scream from my seat. With the next pitch, the batter makes contact and sends the ball flying toward the outfield, where Randy acrobatically catches it, resulting in an out. The second batter strikes out. The third batter hits the ball deep to center field. Randy catches it, then throws to Joe while the runner rounds third base. Come on. Come on. I wring my hands together. Joe throws to Garrett, and within seconds he snatches the ball out of the air, swoops his arm down and tags the player out. I jump to my feet, cheering and clapping.

The Warblers win four to two. After the game, Melanie and Tori take me to the family room where we'll wait for the guys to finish their post-game workout. They introduce me to some of the other players' wives and girlfriends. I exchange numbers with Melanie and Tori, and they tell me they hope to see me at more games. Garrett's signature scent wafts around me seconds before he wraps his arms around my waist from behind and presses a kiss to my cheek.

"The best part of the day was knowing you're here waiting for me," he murmurs next to my ear.

I spin around in his arms. "The best part was watching you play. You did amazing."

His fingers graze my temple, sending a flutter through my chest as he brushes a strand of hair behind my ear. "It's because you were in the stands watching. I had to impress you."

"Get a room!" Joe yells from the other side of the room.

Garrett laughs, and I drop my forehead to his chest to hide my embarrassment. He twists his head to the side to face Joe. "That's an excellent idea. I think we'll do just that."

Chapter 35

SO FUCKING SCREWED

Dessa

It's been a month since I visited Garrett in Arizona. We chatted almost every day, either with a phone call or FaceTime. Of course, it got difficult to sync our schedules especially when his games can either be in the afternoon or in the evening. In between work and talking to Garrett, I got drinks with Georgia. She told me she filed for a divorce from Tony. While he never admitted to trying to kiss me in Chicago, she caught him blatantly flirting with other women. She's served him the papers, but he's been dragging his feet on signing them. I'm sure it's to squeeze out whatever he can from Georgia like the snake he is. The last she heard, he left Harbor Highlands and has been spotted in Chicago. Since Georgia recently opened her new handbag boutique in Harbor Highlands, she's decided to stay here instead of going back to Chicago where her family is. She says Chicago may be big, but it's not big enough if Tony's there. I reassured her she'll always have a place with us.

I change the channel to the Seattle-Houston game at Porter's. If I can't see Garrett in person, watching him play on TV will have to suffice. They're still doing warm-ups while the announcers discuss the game. My heart flutters every time I get a glimpse of Garrett in his uniform. Is it wrong that it turns me on as much as it does? I wonder if that's some sort of fetish other baseball players' partners have. I'll have to ask Melanie and Tori. He does like seeing me wearing his jersey, so I guess it's the same for me to see him wearing his.

"I've never seen anyone with actual hearts in their eyes." Nora rests her elbow on the bar next to me. She picks up a cardboard coaster and fans me with it.

I twist to face her. "What are you doing?"

"You're panting. I thought I'd cool you down."

I laugh and yank the coaster from her hand. "I am not."

She studies me with a quizzical raised eyebrow. "So, when did you know you were in love with Garrett?"

My heart skips a beat. "Love? What are you talking about?" The words have been on the tip of my tongue several times, but it sounds so much different when someone else says them. I love that we've reconnected. I love watching him play a sport he loves. My pulse races whenever I'm with him. He sends tingles through my entire body whenever he touches me. He's constantly on my mind. Anticipation bubbles within me thinking about hearing his voice or catching a glimpse of his smile on video chat. He's the only one I want to be with.

"If the way you're staring at the TV, at Garrett, isn't love, then all the books and all the movies have been telling me nothing but lies." She quirks an eyebrow at me before she adds, "Go for it. It's clear he loves you just as much." Without another word, she turns away and helps a customer at the other end of the bar.

I do love him. I'm screwed. So fucking screwed. My gaze flits to the TV as the camera pans his way. He removes the Warblers cap and flips it backwards before setting it on his head. He's talking animatedly to one of his coaches and then his face lights up with his signature dazzling smile. I miss him. So damn much. Two weeks. I'll get to see him when he plays in Minnesota in two weeks.

It's Friday night, and I settle in to watch tonight's game on the TV. Since I had to work earlier, I wasn't able to make it to today's game in Minneapolis, but Garrett got me tickets for tomorrow. I click the button on the remote and flip to the channel for the game when a scrolling banner on the bottom of the screen says tonight's game has been canceled. I check my phone, but I have zero messages from Garrett about the game getting canceled. My heart sinks. I was looking forward to watching Garrett… er… the game, tonight. I guess I'll have to wait until tomorrow to see him.

A knock on my front door startles me. Mentally, I do a quick rundown of everyone who could possibly be knocking on my front door right now. Lach and Nora are both at work. I just got off the phone with Rylee, and she's at home. Jake would never come to my house. Tony's gone AWOL, and Georgia is meeting with some investors. Another knock echoes through my townhome, only louder this time. I throw the blanket off my lap and race to the front door. I rise to my tippy toes and peek through the peephole. All that comes into view is the top of a Warblers baseball cap. My heart does a backflip. My fingers fumble to unlock the deadbolt, and I yank open the door. His head drifts up, deep emerald eyes stare into mine.

"W-what are you doing here?" I ask.

"It's pouring rain in Minneapolis and not letting up anytime soon. Since they canceled the game, I told the manager I was going to make a drive two hours north."

I hold the door open and motion for him to come in. "You drove all the way up here to see me? What did your manager say?"

He laughs. "He told me if I'm not on the field by one, he'll be using my balls to throw the first pitch. When Skip makes a threat, you don't take it lightly. And I'd rather not have to catch my own balls."

I scrunch my nose and giggle. "That sounds exactly like Jake. When he says something, he means it. Plus, I kind of like your balls. So, your manager's name is Skip?"

"His name is Cory Lockwood, but Skip is a nickname some managers go by." I nod along. "Anyway," a slow grin spreads across is mouth, "I have eighteen hours before I need to be at the field."

"And two of those will be spent in a car. So, what are you planning on doing with those sixteen hours?"

"Well first, I'm going to kiss you because it's been way too long since the last time." He presses his lips to mine in a soft, lingering kiss. He pulls back, entirely too soon, and rests his forehead against mine. "Next, as much as I want to ravish every inch of your naked body, it will have to wait until later. I have other plans first."

I drag my fingers over his chest. "I really like the first option."

"I promise," he kisses me again, "the wait will be worth it." His heated gaze drops. "While I love you in this white Warblers tank top," his finger hooks under the strap, slides it over my shoulder, and presses a warm kiss on my bare skin, "I certainly won't be able to keep my hands to myself. So, I'll need you to change."

I press my hips into him. His growing erection digs into my belly. "What should I wear?"

"Something warm. We'll be outside."

"Oookay," I drawl out, not entirely sure what he has planned, but I trust him. I spin around and he smacks my butt before I run up the stairs and tug on a pair of dark skinny jeans and a cream colored sweater. When I make my way downstairs, Garrett's standing by the door.

"Now that I'm dressed, are you going to tell me where we're going?"

"The Harbor Highlands Huskies are playing tonight. Their pitcher has been drawing a lot of attention. I'd like to see him play."

"So, on your night off from baseball, you want to watch baseball?" He nods. A soft smile forms on my lips. "Baseball really does flow through your veins."

"I eat, sleep, dream of nothing but baseball. And you." He winks.

A laugh bubbles out of me, and I playfully slap his chest. "Good save."

Garrett drives us across town to Atwood Stadium, where the Huskies play, a Double-A minor league for the Mallards. Garrett buys our tickets, and we find a spot on the steel bleachers. Stadium lights flood the field as the sky darkens above us. I've never attended a Huskies game, but they appear to be fairly popular since a majority of the seats are taken. After we sit, Garrett wraps his arm around my shoulder, and I snuggle into his side. I love the warm comfort of him next to me. It's becoming my favorite thing in the world. Being with him feels so natural, like we're meant to be.

Since we got here late, we catch the last five innings.

Throughout the game, he tells me what they should have done, what they did right, and what they did wrong. Some people may take that as arrogance, but Garrett's anything but. Baseball is his life, people should listen to what he has to say about the sport.

"Have you ever thought of going into coaching? Once you're done playing baseball."

He taps his chin. "I haven't put a lot of thought into it. If all goes well and I avoid injury, I could still play another ten years."

"With your knowledge, I think you would be great at it. It's something to consider."

He nods.

The Harbor Highland Huskies win eight to five. When the game is over, everyone shuffles out of the stands, including Garrett and me. Before we reach Garrett's rental car, he stops and turns to me. "Aren't the Hillside ball fields close to here?"

"Yeah, it's only a couple of blocks." I point toward the sidewalk path that leads in that direction.

"Let's check it out. I haven't been there since high school."

A light breeze kicks up, and I wrap my arms around myself.

"Are you cold? We don't have to go."

"No, we can keep going. You'll just have to keep me warm."

"My pleasure."

He wraps his arms around my shoulder and pulls me to his side. His scent invades my senses. It's comforting. It's my home. *He's* my home.

Chapter 36

THIS IS THIRD BASE

Garrett

With Dessa tucked against my side, we continue to stroll down the tree-lined sidewalk. We've lost a lot of time, but I'll spend the rest of eternity giving her the sun, the moon, and all the stars. We arrive at an opening flanked by two baseball fields and a couple of concession buildings. The field lights are off, but the streetlights illuminate the ground enough to light our way. It looks exactly how it did all those years ago. Then I freeze, and Dessa jolts to a stop.

"What the hell? They're selling Hillside Fields?" I stare up at the giant yellow and white For Sale sign.

"Oh yeah. They're trying. It's been for sale for close to eight months."

I drop my arm from around Dessa and slide through the opening of the gate and onto the field. Dessa trails a few steps behind me. My gaze wanders over home plate, past the dugout, and to the outfield. "I have a lot of good memories here. I won my first Little League tournament over on field number two."

"And rumor has it you scored a home run with Lauren Pierson in the dugout on field one." Dessa playfully elbows me in the side.

"Keyword *rumor,* and that's all it was. She wanted to, but I turned her down. She lived up to the name base chaser. When I said no, she got cozy with Clint Walker, who was more than willing to give her what she wanted."

I stroll behind home plate and crouch so I'm balancing on the balls of my feet, nostalgia hitting me like a sack of bricks. "For some reason, it looks so much smaller now."

"Probably because you're in the big leagues."

"I also hit my first home run on this field. My parents still have the ball in my old bedroom. I should pick it up and bring it back to Seattle with me." I stand next to home plate and swing a pretend bat. "What do you say, want to play a game?"

"Um. What kind of game? Because I don't think a game of hide the bat is appropriate for a public baseball field."

A deep laugh rumbles out of me. "I get you can't keep your hands off me, but this is an innocent game of baseball."

"It's rarely ever innocent when it comes to you." She side-eyes me with a playful half smile. "Wait. There's not a bat or balls."

I shrug and return a smile of my own. "Use your imagination. Stand at home plate and pretend you're the batter." My hands grip her shoulders, and I move her into position.

"What is this? Some sort of kinky role-play you're into?"

"You've always had a smart mouth. Later, I'll be sure to

put that mouth to work." I press my lips to hers in a chaste kiss. "For now, just go with it, Tates."

She rolls her eyes but does as I say. Standing next to the plate, she squares her shoulders and bends her knees, exactly how I showed her in Arizona. I stroll to the pitcher's mound and turn to face her. "Are you ready?"

"For the imaginary pitch? Yes." She wiggles her butt.

I laugh. I hold my fist in one hand, lift my knee, and sling shot my arm forward. She swings the bat. I yell, "Strike one!"

She drops her arms to her sides and rises to her full height. "Why was that a strike?"

"You need to be quicker than that."

"That's total bullshit." She laughs.

"I'm just calling the plays like I see them."

"But it's imaginary! Fine," she throws her hands in the air, "we'll call it a strike since I swung." She gets into the batter's stance again.

"Also, I need my ball back."

"But it's imaginary."

"I still need it for the next pitch." Even from the mound, I can see her roll her eyes. She bends over, giving me a nice view of her ass as she picks up the imaginary ball and throws it to me. I jump and with one hand in the air, I catch the imaginary ball. "When did you get an arm? Maybe you should pitch."

She laughs. "Just throw the ball."

"Widen your stance a little. Wiggle your ass for good measure." She laughs and gives it a little wiggle. "This one is going to be a curveball to the inside. Are you ready?"

"I'm always ready."

"That's my girl." I pitch the ball again and with all her might, she swings. From the pitcher's mound, I cup my hand on top of my eyes and look into the sky, following the pretend ball. I swing my gaze to Dessa as she stands at home plate. "What are you doing? Run!"

Dessa starts to run, then freezes before throwing the imaginary bat into the dirt. She jogs the baseline toward first base.

"You have to run faster than that!"

"I can't! I'm wearing three-inch ankle boots!"

With a sudden burst of speed, I dart to the left and close in on her, meeting her halfway to the base. I wrap my arm tightly around her waist, effortlessly twist her around, and hoist her over my shoulder. My arm locks her legs in place against my chest. She laughs in surprise. I continue to run the baseline until my foot lands on the base. Slowly, I lower her to her feet. Her body slides against mine the entire way down. I grab the bill of my cap and flip it around, shoving it back on my head. With both hands, I cup her cheeks, and press a kiss to her soft lips. "First base." I hoist her over my shoulder again and she giggles as I jog across the field to second base. Once my feet are on the base, I lower her to her feet. I slide one hand to the back of her head and the other around her waist and to her ass. I pull her to me and kiss her, pressing my tongue against the seam of her lips. She opens and moans into my mouth. My tongue curls around hers for a few strokes before I break away.

Her eyelashes flutter open. "Let me guess, third base is next?"

"You're catching on." I lift her over my shoulder again. She giggles as I follow the baseline to third. Once I'm on the base, I lower her to the ground.

"And this is third." She reaches down and cups my dick over my jeans. Softly, she strokes me as my dick strains against the zipper.

I groan. "There's only one problem. We're wearing too

many clothes." I slide my hand under the hem of her sweater, and my fingertips trail up her stomach. Her breath hitches when I palm her breast over her lace bra, brushing my thumb over her stiffening nipple.

Her mouth falls open slightly. "If you keep that up, you might just make it home." A bolt of lightning zigzags across the sky, lighting up the entire field. Both of us tilt our heads up to the sky. "It's going to rain," she adds.

A droplet of water splashes onto my forehead. "Or we just have that much electricity between us."

She laughs. "Would you like some wine with that cheesy pickup line?"

I throw my head back in laughter. "Only if I can lick it off your body." I nuzzle my nose into her neck and press my lips against her skin under her ear. "Should we take this all the way to home plate?" Another bolt of lightning flashes across the sky.

"Yeah, and we better make it quick."

I pick her up again. This time she rests her hands on my shoulders and twists her head around so she can see where we're going. When I'm only a few steps from home plate, I slow my pace. As soon as my foot lands on home, I release my grip, and she slides down my body. Her hands roam my chest and abs, leaving a tingling sensation in their wake as her feet find solid ground on the base. "Look at that, you got a home run."

"We got a home run." She stretches on her tippy toes, wraps her hands around my neck, and tugs me down for a kiss just as another bolt of lightning dances across the sky. Seconds later, the roar of thunder echoes over the field. With her lips still pressed to mine, the skies open and rain pours over us. I wrap my arms around her waist, holding her to me, neither of us caring about the rain or getting wet. The only thing we're concerned with is each other.

Holding each other. Kissing each other. Loving each other. I know without a doubt, I love Dessa. I always have. For the rest of my life, I always will.

She pulls away, her lips a hairsbreadth away from mine. "Should we continue this in the dugout until the rain passes?" I nod. She grabs my hand and leads me toward the third base dugout and through the open gate. Rain pings against the metal roof as it shields us from the downpour. I sit on the steel bench and guide her to straddle my lap. As she sits, I slide my hand along her upper thigh, around her waist, and link my fingers together at the top of her ass. Her arms drape over my shoulders, and I drop my head into the crook of her arm, resting my cheek against her chest.

"I can't believe they're selling this place."

"I know. We've had a lot of great memories here. I remember you forcing me to throw pitches to you, even though I had to be like five feet away from the plate so I could throw you a semi-accurate ball."

My shoulders bounce with laughter. "Are you telling me you didn't have fun?"

Her fingers play with the wet hair at the back of my neck. "No, I did, mostly because I got to spend time with you."

"By the end of summer, you were able to throw the ball fifteen feet with pretty good accuracy."

Her gaze drops to my chest. "We've come a long way since then."

"My biggest regret has been the last ten years without you." I hold her tighter, afraid to lose her again.

"My biggest regret was not smacking you upside the head and telling you to kiss me at the dock."

We laugh. "But we can't live with regrets. We're here now and I fully intend to spend the rest of my life with you." I lift my head and peer up at her. "You're my everything. You're all I need." My thumb brushes against the bare skin on her lower back from where her sweater has ridden up. "I don't know how I survived ten years without you in my life. I was a shell of a man, only going through the motions. The last four months with you has resuscitated me. You're the sunshine after the rain, and I've had nothing but rain clouds looming over me." With one hand, I reach up and cup her cheek, forcing her gaze to meet mine. "I love you, Dessa. I've loved you for over half my life, and my biggest regret is not telling you sooner."

She cups my cheek, her thumb brushing over my two-day stubble. "I love you, Garrett. As much as I wish we could rewind and rewrite history, we may not be here without it. Right now, it's pretty perfect."

"I know we've been keeping it casual, and I haven't been casual with anyone else."

Both her palms cover my cheeks, and I lean into her warmth. "Me either," she murmurs.

My mouth goes dry. I've done this before, but this time it's different. My fingers play with the belt loop on the back of her jeans. "What do you say we turn this casual into exclusive?"

Her fingers drop to my shoulders and freeze. "Is the Home Run Playboy asking me to be his girlfriend?"

What I really want to ask is for her to be my wife, but it might be too soon for that, so I nod so those words don't accidentally tumble out instead.

She giggles. "Use your words. Ask me."

The corners of my lips tip up in a smile. She used my own words against me. Again. I sit up straighter and pull her closer to me. "Dessa, will you do me the honor of being my girlfriend?"

She tilts her head and taps her lips, pretending to contemplate her answer.

My heart jackhammers in my chest. The anticipation is killing me. I thought her answer would be yes, but as the seconds tick by without a word, I wonder if she actually has to think about it.

"I guess they'll have to start calling you the Home Run Boyfriend."

Heat radiates through my chest. "One correction. *Dessa's* Home Run Boyfriend." I tilt my head up and press my lips to hers. This is our story. But it's only a matter of time until I change boyfriend to husband.

Chapter 37

BECAUSE I HAVE YOU

Garrett

The following day, I arrive back in Minneapolis and stroll into the clubhouse with thirty minutes to spare. Fortunately for me, Skip will have to use actual balls instead of mine for the first pitch. Dessa followed me in her vehicle, and when we parted ways, I left her with Melanie and Tori until after the game.

After our pre-game warm-up, I'm in the locker room with Smokey, Joe, and the shortstop, Bishop, as we all change into our uniforms. Since last night with Dessa, I've thought a lot about the future and what I want it to look like. Without a doubt, I want Dessa by my side. But will the baseball life be too much for her? Is that something she'll want for the long term? She's gotten a glimpse of it over the last month, but half a year, every year, is a lot to ask of someone. Then what happens when we start a family? Growing up, Dessa's always talked about wanting a big family since she's an only child. She said it got lonely. I want to be the man who gives that to her. My locker door slams with a heavy clank, and I turn to Joe, who's sitting on the bench tying his cleat.

"Is it hard starting a family while playing baseball?"

He peers up at me and freezes. "Starting a family? Where is this coming from? Is there something you're not telling us?"

I rub the back of my neck. "You guys know Dessa—"

"Shit. Did you put a ring on her finger?" Smokey asks.

"No." I drop my hand. "Not yet anyway, but I know she's the one I want to spend the rest of my life with. Eventually, that life will include kids."

"I'll be honest," Joe says, "it's not always the easiest since you're gone half the year. Sometimes you'll miss out on birthdays and other holidays."

"Didn't Ramirez miss the birth of his child?" Smokey adds.

"Oh yeah, his wife went into labor a month early. He was halfway across the country and couldn't get there before his daughter was born," Joe says.

Bishop chimes in, "I missed my son's first steps and his first word. Luckily, Sara recorded a video to send to me. While it wasn't the same, it was still exciting to see."

"I know Tori was a little apprehensive when she got pregnant. She wasn't sure how everything was going to go. But a lot of the other wives and girlfriends have been a great support system for her. They welcomed her with open arms. She's told me their support has really eased her fears," Randy says.

I nod. Not only do the players become like family, but so do everyone's partners. It's a baseball family. I know Dessa enjoys hanging out with Tori and Melanie whenever she comes to a game. Maybe my own fears are getting in the way. If others can make it work, I can too. I know

Smokey takes over parenting duties for Melanie after a game so she can have a break. It's a true test of compromise. The post-game party scene isn't me anymore, so I don't have to worry about that. The hardest thing might be convincing Dessa to shift her life to follow my dream.

When I step out onto the illuminated field, the brim of my cap shields my eyes as I stare up into the stands and immediately spot Dessa wearing a dark blue number seven jersey. Cora sits on her lap giggling and kicking her feet as Dessa tickles her. The smiles on both their faces make my heart swell. One day, that could be Dessa and our daughter.

The start of the game begins like every other game. While in the dugout, I rub my thumb on one of the pennies Dessa gave me before tucking it into my back pocket.

Joe's at bat first. He drops the ball behind the third baseman, giving him a single. I'm the second batter in the lineup, and when I'm at the plate, Joe steals second base. Like a ninja, the Minnesota pitcher catches him and throws to the second baseman, tagging him out. That was the start of our comedy of errors… for the entire night.

I manage to get on base with a single, but Ramirez hits the ball to the second baseman, forcing me out, who then throws the ball to first for a double play.

When we take the outfield, Minnesota hits a home run on the first pitch. Two more players get on base before Holloway, our pitcher, delivers the last strike.

At the next inning, I'm squatting behind the plate. I signal to Holloway for a slider. As the ball soars toward the plate, the batter swings, nicking the ball with the top of his bat. The ball spins backwards and smacks my catcher's mask, getting lodged between the metal wires. Five minutes later, and with help from the ump, we release the ball. Minnesota scores two more runs, one because of an erratic throw to home plate even Stretch Armstrong couldn't catch.

When I reach the dugout, I peel off my mask and slam it against the bench. "What the fuck, guys? We need to get our shit together."

"Same goes for you, Playboy," Carlson, the right fielder, snarks.

"That's why I said 'we.'" I yank off my cap and run a hand through my hair. The whole situation with Dessa has my head swimming. I need to talk to her, and the sooner the better. I'm chalking that up to my shitty playing, but I don't know what everyone else's excuse is. Throwing myself onto the bench with a thud, I reach next to me and grab a handful of BBQ sunflower seeds and shove them into my cheek like a chipmunk. I'm desperate for anything to calm my frustration and sometimes my favorite snack, that I can only get in the Midwest, helps me. Mom even sends me the occasional package stuffed full of bags of the sweet and salty snack, so I'm not without while in Seattle.

At the seventh inning, we're down four runs. As in we haven't scored a single run. We can still come back—we just need a few good at bats. I rake my hand through my hair as my leg bounces on the balls of my foot. From next to me on bench in the dugout, Ramirez backhands my bicep to get my attention.

I twist my head toward him. "What the hell, man?"

He points across the field to the jumbo screen. I follow the imaginary line outside the dugout, across the field, and to the enormous screen spotlighting Camila.

"Is that your ex-girlfriend?"

My stomach plummets to the dirt. Fuck. What the hell is she doing here? She's only ever been to one game of mine, even though I invited her to all of them. And I certainly didn't ask her to this one. This is the cherry on top of my shitty evening.

By the ninth inning, we've scored one run but still get decimated six to one. We haven't experienced a loss this devastating in quite some time. It fucking sucks. As much as a debilitating blow the loss is, I tell myself it's part of the game. Overcoming the loss will always be the greatest challenge.

After my shower, I throw on sweatpants and a hoodie. I sling my backpack over my shoulder and make my way to the family room where Dessa's waiting. As I enter the room, people mill around with whispered condolences, and we'll-get-them-next-times.

When Dessa spots me, she excuses herself from the conversation with Melanie and Tori and greets me, wrapping her arms around my waist. "Sorry about the loss."

I press a kiss to the top of her head. Having her here with me takes a little bit of the sting away. "Thanks."

"Do you want to stay for a while?"

"Nah. Let's get out of here." I nod toward the exit.

"Okay." Dessa waves goodbye to Melanie and Tori before lacing her fingers with mine.

As we stroll across the stadium, I'm thankful one nightmare is over, and I've escaped the other. It's still a mystery why Camila showed up tonight, but I have Dessa so it's irrelevant.

"Garrett!"

I pinch my eyes shut. My name coming out of her mouth grates on my last nerve. Our breakup, if you can call it that, was amicable. But after being with Dessa, I now know it would have never worked with Camila, and she's not who I want. I increase my stride, but Dessa stops, forcing me to halt in my tracks, and she spins around.

"Oh…" Dessa's voice trails off.

"Garrett! Wait!" Camila's heels clack against the cement floor atrium.

I turn on my heel and face her since running away isn't an option. "What are you doing here, Camila?" I try to keep the bite out of my tone but fail miserably.

Her brows draw together as she purses her bright red, stained lips. "You invited me here. At first, I thought it was weird that you were sending me messages telling me you weren't over me and you wanted to see me again. But it was kind of cute. Like pen pals, sending love messages to each other."

Now it's my turn to be confused. "I never messaged you." I peer down at Dessa as she meets my gaze. "I never messaged her."

Dessa nods in understanding.

"You did," Camila exclaims. "You told me how sorry you were that we broke up and you want to try again. That's why I'm here."

"Look." I rub the back of my neck. "I don't know who you were talking to, but I assure you, it wasn't me. In fact, I'm with someone." I nod at Dessa.

Camila's face falls. "Oh." She holds her hand out to Dessa. "Nice to meet you, I'm Camila."

Dessa clasps her hand. "Hi. Dessa."

After they shake hands, I pull Dessa against my side, making it clear I'm taken.

"What was the phone number that messaged you?" I have a hunch, but I want Camila to confirm my suspicion.

She pulls her phone from her purse and unlocks the screen.   "Two-one-eight-five-five-five-two-two-six-one."

Turning the phone around, she flashes me the screen. "You told me you changed your number."

Dessa tenses against me and I shake my head. "Fucking Tony," I mutter. "Look, I'm sorry you got dragged into this. Unfortunately, you were a pawn in someone's game of fuck with my life. It's best if you ditch that number."

Camila's shoulders drop and she nods. Her gaze flits to Dessa and back to me. "In that case, it was good to see you. It was nice to meet you, Dessa." She offers her a small wave, and Dessa gives her one in return. She turns and strolls in the opposite direction.

Dessa's eyes widen. "What the hell is Tony doing?"

"I don't know, but he's not getting away with it." Yanking my phone from my pocket, my fingers twitch as I pull up Tony's number. It rings several times before the voicemail picks up. I step away from Dessa, mostly so she's not subject to what I'm about to say. "I don't know what the fuck you're doing, but it's best to cut the shit," I seethe through gritted teeth. "You're dragging innocent people into your bullshit. If you haven't guessed, I'm not dealing with your shit either. Leave us alone."

As I end the call, Dessa's arms wrap around my waist. I shove my phone into my pocket and drape my arm over her shoulder.

"Do you think he'll do anything else?"

I huff out a deep breath. "I don't know, but it would be in his best interest if he didn't."

When we reach the hotel, I hold the key card to the pad until it turns green and push the door, holding it open for Dessa. This whole thing with Tony has rattled my brain, but he's not my focus right now. Dessa's here and she's my number one priority. After we both step through, the door clicks closed behind us. I drop my bag to the floor. "I want to talk—"

She spins around, a sultry gleam in her eyes, before she stalks toward me. Her palms rest on my chest, pushing me until my back hits the door with a heavy thud.

"What are you doing?" My voice is low.

Her fingers run along the waistband of my sweats. "I won't always be around when you have a bad game or a bad day, but I'm here now, and I want to make you forget about it, so you'll have a clear head for the next one."

Her hooded eyelids lift. Brown eyes meet my green ones. Her hand roams over the front of my sweats until she's cupping my dick. She slides her hand up and down, stroking me over the fabric. I groan and drop my head against the door. She hooks her thumbs under the waistband and lowers herself to her knees, taking my sweats with her. My dick springs free, jutting out between us. I suck in a sharp breath when her hand wraps around me. I love her hands on me. Her tongue peeks out, wetting her bottom lip. I thread my fingers through her hair, pushing it out of the way for a better view. Her full, pink lips wrap around the crown and she sucks. My eyes roll back. The next best thing to having her hands on me is having her lips wrapped around me. Her wet, hot mouth continues to slide over my shaft. She pulls off with a pop and with her free hand, she continues to stroke me while she wraps her lips around my balls and swirls her tongue.

"Fuck Tates. Your mouth feels so fucking good sucking me." She hums around my balls, and I swear I'm about to burst. Another guttural groan escapes my throat when her lips slide down my length. "I want to fuck your pretty pink lips." She moans her approval. I tangle my fingers in her hair and slowly rock my hips. The tip of my dick hits the back of her throat. She gags around me but opens her mouth wider.

I'm seconds away from exploding in her mouth, but I want to be inside her when I come. I release my grip on her hair and pull away.

She whimpers before glancing up at me through her lashes. "What's wrong?"

"I want to be inside you." I bend down, shoving my arms under hers and lifting her to her feet. She shrieks in surprise. I change positions and spin us so her back is against the door. She rolls her lips between her teeth.

"Strip." I leisurely stroke my dick as her fingers reach the hem of her shirt and she tugs it over her head. My gaze drifts to the black lace covering her tits. Her chest heaves as my eyes devour every inch of her. She pops the button on her jeans, shimmies them past her thighs, and kicks them away. Standing before me, she's wearing nothing but black lace.

"Fucking gorgeous." My lips meet hers in a soul-crushing kiss. My mouth moves to her neck, eliciting a sensual moan from her as her fingers intertwine in my hair. I continue moving south, peppering open mouth kisses across her chest until I reach her ample cleavage. With a swift motion, I tug down both cups and eagerly latch onto one nipple, then proceed to do the same with the other. I continue to slide down her body, hooking my fingers in the straps of her panties and taking them with me as I drop to my knees.

"Don't worry, I'm still going to fuck you, but first, I feast." I hike her leg over my shoulder. Her hand threads through my hair. A sharp sting bites my scalp as she positions me exactly where she wants me. Once in position, I lick up her center, and her back arches as she moans.

"So goddamn sweet." I flick her clit with the tip of my

tongue, and she squirms. I'll never tire of licking her pussy. Watching her come undone is an addiction, especially when she screams my name. I wrap an arm around her thigh to hold her in place. I spear her entrance with my tongue and continue to fuck her as she whimpers above me.

"Ah! Yes! Oh Garrett." She pants and moans while her nails dig into my scalp.

I continue lapping her pussy harder and faster with every pass. Her body shudders as she cries out her orgasm. Before she can catch her breath, I drop her leg to the floor and stand. With my hands on her hips, I lift and she wraps her legs around my waist. Using the door for leverage, I impale her on my dick.

Her mouth falls open in a silent moan as her nails claw at my shoulders. With an arm around her waist, I rest my other palm on the door and slide in and out of her.

"You feel so fucking good choking my dick."

"Fuck me, Garrett. Fuck me."

I nuzzle my face into the crook of her neck and pound into her. Our slapping skin mixes with my grunts and her moans. I drive harder and faster into her as her pussy clamps down hard on me, sucking me in. She arches into me as I lick and suck on her heated skin. She clenches down around me as her thighs lock around my waist. Her pussy spasms around my dick as another orgasm rakes her body. My balls tighten, and I can't hold on anymore. Her wet heat feels too damn good. I roar out, slamming my eyes shut as I come inside her. I glance at her face as my thrusts slow to a stop. Her chest heaves as she collects her breath. I brush my fingers over her temple, tucking a strand of hair behind her ear.

"I'm the luckiest man in the entire world."

She raises an eyebrow. "Because you get sex after a game?"

"Because I have you."

She claps her hands over my cheeks and presses a soft kiss to my lips. "And I have you." Her breath skates across my mouth.

I slide out and set her on her wobbly feet. "I'll clean you up."

I stroll to the bathroom and wet a washcloth with warm water. Afterward, we climb into bed. Dessa has gotten used to sleeping naked when she's with me, and I certainly won't complain.

She snuggles into my side, resting her cheek on my chest. "What did you want to talk about earlier?"

"Before I was rudely interrupted?"

"I don't recall you putting up a fight."

I slide my hand over the smooth skin on her back. "Yeah. What I had to say could wait."

Her shoulders shake with laughter. "What did you want to say?"

I blow out a breath and stare at the ceiling. "I know the relationship between us is new, but I've known you for over half my life. You're still the sweetest, kindest, caring, compassionate, and most beautiful woman now as you were back then. When I look five years, ten years, twenty years into my future, you're the one I see myself with." She twists in my arm and rests her palm against my cheek, and I lean into her warmth. "I love you Dessa. I always have, I always will. And I know I want to spend the rest of my life with you." Her breath hitches as fear and anxiety flit through her eyes. The corner of my mouth turns up into a half smile. "I'm not asking you to be my wife. Not today anyway. But I will."

Her features soften, maybe in relief. "I love you,

Garrett. I'm elated that you came back into my life, and we were able to work things out. You and me in a relationship is a lot and fast. As much as I want to be there with you every step of your career, I hate the idea of giving everything up. My life. My friends. My identity. I don't want to only be known as Garrett Dawson's girlfriend."

"I mean, that's a pretty cool title."

She laughs. "It's the best title. But I don't want it to be my only one. So, can we continue as we are for now while we find our footing?"

"Of course." I press a kiss to her forehead. "I'm always here, and always will be."

Chapter 38

OOPS

Dessa

It's been a month and a half since Garrett was in Minnesota. It's been a month and a half since we've seen each other in person. Long-distance relationships are not for the faint of heart. I think the one thing that's made it easier is we sort of started our relationship as long-distance. We've grown used to the phone calls and video chats to communicate, especially as a way of being intimate. Right now, it works for us. But it kind of has to.

Since I last saw him, Garrett's been to Philadelphia, Detroit, Seattle, San Francisco, New York, and Arizona. We've done our best to sync our schedules so we can have more than a few minutes of alone time. I found it works best when he has a night game on the West Coast because he only has to wait around an hour until I'm done with work.

After my shift today, I'm boarding a plane and flying to Seattle. Since I'm landing before him, he's arranged for a car to pick me up and he gave me the code to his condo so I can meet him there. He has a night game in San Diego and once it's finished, he'll do his post-game workout and interviews. Afterward, they'll board the plane and touch down in Seattle around one in the morning.

Behind the bar, I busy myself with anything and everything to make the time go by faster.

"I don't think I've seen the bar as clean as it is right now." Nora steps up next to me and grabs a pint glass, holding it under the tap until the golden beer kisses the brim.

I laugh. "I'm counting the seconds until I leave to see Garrett."

She passes the beer to a customer. "So, things are going well between you two?"

I nod. "Really good. Obviously, the distance throws a wrench into our relationship. I know he wishes we were closer, and I'm sure he'd make room in his closet if I asked him to."

She rests a hand on her hip. "Then why are you still here? Go be with him."

My shoulders slump. "But it's not that easy. Am I supposed to drop my entire life and stand in his shadow?"

"You will never be in Garrett's shadow. He would physically pick you up and move you to the sunlight before he let that happen."

I press my lips together. Who am I kidding? That's exactly what he'd do. I drop my gaze to the floor. "I'd hate to give up everything here."

"Look, I get that Porter's is awesome and everyone here is awesome, but Garrett's giving you an amazing opportunity. Why haven't you carpe diem-ed the fuck out of here, yet?"

"It's hard to explain."

"Lay it on me. Rylee has been giving me tips on how to help customers with their problems." Nora crosses her arms over her chest, waiting for my answer.

"But I'm not a customer."

"Humor me."

"Okay. For starters, my friends and all my family are here. I've never lived anywhere besides Harbor Highlands. Everything here is familiar and comfortable." I shrug. "It's what I know."

"All I'm hearing are excuses. I understand. It's hard to upend your life and do something completely different. Go somewhere completely new. Where you don't know anyone. When I came here, I was alone, but I found my place. In Seattle, you won't be completely alone because you'll have Garrett. And the way he looks at you, he is not going to let a single bad thing happen to you. Go be wild and free. Try something new. You know we'll always be here for you, no matter how many miles are between us." She gives me a warm smile.

She's right. Everything she said is right. Apparently, I needed someone else to tell me in order to believe it. I wrap my arms around her shoulders. Her body stiffens. "Thank you."

She blows out a slow breath. "You can make it up to me by getting tickets to a baseball game. Or hooking me up with a hot baseball player. I'm sure Garrett knows a few."

I pull away, a wide grin on my face. "I'll see what I can do."

When I arrive at Garrett's condo, I punch the code he gave me into the door lock, and it opens. I roll my suitcase across the threshold, and the door softly clicks behind me. I flip on the first light switch, and sconces light up a short hallway. On either side of me is a half bath and a laundry room. A den with a desk and bookshelves is on the right, and the end of the hallway opens up to the living room and open kitchen. I never imagined what Garrett's condo would look like, but the sleek and modern design with touches of gray and white fits him. I drop my suitcase off next to the couch and continue to meander around in the living room.

A few art pieces decorate the walls, otherwise, it's mostly bare. A dark gray leather sofa sits in front of the TV. I drag my fingers over a few men's health and lifestyle magazines sitting on the coffee table. Next to the TV are a few framed pictures of Garrett and some teammates, and one of us he took at the wedding. I pick up the picture of us and stare at his smiling face. Even though the picture was taken only months ago, it feels more like a lifetime. We've come a long way since then. I gently place it in its original spot. Lastly, there's one of his parents. Tony is missing, which doesn't surprise me.

I pass through the kitchen, turning on more lights until I reach a bedroom and a full bath. Everything is too clean and tidy to be Garrett's bedroom, so this must be a spare. I spin around and leisurely stroll to the other side of his condo, collecting my suitcase as I pass by.

With the flip of a switch, the darkness is replaced by a warm, inviting glow. Everything is neat and tidy, except for his bed, which is haphazardly made. A smile flits on my lips. Even all these years later, he still hasn't learned to make his bed. Growing up, his mom always got on his case about not making his bed and many times forced him to make it before he left the house. I drop my suitcase off in the corner of the room and flip on the switch to the en suite bathroom. The vanity is mostly clear except for a comb and a bottle of cologne. I lift the bottle up to my nose, basking in the familiar scent, before I spritz a little into the air.

Back in the bedroom, I spot a baseball sitting under a glass case on his nightstand. I bend at the waist to read the inscription on the plaque. "First Home Run Sophomore Year." My lips pull into a soft smile. It only feels like yesterday that I was sitting on the bleachers, watching him hit his first home run. We've come a long way since then.

My gaze drops. I bite my lips between my teeth, contemplating if I should open his nightstand drawer. I don't want to invade his privacy, but we're dating, so there shouldn't be any secrets. What's wrong with a little snooping? I hook my finger under the handle, twisting my head to the side, so I'm not looking, and I tug it open. *Oops.* I peek with one eye closed as if I'm waiting for a bomb to detonate at any second, but when nothing happens, I open my other eye for a closer inspection. All that sits inside is a remote control next to a couple of batteries, a book, and an unopened box of condoms. My heart does cartwheels when I catch sight of the plastic bag filled with all the pennies I gave him. With my hip, I slide the drawer closed before walking to the living room. I flop down on the cool leather couch, a neon pink sticky note on the remote control drawing my attention. Then I read the words, "The TV is already on the channel for the game. Love you, Tates. See you soon." My heart swells that he was thinking of me.

For the rest of the evening, I watch Garrett's game while chatting on the phone with Rylee. Of course, Garrett plays amazingly. He doesn't hit a home run, but he hits a few doubles which lead to runs by other players. Seattle beats San Diego eight to five. After the game, I strip out of my clothes and crawl into Garrett's bed. With my nose to the pillow, I inhale deeply, knowing when I open my eyes, he'll be here. I drift off to sleep with my arms wrapped around his pillow.

My eyelids flutter open, and I twist my head to peer over my shoulder. Garrett lifts the blanket and crawls under the covers. He wraps an arm around my waist as he tucks his warm body against mine.

He nuzzles the back of my neck. "It feels so good to be home."

My heart flutters when he says "home."

Chapter 39

ONE LAST SCARE

Garrett

Coming home to Dessa in my bed and waking up with her next to me is my new favorite thing in the world. I don't know how I survived the last ten years without her. Looking back, I was living, but wasn't truly experiencing life. Not until Dessa entered my world again. She's my home. I press a kiss to her bare shoulder.

She stirs awake and rolls to face me. "Good morning."

"It certainly is." I lift my chin and stretch to press my lips to hers.

A low moan sounds from her throat as she snuggles closer to me.

"Can this become a permanent thing? Waking up next to you in my bed? If I can have one thing, it would be this."

"It is pretty amazing." Her fingertips brush across my temple, swiping a strand of hair away. "But I do have a confession." Her hand falls and rests on my chest. Her gaze follows suit. "I snooped in your nightstand."

My heart lodges in my throat, and I freeze while trying to keep my expression neutral.

"I didn't dig around or anything. My finger just accidentally pulled the drawer open." She giggles.

I roll over and take her with me, so her back is against the mattress. Her dark hair fans over the pillow as my palms rest on either side of her, caging her in. "Oh, is that so? Accidentally pulled it open. You know what happens to bad girls who like to snoop around?"

She shakes her head, a sultry smile on her lips. "But I bet you're going to show me."

I nudge her leg open with my knee. "Someone has to teach you a lesson." I lower myself until I'm inches away from her mouth. Before my lips touch hers, I move to the right and graze her cheek until I'm placing open mouth kisses on her neck. Slowly, I move down her body, kissing every inch of her until I reach the apex of her thighs.

Several hours and even more orgasms later, we're still lying in bed enjoying each other's company. A deep growl rumbles through her belly. "I guess I can't continue feeding you only orgasms. I'll order us some real food."

"Can I have both?" She giggles.

"Always greedy." I press my lips to hers.

After the food is delivered, she meets me in the kitchen. She sits at the island looking smokin' hot in nothing but my jersey, and I'm standing on the opposite side. I stab my fork into my chicken teriyaki, scooping up some brown rice along with it.

"Have I told you Dawson is a good look on you?"

She smiles around a mouth full of tofu teriyaki and peers over her shoulder, even though she can't see the words. "It's growing on me."

"We can always make that a permanent change." I test the waters to gauge her reaction. If I had it my way, I would have put a ring on her finger months ago. I don't need all that get-to-know-each-other crap. I've known her for over half my life. She's the only person I see a future with. The sun rises and sets with her. All the stars were individually placed in the sky just for her. Before she seemed a little apprehensive, but now, not a single flinch.

"Dessa Dawson does have a nice ring to it." She smiles as she scoops up another bite.

"It sure does." I shove another fork full of chicken in my mouth to stop myself from grabbing the ring from my nightstand and asking her to be my wife right now.

"I never would have imagined Seattle as a place to eat good teriyaki, but this is delicious." Dessa moans around a fork full of tofu.

"Not only is it good, but it's also the best. Philadelphia has cheese steaks. New York and Chicago have pizza. And Seattle has teriyaki."

We continue eating and making small talk. Dessa tells me about some new drinks she's been working on while I tell her about the season so far. After we finish our lunch, I clean up our dishes. "There's somewhere I want to take you tonight."

"Where are we going?"

"If I tell you, I'll have to kill you… with orgasms."

She dramatically presses the back of her hand to her forehead. "Oh no! That sounds terrible." Her voice is high-pitched. "I'd be willing to take the chance for that punishment."

I bark out a laugh. "I bet you would." I lean in so my lips are next to her ear. "But you won't get it that easy."

She throws her head back in laughter.

My phone buzzes from the living room. Dessa turns her head. "Are you going to get that?"

"Nah. The only person I want to talk to is sitting next to me." I shove another fork full of rice into my mouth. The buzzing stops, but soon starts up again.

Dessa rises from her stool and strolls into the living room, picking up my phone from the couch. "It says Skip. Isn't that your manager?"

I swallow down my last bite of food. In a few short steps I'm meeting her next to the couch. Why the hell is Skip calling me on an off day? She passes me my phone and I pull up his number. It rings a couple times before he answers. "Hey. What's up?"

"Sorry to bother you, but there's something important I need to go over with you. Can you come to my office at the stadium?" Skip's tone is flat.

I can't decipher if I've fucked up or if there's another problem. Either way, it's a little unnerving. "This can't be said over the phone? I have company at the moment."

"It's best this is done in person. I promise it won't take long."

Something with his tone is off. Skip is either yelling at you because you fucked up or because he's proud of you. There's never an in between. Whatever this is, it must be serious. "Okay." I spin on my heel and walk toward my bedroom. "I can be there in twenty minutes." I end the call and toss my phone on the bed.

Dessa leans on the door frame. "Is everything alright?"

"I don't know." I yank a t-shirt from a hanger in the closet and pull it over my head. "I have to go the stadium for a brief meeting with Skip."

She strolls into the room and takes a seat on the edge of the bed. "For what?"

"I'm not entirely sure, but he wouldn't call if it wasn't serious." I grab a pair of jeans from the shelf and pull them on. "I'll be back in an hour or so. Will you be alright?"

"Yeah. Don't worry about me."

Bending down, I place a kiss on her lips. In the foyer, I pluck my hoodie from the bench, slide my feet into my shoes, and I'm out the door.

When I reach Skip's office, I knock on the door frame before poking my head through the doorway. "You wanted to see me?"

He lifts his head. "Garrett. Come in. Close the door behind you."

My palms sweat as I shut the door with a click. He motions for me to take a seat in the leather armchair in front of his desk. Once I'm seated, he clasps his hands in front of him. His hard steely gaze meets mine. "I'm going to cut to the chase. You know it's against club policy for any players or staff members to be associated with any gambling involving the sport?"

I'm clueless as to why he's asking me this. My heart is one beat away from busting through my chest. "Yes."

"There are rumors along with an anonymous tip that crossed my desk involving a G. Dawson placing bets against the Seattle Warblers. With the possibility of you throwing last year's game."

"That's bullshit!" What the fuck? Bets? "I didn't place any bets! And I certainly didn't purposely sabotage the game." I shove the chair away and rise to my feet. "It wasn't me! You're just going to believe some fucking rumors?"

"Garrett." His voice is stern. He nods at the chair. "Take a seat."

"Then tell me what's happening." I hook my foot around the chair leg, pulling it closer before I sit.

"The club investigated these rumors because players can't place bets on baseball."

"I know." I can't keep the bite out of my tone. My irritation grows stronger every second he doesn't tell me what this is about.

His hard gaze meets mine. "After the investigation, the name was traced back to a Georgia Dawson. Is that name familiar to you?"

My blood boils. Fucking Tony. This has his name plastered all over it. I pinch my lips together. "Yeah. That's my brother's wife—or ex-wife."

"It seems like he has some animosity toward you. At this time, he hasn't done anything illegal against the club, so there isn't anything for us to do, but if you need anything, let me know."

I nod before dropping my head in my hands. I'm done with Tony and his shit. This needs to stop. I rake my fingers through my hair, then meet his gaze. "Thanks, Skip."

On the drive back to my condo, I white-knuckle the steering wheel wishing it was Tony's neck instead. He's gone too far this time. Trying to jeopardize my career and involving innocent people while he does it. He has zero regard for anyone but himself.

I shift my SUV into park in the underground parking garage at my condo. Before stepping out, I unlock my phone and pull up Tony's number. I don't know if he got my previous message because he never responded, but I hope he gets this one. And that it's loud and fucking clear. My jaw clenches as the phone rings several times. His voicemail picks up. I steady my breathing before it beeps.

"I don't know what the fuck your agenda is, but it's not going to fucking work. Leave me alone. For good. I'm done putting up with your shit. As for Dessa, you better not touch her. Better yet, don't even go near her," I seethe. "It won't end like you want it to. It's time to move on." I end the call. I'm not sure if he'll stop, but I hope so.

When I push open the door to my condo, Dessa, who's now fully dressed with her hair pulled into a ponytail, races to meet me in the foyer.

"What happened?" Concern laces her voice.

"Tony. Tony happened."

"What do you mean?"

I intertwine our fingers and lead her into the living room, taking a seat on the couch. She sits cross-legged next to me as I fill her in on the whole story. For the rest of the afternoon we shove anything to do with Tony behind us. Dessa assures me we're strong together, and he can never break what we have. Never again.

Later in the evening, we exit my condo and head to the parking garage. Buildings zoom past us as we make our way across the city. Her face is glued to the window taking in all the sights, especially when the Puget Sound comes into view. I pull into an alleyway that opens to a small parking lot behind a large steel building.

She turns to me. "What is this place? Some sort of indoor batting practice to embarrass me?"

I laugh. "No, but we can do that next time. This is something more for your benefit than mine." Her legs press together as she squirms in her seat. "Are you okay over there? You're doing a lot of wiggling."

"When you said it would be more for my benefit, I imagined you taking me to a sex club and offering me multiple orgasms over and over again."

The corners of my lips tip up into a smile. "I can offer you the orgasms, but I don't need a sex club to do it." A pink blush covers her cheeks. "All the orgasms will have to wait because we're here."

I park the SUV and push my door open. I round the hood and meet her at hers. With her hand in mine, I help her out, and we stroll to the entrance. As we reach the awning-covered doorway, a small sign with Northwest Distillery on it catches her attention.

Dessa halts in her tracks. "Wait. I've heard of this place. They were voted the number one vodka distillery in the United States."

"And I got you a meeting with the owner."

Her eyes bulge with terror, and her face pales as she slowly turns her gaze to meet mine. Then she peers down at her outfit. "We're meeting Rebecca Langley, and I look like I just rolled out of bed."

I lift her hand up and place a kiss on her knuckles. "First off, you look absolutely beautiful and second, she's not here to judge you on your outfit." Her hand trembles in mine as her eyes flit back and forth as if she's on the verge of a panic attack. "We don't have to do this if you don't want to, but I thought it would be a great opportunity for you."

She blows out a deep breath and nods. "I really wish you would've given me a heads-up so I could prepare."

"So you could over analyze every detail, including your outfit?" I raise an eyebrow.

Her shoulders sag. "No. So then I would know what questions to ask instead of gawking at her like an obsessed fan."

"Be yourself. She'll love you. Just as much as I do."

A small smile spreads over her lips. Dessa is the most amazing, fearless woman I know. There isn't anything she can't do when she puts her mind to it. Including this. She shines the brightest when she's herself. I want her to move out here with me, and since she doesn't want to lose a part of herself, I'm hoping this meeting will help make that decision a little easier.

Chapter 40

CARPE DIEM THE FUCK OUT
OF MY LIFE

Dessa

Garrett pulls the handle and holds the door open for me. With his warm, comforting hand on my lower back, we stroll down a dimly lit hallway until it opens to a large bar area. Behind the floor-to-ceiling glass wall sits large stainless steel fermenter vessels for the vodka. Pipes run back and forth from one distillation system to another. In the middle of the room sits a dark mahogany horseshoe-shaped bar with small chandeliers dangling from the ceiling creating a warm ambiance.

On the far side of the room, a woman with light brown hair spots us from behind a small private bar. She strolls out wearing jeans and a Northwest Distillery t-shirt.

She stops in front of us, and Garrett holds out his hand. "Good to see you again, Rebecca."

Her hand clasps around his. "Likewise."

My heart hammers in my chest as I try to control my breathing so I don't pass out. It's like meeting Isabella

Rossi all over again, except without the notice. Garrett turns his attention to me. "This is my girlfriend, Dessa."

"It's so nice to meet you," Rebecca says.

I blink away my shock. "You too," I stammer, "I'm a huge fan of your vodka. It's one of the smoothest I've ever tasted."

"Thank you. That means so much to me. It's something we strive for here at Northwest." Rebecca waves for us to follow her to the private bar. "Let's get a few drinks and chat."

Garrett pulls out a stool and motions for me to sit as he takes the seat next to me. Rebecca stands behind the bar, grabs a couple of glasses, and proceeds to make us a drink using a bottle of vodka from the private collection. I lean forward for a better view of Rebecca artfully crafting our drinks when I spot the same book Garrett gave me with all my drink recipes. A giant knot sits in the pit of my stomach, and my wide-eyed gaze shoots to Garrett. "Why does she have my book?" I mouth.

All he does is smile smugly. He's up to something, and I don't know what it is.

Rebecca slides the drinks across the bar to us. "So, Garrett tells me you're a mixologist."

My fingers grip the glass. The cocktails sloshes back and forth as my hand shakes with nerves. Garrett's hand brushes over my shoulder, offering a comforting touch, and it helps. Knowing he's here with me, by my side, I know I have nothing to be nervous about.

"I dabble in mixing drinks." I take a sip of the drink she made. Maybe the alcohol will calm me.

"Let me say, I've made some of your drinks, and they are phenomenal." She grabs the book and sets it on the bar.

"Where did you get that?" I ask.

"Garrett passed it along to me and threatened that I needed to try these drinks because I'll never drink anything better."

Garrett laughs. "'Threatened' is a strong word. I advised her that it's in her best interest to try some, as they are some of the best drinks I've ever had."

"And he wasn't lying. I've tried several. The Backseat Smash is one of my favorites."

My cheeks flame red hot. I don't know if it's from the alcohol or because the CEO of a major vodka distillery tried one of my drinks and loved it. "Thank you so much. It's such an honor to receive a compliment from someone with your accolades."

Over the next hour, we chat about the various drinks from my book. Rebecca made a couple of them using Northwest Vodka, and they were incredibly smooth. It was a little dance party for my taste buds.

Rebecca clears our empty glasses and uses a rag to clean off the bar. "I'm glad you could come here today because a great opportunity has come up, and you would be perfect."

My brows pinch together, and I turn to Garrett, hoping his expression gives something away, but all he does is shrug.

Rebecca continues, "We're trying something new at the distillery by creating a line of flavored vodkas, and with that, we would like to launch a series of signature drinks to go with each flavor."

My anxiety spikes. "What does this have to do with me?"

"Garrett was very convincing that you would be perfect for the job."

Oh my god. If I was told this was going to be a job interview, I wouldn't have had all those drinks. My brain is currently doing a leisurely backstroke in vodka and cranberry juice.

"Chatting with you solidified my decision. We would love for you to create those drinks for us."

I blank. I forget all the words in the English language. I possibly forget how to breathe.

"Of course, we'll work out compensation. We can even arrange for a condo for you in the city and moving expenses."

"The condo won't be necessary," Garrett interjects.

Finally, everything she says sinks in. She's offering me a job. Offering me an opportunity to be closer to Garrett. All of this while doing something I love. "This is an amazing opportunity. Do you need an answer right now? I would like to think about it."

"It's a big decision. I'd expect you to take time to think it over. I'll let you two finish your drinks. It was so wonderful to finally meet you in person, Dessa. I hope to talk soon."

"Yes. We will." I shake hands with Rebecca, and before she leaves, she passes me her business card. Once she's out of sight, I turn to Garrett. "I can't believe you blindsided me like that. A heads-up would've been nice." I playfully smack his arm.

He laughs. "If I told you beforehand, you would've gotten in your head, and I just wanted you to be one hundred percent yourself. Remember in high school, you had to give a presentation on molecular biology. You spent an entire week preparing and organizing, and when it came time to give your presentation, it was bland. I was ready to fall asleep."

I spit out a laugh. "Thanks for that. But I got through all my bullet points."

"But what's the point if everyone was sleeping? It made the entire presentation stiff and robotic."

"I didn't want to miss anything."

He swivels in his stool to fully face me, clasping his hands with mine. "Then there was another time at lunch, someone asked about mixing different flavors of soda, and you animatedly talked and talked about it. That was engaging. That was you."

"It's a lot easier when it's something I'm familiar with. But how do you remember that?"

"I remember everything when it comes to you." He lifts our linked hands and places a kiss on my knuckles. "I'm sorry I caught you off guard, but I'm not sorry I did it. I knew you'd thrive."

I blow out a deep breath. "This is an amazing opportunity. This is something I could envision myself doing."

"And it would bring you closer to me." His hopeful green eyes meet mine.

"That is a huge bonus."

"And we could take the next step in our relationship."

Maybe it's time to take a play out of Nora's handbook and carpe diem the fuck out of my life.

Chapter 41

BETWEEN THE RED
STITCHING

Dessa

The next day, Garrett goes to the stadium early to prepare for the game. He's arranged for Melanie and Tori to pick me up at his condo to head to the game this afternoon. I love spending time with both of them. They've become two of my really close friends, and it's nice to have a few friends outside of Garrett.

During the seventh inning stretch, Garrett strolls onto the field, tossing a baseball into the air. He stops where I'm seated and motions for me to come to the railing. I glance at Melanie and Tori and they both shrug, but their knowing smiles tell me they know something I don't. Slowly, I rise from my seat and walk the few steps until I'm at the railing. He motions as if he's going to throw the ball to me, and I nod. He tosses the ball underhand and I raise my hands, catching it between my palms. Glancing down, black marker catches my attention. I rotate the ball and freeze. I repeatedly scan the seven letters, not sure if they're real. Between the red stitching are the words *Marry Me.* Tears instantly well up in the corners of my eyes. I tear my gaze away from the ball and meet Garrett's staring back at me. Love and adoration written all over his face. This is the man I want to spend the rest of my life with, the one I want to be with. The one I want to start a family with. He's the air I breathe. Every heartbeat in my chest. The only man I want to be with. My lips split into a wide smile, and I nod. An ear-to-ear grin splits Garrett's face. He mouths, "I love you" and I do the same.

He struts to the dugout, and I practically float on cloud nine back to my seat. My fingers run over the soft leather, tracing the letters. When I sit, Melanie and Tori are staring at me, anticipating my answer.

"I said yes." They both squeal with excitement and jump out of their seats, both of them wrapping their arms around me, giving me their congratulations.

For the final two innings, Garrett played amazingly. He even got a two-run home run in the eighth. As he jogs from third base to home plate, he points at me in the stands, a wide grin on his face, and I know that one was for me. The Warblers win nine to five.

After the game, I anxiously wait in the family room for him to finish. I want to wrap my arms around him and tell him yes, one million times yes, in person, but he never comes through the door.

Instead, Joe greets me. "Garrett is requesting your presence on the field." He's silent the whole time as escorts me from the family room to across the stadium. Every time I asked a question he'd either nod of press his lips together.

When I stroll onto the empty field, the only stadium lights on are the ones near home plate where Garrett's waiting for me, in a clean baseball uniform. I turn to Joe, and he motions for me to continue before he turns around and leaves the way we entered.

When I reach the plate, Garrett lowers himself to one knee. My hands fly to cover my mouth. My heart skips a beat and my entire body feels weightless, like I'm going to float away. Even though, I know what he's doing, one can never be prepared for it to actually happen.

Garrett grabs my hand and keeps me grounded.

"I know there are still a few uncertainties in our lives, but one thing I'm certain of is I want to spend the rest of my life with you. We can take this as fast or as slow as you want. The only thing I want is to have you by my side."

Tears well up in the corners of my eyes. Everything he's saying, I want, too.

His thumb brushes over the back of my hand. "I know you don't want to leave everyone in Harbor Highlands, so we can keep your townhouse or buy a house together and stay there during the offseason. Whatever you'd like. I'm here to support you, just as much as you've supported me."

Garrett is my everything, and I'm more than ready to take this leap with him. With him by my side, anything is possible. "Will you just spit the words out already?"

He barks out a laugh. "Always impatient." He clears his throat. "Dessa Marie Mitchell I once asked you to be my girlfriend, but now, I'm asking to be your husband."

His gaze meets mine. Love and adoration fills his irises. The day he strolled into Porter's, I knew my life was never going to be the same. And it turned out to be in the best way possible. Without any hesitation, I answer, "Yes!"

He pulls a diamond ring from his pocket and slides it on my finger. Before he can stand, I wrap my arms around his neck, tackle him to the ground, and crash my lips to his. I pour my entire soul into this kiss so he knows I'm all in. I'll always be all in with him. Through the good games and bad. Through the traveling and the grueling schedule, I'll be by his side. Maybe not always physically, because it's a lot of travel, but I'll be just as supportive of him as he is of me.

With his arms still wrapped around me, holding me to him, he breaks our kiss. "Also, since we're going to be married, I thought you should know I bought a baseball field."

"A what?" My brows knit together.

"Technically it's two. The fields in Harbor Highlands…"

"Shut up! You bought Hillside!"

He nods. "I still need to finalize the paperwork, but yes. Soon, I'll be the proud new owner of a baseball complex."

I scan his face, trying to determine whether he's telling the truth or not. "What are you going to do with it?"

He shifts me as he sits up and sets me on his lap, my legs straddling his. "When you mentioned I should go into coaching after baseball, it got me thinking about what I want to do with my life when I retire, and I thought this would be the perfect opportunity. Baseball's imprinted in my DNA. Growing up, it was my coaches who inspired me, pushed me, and encouraged me to fall in love with the sport. I would love the opportunity to do that for other kids, and maybe even our own kids one day."

Moisture pools in the corner of my eyes. I want nothing more than to start a family with Garrett. Hell, we can start tonight.

He continues, "Playing baseball won't be forever, but I would still like to be involved and I think this would be an amazing opportunity to do that. I don't want my legacy to be only what I do on the field. Instead, I want it to be what I leave behind in the world. My family, one day our children, and now this baseball complex. Something that lives on for years after I'm gone. Something that helps others."

"Garrett, that's amazing. You're amazing. I love that I get to go on this journey with you. There is no one else in the entire world I'd want as my husband." I clasp his cheeks. "I love you. So much."

"I love you, Tates."

Epilogue

ONE MONTH LATER

Dessa

We set the wedding date two weeks before Thanksgiving, planning on Seattle going to the world championship, but they lost the last game that would have taken them there. Rightfully so, Garrett was upset and frustrated they lost even though they played one of the best games they have all year. San Francisco simply outperformed them. As he prepares for the next season, we also prepare for the start of our lives together as husband and wife. Even though Garrett put the timeline in my hands and didn't want to push me, I was ready. More than ready to be his wife. Time wasn't going to change my feelings for him, so why wait any longer than we already have? My only request was to not have a snowy wedding, so we decided to have a small, intimate ceremony with only close family and friends at a small beach resort in Siesta Key.

As I stare at myself in the mirror in the bridal room, I run my hands over the silky-smooth fabric of my wedding dress with delicate spaghetti straps, a V-neckline, and a lace-trimmed slit that adds an element of romance. The simplicity is everything I wanted.

A knock on the door startles me, and I spin around, hoping it's not Garrett. Luckily, it's not.

"Hi Nana. You look so beautiful in your dress." I wrap my arms around her in a hug.

"Dear, you're the one who looks beautiful."

I give her a soft smile. "What can I help you with?"

"I wanted to give you something." She reaches into her clutch and pulls out a long black box. Holding it toward me, she lifts the top. Inside sits a gold infinity linked diamond tennis bracelet. I gasp and my hands cover my mouth.

She pulls it out and sets the box on the table next to us. "Hold out your hand." My hand trembles as I do as she says. "Magic happens when all the pieces fall perfectly together. Garrett's grandfather gave this to me the night we consummated our marriage. In fact, Garrett's father was conceived that night." She carefully clasps the bracelet to my wrist.

My eyes go wide for a brief second. I won't break her heart by telling her we've already consummated many times, including once this morning. "Oh wow. This is beautiful." I trail my fingers over the shimmering diamonds as tears prick the corners of my eyes. Don't cry. Don't cry.

"And only the most beautiful women should wear it. I'm happy to have you as part of the family, even though it took so long." She winks.

"Thanks Nana." I wrap my arms around her in another hug. I blink up at the ceiling, willing the tears not to fall so I don't have to do my make-up again.

She pulls away and sandwiches my hand with hers.

"Now go make my grandson the happiest man in the world."

I give her a warm smile. "I will, and know he does the same for me."

After Nana leaves, I have a few minutes before the wedding planner comes in to tell me it's time. She escorts me out of the room and outside to a brick patio. The music starts, and Rylee and Joe walk first, followed by Melanie and Randy. The music changes, signaling it's my turn to walk down the aisle. A calming euphoria washes over me. I'm marrying the love of my life. My best friend. My everything.

At the reception, lanterns illuminate the wood patio overlooking the Gulf. The soothing sound of the waves crashing on the beach fills the air. Garrett's arms are wrapped around my waist, and he nuzzles the crook of my neck. We sway back and forth as "My Best Friend" by Tim McGraw plays through the speakers. I glance around. Rylee is dancing with Trey, Melanie and Joe are doing the same along with Tori and Randy. My parents, Garrett's parents, and all of our close family and friends are here. Most of them, anyway. We still haven't heard from Tony. To us, he's just a ghost that disappeared into the night. His parents occasionally talk to him. They're disappointed in his actions, but he's still their son. Garrett made it crystal clear he and Tony would never be in the same room again. Currently, Tony's bouncing between New Mexico and Arizona working various coaching jobs, but he's evidently unable to keep a steady one. Georgia is busy with opening her new boutique. She regrets marrying Tony but is thrilled to have made new friends. I told her we're adopting her so she can't leave. Jake told me congratulations, but he wasn't closing the bar to attend a wedding. Nora volunteered to stay in Harbor Highlands to help him so Lach could come. Instead of finding Lach on the dance floor, I spot him locking lips with a blonde woman at the bar. I nudge Garrett, and he turns his head.

"You know who she is?" I ask.

He shakes his head. "He always said he likes to keep things casual, and there's nothing more casual than a vacation hookup."

The night carries on with drinks and dancing next to the beach. By midnight, everyone is exhausted, including me, but I also don't want to deplete my entire energy bucket so Garrett and I can put the powers of Nana's bracelet to work tonight.

I glance around. "Has anyone seen Lach?"

Lach

I didn't intend to come to Florida to hook up with someone, but when I locked eyes with the blonde bombshell at the bar, that idea was shot to shit. When I offer to buy her a drink, she slides her hands over my thighs and tells me she'd rather have some of mine. Before I can ask her what she meant, her arms wrap around my shoulders, and she kisses me. I hope she likes a whiskey sour since that's all she's going to taste as her tongue strokes against mine.

She inches closer to me, deepening the kiss. In all my life, I've never had a girl take charge like this, and I'm here for it. One hundred and twenty percent. What's even better, tomorrow we'll go our separate ways as if nothing happened. Nothing but a vacation memory.

She pulls away. Her pink, plump lips swollen from our kiss. "Do you want to get out of here?"

"Wait. Should we exchange names or something first?"

Her eyebrows lift. "Are names necessary?"

I shrug. "How will you know what to moan later?"

She giggles. It's so fucking soft and sweet and it makes my dick twitch. "How about this?" She drags the tip of her finger down my chest as her long lashes flutter against her cheeks. "I'll be Kat," she reaches the waistband of my slacks, and her tongue peeks out, wetting her bottom lip, "and you can be Patrick."

Fuck. She can call me Bob, Jim, Harry, or whatever the hell she wants. I clear my throat. "Now that's established, where are we going?"

Her teeth sink into her bottom lip for a brief second. "Where's your room?"

Damn. She's not a stroll-on-the-beach first kind of girl. I can work with this. I push my stool away and rise to my feet, and she does the same. With the heels she's wearing, she's about the same height as me, maybe an inch or two shorter. On the entire walk to my room, her hands roam over my chest and down my abs. Several times, her fingers graze my hardening dick. She throws her arms around my neck and continues to walk while kissing and sucking on my neck. My hand roams over her ass until I reach the hem of her short, flowy dress. I slide it up, brushing my fingertips over the bare curve of her ass.

When we reach my door, she continues to distract me with open mouth kisses along my jaw while her fingers toy with the waistband of my slacks. My fingers fumble to pull the keycard from my pocket and press it to the keypad. It's not an easy feat while a woman is rubbing herself all over your dick. Finally, it flashes green and I push through the door. Once inside, I spin us around and give her my undivided attention. With her back against the door, I meet her lips in a searing hot kiss. Without breaking contact, I slide my hand down her leg until I reach her knee. I lift, hiking her leg over my hip. I want to find out if she's wearing a thong or nothing at all. She moans into my mouth as I thrust against her. Her fingers wrap around my wrist, and she tugs my hand away. I'm convinced she's changed her mind and wants to put a stop to this, so I break our kiss. Scanning her face, I wait for her to say something, but instead her lips tip up into a smile as she slides my hand under her dress. My fingers graze her bare pussy, and there's my answer. I crash my lips to hers in a bruising kiss. I slide two fingers through her wetness, she moans into my mouth, and I swallow the sound. Her hips gyrate against my hand, pleasuring herself. I've never been with a girl who takes exactly what she wants. It's fucking sexy as hell.

Her head falls back, breaking our kiss. "Oh! Yes! Patrick! Fuck me with your fingers."

My strokes falter. I won't lie, it's a little jarring to hear someone else's name, but this is her game. I'm just here to play. Without notice, I spear her with two fingers.

"Ahhh! Yes! More!"

I continue to thrust into her, harder and harder. The palm of my hand rubs her clit, and she moans and whimpers, and her wet heat coats my fingers. I kiss her neck while pressing my nose to the sunflower tattoo behind her ear, inhaling a whisper of sweet honey and citrus. Her chest heaves as she rocks against my hand as I continue to finger fuck her.

Her nails dig into my shoulder as her pussy clamps around my fingers. "Oh. Oh. Yes!"

I pull back so I can watch her come undone. Her pink, plump lips falls open on a gasp. Slowly, her eyes flutter open.

I remove my hand from under her dress, and her leg drops to the floor. Lifting my hand to my mouth, I smear her orgasm over my bottom lip before sticking my fingers in my mouth. She watches my every move as I suck off her orgasm. "Fucking delicious."

Her gaze drops to my dick tenting my slacks and then back up. "Do you have a condom?"

I freeze. Do I have a condom? Fuck! Why don't I have a condom? "No. But I can get one." Trey must have one, or Garrett, or someone.

"I suggest, if you want to keep the party going, you do that."

With my hands on her hips, I pull her away from the door, and she giggles. I slam my mouth to hers in a fervent kiss, mostly to give her something to think about while I go on a condom run.

With my lips brushing hers, I whisper, "I'll be right back." Spinning around, I fling open the door and race down the corridor to Rylee and Trey's room. With my fist, I pound against the door, willing him to answer and to answer quick. Time's wasting. When he doesn't answer, I try again. Shit. I bet they're still at the reception. My forehead drops to the door with a heavy thud.

Voices from down the hall catch my attention, and I roll my head to the side. Strolling down the hallway is a man and woman, around my age, holding hands. Maybe they also have sex? Protected sex. Would it be weird to ask strangers for a condom? I don't know, but I'm about to find out.

"Um. Excuse me?" I ask as the couple approaches.

They come to a stop a few feet away. "Can I help you?" the man asks.

I rub the back of my neck. "This is going to sound strange, but would you have a spare condom I could get from you? I have a girl back in my room," I hike my thumb down the hall, "and I'm fresh out."

They glance at each other, and the woman shrugs a

shoulder. The guy nods. "Yeah. We're just a few doors down. I'll get you one."

"Thanks. You made my evening." I give myself a fist pump. The night is turning around.

Once I secure the condom from the kind strangers, I strut through the door of my room. "Kat! I got a condom!" I stop dead in my tracks. The room is silent, and the blonde bombshell is nowhere to be found. I glance around the room, and there's no sign of her. I stroll into the bathroom and flip on the light. Empty. I sit on the edge of the bed and toss the condom on the comforter next to me. She left. After waiting for twenty minutes, I'm certain she's not coming back.

Thank you for reading Make My Heart Malt! Want more Garrett and Dessa? Claim your copy of their fun and steamy bonus scene when you join my newsletter! https://www.authorgiastevens.com/bonus-mmhm/

MAKE MY HEART MALT COCKTAIL

Bang-Bang Play

Ingredients:
- 16 ounces Lemonade
- 1 Blue Raspberry Drink Packet*
- 1 1/2 ounces Vanilla Rum
- Grenadine

Directions:
Mix the lemonade and drink packet. Over a glass of ice pour in rum them the lemonade mixture and stir. Top with a splash of grenadine. Enjoy!
*Suggestion: Jolly Rancher Blue Raspberry Packet
*Substitute vanilla run for coconut rum or regular rum

Drink Created By: Cindy C. -Cocktail Concoctionist

Acknowledgments

First and foremost, I want to thank everyone who picked up this book. I think I will forever be in awe that you want to read my stories.

I have to thank my husband. I don't know if I would have ever started writing without his words of encouragement.

A big shout out to Brandi Zelenka. You were there for me every step of the way and I don't think I could have done this without you.

To my creative team, you pushed me to put out the best book possible and I am so thankful to have you on my side. Thank you to my editor, Brandi at My Notes in the Margin. I tend to give you a hot mess and you make it brilliant. And thank you to Maddie at Davenports Edits for all your extra helps on polishing this book.

Thank you to Katy Cuthbertson for all your work and support, especially your eye for commas. You've been a huge help.

Thank you to my beta readers Rachel Story, and Randi Gauthreaux. You gave me invaluable feedback to help make my manuscript sparkle. Thank you to my proofreaders Jessie Bailey and Tonya Fender. You've helped me out so much.

Thank you Indie Pen PR for your amazing PR work. You made everything run smoothly.

Thank you to my wonderful Sassy ARC Readers! I appreciate you so much.

Most of all thank you to all the bloggers, bookstagrammers, and booktokers for reading and sharing your excitement for this book. It means the world to me and I can't thank you enough. And of course, thank you to all the readers for reading my words. I hope I've been able to give you a fun escape for a few hours.

See you at the next book! Stay sassy!

About The Author

GIA STEVENS

Gia Stevens resides in Northern Minnesota with her husband and cat, Smokey. She lives for the warm, sunny days of summer and dreads the bitter cold of winter. A romantic comedy junkie at heart, she knew she wanted her own stories to encompass those same warm and fuzzy feelings.

When she's not busy writing your next book boyfriend, Gia can be found binge watching TV shows that aired five years ago, taking pictures of her cat, or curled up with a steamy romance book.

Visit my website for more information.
https://www.authorgiastevens.com

Also By

GIA STEVENS

Want to read more sassy heroines, swoony heroes, and fun and flirty romance books?

Visit Gia's website to find a complete list of all her books.

www.authorgiastevens.com